# THE
# LAST
# SUNRISE

# THE
# LAST
# SUNRISE

## Anna Todd

G

Gallery Books

New York   Amsterdam/Antwerp   London
Toronto   Sydney/Melbourne   New Delhi

# G

Gallery Books
An Imprint of Simon & Schuster, LLC
1230 Avenue of the Americas
New York, NY 10020

First Gallery Books trade paperback edition May 2025

GALLERY BOOKS and colophon are registered trademarks of Simon & Schuster, LLC

Simon & Schuster strongly believes in freedom of expression and stands against censorship in all its forms. For more information, visit BooksBelong.com.

For information about special discounts for bulk purchases, please contact Simon & Schuster Special Sales at 1-866-506-1949 or business@simonandschuster.com.

The Simon & Schuster Speakers Bureau can bring authors to your live event. For more information or to book an event, contact the Simon & Schuster Speakers Bureau at 1-866-248-3049 or visit our website at www.simonspeakers.com.

Interior design by Julia Jacintho

Manufactured in the United States of America

10  9  8  7  6  5  4  3  2  1

Library of Congress Cataloging-in-Publication Data has been applied for.

ISBN 978-1-6680-7953-9
ISBN 978-1-6680-7954-6 (ebook)

To those of us who journey through the tangled and complicated path of forgiveness, may you find hope in the pages of this story. To the lonely hearts that long for connection and to be understood, may you find the love and acceptance you crave and deserve. May this book remind you of the power of healing, self-love, and the undeniable beauty of second chances and letting go of expectations placed by others and, more importantly, yourself.

# Playlist:

"Where's My Love," SYML

"It's Always Been You,"
   Caleb Hearn

"Here's Your Perfect,"
   Jamie Miller

"Those Eyes," New West

"Drunk Text," Henry Moodie

"everything everywhere
   always," Elijah Woods

"The 1," Taylor Swift

"Bleed," The Kid LAROI

"Satellite," Harry Styles

"Cinnamon Girl," Lana Del Ray

"Yes or No," Jungkook

"Pluto Projector,"
   Rex Orange County

"Closure," Henry Moodie

"We Can't Be Friends,"
   Ariana Grande

"Ready for Love," India.Arie

"Memory Lane," Haley Joelle

"Oceans & Engines," NIKI

"The Truth Untold," BTS

"Sunday Morning," Maroon 5

"I Don't Know You Anymore,"
   sombr

"Give Me Your Forever,"
   Zack Tabudlo

"Off My Face," Justin Bieber

"My You," Jungkook

"U Got It Bad," Usher

"Only," LeeHi

"Let It Go (acoustic)," James Bay

"Invisible String," Taylor Swift

"Pick Up the Phone,"
   Henry Moodie

"Dancing with Your Ghost,"
   Sasha Alex Sloan

"Blame's on Me,"
   Alexander Stewart

"Fallin'," Isaac Hong

"Atlantis," Seafret

"Good Graces,"
   Sabrina Carpenter

"Sunset," DAVICHI

"Infinitely Falling,"
   Fly by Midnight

"Big Girls Don't Cry," Fergie

# Prologue

I close my eyes as I float, light as a feather, becoming one with the waves. I let the warm, salty water wash away my fear and my fate, take control of my sadness and my pain. My body has become my enemy, perhaps it always has been, but now I've accepted it. The scale of fairness has tipped for me, and I can barely stand it, the injustice, the resentment. The only place where I'm just another particle of the earth is here in the water. The ocean doesn't care about sickness or health, life or death, love or hate. It's balanced, ever changing, never longing for more or less than it has, never lingering or stagnant. It keeps roaring, keeps us floating.

If I wasn't such a cynic I would be inspired by its forgiveness, but I've become bitter and find it hard to appreciate something so graceful, so fair. Naïve and easily taken advantage of. There is nothing lavish or luxurious about water, and even though our survival depends on it, we mistreat it, drain it, pollute it, but even still, it comes back to us, always, to nourish and keep us alive while we go out of our way to destroy it. If I were the sea, I would wash away every inch of this world, no regret.

# Chapter One

The airplane seat belt signal dings me into consciousness. My eyes slowly blink open, welcoming the sunlight bursting through the small airplane window. The flight attendant approaches with a warm smile, her heels clicking as she leans over to speak to me. She smells like coconut and sunshine, though we've been on an airplane for over twelve hours.

"Do you need anything else before we land, Miss Oriah?" she asks.

I shake my head, quietly thanking her.

Her accent is beautiful, Italian, maybe? I slept most of the flight, so I had little to no interaction with her during our trip across the North Atlantic sea. I hope that made her day easier and that my mother didn't hassle her too much during our private flight. When my mom told me we were flying, which I haven't done often and barely remember the trips, I was excited for the hustle and bustle of the crowded airport, eavesdropping on strangers' conversations, and people watching. Even the lines and the stressed-out flyers who left their houses too late, huffing and puffing as they make their way through security. The chaos seemed exciting, but my mom's company, SetCorp, graciously afforded us one of their many private company jets to Spain, which I would never complain about to anyone but my mom, but it felt a bit excessive and wasteful. The trip was seamless, quiet and luxurious, the way my mom loves her business trips to be.

Looking over at my mom seated across from me, neatly applying a layer of deep burgundy lipstick, I'm not remotely surprised. She packed her carry-on full of beauty products to make sure she didn't miss her ritualistic skincare routine. I respect the discipline and it's absolutely paying off, but a few steps in the morning is enough for me, I don't have the energy. I do love watching other people on the internet do their fancy nighttime routines, but for my life, it's not realistic.

I lean over and grab the handle of my mom's Dior tote, embroidered with her name, another gift from her boss, and drag it toward me. Taking the pack of makeup wipes to clean my face with, I rip one out and swipe it across my bare skin. The smell of cucumber fills my senses, making me sneeze, causing my mom to panic mildly momentarily. My sensitive sense of smell should be the least of her worries, yet even a sneeze makes her body react.

"I saw a video that wipes are harmful to our skin barrier and oil cleansing is the new thing," my mom says, her dark eyes moving from the wipes to me. She keeps up on every single beauty trend, religiously following them. I'm more of a *love to watch cat videos and people falling off things* kind of woman, but to each their own.

I smile, ripping one out of the little crinkly holder. "I don't have an oil cleanser on hand, but I'll keep that in mind for the future."

She smiles, gently rolling her eyes at my sarcasm. We're two sides of different coins, always have been, always will be. We quietly exist in each other's worlds but aren't quite connected. A hopeful bubble floats across my chest that being in the town she was born in will change that. That a little bit of her walls will come down.

"Did you take your medicine?" Her voice is a bit more tired than usual, from working the entire flight. She's always on a call, a Zoom, or making voice memos, I've learned to completely drown her voice out 99 percent of the time.

I nod, gulping down the slight guilt. Her eyes move to the flight attendant, and she nods, joining me in my deceit. I smile at her.

"Did you even sleep at all?" I ask my mom.

She presses the lid of her lipstick back onto the tube and makes a popping sound with her lips. "I'll sleep tonight after our meetings. I didn't want to mess up my cycle."

What cycle? She never sleeps, I know that for a fact. I roll my eyes and look directly at her so she knows I'm not buying it. She's completely unbothered and moves to putting mascara on her long lashes. She drags the wand up and down, dotting the corners with the jet-black liquid. I put in my contacts methodically, wanting to avoid the constant comments about my eyes, even across the globe.

I sit back and sigh, looking out the window of the company jet at the calming and vibrant deep sea below us. We're about ten minutes from landing, and I can't help the smile pulling at my lips. It's finally here, my summer of freedom, my great hurrah. My coming-of-age story is beginning at twenty-three, and I've never been more ready. Just like the main character of a nineties film, this trip will be life-changing. Finally, I'll discover who I am, what the purpose of life is . . . maybe even fall in love. I laugh quietly, covering my mouth at such an absurd thought. How pointless that would be.

"Isn't it just stunning?" the flight attendant softly asks.

I nod, gawking at the view, and we haven't even touched the ground yet. "It's my first time in Europe. First time leaving the US, actually," I tell her.

Her hazelnut eyes widen. "Really?" she asks in disbelief.

"Yeah, I know, it must seem like I travel often, given the whole *private jet damaging the ozone and my mom's in-flight skincare* routine, but I've only been on a few planes, and never for fun, but honestly, I barely remember them." I don't tell her why. The last thing I need is any more pity.

She laughs, and we both look at my mom in all her beauty. She's now putting on a pair of earrings, thick gold hoops. She really is striking, in a frightening, evil-queen kind of way, but one of the most beautiful women I've ever laid my eyes on, and she knows it. One thing that I admire about my mom is her confidence, not only about the way she looks, but her ability to rise from less than nothing to one of the highest-paid women in her industry. Granted, there aren't many women in luxury hospitality real estate development and investment, but it's still a massive accomplishment.

"You're going to love it here," the attendant tells me, pulling my attention back to her.

I smile from ear to ear. "I really hope so. I'm so excited," I admit. "You must have a passport full of stamps. Have you been a flight attendant long?"

She pulls out a dark red passport, and I read the words *Italiana*. I was right, she's from Italy. She flips through page after page full of stamps and hands it to me.

"I promised my twin sister I would travel the world for both of us," she tells me with a small smile, proud of herself.

I run my finger over the Paris passport stamp on one of the pages. "It's a shame they don't stamp them much anymore, but you should buy the stamps and do it yourself. I do that now," she tells me.

"She must be so happy, you've been everywhere." Russia, Brazil, Mexico, the stamps and visas go on, and her passport has double the pages of mine.

"She's . . . she passed away last year."

*Shit.*

"I'm so sorry. I—"

She shakes her head, her dark hair moving off her shoulder.

"Don't worry, I don't want you to be uncomfortable. People always get that look on their face when I talk about her, but she was at peace and death is sometimes a relief. I had wonderful times with her, life-altering memories that I'll cherish forever. I'm grateful to have them and to have had her in my life for the time I did. She was a gift to me, and not all gifts last forever."

I soak her words in for a moment. What a healthy way to look at and appreciate something with the most intense stigma around it. Death is always dreaded, but her take on it was refreshing to me.

"You're right. We tend to have such fear and judgment when it comes to losing someone, but you're doing it right. This is amazing, you're amazing," I tell her, full of honesty, wishing I had taken that approach when I lost the person, outside my mother, who was closest to me.

"Thank you." Her deep olive cheeks turn slightly pink, and she gently cups my hands while taking her passport back. "You'll fill yours soon. This is just the beginning." I don't say anything. There is nothing to say, so I return her smile and sit back, enjoying the view as we get closer to the ground.

"Just the beginning." I repeat her words as the jet's wheels touch the ground.

# Chapter Two

The ride to the hotel is about a half an hour, and my mom spends it on the phone. I stare out the window trying to capture every flicker of beauty I can. I can't believe I'm here in Europe, in Spain, on the beautiful island of Mallorca. It's surreal. It's so different from what I'm used to in Texas, and nothing like what I imagined it to be. All of the Google Maps Street View searching, Instagram reels, and TikToks didn't prepare me for the real thing. The air inside the car is cool, and yet I can smell the sea. When we arrive at the hotel, it's also more beautiful than the internet prepared me for. It looks like a castle, completely made of stone, and rests on the edge of the sea, and the crashing waves can be heard from the valet circle. Luxurious cars are lined around the curve of the cobblestone driveway, and the valets are so quick to open our doors, grab our bags and haul them onto a rolling cart, escorting us to the lobby before I can catch a breath. Once inside the lobby, a handsome man dressed in a white shirt and khaki linen pants offers us a welcome drink. It's dark red with a lot of ice and a giant orange slice on the edge.

"Calimandria for you; it's our delicious and refreshing specialty here. Welcome to Mallorca." His smile is so welcoming and warm as I reach for the drink.

My mother's hand gently pushes at my wrist, pulling the drink toward her.

"You shouldn't—" she begins.

I yank the glass back rebelliously. "It's also *my* summer, remember? And it's one drink." I pretend to plea, but either way I'm having this damn drink.

With a heavy sigh she grabs the other one and raises her glass to clink it to mine. I realize, with a bit of sadness weighing on my chest, we've never cheersed before, and this would likely be the last time. *Stop being so ominous*, I tell myself, plastering on a smile.

"Cheers to your summer, *our* summer, in my favorite place on earth. I do hope you make lasting lifetime memories. Let's enjoy our time here together?"

I nod, smiling and taking a sip of the ice-cold cocktail. It's slightly bitter but in an addicting way. It tastes so fresh and exotic. I'm already beginning to feel like I'm morphing into a different woman here on this island, and we just arrived. I'm easily influenced by the small things in life, which I hope will make every moment here even more life-changing.

"This way, Señora Pera." The man who gave us our drinks waves the hand that isn't holding the empty tray.

I follow his eyeline to the reception desk as my mom corrects him to say "Miss." There's no one behind it as we approach. My mom's phone rings in her bag, and she digs in it while we wait, downing the rest of her drink. I try to keep up and decide to just chug it. It's refreshing and warms my stomach. I hand the glass back to the man and my mom does the same. Leaning my elbow and forearm onto the empty counter, I try to ignore my growling stomach as the cocktail slowly kicks in.

I jump in surprise when a young woman with bright red curly hair pops up from behind the counter.

"Sorry." She lets out a loud laugh.

The sound is so unique that I instantly smile.

Her eyes are bright green, so light that I wonder if they're contacts. One of her eyes has a half-finished black line across the lid and she's holding an eyeliner pen in one hand. There's a shiny piece of tape stuck to her eyelid.

"I saw this tutorial on TikTok where you use tape to get the perfect cat eye!" Her voice is as full of energy as her laugh. "But I haven't mastered it yet . . . obviously." She shrugs, beaming from ear to ear.

My mom groans and taps her credit card against the counter. I read the girl's name tag. Amara. What a pretty name. It matches her perfectly.

"Sorry . . . Sorry, Mrs.—" she begins, but my mom cuts her off.

"It's Miss Pera. Not Missus."

"Sorry, sorry." Amara's eyes drop to the graphite counter her computer is resting on.

"It's okay. Don't worry, she's just crabby because she didn't sleep on our flight." I try to make the receptionist feel better. "And calling her 'Missus' is a sore spot for her."

My mom isn't always rude to strangers, but when she is—it's incredibly embarrassing. For someone who came from nothing, she sure seems to forget that sometimes. Just like she suddenly isn't speaking her native language, as if to prove a point that she is far removed from this place and her past.

Amara tries not to laugh, or even smile, but she can't contain it. I grin along with her, at my mother's expense.

"We have the suites. Under SetCorp, but my name is Isolde Pera, and both rooms are under my name." My mom slides the credit card to her.

"Ohhh, SetCorp people in the flesh. You're technically my boss then. Fancy," Amara responds with humor and sarcasm.

God, I love this woman's energy and fire and I've only been in her presence for a few minutes. She's bold; even working in hospitality at a luxurious hotel, she doesn't seem to water herself down for all the obnoxious wealthy people she must have to deal with daily. I love meeting authentic people, which is sadly rare in my small world, but I can already feel myself being inspired by her and her carefree sense of self.

"Here are your room keys." Amara hands us small, circular pieces of wood.

"What is this?" My mom turns it in her hand, studying it.

"We're eco-friendly now, so our keys are made from recycled wood particles. We don't use any plastic bottles, and we even compost the food that people don't finish. We're one of the first hotels on the island to have such extreme eco vibes," she explains to my mom.

My mom, who tries to keep up with everything new, nods, looking a little confused, but I know for sure that the moment she's in her room, she will be looking up the environmentally friendly wave coming across Europe. It's not so big in Dallas but hopefully will be someday, and knowing my mother, she will certainly find a way to help SetCorp capitalize off of it for their future properties.

As we follow the doorman across the lobby, I try to take it all in. There's just so much to look at. I can't believe this place will be my home for the summer. The lobby walls are all made of gray stones from floor to high ceiling. Ottomans and couches are arranged throughout the massive space, and huge mirrors and chandeliers wrapped in what looks like moss dangle from above. There are plants everywhere; it's modern and earthy and perfect. I don't want to think about how much money SetCorp is losing for us to be here this long, since half the hotel is being occupied by this team, but I know the reason we came will make their money back tenfold, that's Isolde Pera's specialty. Plus, since they own this hotel, it's probably a tax write-off anyway. Another example of the way the rich always get richer.

I wave goodbye to the lively woman behind the desk, and she tells me to come find her if I get bored, as the elevator doors close. We ride to the tenth and highest floor, and the doors open slowly. I follow quietly, reading the lit-up room numbers on the floor in front of the doors. There seem to only be a couple rooms on this floor, but of course my mom's and mine are right next to each other.

"You can have whichever you like more." She waves her hand toward the doors.

"1011 has the best view of the water and the garden, and 1012 has the best view of the street and the coast," the doorman explains.

Our home in Dallas has a beautiful, quiet garden. I want to see people, hear them, and feel like I'm a part of the city.

"I'll do 1012, please?" I'm positive both rooms are spectacular, but since my mom gave me a choice, I'm going to take it.

"If it gets too noisy, we can switch," she tells me.

The doorman opens the door with his own wooden chip and rolls my suitcase inside. The first things I notice are how high the ceilings are and how light and bright the room is. The thick forest-green curtains are pulled back, allowing the sun to cast onto the hardwood floors. There's a sitting room with a couch and two chairs, a coffee table, and a television hanging on the wall. I can't imagine that I'll use it while here, but maybe I'll just turn it on for the hell of it, so as not to waste it. The color pallet of the room—green, beige, cream, and brown—is calming and comforting, washing away the awkwardness of staying in such an expensive room for such a long time. I already feel at home in a way, excitement buzzing under my skin.

"Wow. This is . . . the room is so beautiful," I say to my mom, turning around to thank her, but I find my room empty.

No surprise. I shrug, relieved to be alone and able to take in every single detail uninterrupted. I touch nearly every inch of the living room before making it to the bedroom area. The bed has more pillows on it than I can count and looks as soft as a cloud. When I plop onto it, confirming its cloudlike texture, my body melts into the mattress. I spread my arms and legs out and wave them, like I'm making snow angels. Staring up at the ceiling, my chest feels like it may explode with excitement. Have I ever felt this alive, this awake in my life?

I roll over and look out the massive window at the people on the street. "Nope. Absolutely not," I audibly reply to myself, my voice echoing through the empty rafters, filling the room.

# Chapter Three

After unpacking my suitcase, hanging up all my clothes, and setting out all my toiletries, I take the longest, warmest, most refreshing shower in my life. I check my phone, knowing my mom has added all our appointments for today into my Google Calendar. My life back home is always empty, but my mom lives off her Google Calendar, and while here, I'm expected to do the same. As foreseen, my calendar for the day is full, yellow for meetings with my mom's work stuff that she wants me to tag along to, green for meals—guaranteed to include at least one SetCorp employee or lawyer—and red for commute time. Thankfully, most of the meetings are at the hotel with the event planners, so I won't have to go far today. As much as I'm looking forward to sightseeing, my body is exhausted from traveling, even though I slept most of the time. My mind is wide awake, but my body, as usual lately, isn't on the same page.

My usually pin-straight hair is waving a little as it air-dries with the sea so close and the humidity of the Mediterranean mixing. I stare at myself in the mirror. Putting on a little sunscreen, I brush my unruly, thick brows, another gift from my mother's Spanish genetics. I put in eye drops to freshen up my contacts and dot a little blush on my cheeks. I didn't bring many clothes with me, assuming my mom will force me to shop with her at least three times, so I pull a comfy, oversized pin-striped button-down and white shorts from the closet. I stare at the little blue container on the counter, debating what to do. I had made my mind up before getting on the plane, so now that I'm here, I want to stick to my choice. I won't spend the rest of my life in a fog; I'm taking control of the time I have left. So I walk away, leaving it be, and find the minibar for some water. Amara's reminder of how environmentally focused the hotel is becomes more obvious as I open the fridge. There are some sparkling waters, sodas, juices, and more alcohol than any one person needs.

Where on earth is the still water? I look around and find a refillable cup with a little tag on it.

"Please reuse me during your stay. Join us in conserving plastic waste, one bottle at a time," it says on a little attached tag.

Next to it, there's a built-in waterspout coming from the wall. As a self-proclaimed water connoisseur, I'm amazed by it. I fill the bottle and drink half of it at once. I refill it. It doesn't take much to make me happy here, I realize with a smile. Maybe my cynicism and harshness have been products of my environment back in Texas? Unavoidable personality traits caused by loneliness and lack of human interaction. I'm not sure yet, but one thing is clear: Oriah Pera is going to thrive and make final memories in Mallorca.

I don't have to open it to know what the manila folder on the entry table contains. My mother is thorough with her planning, so I leave her printed-out schedule sitting untouched and head to meet her in the lobby. Amara greets me again, and this time, both of her eyes have liner.

"Seems like you figured it out." I point to her makeup. "Looks great."

"Thanks! It took fucking forever, but it does look good, right?" She holds her phone up, using the camera as a mirror even though the entire wall behind her is a mirror.

"You're American, right?" I ask her. Since she barely has an accent and uses such casual English slang, she must be.

She laughs, that unique sound filling my ears.

"Actually, no. I'm German; a bit of a nomad, really. But I've been learning English since I was a kid and watch tons of American shows. I tried to live there once, in New York, but it was not my vibe." She shudders, speaking a million words a minute. "Have you been there? I bet you're from LA; you have that West Coast vibe."

I try to count how many times she's said the word "vibe," but laugh instead.

"I'm from Texas, actually. I've been to New York once when I was a kid," I tell her, not wanting to go into detail of why my trip there was anything but a vacation. I spent it hooked up to wires for six days and got to see the Brooklyn Bridge only on our drive back to the airport.

"Texas? I wouldn't have guessed. But I haven't met anyone from Texas before. You seem so sweet compared to the news."

"Everyone seems sweet compared to the news, no matter where they're from," I tell her, wondering what the rest of the world is saying about Texas, but it's easy to guess. The news is the news no matter where you live or what you believe. Hysteria caused by negativity boosts ratings, which in turn boosts money for the mouthpieces in front of the camera.

"True, true. Anyway, I know every inch of this island if you get bored with corporate life."

"I'm already bored with it," I admit, looking toward the lobby door and immediately spotting the driver my mom has designated to mildly babysit me this summer. He tips his hat to me, and I politely smile back.

I can't drive myself, but I'm sure I can figure out the public transportation here. According to the social media research I've done, nearly every country in the world has better public transportation than the US. In Dallas, everyone I know drives. It's impossible to get around without a car or a driver.

"If you want a cure for your boredom, I'm having a few friends here tonight if you want to join us. The garden in the back; we hang there and drink and talk. We all love to meet new people and we're from all over. Only one of us is a local, but he barely comes around anymore anyway. Blah, blah, blah, I'm probably overwhelming you." Her bright eyes meet mine.

The very garden that my mom's suite overlooks, I realize with disappointment. "I . . . can't tonight, but rain check?" I should have taken the other room.

"Rain check . . . like, next time, right?" she clarifies.

"Exactly."

"Deal. Rain check. Even if you're not the social type, I know the best food and views, anything you want to do, just ask me. I'm your girl." She raises her hand to a salute at her forehead and we share a laugh.

"Ry." My mother's voice cuts through our cheer.

I spin around to see her with two men in suits and Lena, her robotic executive assistant, at her side. Lena arrived here a week ago to get everything moving. I've known her half my life and she's never missed a beat. Lena hugs me, placing both of her hands on my shoulders and squeezing gently. She smells like bergamot and red wine. She's less of a machine when it comes to me, but I'm doubtful there's a warm, flowing human brain in her skull if it were to be cut open.

"Are you settled in? Do you need anything? How's your room? Did you choose the street view or the garden view?" Lena asks with a comforting smile, trying to remember all the questions she asked.

"Street. I'm totally settled in. Thank you, though. What about you? Are you liking it here so far?"

She nods with enthusiasm, an emotion she rarely shows. "It's so beautiful here. I love it. We have a lot of work to do, but it's incredible, even the weather."

I wouldn't know . . .

"Are you ready for today's schedule?" she asks me.

"Yep. Am I dressed alright? Or should I change?" I ask Lena, but glance at my mom as well.

"Your outfit is perfect." My mom is the one to respond. As I take her in, she's wearing nearly the same outfit I am, a striped blue-and-white shirt, but hers is sleeveless and V-neck, and instead of shorts, she's wearing white pants. On her feet are strappy low heels, almost identical to my brown sandals.

"Thanks," I tell her, pulling my shorts down a little.

Not that I'm not used to her compliments about my appearance, but sometimes I wish she would praise something about me that wasn't surface level. I guess something is better than nothing.

"Try to have fun while you're here, okay?" Lena whispers to me just before she leads us to the banquet room. It's huge. Bigger than I realized this hotel could hold. The high vaulted ceilings, the floor-length windows, like the ballroom itself were carved out of stone from an ancient fairy tale, yet clean and almost modern. Metals and woodwork pieced together to create a sleek but warm space, full of texture. Plants and trees are scattered throughout the room. There's so much to look at, but I'm entranced by the plants hanging from the corners of the room, the massive tree in the center. Everything's immaculate and smells real. I study one of the closest hanging leaves and touch it with my thumb and forefinger. It's silky and is in fact real. Wow.

As I take it all in, my mom starts rambling off work stuff, telling people where to go and what to do, and I wait for her to ask my opinion on something. It finally happens as one of the event planners lines up six white chairs.

"Eggshell, Bone, Vanilla, Seashell, Snow, Ivory." She lists them as she walks behind them, her hand running along the edge of the fabric draped over them.

As I step closer, I try my damnedest to find a difference in them. I want to be involved in planning the event, not only because the causes—art and children—are obviously great, but I want to feel like I'm doing something to make a difference here. Not just taking up space while a team of planners line up chairs, and my mom, who's crankier than ever since landing in her hometown, points and scoffs for hours on end. I want to be part of something important, part of something helpful, but choosing between white and white wasn't exactly what I had in mind.

"Um, bone?" I say, noticing it has a tinge of gray.

"Bone it is," my mom agrees, typing furiously on her phone.

It starts to ring but she swipes, ignoring it. Her apple-red thumbnail is chipped, and I take note of it, betting to myself that she'll have it fixed by the end of the day. Hell or high water, she's never not polished in every sense of the word.

"Great! Now to the curtains. We will cover all the plants here," the woman tells my mom, and I politely interrupt.

"Why would we cover them? They're beautiful." I look around to the branches and greenery layered through the ballroom. "They're the best part." My cheeks heat, not wanting to be rude or make a bad impression. Lord knows what they already think of me, the spoiled daughter of the rich, bossy, clipped-tone woman with the bright red nails and matching heels.

"Most people want them covered or moved for their weddings. To make the room more elegant," the woman explains, her eyes soft but nervous.

My mom agrees with me. "Let's keep them. It's charming."

"We can incorporate them into the theme. Like a forest at night?" I say as it comes together in my mind.

My love of interior design and putting things together to create something beautiful is blooming at full force. I haven't felt this way in so long. My imagination has been dormant for months, so I have been taking stock. Numb and nonexistent. Dance, my number one love, is long gone now, only serving as a distant and painful reminder of what I'm no longer able to do. Pushing that thought aside, I try to focus on what I can do, which is visualize a concept and execute it. My sudden confidence and boost of energy surprise me, so I'm running with it.

"This is exactly why I wanted you here," my mom tells me.

Turning to the small group of planners, she waves her arm toward me. "My daughter led and decorated the entire remodel of SetCorp's main office in Dallas when she was barely twenty-one. She has remarkable taste, so just follow her opinions and everything will be fine."

Despite the smile on her face, her tone is mildly aggressive. Since these women don't know her, they can't decode that she's using her fakest of smiles right now. They don't know that if she waves her hand, they will lose their jobs and she won't lose a wink of sleep.

"Great," one of them responds.

We move on to the linens and curtains, which I gently suggest we drape from the ceiling instead of covering the beautiful windows. The event will be held at night, so I suggest small, soft, twinkling, yellow-toned lights to avoid too much reflection from the glass. I'm high off the feeling of doing something, and the day flies by.

My mom, Lena, and I head out for a late lunch. The waitstaff have brought us a table full of dishes I don't recognize, but my mom's eyes light up as each one arrives. Despite her Spanish roots, she's never introduced me to her native food, or any seafood, with the exception of lobster once or twice at a steakhouse. My palate is embarrassingly limited, but I plan on working on that while in Mallorca. I take photos of the food, like I always do, and grab a fork.

I've never seen my mother eat as much as she is now, her eyes closing as she inhales the meal. It makes me happy, to see her this way. The chipped paint on her fingernail is now fixed—no surprise. I try not to stare at her too long, so that she doesn't notice and put her guard back up, but I can barely help it. Lena makes eye contact with me from across the table, and a subtle smile lifts the corner of her mouth. She must notice my mom's sudden appetite too. She scoops some pasta onto my plate, knowing me well enough that she doesn't give me any of the seafood, just some bow tie–shaped noodles with a white sauce and peas. I take a bite; it's creamy and delicious, but the smell coming from the steam off the shrimp in front of me is begging me to at least try it. Hesitantly, I grab a piece of shrimp from the plate and pop it into my mouth. The flavor bursts as I chew, my taste buds dancing as the garlicky, buttery flavor fills my senses. Sometimes my sensitive sensory awareness can be such a burden, but the thick smell of garlic and lemon and spices has me grateful for them. I grab another piece, feeling ridiculously proud of myself for such a small thing, and my mom takes notice.

"You like it?" She seems more surprised than I am.

I nod, chewing and smiling. Her lips twitch at the corners and I can tell she's keeping herself from smiling back, but even so, I can feel her pleasure at me enjoying the food she grew up eating. It might be ignorant to assume the food is the same here as where she grew up, but I wouldn't be so naïve in my thinking if she was open with me about her life. She doesn't talk much, if ever, about her childhood and teen years, but the few times she has, there's a passion within that doesn't exist in her current life. I'm on a mission to find out more about my mom this summer, whether she agrees or not. I'm determined to get to know her before we run out of time.

# Chapter Four

skipped dinner with my mom and Lena to have room ser-vice, and it was the best choice, even though my mother took the liberty of deciding what I wanted for dinner. The extravagant rolling cart is full of shrimp, pasta, and thick, crunchy, delightful bread. The silence in my room is comfort-ing after a day full of talking. I snap pictures and videos of the food and nearly every inch of my room since I didn't earlier, then scroll through the photos from the day. I love capturing every moment that I can. My photo album in my phone has almost one hundred thousand photos of even the most mun-dane moments in my life. I zoom in on one of the pictures I snuck of my mom at lunch and smile. Her brows are relaxed, her phone away from her ear. Maybe this trip is just what we need to become closer. My nightly alarm goes off, making me drop my phone on my chest in surprise. I swipe to silence it, roll out of the comfy bed, plug my phone in, and head to the bathroom. My nightly routine is always the same: shower, pajamas, brush my hair and teeth, take my meds.

Like a zombie, I go through the motions without emotion or having to think about the next step. Every single night. I open my blue pill organizer and take out a sleeping pill, even though I'm so exhausted already and not entirely sure I need it. The clock says ten thirty, so I check my calendar for tomorrow. Legal meetings, on-location walk-through of the new land SetCorp will build the resort on. It's endless and starts at seven a.m. As I move to close the thick forest-green curtains, I hear voices from the street below and tighten my grip on the fabric, pulling it back open.

Curiosity has me sitting on the ledge, which is perfect for people watching. In my suburban neighborhood at home, the streets are practically always empty, so this is fascinating. There are people everywhere, and the streetlights are bright, allowing me further into the busy nightlife. Laughter rolls through the air, couples young and old hold hands as they walk, and my heart aches a little seeing a couple dancing on the sidewalk. Not really for myself—that ship would never so much as set sail—but it makes me think of my mom and how lonely her life must be. She's still so young, not even halfway through her forties, and there's still so much time for her if she would open herself up to the possibility. I, too, have longed to be loved—at least once—but the universe has other plans. Plans I accepted a while ago.

As far as I know, my mom hasn't so much as gone on one date since I was born, and my "father" was a man she met at a bar but fell head over heels for—how cliché. My mom says she never gave a shit, but I overheard her talking to Sonia about how much she cared about him and wanted to be a mother, a family, but he bailed. Trying to imagine a version of Isolde Pera who meets a random man at a bar makes me laugh, and I lean my cheek against the cold glass of the window, enjoying the voyeuristic view of the people below. Like a spoiled princess trapped high in a castle tower, I close my eyes and try to imagine what it would be like to be one of them.

I wake up to the sun warming my skin against the window. Panicking, I grab for my phone and check the time. It's only six forty-five. The street below is already filled with vendors, tourists, and locals alike, starting their day as the sun rises. The reflection of deep orange burns my eyes, but I refuse to look away. I want to be out there; I want to feel the breeze and the buzz of energy from roaming around the full streets.

The desperation to join them pulls at me, and I mentally weigh the potential consequences of ditching my mom's schedule for the day. Will she even care? Today isn't like yesterday, there aren't any plans that include the charity gala, so I'll just be tagging along, taking up space in the car.

I begin typing a long paragraph of excuses to my mom and pause. What the hell am I so worried about? I'm twenty-three years old and I'm not here for the summer to work for or be shackled to SetCorp. I jump off my bed before I can change my mind and go to my mom's room, knocking at the door. She opens it, already ready for the day. Her makeup is bold today, maroon eye shadow swept across her eyelids, her high brow bones accented with a shimmery bronzer. Her outfit is more business-centric than yesterday, a deep mauve suit with black pointed-toe shoes peeking from the bottom of the pants.

"Is everything okay?" she asks before I start my plea.

Nodding, I pass her and walk into her living area. Her room smells like jasmine, her favorite note in perfume.

"Yeah, I feel fine," I respond, knowing that's what she wants to know, not mentioning that I forgot to take my medication last night. It's been in my system so long that one night won't hurt me. "But I really want to go to the beach today. I can see the coastline from my window and it's driving me crazy that I haven't seen it yet."

She takes me in, silently assessing me. "We can go to the beach between lunch and the land walk-through?"

"Mom," I sigh, knowing she doesn't mean to control me, but that doesn't change the fact that she does. "I want to go to the beach alone. And walk around. I really, really want to have one day without SetCorp stuff."

"It's only been one day since we arrived, Ry," she coolly responds, pushing a gold earring through one ear, then the other.

I pace a little around her room, noting that it looks like no one is staying there; not one thing is out of place or on the counters. She's already made her bed, perfectly tucked corners and arranged pillows. Not a wrinkle or crinkle in sight.

"I know, but I want to make each day count. You told me this was my summer to experience life and Spain, remember? Don't make me beg. Please."

I reach out to touch her hands but stop short as she takes a step back from me. Physical affection has never been our thing. Well, her thing. I wouldn't know if it's mine or not.

"Okay. Okay." She sighs through her nose. "I get it. Just make sure you use the driver; I'll get another one. And don't take anything from anyone, even if they say it's free, it's not. And wear sunscreen and don't smile at anyone; they'll target you as a foreigner straightaway."

I let her go through her list of warnings as if I don't have any street smarts, nodding along and smiling in agreement. Her phone buzzes, interrupting her, giving me the perfect escape.

I wave at her as she snaps at someone on the other end of the line and dip out of her room as fast as I can.

I find myself dancing around my room, my feet gliding across the cool concrete as I turn the shower on, lay out my bathing suit and tote bag. The essentials—a book, sunscreen, sunglasses, my phone, and wallet—get tossed into the tan woven bag, another hotel freebie, biodegradable bags made from recycled straws. As I close my suite door, freedom rings in my ears, a beautiful melody.

Half dancing, half walking through the hall, I rush to the elevator just in case luck isn't on my side and I end up with my mom. When I get to the lobby, I find Amara behind the desk, looking down at her phone, scrolling with her index finger, looking bored out of her mind.

"Good morning," I greet her quietly, not wanting to startle her.

Her phone crashes onto something behind the barrier and she jerks up.

"Sorry! I tried not to scare you," I tell her, my hands in the air.

She bends down to grab her phone and laughs at herself. "It's okay. I thought you were my boss, and we aren't supposed to be on our phones . . ." She looks up toward the ceiling. "Even though there are cameras everywhere, he never watches them." She winks at me, waving her hand toward the red light on the ceiling.

"Wait . . . are you actually doing something fun today?" she asks, noticing my bathing suit peeking out of my cover-up.

"I am!" I can't contain the excitement in my voice. "I'm going to the beach. Which is why I'm here, to ask you where the best one is. I want to go somewhere without my mom's co-workers swarming around."

Amara's fingers tap on the counter, and I can almost see her ideas flying through the air, full of excitement. She must really, really enjoy acting as the local tour guide. Her petite body bounces as she taps her index finger against her temple.

"I know the perfect place. Let me see your phone." She holds her hand out and I notice a small moon-shaped tattoo just under the cuff of her sleeve. I unlock my phone with face ID and place it in her open palm.

"Thanks." I look at the directions she put in my phone: only an eighteen-minute walk. Perfect.

"I hope you had fun with your friends last night. Sorry I couldn't join."

"Ugh, you didn't miss out on much. One of my friends— the only local one—he caused a scene and ruined everyone's night." She takes a gulp from her own water bottle the hotel provides. Tilting the bottle toward me, she says, "Spoiler, it's not water. Want some?"

I shake my head, thanking her anyway.

"Is there another exit I can use?" I nudge my head toward the door where my driver is standing, waiting, looking grumpy today and more like a watchdog than a driver.

Amara's face breaks into a smile, the light above reflecting onto the light freckles dotting her cheeks. They're fainter than mine and add to her cuteness.

"I really like you!" She smacks her hands together and helps me escape.

The moment I step outside one of the EMPLOYEES ONLY exits, the sun dancing across my skin feels like a gentle kiss. I put my sunglasses on and follow the directions on my phone. The June sun is unforgiving, and I reach into my bag to spray sunscreen across the tops of my shoulders and face where I always burn. Each summer, I get at least one sunburn that turns into a tan, but the first is always the worst. Throbbing, peeling skin and all. I rub my hands over the white dots of sunscreen on my skin and keep walking toward the smell of the ocean. Does my mom notice I'm gone without the driver yet? The thought keeps crossing my mind, so I check my phone. No texts. What a relief.

The neighborhood my hotel is in is clearly designed for tourists. I have to keep myself from stopping at all the little tents full of jewelry, pottery, notebooks—all the things I want to buy while here, but not today. Today is my beach, and beach only, day.

The closer I get to the water, the breeze picks up. I cross the street and finally see sand. My heart swells. I don't know why, but I've always felt so at ease, so touched and welcomed by water and its surroundings. I've only been to the ocean once, on a trip with my old neighbor and her family to Galveston when I was in grade school. It was gray the entire time, but I couldn't stay out of the water. Pools, lakes, rivers. So much so that my mom bought us a boat and promised to take me to the lake every weekend.

As time passed and she got promoted and promoted again, and again, we gradually went less and less, and the boat just sat there for months at a time, full of cobwebs and promises that never came to life. The last few memories I have from going on the boat with her are full of phone calls, her frustration over the bad cell service, and her snapping at me when I accidently got her laptop wet when I climbed back onto the boat from the water. During my formative years, she morphed from a hardworking woman to the typical stereotype of a "Boss Babe" whose life doesn't exist outside her job, forgetting to teach me anything but how to put her career before herself and her daughter.

By the time I was sixteen, my mom sold the barely used boat, saying that the lake was too crowded now that tourists had found it, and the drive "wasn't worth it." Even though the highlight for me was stopping at Buc-ee's, a Texas staple that's essentially a gas station as big as a supermarket and has everything you could ever need, from snacks and coolers to clothes, as well as everything you absolutely don't need, like a beaver-shaped yard sign. I loved getting to choose all the snacks I wanted, from fresh beef jerky to brisket sandwiches, drinking so much soda that my stomach hurt, and listening to old songs in Spanish that reminded my mother of her childhood. All of that was worth the drive to me, anyway.

What she really meant when she said it wasn't worth it, was that she valued her time for work more than taking me to the lake or spending time with me. The boat sold in one day, and I still remember the taste of the salty tears that fell down my cheeks as I watched from my window as it got hitched to a big red Ford and disappeared down the street.

My mother hasn't mentioned it since. There's a framed photo sitting on the fireplace mantel of us on the boat from when I was about ten, I guess to remind her that we once had done something together. I've always loved that picture, though it caused me pain, because it permanently stamped one of my favorite memories. My mom had less worry etched into her face, more emotion in her eyes. I was tanned and happy, unaware of how much would change as the years went on. Ignorance truly is bliss.

A motorbike honks and makes me jump, startling me from the memory. Coming to, I look around, ignoring the stares of locals as they make sure I wasn't hit by the bike. I gather myself, or attempt to, even though my hands are still shaking as I step onto the sidewalk and the shore comes into view. The beach isn't as crowded as I'd assumed it would be as I make my way down the white, soft, warm sand. The cove is lined with rocky cliffs, and I watch as a handful of people jump off them and into the bright blue water. I feel the tiny flakes mold around my feet, step after step. Umbrellas and blankets are sprinkled along the small coastline. Bodies sprawling out in the scorching sun, soaking up the rays, enjoying their day. It takes my brain a few seconds to realize that most of the women are topless. Well, okay . . . I look down at my white swimsuit, a one-piece that goes all the way up to my collarbone. Of course Amara would send me to the nude beach. She's probably cracking up right now imagining me here. Embarrassment warms me from the inside out.

Texas obviously doesn't have nude beaches, but we sure have a ton of laws against women's bodies. I shake the frustration of that away and spend a few seconds considering what it must feel like to have the sun touch my bare skin. The idea grows on me, and who knows? Maybe a few weeks in Spain will have me topless on the beach, my scars out in the open and all. The thought makes me laugh to myself, and I try not to look too long at the naked bodies and make my way closer to the water to find an empty spot. No way am I leaving this gorgeous place.

Who cares if everyone except me is naked? Bodies are bodies and this is a new experience, which is all I want for this summer. The white sand sticks to the crevices in my sandals, so I shake them off, knock them together, and toss them into my bag as I walk closer to the water. The shoreline is incredible; it's more like a pocket beach, hidden in the middle of a long coastline. The waves gently brushing against the shore. The skyline isn't blocked with huge sprawling hotels. The sound of the waves caressing the sand and the voices around me is alluring, lullaby-like. I wish I could bottle it up and take it back home with me. Listening to ocean waves on Spotify to fall asleep just isn't the same.

Finally, I find the perfect spot between two couples, giving them enough space to not feel bothered by me. I dump my bag out onto my towel and sit down on it. After lathering more sunscreen across my skin, I open my book. I've been so mentally distracted by the overwhelming pressure about my future that I've barely been able to read or dance, two of my favorite things in the world. I turn to my dog-eared page and try to transport myself to a world full of dragons and magical romance. The sun is so bright that even my sunglasses aren't helping much, so I try to squint while reading the pages. I'm so distracted by the lively voices around me, mostly in Spanish and full of laughter, lightness, and vibrance, that I find myself rereading the same paragraph over and over before shutting the book and putting it down.

Keeping my eyes off strangers' bodies, I look up at my surroundings. Everything feels so vivid, so colorful and alive. From the orange umbrellas to the rainbow of beach towels, fruit carts, bathing suits, and skin. The couple closest to me are captivating. The woman has long black hair and dark skin touched by the gods. She's glowing as she props herself up on her elbow to look at her lover. He's beaming back at her like she is the sun. My heart aches. He laughs, wrapping his arms around her back, pulling her to his chest, and she says something that the wind erases before I can hear it. They are so intensely enthralled with each other; I can physically feel the passion between them from twenty feet away. The two of them are in their own world, and I find myself a little envious. What must that feel like? To be someone's sun?

I tear my eyes away from them and look to the British couple on my right. They couldn't be more different, beers in their hands and sand sprinkled across their skin. They're loud, arguing over the song playing from their portable speaker. She swears it's a classic, he swears that it's shit. Their voices are louder than the music they're debating, speaking in English, and finally the man agrees that the woman is right, and I look away just as she begins a little dance on the blanket they're standing on. I feel incredibly lonely as I stare out over the water. It's not as simple as wanting to be with someone at the beach, kissing them or arguing in the sand, it's more that the choice and possibility of having an epic, brain-chemistry-altering, lifelong love story have been taken away from me.

I've been working really damn hard to grow comfortable with the idea that I will never have the thing that people want the most and being okay with it. I'm mostly there, resigned and accepting my fate, but I'm only human and have my moments. There are many types of love anyway, and I'm going to start with myself. According to the TikTok and Instagram Reels I've been consuming, that's the most important anyway. I get myself situated and open my book, trying to become lost in the pages. After a couple of chapters, I get to a confession of love from the main male character, one that makes my heart race and ache, one that I'll never experience. I slam the book closed and roll onto my back.

Ending my pity party, I stand up and look around again. Tons of left belongings are sitting on towels, cell phones and laptops are left abandoned under umbrellas, so I decide to ignore my mom's voice in my head telling me to never leave my stuff unattended. I look back one time, just out of habit, and let the ocean call to me, drawing me in. The water is bath-water warm as it touches my toes. I take another step.

The waves are predictable, and I love them for it. Each one touches me differently, then disappears, but always comes back. I walk out farther, until my body begins to float under me. I try to relax my mind, shutting out all the noise, and focus only on the sound of the water rushing around me. I lift my legs up and push my body out. The salty water tastes like a candy I've missed since childhood, and I lick my lips again before going completely under. When I rise, I let the water carry me and turn on my back to look at the bright sky as I float. There are only a few clouds above me, one in the shape of a rabbit and one that reminds me of a teacup. Silly, juvenile thoughts of rabbits drinking tea and sharing with me fill my head and I don't resist them. Instead I revel in them, smiling and imagining things that are whimsical and allow myself to explore them. I'm Alice in Wonderland, without the potions and shrooms.

After what only feels like a few minutes but also hours, the sky begins to turn a light shade of orange above me. I keep floating, the waves slowly bring me to the shore, and I make my way back each time. I have no concept of time or rules or schedules. The sun is setting, and I want to watch it from the shore, so I finally decide to get out of the water. My skin is pruned like raisins on my fingertips and toes and my hair is heavy from the salt water as I make my way to my towel. The beach has mostly cleared out; both couples are gone now, no trace of their love or affection left behind. I wring out my hair and rub my burning eyes with my wet hands. When I open them, a man is standing in front of me. My eyeline is at his chest and I trace up to his face. He's looking at me like he's concentrating on an essay or trying to figure out how to interpret an abstract painting in a museum. I'm not sure if I should speak to him or not, if it's safe or not.

"Can I help you?" he says, accent thick but clear.

"No, I—" He looks directly into my eyes as I respond, and my chest tightens. "I . . . it's nothing, I was just looking . . . at him?"

He turns to find a nude, older man, who I was certainly not looking at and is so far from believable that the man laughs, "Is that so?"

"Uhm." I want to crawl into the sand and never reappear. "I mean I was looking for my stuff." I scramble.

"Is that not your stuff?" He points at my hotel-branded beach towel that I'm standing directly on.

I feel so flustered, maybe because Amara is the only person here who I've spoken to without my mom's presence?

"Technically, yeah, but . . . I was just making s-sure," I stutter, and notice his grumpy expression.

It annoys me, and I flip my tone to sure, sarcastic, and strong. "You were the one standing here in the first place," I remind him.

He continues to look at me with a blank expression.

"What are you looking at?" I put my hand on my hip, tilting my head dramatically. If he can be rude, so can I.

"You look familiar. Are you sure we haven't met?"

"Oh, I would remember if we had." I give him my hardest glare, hoping it's half as intimidating as I mean for it to be.

The setting sun casts an orange glow across the stranger's skin. His hair is dark and messy, curling at the ends and touching his forehead and the nape of his neck. His eyes are the color of fresh, frothy espresso. I don't think I've ever seen anyone who looks like he does, like he was made to stand in the sunset. I look down his chest, down to his faded navy-blue swimming trunks and to the book in his hand. Out of nothing but curiosity, I look for the title, only to find that it's a crossword puzzle book. The book is in English: the black-and-white boxes are easily detected, no matter the language. Is he American? He doesn't seem American. The book is worn, the pages curled at the sides, the binding bent many, many times.

What kind of person does crossword puzzles on paper these days? Before I can answer my inner monologue, he smiles at me, and my toes curl in the sand. I smile back at him, instantly abandoning my feisty attitude, watching him as he turns and walks away, disappearing as if he was never there in the first place.

I blink a few times, still in a daze from floating in the water for hours, and the strange encounter with this random man. Feeling a little dizzy, I sit down on the pillowy sand. I gulp down the water in my bottle from the hotel and close my eyes, remembering how free I felt in the sea and how attractive that man was. Weird? Yes. Hot? Also yes. I've never been instantly attracted to someone before, but I guess my Season Two Summer is in full effect—that, or being in the water for hours brought me to a new level of exhaustion. But I decide that Season Two Ry would have sauntered over and asked him back to my room. Lost in my own *fake it till you make it* fantasy that I coined from TikTok, I set my eyes on the lowering sun. Long after he's gone and the sun sets, I find myself still thinking about his eyes and how a simple gaze made my body react. Maybe it was that he was clearly arrogant, something I wish I could be. I'm confident, sure, but that free feeling of just not giving a shit about other people or their opinions of you— what a dream.

Feeling like I need a bit of reality to bring myself back to solid ground, I reach into my bag and find my phone. The screen is pitch-black, which is strange since I didn't turn it off, so I press the side buttons and wait for the little apple logo to come on the screen, but nothing happens. I wait a few seconds and try again. Still nothing. Because I fell asleep on the window ledge last night, I didn't plug my phone in.

*Well, shit.* I look around at the empty beach and gather my things. I shake the sand from my towel and roll it back up, shoving it into my bag. I try my phone again, hoping for a miracle. I'm out in a new place with no clue how I got to the beach, let alone which way I should go to get back to my hotel. I'm so dependent on my phone and technology that the idea of trying to find my way back to my hotel is embarrassingly terrifying.

I cross the street where I came from, trying to remember something, even a tiny detail of my surroundings on the way to the beach. I remember the smell of the food cart, the sound of the sizzling meat on skewers, and the crunching of ice being chipped away and rattling as pieces of it hit the concrete, instantly melting. I remember the fish lying on that ice and the friendly look in the vendor's eyes as I passed by. The sounds of scooter horns, and the way the stone street felt beneath my sandals was as clear as the daylight was, but none of the buildings or streets look familiar as I wander. I turn right, then left, then right again. I'm lost.

I look and listen for English speakers who could possibly help me. I don't even remember the name of my hotel, so I pull out the key and read it. Hospes Maricel. The streets are becoming more and more empty as I roam, a clear sign that I'm going in the opposite way of my hotel's busy area, and I become unable to ignore the bubble of panic growing inside me. I pass a pay phone but have no coins, and I only know one phone number by heart and it's my mother's, the last person on the earth I can call right now. I'd rather sleep here on the street than call her and tell her I'm lost on our first full day here; she will tighten the reins even more if I do that, and I want my freedom. I need my freedom. A man and a woman stumble out of a restaurant, and I try to get their attention. They wave me off, too busy holding each other and pointing up at the sky. A car honks and I jump out of my skin.

Why am I being so skittish? I wanted adventure, I wanted to explore. I'm a capable adult woman, and I've been through way worse shit than being lost on a street, I remind myself as I try to ask another person for help.

"No English," he politely tells me, an apology clear in his eyes.

I should have listened to my mother and taken more Spanish classes before coming here. Or she should have taught me some since she's fluent, but honestly, the whole trip didn't feel real until we landed on the runway, so I spent my time dancing around my bedroom and dreaming of the possibility of having the type of summer I've only read about and seen on screens. On top of that, I didn't think I would have much freedom outside the hotel; now it just feels like I'm the stereotypical entitled American tourist expecting people to speak my language.

"You lost?" a voice calls to me, making me lose my breath.

I turn around to follow where the sound came from, and standing under a streetlamp is the dark-haired, beautiful man from the beach. The one with the espresso eyes and sun-kissed skin and the book of crosswords. The one who immediately made the blood warm beneath my skin. The one with an annoying-ass attitude. Now that I'm frustrated and my feet hurt, I have even less patience for his grumpiness.

I shake my head, lying because I am no damsel in distress.

"I'm just exploring." I can't think of a remotely credible lie, and at the same time, I have no idea why I care if this man knows I'm lost. It's not like I need to impress him and not let him know I'm not capable of finding my way back to my hotel.

"You're lost," he says with certainty.

My throat tightens and I give in with a huff, nodding my head slowly. The streetlamp above him flickers, and he steps closer to me. My heart races.

"You." I point an accusing finger at him. "How did you find me?"

His eyes squint slightly as he approaches me. He's wearing a shirt now, a beige one without sleeves that has a faded sailboat and words that are beyond recognition on the front, and the same *navy-blue faded from sea salt* shorts. His sandals are worn, and his hair is still messy, his eyes soft despite the annoyed turn of his jaw.

"I didn't *find* you. I was going home and saw you wandering around here, and there." He points his finger into the air, toward nothing in particular, but in the opposite direction we're facing.

Hmph. Well, he speaks very good English and seems . . . a tiny bit friendlier than earlier? I stare at him. I shouldn't trust a stranger. Especially at night, and a man at that. Double especially in a foreign country with a dead phone. When the smirk on his face grows into a full grin, I shake my head.

"I'm fine, actually," I say, but internally know that I'm a liar. Why am I so nervous?

"You sure? You don't seem fine."

"Are you stalking me?" I ask, and he laughs, bringing his fist in front of his mouth to hide his smile.

A car passes incredibly close to him, but he doesn't move or even flinch as it nearly brushes his arm. I'm used to wide Texas roads with plenty of room for the gigantic, lifted trucks; he must be used to these tiny lanes with tiny cars squeezing through.

"Why would I stalk you?"

The offended tone of his voice makes my skin crawl. With fear? Or excitement? I'm not sure. All my responses feel conceited or paranoid, so I stand with my hands on my hips, running through potential comebacks in my mind. I don't want this to be one of those conversations where I say the wrong thing and lie awake at night thinking about it months later. I have enough of those to last a lifetime.

"Because you're a pretty girl from the States?" he begins, stepping even closer when he clocks that I'm struggling to answer.

The night air is warm between us, no breeze from the beach to give me breath. He taps his index finger on his lips.

"Or because you're alone and lost at night with no phone battery?" His voice is quiet, eerily so.

Ted Bundy pops into my head suddenly, and I remind myself that he was also considered charming and charismatic to women, and he murdered them. Too many true-crime docs, too many enemies-to-lovers novels under my belt, floating around my brain, unsure which type of character this man is, making me delusional and slightly afraid. There's only about a foot between us as he continues. I'm still silent, and my head feels foggy. I'm pretty sure I could outrun him, even in my state of exhaustion. He's much bigger than me, and my dancer's body and yoga classes aren't going to come in handy, but I can run like hell if I need to.

"I know American people are arrogant, but trust me, I'm not stalking you or following you. You aren't that important."

"Wow," I scoff. "What's your deal?"

He shakes his head, sighing, as if he doesn't know the answer.

"My deal? You accused me of stalking you when I'm trying to be a Good Samaritan and help you get back to your hotel." He groans, clearly debating within himself if he should be helping me or not.

"I wasn't being arrogant. I'm not used to . . ." I start to tell him that I'm not used to traveling or strangers being nice for no reason, but I don't want to sound desperate or vulnerable. Also, it's none of his business.

Why on earth do I care what he thinks about me? I don't know him and have never been the type of person to put too much emphasis on other people's projections of themselves that they force onto me. That's what most unsolicited opinions are.

"I'm not used to this area." I continue my lying streak with a half-truth. "Anyway." I look everywhere and anywhere but his face. "I'll find my way. Have a good night." I wave to him and force my feet to move.

That was stupid. I have no idea where I'm going, I know that and I know he knows that, but still I walk away with my head held high. My feet are aching. I should have worn more comfortable sandals but I didn't realize I would be walking so damn much today.

"You're going the wrong way!" His voice carries to me through the night wind. Shit.

"How do you know where I'm going?" I whirl around.

What is going on with me? I feel so defensive and embarrassed.

He points to my hand. "Your towel, your bag, your key in your hand? You're a walking advertisement."

Obvious answer.

I quickly drop my hand, turn the key over, and he smiles, proud to have embarrassed me.

"And my phone— How did you know it was dead?" I continue to interrogate him even though I know he's likely to have a logical answer to this as well, but the words are out before I can stop them.

He rolls his eyes. "Because you kept trying to turn it on at the beach, and if it worked, you would be using it to get back to your hotel." Another obvious answer. This freaking guy . . .

"Here." He types something into his phone and extends his arm toward me, a small phone in hand.

I look at the screen and see that it's on navigation. The screen is cracked like a spiderweb, and everything is in Spanish, including the voice coming out of the speaker, but I can see the blue line and can most definitely find my way with it.

But should I accept his help?

What does he want in return?

People don't just go out of their way to help strangers. I know better than that.

"What? Is my phone not fancy enough for you?" he presses before I can respond. "Just take it and get back to your hotel. I won't speak to you while we go, but just go. M'estàs tornant boig." He shakes his hand, emphasizing the phone in it.

"I don't know about this . . ." I voice my hesitation.

"My patience is running out, Miss America."

"Then why are you offering to help me?" I roll my eyes at the ridiculous and slightly flattering but insulting nickname.

He shakes his head, crosses his arms, and runs his hands over his muscle-defined arms. "I don't know." He scratches his head. "But my offer is about to end."

"What's your name? Just in case," I ask him.

Maybe if I know his name, the likelihood of him trying to murder me will decrease? Then again, if I'm dead, I can't tell anyone his name anyway.

"My name doesn't matter, Miss America. I already know your hotel, so if I was a danger to you, it would be clear by now. My offer expires in about ten seconds." He begins to count down from ten in Spanish.

"Fine." I snatch the phone from him just as he says "dos."

I begin to follow the navigation and walk on the limestone street, trying not to think about him walking behind me. My sundress feels shorter, my steps wobblier, the blister on the bottom of my foot is throbbing, and I unconsciously smooth my hand over my frizzy, sea-salt-filled, air-dried hair. Following the arrow on the screen, I navigate the curve of the small streets from one to another. Thankfully, my hotel is only ten minutes away. The smell of sugar fills the air and my stomach growls.

When was the last time I ate?

I skipped breakfast this morning and picked at my room service last night.

"Hungry?" the not-stalker asks from behind.

When I turn around, he has some sort of bread in his hand. It's wrapped in a white paper bag. How did he even mange to stop and grab it as we walked?

I shake my head, ignoring the rumble of my empty stomach.

"You sure? Ensaïmada is a local delicacy." He tears at the spiral-shaped bread with his teeth, and I groan.

"Is that the sugar I smelled?" I ask.

He nods. "It's similar to a croissant but much better," he tells me, noticing my skepticism. "Have some. I didn't poison it."

"Ha. Ha." I walk a little closer to him and reach my hand out, hunger getting the best of me. Bread and sugar? Who can pass that up, even from a stranger? Not me.

"Say 'please,' Miss America." He grins, waving the pastry in front of me to taunt me.

I yank it from his hand, and the surprise on his face is more than satisfying.

I take a huge bite and—holy hell!—it melts in my mouth. It tastes like a croissant and a funnel cake had a delicious baby. I eat more and ignore the way he's staring at me as I devour his food.

"Are you always this ravenous and steal people's food?" he asks, amusement clear in his voice.

I nod my head. "Especially when I'm starving and in the sun for hours without eating."

"Well, I'd say help yourself, but it's gone now." There's a gleam in his eye that is way too charming, and I've had way too long of a day.

"You offered." I shrug. "That's what you get for being nice to an arrogant tourist." I stick my tongue out, and his eyes narrow in amusement, like he's studying a species he's never encountered but is curious nonetheless.

"Are you still hungry?" he asks. "We eat dinner here much later than you're probably used to. We could—" He stops himself mid-sentence and shakes his head. It seems to be a habit of his.

"Your hotel has room service," he says coldly, retracting his offer before he even finishes the suggestion.

"Were you about to ask me to eat dinner with you?" I ask boldly.

"No. I was just . . . no. I wasn't. Let's walk." He points straight ahead.

"Surrrrre." I turn my back to him, slightly disappointed but aware of how out of character it would be for me to eat a meal with a total stranger. And my mom is probably losing her shit, since I'm not back and my phone is dead and she can't see my location.

"*Yes, you were*," I add under my breath, not caring if he can hear me or not.

Am I flirting with him? Do I even know how to flirt? Maybe coming to Mallorca has already begun to change me. Maybe my mother is right and this island holds something magical that even the most skeptical can't deny the pull of?

His looks aside. He seems like a walking red flag. Physically safe, my gut tells me that, but not the kind of guy I want to be kept up thinking about at night, or ever see again.

"How long have you been in Mallorca?" His voice travels with the breeze from being so close to the shore.

"Not long enough to not get lost." I keep facing ahead, my back straight and feet absolutely screaming at me for not breaking in my sandals before wearing them out all day. I look down at them, at the blisters forming, and groan.

"Do you want to borrow my shoes?" he asks.

What the?

"You can barely walk," he simply points out.

I don't turn around. I'm already having him help me back to my hotel. Putting his sandals on would be too much, wouldn't it?

I nod to myself, yes. Yes, it would. He's a random man who I don't want to owe a favor to.

"You want me to wear your shoes, but you won't tell me your name?" I call to him as we turn the corner, passing a stunning abandoned church.

"I never said I wanted you to wear my shoes," he corrects me. "I offered them to you because your feet are bleeding. You haven't told me yours either, by the way."

I look down again and shake my head. He doesn't need to know my name, and I don't need his stupid, comfortable, padded, not-torturous shoes.

# Chapter Five

When we arrive in front of my hotel, I can't help but pause, taking in its beauty at night. It's a literal castle hanging right off the shore. The light washed stone is perfectly imperfectly built and entrancing. It's an architectural dream. From the front entrance I can hear the soft crash of the waves below. Shiny luxury cars are parked in a row, my mom's driver is luckily nowhere to be found. I can hear music . . . a violin maybe, coming from inside the hotel lobby.

"Thanks for your help, Mr. No Name." I turn around to my surprising saving grace tonight.

Not only for the walk back but for the delicious snack. I try to remember what the name of it was as I wait for him to respond.

"Have a good night, Miss America."

I want to tell him that his nickname is starting to piss me off, and part of me, a really random and out-of-character part, is a bit bitter that our time's ending and that I'll never see him again. This is what happens when people travel: they have unrealistic and whimsical fantasies of a whirlwind romance that changes the course of their lives. But I, Oriah Pera, live in a completely different reality, one that suffocates daydreams until they lose their breath.

"You know, Miss America is a really sexist, degrading competition for the most part, and the men who own, profit, and run it are absolute pigs," I tell him as I walk closer to the lobby door. My feet ache with every step.

I hear him make a noise. "Is that so?"

"Yeah. And I grew up in a house that didn't sexualize women's bodies but focused on their minds, so that nickname is insulting."

He studies me for a moment. "Hmm, well, it's also insulting that the chemicals used to keep this grass so green leak into the water canals we use for fishing. It's insulting that you intruded on our local beach and probably left a plastic water bottle or glass there without thinking. The price for your hotel per night is more than most of us make in two weeks of work, and the skyline and working class have been destroyed by your American greed. I could go on and on."

"My American greed? My mom and I are here for a charity event and to build an Arts Center for the children in Mallorca. You have no clue what you're even talking about. Judgmental without having a clue of the context. You don't know me," I snap, thinking this isn't the time to mention the Arts Center is tied to a new luxury hotel . . .

"Good for that," he replies, his lips twisting into a snarl.

What a hostile turn of personality from the guy who just helped me get back to my hotel. He's confusing and I'm tired, my head aches, and my stomach is dying for food. My fuse for rude locals—hot as sin or not—is running out.

"Yeah, good for that." I straighten my back. "Have a good night. Actually, don't. Have a shitty night," I say as rudely as I possibly can.

I hope it starts raining before he gets home. Or his stupid sandal breaks or his pants rip and fall to his ankles or those sprinklers he complained about turn on and spray the crap out of him. Asshole.

I turn on my heel and the friendly bellmen wave to me. I manage a smile for them as I cross into the air-conditioned lobby. I jerk in surprise when a hand grabs my arm as I press the up button on the elevator.

"What are you doing?" I yank my arm away from him. Somehow I knew it would be him. "And what could you possibly want? To berate me more? Look, I appreciate you helping me get back, but I'm over your attitude and I'm too tired and literally starving. So if you could leave me alone, that would be great."

His face bunches up, and his dark lashes are so thick on the bottom rim that it almost looks like he's wearing makeup. Under the bright lights, I can see a series of dark freckles across his arms and neck. It's beyond annoying that I can't stop noticing the details of his physical appearance.

"I want nothing more than to leave you alone, Miss America," he mocks me *again*.

Anger bubbles up and I briefly think about slapping his arrogant, beautiful face, but I don't want to get arrested for assault on my second day here, and this isn't a nineties romcom where we let physical abuse slide for the sake of comedy.

"Then why the hell are you still here?" The elevator dings and opens in front of us. The interior is covered in mirrors, making four of him. One is enough.

"You have my phone. Or is stealing another one of your many charming American traits?" His eyes move to the phone in my hand.

Ugh, if he hadn't been so obnoxious and distracting, I would have realized earlier that I hadn't given his phone back.

"Here." I push it into his hand, just a bit too hard, but he doesn't react at all. His hand wraps around his cell phone and he pushes it into the pocket of his shorts.

"Adéu, let's not see each other again, okay?" His words press into my chest, though it's ridiculous.

The elevator closes and I turn to face him. "Gladly. This island is big enough; I don't think that will be a problem. And I'm sure you don't spend your time at tourist hotels that ruin your homeland."

"And I'm sure you don't spend your time anywhere but here. Have a shitty night." He grins and my vision goes red.

I press the button again, harder this time. My eyes burning, struggling not to cry. Not out of sadness, but out of anger. I have my mother's temper, and I'm trying my hardest not to lose it on this asshole; it wouldn't be worth the energy. Finally, the elevator opens and dings, signaling my escape.

I step into it and turn around to look at him one last time.

"Adéu." I repeat his goodbye, waving, when what I really want is to flip him off, but I don't want to give him the satisfaction.

He watches me with intensity as the seconds pass, and the tension in his stare makes me press the close-door button as many times as I can. He begins to disappear as they shut between us, and I can't shake this tight feeling in my stomach as I make my way to the top floor, to my expansive suite.

I go through most of my nighttime routine distracted, brushing my teeth but forgetting to put the toothpaste on first, using body wash instead of shampoo, and nicking my legs with my razor more times than I can count. My mind is all over the place but ignited, awake in a way it hasn't been before. I can't find the explanation as I dig into my brain, wondering why he had such an effect on me. I've never, ever been the type of woman who is persuaded or blinded by an attractive man, and certainly not a rude one who hates people just for being tourists. Stepping out of the shower, I towel-dry my hair, Band-Aid my feet, pop my meds and some melatonin to shut my mind off, and tuck myself into bed with my hair still damp.

I can hear the busyness of the streets below my hotel, and some sort of water sound? It's not the waves. I sit up just as my eyes begin to close. I follow the sound and nearly slap myself on the forehead when I realize I forgot to turn the shower off. Whatever is happening to my common sense will be better tomorrow, I just need sleep. I will forget about him and the odd roller-coaster of an encounter we had. I'm not here to make enemies with some local jerk who hates tourists, and I'm certainly not going to spend my time thinking about how beautiful he was in the sunlight and somehow even more striking in the moonlight. Nope, I'm not.

# Chapter Six

"What about sea moss? Or forest harvest?" my mom asks, pointing to a line of nearly identical candleholders in the nearly empty ballroom. Not this again. Not us comparing different tones of colors again.

At least a dozen workers are here, dressed uniformly, standing silently as my mom and the lead planner, who finally got called by her name, Eliza, study each one like they're examining dinosaur fossils. It takes one glance to know that sea moss is perfect.

"Sea moss?" I offer, just to end everyone's misery. Mostly mine.

"Hmm, sea moss is pretty, but there will be a lot of lights around, will it make it look dark in here?" My mom taps her chin, deep in thought.

I'm slightly envious of her attention to detail when it comes to the candleholders. Outside of my medical stuff, I can't remember a time when she put so much thought into me as she is into these decorations, when spreadsheets and Zoom calls are more her thing. I know damn well it's not because of the children she's allegedly raising money for. They won't care about the difference between shades of dark green.

"It's possible. We could always do black?" Eliza suggests, clicking a pen between her fingers.

"No. I hate black for this. It will make the room too dreary."
My mom instantly shuts the idea down.

"Isn't the point of this whole thing supposed to be about the
arts and marine biology for children? Do we think they will give
a crap about the color of the decor?" I roll my eyes. I'm getting
irritable and trying not to be rude, but this is just obnoxious.

My mother's gaze falls on me, annoyance abundantly clear
on her face. One of the women behind her is smiling at me,
agreeing with my statement out of my mom's sight. They, like
me, probably remember that my mom just told them to follow
my lead when it comes to the design for the event. She told
them I have *impeccable taste* and bragged about me redoing
SetCorp's office, but now she's bickering with me over candleholders. My head throbs.

"Oriah," my mom exhales. "The children we are trying to
help are not the ones paying for it. The ones with the check-
books are the ones who will need to be impressed by the
chairs, the candleholders, the cutlery. I get the sentiment, but
we want bigger checks, right? So, at least pretend to help or
you might as well go back to the beach." Her stare drags across
my sun-kissed shoulders down to my slightly red thighs. "And
wear more sunscreen this time."

I remember when I was a teenager, maybe fourteen, and
my mom brought me to a "charity" event in Houston. We spent
thousands of dollars in one day, getting our hair and makeup
done, buying floor-length dresses from the fanciest mall, and
I felt like Cinderella arriving at a ball—for about ten minutes,
that is. The event was supposed to be for sex-trafficking
survivors, and it was at the top of a fancy hotel in the shape
of a circle. There were too many people for the small space,

which I interpreted as more support, only to realize most of the people attending only came for the open bar.

During a poem read aloud by a young girl who was a survivor, the crowd was rowdy and so consumed by their own conversations that I could barely hear her speaking despite the microphone. Her voice was shaking and quiet. It made me enraged, not only because of what she had experienced, but because no one in the room seemed to care enough to even pretend to listen to her. My mother saw and felt my anger, and ended up being the highest, and one of the only, donors of the night. From that moment on, so-called "charity events" pissed me off. My mom and her company are turning this into a fiasco to show off their money and resources. I should have stayed in Dallas and had the house to myself and let my mom come here and waste these people's time. Aside from the home nurses coming to check on me, I loved my alone time when my mom was gone.

"You know what? I think I will do that." I nod to her, turn on my heel to walk out of the room.

"Don't forget to charge your phone this time!" she calls after me.

Once I'm out of her sight line, I roll my eyes and repeat her words in a sarcastic, mocking, and childish way. I got an earful about safety and backup chargers, and *This is why you should have listened to me and taken the driver.* In my effort to prove I don't need her team of assistants and worker bees, it's backfiring, making it obvious to her and myself that I'm not as capable as I'd like to believe.

I end up walking around the hotel and find the pool area. It's empty, which, given my mood, is fantastic. I sit down on one of the dark gray lounge chairs and lean it all the way back to lie down. The umbrellas are already up, even though it's not even nine in the morning, meaning the staff knows today's sun will be brutal. I get the sunscreen bottle out of my bag and rub it on my legs and arms, then face and neck, and close my eyes. The salty air is so nice, and the gentle breeze helps my temper deflate a bit. I drift off into the most peaceful nap of my life but am woken up by the noise of a man's voice. He's on the phone and dressed in a suit, even in this heat. The sun is beaming down onto his bald head. He's speaking in English, so he must work with or under my mom at SetCorp. I turn away from him before he looks at me and face the infinity pool, where the edge seems to disappear into the ocean.

It's so beautiful, even with the man's voice interrupting my peaceful pool time.

"We are working on it. Isolde has it under control. You know this is her specialty. She's got them under her thumb; it will be any day now. The guy is stubborn as hell, but she's a bulldozer. You know that," I hear him say.

Taking notice of my mom's name, I try to listen to the rest of his call, but it ends abruptly, and he walks back inside without even glancing at the beautiful view in front of him. He's either too consumed with work or too spoiled to really revel in the scenery. Getting antsy but not wanting to be around my mom, I gather my stuff and head to the lobby to find the colorful woman with the colorful name, Amara, who works behind the front desk. The hotel isn't massive like the Hyatt and Gaylord outside Dallas, but it's so beautiful and a bit hard to get around because of the floor plan, which makes me love it even more. Sunbeams fall through the floor-to-ceiling windows as I walk down a wide hallway, dust dancing through the air around me like glitter. I might be lost.

I pass through an area that looks like the back end of a kitchen. It's less sparkly than the rest of the hotel. I peek in and see a group of people dressed in chef's uniforms. They're smiling and chatting, their hands busy peeling shrimp, dicing tomatoes, chopping onions. I don't realize I'm staring until one of them makes eye contact, raising their brow in curiosity. I bow my head, quietly whispering an apology and rushing out of the kitchen, finally finding the lobby after another ten minutes of wandering through the mazelike halls.

"Hey you!" Amara greets me with a wave and massive smile.

"Hey! Nice trick yesterday, sending me to a nude beach." I lean my elbow on the counter and playfully glare at her.

She bows, lifting and bending one arm in front of her stomach. "You seemed like you needed a bit of fun in your life. You're welcome." She beams, winking at me.

I roll my eyes, and she giggles. "It was fun, though, right?"

I nod. "And beautiful . . . just a bit surprising at first. Which I'm sure made your day imagining me there."

"It sure did," she proudly agrees. "Most of the best things in life are."

She has a point.

"The only shitty part was my phone died and I met this rude local who sort of helped me get back here but was clearly very against tourists and didn't seem to like Americans." I groan.

"Honey, no one likes Americans. Not even the Americans."

"True. But he was so rude about it. He . . . he was obnoxiously cocky and annoying."

"Ohhhh, do tell me more. Was he hot?"

I sigh. "Does that matter?"

She nods enthusiastically. "That *always* matters."

"I mean, I guess he was. But he was so arrogant and obnoxious."

"You already said that." Her smile grows as she narrows her emerald eyes.

I would typically stop there, but for some reason I feel free to vent around Amara, though I barely know her.

"Right. He was also charming in that asshole kind of way. And he spoke English so well and had a crossword puzzle book, which was weird but makes me think he's smart and—"

"A crossword puzzle book?" Amara's voice changes.

I nod.

"Built like a god . . . dark, kinda curly hair?"

I nod again. Oh no.

"Big brown eyes and thick, feminine, envy-inducing eyelashes?"

My head might roll off my neck if I keep nodding. "You know him?"

It sure sounds like she knows him. Oh god, what if he's her boyfriend?

Amara dramatically slides her elbows and head on the counter. "Yeah, Julián Garcia."

"Is that a good thing or bad thing?" My interest is officially piqued. If she's not dating him, that is.

She hesitates, chewing on the side of her cheeks. "Both? He's great. So fun, but it depends on what you're looking for. He's my friend, so he's a good guy deep down. I'm not friends with assholes, but I wouldn't recommend someone like you to hang out with him if you're looking for emotional connection."

I take her words as a slight blow. "Someone like me? What does that mean?"

She lifts her arm up and places her hand on my shoulder.

"Not what you're thinking it does. I'm not labeling you, but I don't get the feeling you're someone who's down to hook up and never speak again. Unless I have you totally wrong and that's exactly what you're looking for?" She raises her brows suggestively and I loosen up, my defensiveness slipping into a smile.

"No, I'm not really looking for anything, actually. Is that what he's known for around here?"

"Mostly. But also, his family's business is our biggest local fishing producer. Most of the local restaurants and even our hotel get their seafood directly from them. He works all the damn time, so he doesn't hang out as much in the summer as he does in the offseason, but when he's not hiding out on his boat, he's the life of the party. Julián Garcia is pretty much a tourist destination himself."

The pit of my stomach aches. He almost, almost, almost got me. I was so easily charmed by his confidence and energy. I can totally see why many women want to hook up with him. Not me, though. I will absolutely not let my name be added to his list. I don't have the time or energy to get distracted.

My tries at dating in the past have been massive failures. Turns out, teenage and college-age boys can't and don't want to handle being with a woman with complications. At first, my mom's money and status had boys flocking to me, but after my first public seizure, they practically ran the other way. In college I managed to keep a boyfriend for a few months, but he was an athlete and constantly restrained by my lack of ability to join him in his adventures. To his credit, he did try to adjust, but after meeting his parents, his mom pulled me aside and kindly begged me to end things with him.

*His grades are slipping*, she said. *His future is bright*. As if mine wasn't. I agreed because in a way she was right, so I broke up with him the next day and we never spoke again. If someone who I'd spent a few months with couldn't handle the possibility of a life with me, there's no way some random guy who lives on the other side of the world can see me as more than just a liability. Maybe picking out chairs and curtains with my mom is the best use of my time here after all. Though I had planned to enjoy the island and find out more about myself and my mother.

"Anyway, just don't hang out with him if you aren't into that. Sorry, hang on," she says, pulling her cell phone out of the pocket of her slacks.

Her phone case is bright green and covered in rhinestones. So cute. She speaks Spanish into the phone, looks at me, nods, and hangs up.

Her eyes blink slowly. Something is up.

"What?" I ask, tilting my chin to her.

"Let's have some fun tonight."

"Don't you have to work?" I ask her, looking around the nearly empty lobby.

She points to the clock on the wall behind her. "I'm off at nine."

"Nine? Isn't that late to go out?"

She looks at me like I have three heads and twenty eyes.

"That's early here. So try to stay awake." She smiles.

"Ha. Ha." I roll my eyes at her, knowing good and well I'm usually in bed by then.

By the time eight comes around, I'm getting sleepy. I scroll and scroll on my phone, growing bored to death. My mom has some dinner with Lena that I declined so I can go out, without her knowing. I end up pacing around my room, jumping up and down a few times, splashing cold water on my face, anything and everything to keep my energy up. I open the minibar and wonder how my body would react to a Red Bull, but decide against it. At eight forty-five, I'm restless and go down to the lobby early. Amara's on her phone, scrolling, looking bored out of her mind, just like I was in my suite.

"You're awake!" She claps her hands.

"I am." I lean against the cool stone counter between us.

"I'll just leave early. No one will care and Marian just got here, so I'll sweet-talk her to clock in a few minutes early." She winks at me, noticing my hesitation.

Why do I care? It's her choice and her job. I need to lighten up, live a little, and do what I promised I'd do this summer, which is step out of my comfort zone as much as I can.

"Come on. Let's get you changed, and I'll introduce you to some of my friends here and show you why I found it impossible to leave this island since I came here on holiday."

I look down at my gray tank top and jean shorts, wondering what she expects me to change into. "Not Julián, though, right?"

She shakes her head. "No. He never comes out on a week-day," she assures me.

*He did last night*, I want to say, but I just nod, and we head up to my room.

"What's it like to stay in here?" she asks, looking out the window. "I've only helped guests bring their luggage in and bring them ice and stuff. It must be so different sleeping here, especially for the entire summer. I think the Obamas are the only ones who have ever stayed that long, them or one of the Kardashians."

"They stayed here?" I ask, pulling out a couple shirts from my closet.

"Yeah, tons of famous people have, but a lot of them were rude and entitled, except the Obamas, and ironically which-ever Kardashian it was. I think it was Khloe. Anyway, it must be so nice to have this view every day. My flat here is the size of your bathroom. Oh, to be rich!" She twirls around, into the bathroom and back out, smiling.

"It's really incredible, honestly. Staying here, I mean. Not being rich. I'm not rich, my mom is." I stare out the window at my view of the expansive sea.

"Well, my mother only calls me to borrow money that I don't even have so she can buy a liter of scotch. Wanna trade?" Amara's tone is light, not bitter.

I try to imagine her family, how warm her mother must have been, addiction or not, to raise such a sunshine of a daughter.

"My mom's entire personality is her job, so I might take you up on that," I tease back, kind of meaning it.

I use the reflection of the window to pop out my contacts and turn around to grab a new pair.

"What the! No shit! Your eyes, oh my god." Amara's petite hands wrap around my shoulders as blood pools in my cheeks.

Here we go. There have been times when having hetero-chromia felt cool and unique, but having people constantly commenting on my appearance, whether it was positive or not, got old quickly, and I eventually just wanted to fit in. That, and I have other medical *uniqueness* that's enough for one woman. "I know, they're—"

Her hand zips up to my mouth, gently covering it. "Don't you dare say anything except they're cool, stunning, beautiful, rare . . . and don't even think about putting those brown contacts back in." She eyes me, lowering her hand from covering my mouth. "At least for one night, be you. Don't cover them, and if people annoy you about them too much, I'll fuck them up. I love a good bar fight," she says, making both of us laugh at the idea of her in such chaos.

I don't know how to react, but man she's good at convincing me. I look back out the window and she claps her hands, proud that I'm not protesting. If only she knew that I came here to be anything but myself, to live a temporary fantasy life.

A few boats are in view, and for some reason my mind goes back to Julián. What a small world that Amara, the only person I know on this side of the earth, knows him. I can't seem to get his face out of my mind, but she's good at distracting me.

"This one." She holds up a silver shirt, one I brought thinking I probably wouldn't wear it, but here we are. When the light hits it, it looks black.

"Is the place fancy? Or like a club? I can't do strobe lights, just to let you know," I tell her, hoping she won't ask a ton of questions.

"Not a club. It's like a lounge-type place. I know the whole staff, so if there are too many lights, I can tell them to turn them off. I'm usually drunk as hell, so I can't remember if the lights are strobes or not, but we will figure it out. Everyone has their phobias," she says, handing me the shirt.

Phobias . . . *if only*.

I take my tank top off and pull the shirt over my head. It's tight, and the sleeves are long and bell-shaped. The material isn't see-through but gives off a shimmery vibe and is super sheer, cutting off just above my belly button.

"Can you take your bra off? No pressure if you're not comfortable, but it's going to be hot, and you have the boobs for it. This is Europe. Not only Europe, but summer in Europe." She smiles.

I reach up my back and unsnap the hooks, feeling immediate freedom. Not wearing a bra is the definition of happiness. I would feel beyond uncomfortable walking around my local Target braless, but when in Mallorca . . .

"Hot. So hot. You won't have to pay for a drink all night. Guaranteed."

Amara is such a girls' girl and I love that. I've always yearned for a friendship like this, where the compliments aren't filled with comments for me to overthink. Even though I've only known her for a little over forty-eight hours, she makes me feel so comfortable and so safe. I had the best friend a woman could ask for, but . . . I shake the memory out of my head. I knew I couldn't think about her without breaking down, and this wasn't the time or place for my heart to break for the thousandth time. Their names being so similar doesn't help, and the deep ache of loss will never go away. There will always be a hole there, but I'm trying to learn to shut off the endless bleeding tap when I can.

"Jeans or shorts?" I clear my throat as I ask, "And what are you going to wear?"

"Jeans. Sometimes the seats are sticky." She shrugs, opening the yellow bookbag she brought up to my room, pulling out a burgundy tube top and black pants. The bookbag is sprinkled with little metal pins of animals—a koala, a horselike thing, a yellow animal that looks sort of like a teddy bear. There are seven of them.

She notices me staring at them, trying to figure out what they are. "They're a K-pop group I love. It will take hours to explain, but if you're looking for a new obsession, let me know. This is what I'm wearing; what do you think?" She starts to get dressed carelessly and, of course, her outfit is killer.

The burgundy contrasts with her bright hair and the paleness of her skin sprinkled with freckles is so stunning. Her black jeans are loose around her frame, with two wide slits across the knees.

"You look so good. I haven't seen a tube top in a while. You're making me want to get one."

She smiles, admiring her reflection in the mirror. "I love a tube top moment. Do you have a ribbon or something?" she randomly asks as I pull my blue jeans over my legs and shimmy into them.

"A ribbon? No," I tell her.

"Hmph." She looks around the room. "Can I pretend to be you for a sec?" she asks.

I nod, having no idea what she's up to, but excited to find out. She picks up the phone on the nightstand to call down to the concierge and asks them for a pair of black shoelaces.

"They'll be here in ten minutes," she says proudly.

"Really? I didn't know I could make requests like that."

She laughs. "You're staying in one of the best suites for the entire summer. If you want a group of flamenco dancers at your doorstep daily, your wish is our command. Trust me, we've gotten much crazier requests than a pair of laces."

Within ten minutes, a man brings the laces to the door, and I can tell he and Amara have a close relationship by the way he laughs when he realizes it's her. He's slightly confused as he glances around the room, but when his eyes meet mine and I wave, he lights up and waves back. They speak in Spanish, and he disappears.

She walks over to me, laces in hand.

"If you hate it tell me and I'll use them for something else." Her warm fingers brush my skin as she ties them together and wraps them around the bare skin of my torso, tying them again in the back. I stare in the mirror, and I love the way it looks.

"How did you even think of this?"

"I love finding cheap ways to look hot and make my friends look hot." She shrugs.

"I love it. How random, but cool."

"Yay." She beams. "We should go soon. I'm going to touch my makeup up a bit, but it won't take long. We can walk there; it's only about ten minutes away."

"So, how long have you been here?" I ask Amara as she sticks on little heart-shape rhinestones to the highest part of her cheekbone.

"About two years. I came for fun, stayed a little longer for instalove, then moved here for the hell of it."

"Instalove? Do tell." I brush my hair back, pulling it tight into a high ponytail so it doesn't get in my way tonight.

When my hair is pulled back like this, I look more like my mother than ever. High cheekbones, long chin. The necklace dangling across my collarbone looks like any other dainty white-gold piece, but inside the little seashell-shaped locket is my blood type, my diagnosis, and my mother's phone number. I gently press my fingertips against the cold metal and tug a little, considering taking it off.

Not yet, I decide. One step at a time.

"Her name was Grace. An American who moved here to teach English. I fell haaard," she emphasizes and sighs, rolling her neck in a half circle. "We had an amazing few weeks. Sensual, emotional awareness, all the green flags. Best sex, and I mean *best* of my life." Her eyes widen and her voice draws out to emphasize her point. "I spent my whole holiday with her and decided to extend it. When it was time for her to go back to Barcelona, she started semi-ghosting me, and I did what any rational lovestruck woman would do and found her on Facebook—which she said she didn't have, by the way—and she was freaking married the whole time. Two kids, big fancy house in Florida. Ken-doll husband. Ugh. So I flew to Barcelona and confronted her . . ." She pauses to smile, pointing the tweezers in her hand at me. "I was out of my mind, obviously." She laughs. "She called security on me before I could even get a sentence out. It was so fucked-up! Luckily, I had already made a few friends here—Julián and a few more you'll meet tonight—so I decided to stay. Hotels are always looking for multilingual employees, and I don't have much at home in Germany anyway." She shrugs.

"Just like that? You just moved here?" I ask in wonder at her bravery.

She nods. "Yeah. I moved to Rome for six months just for the artichokes, France because I had the best kiss of my life there with a stranger, almost moved to Greece but it was too expensive . . . I know it sounds cra—"

"Brave," I cut her off. "It sounds incredible and freeing. Wow."

I can't imagine having the freedom to just pop around from country to country, especially over artichokes, but I'm deeply fascinated by Amara's ability to adapt and her independent nature.

"Thanks for not judging me." She leans over and surprises me with a hug.

We just met, yet I feel like I knew her in another life, like maybe she's the mirror of all the things I wish I could be, and maybe she's come into my life as a fairy godmother and is here to teach me to let go and live the rest of my life to the fullest? Whatever the reason, I'm happily going along for the ride. As we go to leave, the pill container on my counter catches my eye under the light, but so far, I'm only feeling better not taking them, not worse, so I flip the switch off and close the door behind us, heading out on my second European adventure.

# Chapter Seven

The walk to the place Amara leads me to is as short as promised. I wore plain white sneakers and made sure to put double bandages on yesterday's blisters and scrapes from the walk from hell. The streets are busier than last night, bustling with lively excitement for a weekday. Amara stops in what seems to be the middle of a small road. If I were walking alone, I would miss the place. There's no sign, just a hanging lantern burning with a real flame inside. I watch it dance in the slight breeze as a wooden door opens. A man the size of a bear steps out of it with his massive arms crossed in front of him. His burly appearance softens when he sees Amara. He smiles at her, greeting us in Spanish.

He doesn't ask for an ID from either of us, but then again, the drinking age here is younger than in the States. The two of them talk for a bit and I smile, clueless about what they're saying but excited to go inside. I've only seen European nightlife on television, and I can feel the subtle vibration of the music inside pouring out into the street.

I can't hear any music blasting, but I can *feel* it, which is a relief. I've only dabbled in the nightclub life, going to a few with some friends during my freshman year of college. They were too loud, too many strobe lights, sticky floors that weren't fun to dance on, and sweaty bodies bumping and shoving into one another. Overall, not for me and not nearly worth the battle with my mom every single time I was out past eight. At first I did like the validation I felt every time a man spoke to me, but I quickly shut them down, which in most instances caused them to immediately insult something about my appearance or declare they didn't like me anyway. It's the ultimate defensive mechanism of fragile men who can't handle being rejected, no matter how politely.

Aside from nightclubs, I'm acutely aware that I'm nowhere near an expert on dating or meeting men, either, but I know that if I were to end up having a love story this summer, I would rather it not begin with a man whose eyes were bloodshot and whose breath reeked of whiskey.

As we enter, I'm shocked by how big the place is. The walls are thick pieces of stone, making it feel like a cave. Yellow lights dangle from the ceiling in the most random patterns and the music, like I gauged from outside, is loud enough to enjoy without being obnoxious or blowing an eardrum. Amara's walk turns into a dance of its own; her curvy hips sway as she leads me to the bar, hand in hand.

The man behind the bar is as tall as the high shelf of liquor behind him. He's free-pouring what seems to be vodka into a purple mixed drink, no measuring glass for the standard two-ounce shot in sight. As if he can feel my stare, he glances over at us, eyes full of life and excitement as he notices Amara and shouts her name. He slides the woman waiting for her purple drink her cocktail, and I hope she has a high tolerance for liquor.

"El meu nadó." The bartender homes in on Amara, rushing to come greet us. He leans over the bar, kissing Amara on the cheeks, then me. I don't think I'll ever get used to being kissed by strangers, and the warmth pooling in my cheeks makes it evident.

"Fabio! Amor meu," Amara coos, hitting him with her bright, stunning smile.

His dark, long hair is tied away from his face in a low ponytail. The tip of his thick hair lands just above the belt around his waist. His white shirt is tight, unbuttoned at the top to show his build and a patch of dark chest hair. His eyes move to me, catching me taking him in.

"And who is this?" He changes to English, his sultry eyes making my stomach flip as he scans my body.

"Fabio, this is Oriah, my American friend. Oriah, my darling, this is the infamous Fabio. Best and most heavy-handed bartender you'll ever meet."

"I noticed the heavy-handedness. You can call me Ry." I laugh, nodding toward the lady with the purple drink who's sucking it down like it's lemonade.

"Hi, Ry. When did you move here?" he asks me.

"Oh, I don't live here. Just here for the summer."

He grins. "Never say never. I came for a summer too. A decade ago."

This place seems to have something magical in the water, in the limestone, something that makes people from all over the world feel at home enough for them to make it their home.

"Where are you from?" Curiosity drips from my voice.

"Milano, but Spain is my home. I hope you'll feel at home too," he says, accent thick and seductive.

I get the feeling he's not hitting on me, even as he reaches for my hand and takes it in his, lifts it to his lips, and kisses the back of it. He doesn't have an ounce of creepy oozing off him.

"Let's have a drink to celebrate your welcome. I'll show you what I'm famous for!" With a wink, he moves like a flash back to the center of the bar.

His hands move remarkably fast. Amara leans her shoulder into mine. "What's your alcohol tolerance like?" she wonders.

"Like medium?" I shrug my shoulders.

I can handle liquor, but after seeing Fabio's idea of a drink, I don't dare to say I have a high tolerance.

"Medium is good. Medium means you'll survive the night," she says as Fabio pulls out a torch and lights our shots on fire.

"What on earth?" I ask myself as he slides a bright blue, literally glowing and burning shot into my hand.

"They taste like candy!" Amara promises, clinking her glass to mine. The fire dies down, leaving a tiny blue flame that I assume is edible? Amara dips her tongue into hers to put it out, so I do the same. It's not hot at all. I don't understand, but I don't need to. Now isn't the time for questioning; now is the time for *fun*.

"That sounds . . ." I almost say "dangerous," but Oriah Pera in Mallorca wouldn't be afraid of anything. "Yummy," I say instead, pouring the drink down my throat in one solid swig.

It's delicious and most definitely dangerous.

"So?" Fabio urges with wiggling eyebrows, knowing he's good at what he does.

There's no way anyone on earth wouldn't love it. It tastes like a Starburst and Skittles without being overly sweet. Not a hint of the burn I'm used to when I take a shot, even as it settles in my stomach.

"Now I know why you're famous." I smile, licking the sugar-coated rim of the shot glass.

He claps his hands, his head falling back, hair swaying. "*Infamous*, honey. Infamous."

"Another round, please!" Amara requests, and Fabio ignores the growing line at the other end of the bar and makes us four more.

One for now, another for ten minutes later, he advises, as we carry them to a table in the corner. The table is made of old wood, not sanded and polished. It's beautiful, and the moisture rings from drink after drink being left on it only make it more unique. The chairs are simple low, square-shaped stools. We sit and I look around the cave-like bar. I can almost feel all the memories that have been made here.

It's not crowded but not empty. Small clusters of people are spread around the space, talking, laughing, a few of them dancing to the music. There are more women than men, that is, until a group of them walk in just as I have the thought. From what I've googled, nightlife here doesn't truly start until much, much later, so this is the calm before the storm.

"By the way, would you mind if I have someone meet me here? I was going to wait to meet her until tomorrow, but she's messaging me and she's sooo gorgeous and seems sane enough, and since you're here, it would be safer," Amara explains. "I met her on Tinder and she's only here for two weeks, but if you're not comfortable, just let me know and I can meet her later."

I shake my head. "No, of course she can come! I don't mind at all."

Amara's face lights up and she pulls her phone out, tapping and swiping the screen. She holds it up to show me.

"Look at her, my god. And she's a medical student. Hot and smart. Killll me." She rolls her eyes back, looking down at the screen with a melty smile, the kind of smile I daydream about someone having for me.

"She's stunning." I swipe through a handful of photos of the woman. Deep brown skin; high cheekbones; thick, perfectly shaped brows. I can see why Amara is in a hurry to meet her.

"Her name's Prisha. She's from India but is living in Sweden right now while going to medical school. Okay," she says, typing on her phone, dramatically breathing in and out. "I'm telling her to come."

"As long as you don't move to Sweden before I go back to Texas," I tease her.

She cackles, a high-pitched lovely sound. "I can't make any promises."

We cheers to that, taking our now-flameless shots.

# Chapter Eight

Prisha shows up quickly and is even more beautiful than her photos. She glows as she walks through the bar, impossible to miss. Her raven hair is so smooth, giving the illusion of glass as she approaches.

"Oh my god, she's even hotter than I thought. She's too hot for me; what do I do? Should I run out the back door?" Amara squeezes my arm, and I laugh at the sudden deflation of her confidence as she attempts to hide behind me.

"She's thinking the same thing about you, I'm sure of it. And no running, you brought me here. Now talk to her." I gently untangle her death-grip on my arm and push her toward the approaching woman.

"Hi." Amara smiles, showing a side of herself that I didn't think existed. A shyness, a nervousness that makes her even more endearing.

"Hi." Prisha's voice sounds like a purr.

Her mouth twitches a little as she smiles, matching Amara's energy.

"This is my friend Ry." Amara touches my shoulder. "She's here for the summer from the States, and she's here to make sure you don't murder me or something."

Prisha's laugh is a musical, low-pitched sound. I love the details of people's laughs. Strangers or friends, you can tell so much about someone by their laugh. It's one of the only moments in human behavior when there's no guard, no walls, just a clear undiluted sound unique to them.

"Hello, Ry, I'm Prisha. Not a murderer, so I hope you won't be too bored." I take her outreached hand and shake it gently.

I'm not the one on a date with her and I'm already mesmerized. I really hope this goes well, for Amara's sake. Amara motions for all of us to sit down and the small talk begins. The warmer their conversation becomes—why Prisha is going to med school in Sweden, why she chose to come to Mallorca for her break, how Amara ended up living here—I begin to drown them out to give them a sense of privacy. Looking around the bar, there are more men now. I'm getting annoyed as I find myself comparing every single one of them to the man from the beach yesterday. Julián. The nameless asshole with the pretty name. Nearly all of them are handsome, but nothing close to him. How obnoxious.

"Ry? Are you there?" Amara's voice pulls me from the maze in my mind.

"Yeah, sorry." I smile, relieved she has no clue that I'm daydreaming about her stupid one-night-stand-loving friend.

"Anyone interesting?" She wiggles her brows.

I shake my head fiercely. "Nope."

God, I need another drink to get him off my mind.

"Let's take some pics together!" Amara pulls out her phone and starts taking selfies of the three of us. I follow their lead of when to smile, when to hold up a peace sign, when to smile with teeth.

"Can you take one of me and Ry?" Amara hands her phone to Prisha, who happily takes at least five photos from every angle.

When she gives the phone back to Amara their fingers brush, and even in the dim lighting I can see the goose bumps rise on Amara's arm. I look away, smiling but trying not to embarrass her.

"I'm going back to the bar, want another round?" I ask them.

Without breaking eye contact with each other, they both nod, and I leave them in their own little world to get us drinks.

Fabio, busy as ever, finishes perfectly pouring a draft beer into a tall glass and saunters over to me, passing the crowd of already waiting costumers. The people in line don't seem to care or are used to the way he works. Without a word, he winks at me and starts pouring the shots, sans flames, which I suppose would lose the novelty after a few. My eyes widen when he hands me a tray with at least ten shots on it.

"Enjoy, lovely, and have the time of your life!" He dashes off to get back to the line.

The music has gotten louder, and it's gotten busier since we arrived, but he's still the only one working behind the bar.

When I get back to the table, Prisha's hand is resting on Amara's thigh, a clear sign that she's into her too. Prisha's dangling gold earrings catch the light as she laughs at something Amara says in her ear. I feel bad ruining their moment, but I'm carrying a tray of shots and have nowhere else to put them and no one else to take them with.

"I'm back with a ton of shots," I say, stating the obvious and nodding toward the tray as I sit it down, trying not to spill any in the process.

"Ry! Look who liked the pic of us within literally ten seconds of me posting it!" Amara holds her phone up and shows me an Instagram profile. There are only two photos, one of the sunset over a calm blue sea and the other of the back of a man's head, which I recognize a little too quickly for my own good.

"Julián?" I already know the answer but confirm anyway.

She nods. "He's definitely got his eye on you."

"Who's Julián?" Prisha asks me.

I shake my head. "No one. I mean no one to me. He's Amara's friend who I happened to meet randomly, and he was such an asshole. Arrogant and hates tourists, which doesn't make sense when you live in a tourist-filled place, but he's grumpy and thinks he knows everything. He's the worst."

Amara's eyes widen like she's trying to tell me something, and I turn my neck to see what she's staring at behind me.

"The worst, huh?" Julián, in the flesh, is standing directly behind me. I track my eyes up to his face, and of course he's got a shit-eating grin spread across it.

"I— Well, I didn't—" I stammer, because there's no way in hell to dig myself out of this hole.

Julián holds his hand up. "I don't care what you think of me, I'm just happy to hear it firsthand, but you sure had a lot to say about someone who is no one," he says with pure amusement, grabbing ahold of another stool and dragging it to sit right next to me.

"Julián, this is Prisha. Say hi," Amara nudges him.

Julián turns on his charm, which makes my skin itch, warmly smiling at Prisha, greeting her way more kindly than he did me yesterday. I guess he only dislikes American tourists?

Julián reaches for one of the shots without asking, and even though they aren't technically mine, it annoys me and I move the tray just before he can grab one.

His eyes snap up to mine. "Now you're guarding the drinks, Miss America?"

"So is it that I'm American that bothers you, since you seem to be nice to everyone else?" I stomp my foot, instantly regretting the choice.

"Nah, it's that you're entitled . . . and American."

"See! Asshole." I look at Prisha and Amara to confirm my statement. Prisha smiles and Amara laughs.

"Let's drink and everyone make nice?" Amara suggests.

I wonder where their other friends are, the ones Amara told me were coming. The ones who were not supposed to include Julián.

"Fine." I take one of the drinks and hand it to Julián, an olive branch of a gesture.

We each grab one and clink our glasses together, then down the shots. I try my best not to look at Julián, but damn, it's hard. He's dressed in a simple salt water–stained T-shirt, linen shorts, and sandals. He has that vibe of not caring what he's wearing and knowing he just looks good. Then again, with that face and that body, he doesn't have to put in much effort. He would look sexy in anything. I roll my eyes, and he catches me, raising a brow in curiosity.

"Something bothering you?" he leans in to ask me, his knee slightly knocking into mine. I don't move.

"Besides you, no," I respond half-heartedly.

"Hey, that's not very nice." When he smiles, I notice the slight overlap of his two front teeth.

"You told me you never want to see me again," I remind him.

"Yeah, and I meant it. But here we are." He puts his hands on his bare knees, rubbing them across his skin.

"Shall we call a truce, then, for Amara's sake? You don't even have a reason not to like me, and I don't want to waste any more energy bickering with you." I grab another shot and down it before he responds.

I watch him count the shots left on the tray. Five. "But it's fun, no?"

"No."

"And I don't need a reason. Neither do you. How many of Fabio's shots have you had?" he asks, his thick brows drawn together.

I try to count . . . one at the bar, another with Amara, then another with Prisha too? Am I missing one? Or two? "I don't know. Like three-ish? Maybe four."

"You should be careful. I've seen a lot of blue vomit coming out of foreigners when they have too many of his shots," Julián warns, as if he actually cares if I get sick or not.

I tilt my head to the side and look into his eyes. "I bet you have seen a lot," I mutter, recalling what Amara told me about him hooking up with so many tourists. It shouldn't bother me. It doesn't bother me.

Does it?

I grab another and hand one to him, hoping he's wrong about the whole vomit situation. I inherited my mom's tolerance, though I don't drink often, but when in Mallorca . . .

"Cheers to a night you're going to regret." He laughs, downing the shot.

I take mine and watch as he licks the sugar rim of the glass. His tongue moves slowly, each flake of sugar melting as he glides it. My belly flips. My imagination runs wild, flashes of his tongue running along my skin filling my mind.

Oh god. I need to get up, get away from him. Him and these shots are not mixing well.

"How do you know her, anyway?" Julián asks Amara, looking at her as if I'm not sitting right there.

"Not such a detective now, are you?" I roll my eyes.

He hasn't connected the dots to the hotel, the way he so arrogantly did last night.

"Ah." A light bulb goes off in his head. "The hotel. You always pick up strays," he tells her.

I have the urge to knock him across the back of his head, but I restrain myself. Something about his personality digs under my typically thick skin. Being raised by a statue of a mother who has zero qualms about sharing her opinion on any and every choice I—or anyone around her—has ever made has conditioned me to be this way. I choose to be thankful instead of resentful, and it's come in handy a few times. Like now, when I want to tell this asshole to fuck off, that he thinks he's way cooler than he is, and that I don't give a shit if he likes me, but he better stop being rude or I'll—

"We're all strays, Julián. Even you," she tells him, cutting off my mental lashing at him.

Her fingers dance on Prisha's open palm. "And strays should stick together, not act like children on a play yard."

"Yeah, yeah. You're usually better at picking friends than this one." He nods toward me, and I reach for another shot.

There's a humor and softness behind his teasing that keep my usual temper at bay. "Clearly she's not or she wouldn't be your friend," I reply, full of immaturity.

The corner of his mouth turns up into a half smile. The hint of a dimple forms in his cheek. Damn it, why does he have to be so hot? I can't even blame the alcohol because I was instantly attracted to him at the beach, and I'm clearly desperately longing for some sort of adventure.

"Touché." He picks up a water bottle and takes a drink, wiping his mouth with his loose T-shirt. It lifts at the bottom, revealing a sliver of sun-kissed skin. The alcohol in my body makes me want to tell him about the cool reusable bottle my hotel gave me, but I get the feeling that would prove his point about me even more, so I zip it.

I start to tune out the small talk again, Prisha telling Amara about her siblings in a low voice that I can barely hear anyway. I watch Fabio behind the bar. He spins and twirls liquor bottles, uses his torch to impress the patrons, dances a little when the song changes. He's a pro.

"You know his name isn't really Fabio, right? It's a tourist trap of a fake name," Julián leans in to tell me, his breath touching my ear.

I shiver, jerking away.

"How do you know?" I ask him, not admitting that I assumed that already.

Julián licks his lips. "I know everything. Just like I finally know your name, Ry. Though I will miss creating new ways to annoy you."

Amara's Instagram post must have given it away. "It's Oriah, so you don't know everything."

He studies me so intensely that I shift in my seat. "Oriah," he says slowly, as if each letter deserves its own moment. "Your name suits you perfectly."

If I keep having to be around this man, my eyes are going to roll out of my head.

"Right. The name Fabio also suits him." I pull the conversation back to the bartender and away from the burn in my chest and the racing of my heart. "He kind of does look like Fabio." I laugh, noting his long hair and thick build, like the shirtless muscleman on the cover of many classic romance novels.

"Do you know who Fabio is, the romance guy? I'm sure your mom has a book or two with him on the cover," I joke, trying to keep the tension between us away.

Something changes in his posture at the mention of his mother. His grip on the bottle tightens and the plastic crunches in his hand. He purposely looks away from me and stares into the distance. I can physically feel him putting a wall between us.

"What's your—" I start to ask, but then decide I don't care.

If he wants to be an asshole, more power to him, but I'm here to have fun, not bicker with him, so I stand up. The room spins a little, but I stabilize myself quickly.

"Anyone want to dance?" I ask Amara and Prisha, who are now only an inch away from each other, lost in their own little world.

Julián smirks, points at his chest, and shakes his head. "Not a chance."

"I wasn't asking you." I snort, grabbing one last drink and slamming it before making my way to the small, tiled area where there are a handful of people dancing.

It's mostly couples. The live band begins a new song, the beat slow, sensual, and jazzlike. My mind is on cloud nine, my hips following the rhythm of the music. I close my eyes, shutting off the last bit of uncertainty of dancing alone, and let the music control my body. Dance has always been my first love since I was a child. Out of all the things I *can't* do, this is one that I can and happen to excel at. Music has a way of crawling under the flesh over my bones and taking over, moving my body without thought. Blossoming, expanding, awakening something inside me. It's been too long since I've felt this, since I've had the energy and excitement to relax enough to let my desire for dance take control and my mind shut off.

The passage of time doesn't exist as one song ends, and another begins, again and again. A pair of hands on my waist pushes through my haze. The corners of reality are blurry, dancing and warping, pulling me further into a pulsing, addictive rhythm. The body behind me is solid. I feel it pressing against me, knowing by the mere size and scent of cologne that it's a man. I don't care what he looks like or who he is; so far, he's a great dance partner. I keep my eyes closed as I turn around to face him, lifting a thigh onto his, our bodies melting together perfectly. The stranger moves his hand to my hair seductively and even in my mildly hallucinogenic state, it becomes clear how long it's been since I've been touched this way. I haven't felt desired in so long, just lethargic and bustling around hospitals, classrooms, doctors' offices.

The music picks up in tempo and I have yet to open my eyes. I don't want to or need to, not yet. I want to soak this moment in, that tiny crevice of rarity that comes when you move in sync with someone else. The connection of two people while dancing is incomparable, speaking the same language without saying a word. He twirls and whirls me, I push my ass against him and rub my hands down his arms, stopping at a thick piece of metal—a watch, I realize—and grab his hands, letting them roam my body. Down my thighs and back up. At this point, I'm so intoxicated, and not just by Fabio's shots, that I don't care what he looks like as long as he's not a creep.

When I blink them open and turn to face him, he's a little older than I expected, but I'm not disappointed by what I see. His black hair is cropped short like an American soldier, but I can tell he's not American. The shape of his jaw is wide, his smile bright, revealing perfect, toothpaste-commercial-level teeth. He's tall and wide, and strong, I add to the list, as he lifts me off my feet, spinning me around.

I laugh, my head falling back as something flashes. A camera? I ignore it for a second, keeping eye contact with my new dance partner. Another flash. And another. I close my eyes, steadying myself. Not now . . . not when I'm having the time of my life. *Please, universe,* I beg, *let me have just one night . . .*

The flashing continues and I pull myself away from the man, trying to explain to him that I need to sit down. Looking around the room, I can't figure out where the table with Amara and Prisha is. I can't remember where the bar is. With confusion in his eyes, the man starts to speak to me in a language that doesn't sound like Spanish.

"I'm sorry, I need to find my friend," I tell him, gently taking his hands off my waist.

His grip tightens as he keeps speaking to me in another language. I shake my head, apologizing again, but really, really needing him to let me go.

"We were having a great time . . ." he finally says in English.

"I know," I pant, desperately looking for Amara's bright hair. "It's not you— It's the lights . . . I need to go." I attempt to pull his hands away again.

It takes me too long to realize that he's not allowing me to. What the hell? I push at his thick arms, but to no avail.

"Let me go!" I yell at him, my panic increasing at the potential of what could happen if I stay here with the lights flashing.

I tug at his wrist, the watch catches between the friction, and I feel the metal push apart. His eyes flare and he shoves at my chest, my body slams against something . . . someone.

I turn around to apologize. "I'm so sorry."

Julián. I'm so relieved to see a familiar face that I don't care if it's him of all people.

"You broke my fucking watch!" the man shouts at me, puffing his chest and huffing his breath in my face.

Now that my dance state has ended, everything feels and appears completely different. The guy isn't hot, not even remotely. He has an aggressive aura around him, especially now that he's shouting in my face about breaking his watch. Any attractiveness he had is vastly outweighed by his erratic behavior.

"I didn't mean to! I told you to let go of me!" I close my eyes again, trying to avoid the flashing.

I press my body against Julián for stability, half expecting him to move out of the way and tell me to fuck off, but he doesn't. He squares his shoulders and moves toward the man.

"I was watching you the whole time. I saw you holding on to her when she told you to stop and you didn't. It's your own fault your shitty watch got broken," he tells him casually but loud enough that the man and everyone around us hear it.

The man's face reddens, embarrassment and anger swirling in his light eyes. He pushes Julián, making us both rock back a few feet. Julián says something to him in Spanish that I can't hear or understand, and motions for me to go to the table. I follow his finger and finally spot Amara and Prisha, who are making out, and rush toward them. I grab my purse, not wanting to interrupt, but I must get out of here.

Neither of them notices me as I disappear back into the crowd, closing and opening my eyes to the match the rhythm of the flash. Not that that will help, but it gives me a false sense of hope. Passing the bar, I wonder if Fabio will be pissed or get in trouble if I don't pay. There's a crowd in front of the bar, so I'll come back first thing tomorrow and pay. If this wasn't an emergency, I'd never do this. Just as I reach the door, I'm pulled back by my purse. Thinking the strap got stuck on something, I yank it, but the resistance is too strong. Fuck me. It's the watch guy.

"Pay me for my watch!" he says, his jaw tightening as he holds up the barely "broken" watch.

"You wouldn't let go of me! I'm sorry about your watch, you can come to my hotel tomorrow and I'll give you money for it, but I have to leave!"

He studies me for a moment. "Which hotel?"

Relief fills me and my shoulders drop. As much as I hate throwing my mother's money around, I will do anything to get the hell out of this place right now.

A warm hand clasps over my mouth just as I say the name of my hotel. I recognize the smell of him without looking. Julián, the man who's everywhere.

"Don't tell him," he says in my ear.

"Here." He throws a bill into the air, and it floats down, dancing between us before it lands on the floor. I can't tell how much it is, but it doesn't seem to be enough for the man.

"I don't need you to rescue me," I growl at Julián.

Even though I'm thankful, there's something about him that still makes me defensive, like I need to make sure he knows I don't need him. I can pay for the stupid watch myself. *Well, my mom could.*

"That's not enough!" the guy says, grabbing Julián's shirt and pulling him closer.

I look toward the door to find the security guy from earlier, but he's nowhere to be found. Fuck.

"It's not a fucking Rolex," Julián tells him, trying to loosen the man's grip on him.

It's not working. Julián's strong, but this man is huge and enraged and way more intoxicated than the two of us combined. Veins popping out on his forehead and forearms, sweat on his oily forehead and the neckline of his shirt. As he draws one fist back to punch Julián, I wrap my purse around my fist and swing, hoping the water bottle from the hotel is strong enough to at least surprise him enough to let go of Julián.

With a cartoon-like WOMP, my purse slaps across the man's face and he stumbles back. I grab hold of Julián's shirt and drag him out the door with me. We run to the end of the street, turn the corner, and stop. I'm out of breath from all the adrenaline, my body instantly melting a little as the night air rolls over me. I bend my knees and put my hands on them, trying to catch my breath but finding myself laughing.

"Why did you do that? Someone's going to call the police." Julián's voice falls on my ears.

I snap my eyes open.

"Because he was about to beat the shit out of you," I remind him. "We should go before he comes out here."

He scoffs, "He was *not* going to beat the shit out of me." He says this as if we were debating a completely unreasonable notion, like whether dogs could fly or not.

"Seemed like it," I huff.

"I saved your ass, and you still have an attitude," he says, laughing into the night.

"Correction, I saved you." Whether or not I was right or not wasn't the point, and I did appreciate him getting the guy away from me, but no way in hell was I going to say it.

"You know you're wrong." He seems a little amused and less annoyed than I expect. "But I don't care enough to argue with you. Were you sick or something?"

My heart stops at the word *sick*. "What?"

He nods toward the direction of the bar. "Back there, when you were dancing, you were fine and then it seemed like you were getting sick. I warned you about those shots."

I laugh, the fakest laugh in my life. "Oh yeah. Totally. It was the shots."

Something about the way he's looking at me makes me squirm. For a stranger, he sure can read me like a book. I can feel it in my bones as he continues to study me. "Anyway, thanks for trying to help. I'll try not to see you again, really this time."

In the distance, I hear a siren. We both look toward the flashing lights reflecting in the sky a few streets over.

"I told you." He shrugs. "Come on." His hand reaches out for me, but before I can grab it, he drops it.

We quickly cross another road, and he stops in front of a motorcycle-looking thing. Of course he drives one.

"Put this on." He pushes a black helmet against my chest.

I look at the death trap on wheels. "What? No freaking way! Plus, you're drunk."

"I had two drinks over an hour ago, and my tolerance is a hell of a lot stronger than yours, but fine. Stay here and get arrested or lost again, Miss Know-It-All." He climbs onto the bike, puts a helmet on, and gives me one more chance to get on.

If something happens and I hit my head . . .

If my mom . . .

I shut off the internal worried monologue and put the helmet on. This is what I'm here for, to do things I would never, ever, typically do. I swing my leg over the side and Julián puts his hands over mine, wrapping my arms around his torso.

"Stop calling me annoying nicknames," I growl into his ear.

I'm terrified and excited as he pulls onto the stone road, whipping through the warm summer wind mixing beautifully with his laughter.

# Chapter Nine

When we finally stop, it's been either ten minutes or an hour, I can't recall. The ride was much less terrifying than I thought it would be, and he didn't do the asshole thing of speeding up to try and scare me. Once we reached the shoreline, the smell of the salt water filled the air and he slowed down, taking the curves slowly enough that I could hear the waves crashing. It became relaxing, freeing. I can see the appeal now. Not that I'm going to make a hobby out of it, but I don't hate it.

"Wasn't so bad, was it? You're alive," Julián says, kicking his foot to put the break stand down.

"Alive, yes. Not so bad," I admit, yanking my hands from his torso and crossing them in front of me, flushed that I kept hold of him a bit too long.

He pulls his helmet off. "I can't believe you were going to tell that guy your hotel name. You're really naïve, aren't you?" he asks, shaking his hair out.

I tug at the helmet on my head, trying to find the clasp to undo it. Julián steps off the bike and it shifts a little, changing the balance, making me uneasy. I reach out and hold on to his shirt, and his hands move to help me. My heart is pounding, reminding me of just how alive I am. I don't need to think too much about whether it's the bike or him that's making me feel so jittery, like I've had ten shots of espresso. He stays standing directly in front of me, my mind jotting down the thickness and dramatic curl of his eyelashes, seeming to shine under the dim streetlamp. His hands reach behind my head as he takes my helmet off in one gentle but swift motion and puts it back into a pouch on the side of the bike. I catch a glimpse of the cover of a crossword puzzle book inside. He must take one with him everywhere. Is it anxiety? Or just a quirky, old-school hobby?

Instead of commenting on it or responding to his accusation that I'm naïve, I decide to change the subject altogether.

"I can't believe you stalked me on Instagram. You don't seem like the type to use social media."

He laughs, a soft whisper nearly lost between the wind and waves. "I did not stalk you. I randomly saw a photo of you with Amara when I was already on my way there. She invited me and our friends before your plane—or hell, probably private jet—even landed on our island. Before you were even thought of."

"That's harsh." Honesty pushes the words out of my mouth before I can catch them.

He stares at me for a beat as if he's trying to figure out what was wrong with what he said. Just as I'm about to attempt to lighten the mood and deflect from my sensitivity, he speaks. "I don't mean you weren't thought of." He rubs his thumbs against his temples, the rest of his fingers lost in his dark hair.

He adds, "We made plans as a group is all I meant."

"Why didn't the rest of the group show up? Amara said you never come out during the week. I didn't expect you to be there."

He tilts his head to the side, looking at me a little too intensely. I look away as he replies, "I don't know why they didn't come, but why are you and Amara talking about me anyways?"

"Because . . . I was complaining about the asshole— Sorry, the not-so-nice guy who helped me get back to my hotel, and she told me she knows you."

"What else did she tell you?" he wonders.

We make eye contact and those damn eyes of his make me want to tell him every word, but logically it would be a bad idea to tell him what Amara said, and I would never want to do anything that would cause her drama or stress. She's been so kind to me, so I decide to lie to the one who hasn't.

"That was it. Oh, and that you're a fisherman or something." I shrug, leaning my hands behind me onto the smooth metal of the bike. The salty air smells incredible as it gently brushes against my face, arms, torso, caressing my bare skin where I've rolled my sleeves up.

"Hmph." He doesn't seem to believe me, but that's all he's getting out of me. "Are you going to stay on my bike, or do you want to go down to the water? You keep staring at it; I can feel you longing for it."

Maybe it's the slight language barrier or his choice of words, but that damn pang in the bottom of my stomach throbs again.

"Let's go, then." I hop off his bike and bend down to cross under the wooden fence between us and the sand.

I spot a narrow dirt path carved out between the low brush and I follow it until my feet touch the sand. Without looking back, I can hear Julián's footsteps behind me. I listen carefully to them, the quiet flip and flop of the sand against his sandals, the way the sound changes when he takes them off. I stop for a moment to take my shoes off, because sandy sneakers are a nightmare, and carry them in one hand. It's darker down here without the streetlamps, but the moonlight is bright enough to make out the line of the water, the sand, the cliffs, and of course Julián's face, as I turn around to look at him.

"Is this beach for locals only too?" I ask with a hint of sarcasm.

He smiles. "All of our beaches are. Sorry, you should go back up to the street. I forgot you're American for a second."

"Ha. Ha." I narrow my eyes. "You're the one who brought me here, betraying your people," I tease, allowing myself to get drawn toward the water.

The shallow waves finally kiss my toes, warm and relieving. Washing over the tops of my feet, in and back out, in and back out.

"Are your feet better today?" He looks down between us at my bandaged feet, my sneakers in my hand.

I nod, surprised that he cared to remember, let alone ask. We're quiet for a moment, and I close my eyes again, a natural reaction when I'm relaxed.

"You like the water, huh?" Julián asks maybe two minutes later. I open my eyes and he's now standing closer to me.

I nod. "That obvious, huh?"

"A little, but I'm very observant."

"Is there anything about you that you would consider a flaw? Or do you just think you're perfect?" I stare back out onto the water before he responds.

There seems to be something soft, almost vulnerable about him, if I didn't know better. "It would take your whole summer to listen to me list all my flaws."

His response quiets me. I don't have a witty or snarky thing to say. There's an honesty to him that I want to see more of, feel more of.

"And you? Do you have any flaws, Miss Know-It-All?"

"Only tragic ones," I tell him, letting him decide if I'm serious.

The silence between us feels soft and safe. Not what I expected when alone with Julián, who just a few hours ago was my enemy. He starts to walk forward, and my eyes follow him to the water, as does my body. I leave my shoes in the sand and roll the bottom of my jeans up.

"I wish I would have worn a swimsuit. I'm dying to swim." I sigh, debating just how annoying it would be to wear heavy, soaked jeans and top on the bike back to my hotel.

Then again, this is Europe, and there's not a soul here on the beach to see me. Except Julián, who's clearly used to going to nude beaches and has seen many, many, many women naked. I won't be fully nude anyway, just in a shirt and panties. Of course, I wore the most boring panties I own, and I'm not wearing a bra for once. I have the urge to slap myself at the thought of caring what he thinks about my panties.

I shimmy out of my jeans, watching him like a hawk for a reaction, but there isn't one. Not even a glance my way after he realizes what I'm doing. I toss my pants next to Julián's shirt and my purse and try to untie the laces that Amara tied around my waist. The knot is too tight, and my nails are too short to get it to budge. Leaving it, I go back to the edge of the water and slip in. Julián's about ten feet farther out than me, the moonlight shining off his bare shoulders and broad back. I walk out toward him, surprised how shallow the water is as I walk.

"Does it feel like a dream to live here?" I ask, breaking the silence between us.

"No. But if I were only here for a holiday, it likely would."

Okay, so we're back to being combative . . .

He seems to notice my defensiveness.

"Not talking about you," he explains. "Just in general. Our island is suffering from the tourists, but on the other hand it's surviving because of them. It's a double-edged sword. Most of our working class can barely afford to keep their homes due to the land value increasing. The pollution, the cultural shift, it's not very dreamlike."

"I'm sorry. Not for asking, but for what's happening. I guess when your livelihood depends on an industry that's harming it, it's not all sunny days, warm water, and yummy food."

"Not at all. But hey, I'm healthy, my pare—that's my dad— is healthy, and our business hasn't been shut down." Sighing, he adds "yet" tacked on to the end, making it known there's something more to say. But he didn't mention his mom, and I've been intrusive enough for now.

"And you? What's it like where you're from? I'm sure your life is night-and-day different from mine. I can tell by your clothes alone." It's his turn to ask a question, wrapped in an assumption.

The water is steady, the waves gentle, as if they've settled only to allow us to have a conversation in front of them.

"It's boring. Everything is the same . . . day in and day out. I feel privileged and bratty saying that to you when you're dealing with bigger things, but I'm so tired of being bored and lifeless. No passion, nothing to look forward to. Life feels like one endless loop of the same mundane day."

"Everyone has a reason to have their own perspective on life. Rich girls can be sad too." He grins. His response is understanding and not judgmental. Who would have thought he had it in him?

"Rich girls can be sad too," I repeat. "I should put that on a T-shirt." I laugh, imagining it going ironically viral online.

"See, you Americans, always stealing ideas and colonizing . . ."

"Hey, I took European history. Spanish people also colonized." I splash a bit of water toward him, and he laughs, a sound I haven't heard from him yet.

I've heard his sarcastic laugh, his annoyed laugh, his trying-to-hold-back laugh, but this one feels deeper, more real, like I can reach out and touch it.

"Fine. Fine. What do you do for work?" he asks.

I push through the embarrassment as I respond. "I don't . . . I was in a local dance academy and had to leave . . . Then I got into a program for business just to have something to do to kill time, but honestly, I've never worked. Even when I wanted to, my mom wouldn't let me, and even though she travels all the time, she would immediately find out. I always have keepers checking on me, so school was my only escape. But I don't even know if I want to go back to school, which is causing a lot of tension between my mom and me. I know how spoiled that sounds, but that's my story."

I hesitate to drag my eyes to him, fully expecting some sarcastic and judgy comment, but it doesn't come. I can't bare the silence.

"What? You don't have anything mean to say about me never working a day in my life?"

He shakes his head. "Nope. Not this time," he says, disappearing as he dives under the water.

A distant beeping noise stops me in my tracks, and I realize it's my phone. My alarm for my medication. I rush to the shore and grab my phone with wet hands, shutting the alarm off. I have a few texts from my mom and a missed call and text from Amara. I text them both, telling them I'm fine and safe, informing my mom I'll see her at breakfast and promising to call Amara in the morning.

I leave Julián out of both conversations for two opposite reasons. I don't want Amara to come here during my alone time with him. The realization of that makes me feel guilty and a little confused, but when I look out at the water and Julián, I can't deny it. I'm increasingly attracted to him, and even though it won't go anywhere or matter by the time the sun comes up, I want every second of alone time with this man I can get.

"Everything okay?" he calls out, his voice echoing through his cupped hands.

"Yeah! Just my mom and Amara, making sure I'm alive."

He stands up and walks toward me, leaving the ocean behind him. "How old are you anyway?" he questions from a few meters away.

"Twenty-three. My birthday was last month. Why do you ask? How old are you?"

"I asked because you've mentioned your mom a lot and I started to get worried that I kidnapped a minor."

"If my mom were here, she would agree. But I'm an adult. How old are you?" I turn his question back to him again.

"Twenty-six. My birthday was yesterday."

My eyes go wide. "Your birthday was yesterday?"

He shrugs his broad shoulders, the definite line of muscles retracting. He's built like a fisherman, that's for sure.

"Yeah, why?"

"And you spent it on a nude beach, alone?"

His bottom lip curls up and he bites down, hiding a smile.

"Don't make me sound like a pervert. I spent it doing whatever I wanted and not working. Don't be so uptight about nudity; it's not a big deal." He gestures to me in my soaked, skin-gripping shirt and panties.

"Stop staring at me." I cross my arms over my bare torso.

"You've been staring at me all night, and right now I have less clothes on than you."

Though he has a valid point, I ignore it and try to look away from the beads of water shimmering on his buff arms, his toned chest . . .

"Why didn't you mention it was your birthday yesterday?" I wonder.

His neck jerks a little; his face changes from cocky to confused. "Why would I? We don't know each other."

Right. We don't know each other at all. It's been a little over a day since I met him, so why does it feel like weeks, months, years even? Is it my lack of exposure to men since I graduated college?

"Feels a little longer, yeah?" he surprises me by saying.

Debating whether to be honest or not, I look at him. His eyelashes are soaked, even more thick and bold than usual. "Yeah, actually."

"Same. I don't know why, but I feel the same."

I can feel it as it happens, my guard rolling down the sand and getting lost in the sea. He's good, too good at this. He steps toward me, making the gap between us less than a few feet. My toes curl in the sand, the granules attempting to stabilize me. I've never met a man who's so insanely versed in the art of seduction.

Even his tone has changed as he asks, "Do you have a boyfriend back home?"

His eyes feel like a paintbrush, stroking gently, leaving traces of watercolor on every inch of my skin in its wake. His tongue slides across his lips slowly as I try to catch my breath.

I shake my head. "Shouldn't you have asked me that before?"

My fingers tug at the knot at my waist as I try to keep a bit of reality within the bubble we're suddenly in. The air has shifted, something between us has changed and ignited.

"Here," he whispers, and I shiver as his fingertips brush my skin. Within seconds the lace loosens and falls to the ground at my feet. I look back up at him, impressed. "Fisherman, remember?"

"Ah, yeah." I can barely speak, my mouth is so dry.

In contrast, he's fully composed as his expert fingers drag along the dip of my hips. I suck in a breath and put my hand on his shoulder to keep my knees from buckling. His skin is cold compared to mine, his chest calmly rising and falling with each breath. Time stops and speeds up at once, and everything in my sight looks so much more vivid, the deep bow of Julián's bottom lip, the freckles on his nose and chin. I begin to count them as he leans in.

I close my eyes, anticipating his lips touching mine, but they don't.

"I don't hook up with women I just met." His teeth graze my ear, gently biting the tender pad of my lobe. I groan, instantly aching between my thighs.

"Really?" I push my hands toward his waistline, pressing my fingernails just hard enough to leave the slightest of marks on his skin. His eyes, full of lust, roll back. His hands pull me closer to press my body flush to his. The intensity is so strong, I think I might faint if he weren't holding me up.

I continue to tease him; this time my hands move across his expansive back.

"Yeah, really." His breath is warm across my lips, my body throbbing.

"I heard that's your favorite type of woman to sleep with," I whisper in his ear, purposely letting my lips touch him.

As the words come out, he instantly pulls away from me, putting at least five feet between us. I'm confused and flustered.

"What did you just say?" he asks, the words coming out in small puffs.

I stare at him, wondering why he's so pissy when I'm fine with his lifestyle of hooking up with random foreigners. Right now, I just want to be one of them.

"Look, I'm not judging you. I'm fine with it. If anything, I'm very, very fine with it," I admit, my body screaming at me in desperation to have him.

I take a step toward him, but he walks backward, making it clear he's pissed off.

His brows scrunch together in frustration. "So, you heard from Amara that I go around sleeping with women and you—" He cuts himself off mid-sentence, like it's not worth finishing his thought. "I'm leaving."

And just like that . . . he leaves me on the beach, with nothing but confusion and his T-shirt on the sand.

# Chapter Ten

As I walk back to my hotel, my fingers twist the fabric of Julián's T-shirt, ringing it out over and over. What the hell is his problem? Maybe I took it too far by talking about his sex life, but he could use a lesson or two in fucking communication instead of just walking away. If I would have known he was so precious about his lifestyle of sleeping with women and ghosting them, I wouldn't have brought it up, or at least apologized if he wouldn't have taken off like a coward. No, fuck that, no apology from me. He's in the wrong here. I would have called him out on his shit and asked why he's fine hooking up with other women but not with me.

And the audacity to leave me at the beach, knowing damn well I didn't have a way back. What a selfish asshole. The walk is only a little over twenty minutes, but the point stays the same. He's a dickhead. A dickhead who embarrassed me and took off like a temper-filled child. Thank god we didn't hook up. I blink my eyes to get rid of the stupid vision of his wet lips, the muscles across his chest . . .

When I reach the main road, my anger has only increased. As I pass a busy restaurant, laughter and music pour onto the sidewalk with the tables and chairs. I consider stopping in and ordering a drink, taking a picture, and posting it on Instagram to get Julián's anger and attention. How desperate of me to think he would even care enough to notice.

I pull my phone out and text Amara, hoping she's still out. There's no way I can go back to my hotel and face my mom right now. It's almost eleven. My mom must be really, really distracted or exhausted with work to not be questioning me this late.

Amara's name pops up on my screen as my phone vibrates in my hand. I slide to accept it immediately. "Where the hell did you disappear to?" Her voice is loud, the background even louder.

"I . . . Julián took me out of there before the cops came. You didn't get in trouble, right? And I swear I'll give you money for the drinks."

"No one got in trouble and everything's fine. Wait, are you still with Julián?" she asks. I can imagine her brows wiggling through the phone.

"No. He—" Something stops me from finishing. "I'm not with him anymore. He basically just dropped me off." I don't know why I'm lying to her, but I can't seem to help it.

"Are you guys still out?" I ask, trying to move the topic from Julián.

"We are . . . but we're on our way to Prisha's Airbnb," she tells me. "You can come?" she offers, like the angel she is, but I want her to have alone time with her date that I nearly ruined and I would be the worst company right now.

"No, no, it's okay. I'm tired anyway and have had enough excitement for one night. I'm nearly back to my hotel now."

I click on the directions on my phone. A little over half a mile to go.

She promises to call me tomorrow, and I tell her to have fun, hoping she has more fun than I did with Julián.

The familiar rumbling of a motorbike engine rings in my ears. Though there are tons of them in this city, I've already memorized his. I refuse to look back, even as he slows to a near stop next to me.

"Hey," he calls to me.

I walk faster. I can see him in my peripheral, but I'm still so pissed, not to mention embarrassed.

"Ry, look, I'm sorry. Can we talk for a minute?"

I shake my head. "No. You said what you wanted to say and left me at the beach alone. Fuck off."

I give him one glance and see he's struggling with the pace of my walking with his bike. He shuts down the engine, the purr going quiet.

"I deserve that. I shouldn't have left you there, knowing you can't get back."

I stop dead in my tracks, the temper I inherited from my mother flaring. "I can get back! Clearly." I hold up my phone to show him. "So leave me alone."

The last thing on earth I want is for him to leave me alone, which pisses me off even more. Something about him is so hard to resist. Especially when I look at him. I guess that's how hot men get away with manipulation so often. All sense of critical thinking disappears in their presence.

"Can I at least drop you off at your hotel? Then I'll leave you alone," he says. I start walking again.

"No. I don't want or need you to take me anywhere. You made it abundantly clear that you don't like me, so why would I get on your stupid bike and wear that stupid helmet for a three-minute ride that will keep me up all night?"

I hear him laugh and I give him a death stare, trying with all my might to ignore that he's shirtless. His shirt is in my hands.

"So, you'll be up all night thinking about me?"

I shake my head. "That's not what I meant."

I start to wonder why I'm lying to this random guy who I almost kissed just so I don't feel even more embarrassed, but what's the point of caring what he thinks of me? We're on a quiet part of the street and it's not likely that anyone around will understand me anyway. My ego loses and honesty wins.

"You know what, yeah, I will be up all night thinking about you. It will drive me nuts wondering why you are so hot and cold, why you almost kissed me and then rejected me. Why you apparently sleep with every woman on the island except me. It's embarrassing, and you're getting under my skin and I don't know why. I'm trying really hard to act like I don't give a shit what you think about me or if you think I'm pathetic, blah, blah, blah. That's how my brain works, and it does bother me that you humiliated me and made me feel awful about myself."

The grip on his handlebars slips and the bike tilts to the side, nearly falling. Apparently, he's not used to women being honest to his face. I'm honored to be the first and hope I'm not the last.

"What? Nothing to say now? You shouldn't have asked if you didn't want an answer," I snap in his silence.

He looks at me, his eyes touching mine and not moving. As he begins, the tone of his voice is so strained, like the words are being slowly ripped out of his chest and off his tongue.

"I'm sorry. Genuinely. I don't know why I got so mad and left. I guess being called out didn't feel great, and I was embarrassed, too, that you think I'm some asshole who fucks every woman I meet. I don't want you to think that. I want you to . . . I guess I wanted you to get to know me, and I thought I was being respectful by not hooking up with you on a public beach."

"You pretended to be into me and then literally left me there."

"I know that was immature of me. But I was not pretending to be into you. I'm very into you and I think that's why I acted like that. It's not an excuse, but I can't stand the idea of making you upset or feel bad about yourself."

I wasn't expecting an honest reaction from him, and he's apologized, so what's left to say? Maybe more honesty . . .

"Well, I appreciate your apology and I'm glad you didn't mean to make me feel like shit. But it still did."

"Are you going to ignore that I said I'm into you?"

I nod, glancing at a woman and her child walking by. The toddler is holding a green balloon in one hand and the woman's hand in the other. I don't think I've ever seen a child out so late, but the culture seems to be so different here, starting dinner after nine, when I'm usually already drowsy from my meds, and staying out until midnight on a casual work night.

"Are you not into me?" Julián presses.

Okay . . . enough honesty for one night. It's overwhelming and I've never had someone flat-out ask me, while making eye contact, if I like them or not.

"I think you are." He pushes again.

"Does it matter? We barely know each other and look how rocky it's already been. Plus, I thought you hated tourists."

"I don't *hate* tourists. I hate rich people who think they rule the world. And yes, I'm aware that they do, but I hate it with every fiber of my being. I hate that spoiled rich people come here and trash our land and drive up the prices and eliminate the working class. But you with your reusable water bottle . . ." He homes in on me. "Something about you . . . you're not like that. Spoiled, yes. But you're different, I can tell, or you wouldn't be driving me so crazy."

"I'm different?" I laugh at how bold he is at making assumptions and speaking his mind. "I'm not like other girls? I'm not the kind of woman who wants to be told I'm not like other girls. I want to be like them, and I'm so sick of men pitting us against each other by—"

"Whoa, whoa. Slow down, Jeanne Deroin. I never said anything about other women. I said tourists. Don't make me out to be a scumbag."

Embarrassment rolls through me. He's right, again. And I jumped to conclusions, again.

"Whatever. And yes, I do know who that is. I'm not as dumb as you think." I roll my eyes, thanking my mom for making me learn about many, many influential women who shaped feminism in history. Him knowing about her is impressive, but I've already given him enough of an ego boost by embarrassing myself.

"I never said you were stupid. In fact, I said the opposite. Do you always jump to conclusions?"

"Do you always have to have the last word?"

"Yes," he admits with a cocky shrug.

"You're annoying, you know that?"

He nods. "Yet here we are."

*Yet here we are.* I'm tingling and excited and enjoying the banter with him. Damn him.

"I'm here for the summer, what's the point of liking each other?" I ask him and myself as we continue to walk.

"What's the point of anything in life? If you only think of the ending, you're unable to take in the present, the point of living."

"How philosophical," I tease, trying to undercut how right he is and how deeply I feel his words.

"I'm being serious. Do you like me so far? Because it seems like you do."

"Are you always this pushy? It's been a day since we met." I can tell by the expression on his face he's not going to let this go.

Do I like him? Yes. Do I want to like him? No. No way in hell. I'm scared of what will happen if I say yes. I promised myself when I boarded the plane to come here that I wouldn't let fear make any more choices for me. At the time I meant diving into the ocean, spending time roaming unfamiliar streets, trying new foods. Not a man on a freaking motorcycle who manages to turn me into a puddle every time he looks at me.

"No. I'm not. Believe it or not, I don't usually chase women around town. It would be bad for my already damaged reputation."

I laugh, allowing myself to enjoy the way he makes me feel. His humor is my favorite type. Self-deprecating and witty, intelligent but not obnoxious. Well, a little obnoxious, but still.

"So, what's so bad about us hanging out until you leave or we get sick of each other? What's the worst thing that can happen?" he questions, having no idea what the worst thing actually could be.

"If you don't agree, you can live with the satisfaction, or guilt, of knowing you drove me absolutely mad by turning me down." A playful glimmer in his eyes makes me smile. "Just for the summer, why not see where it goes and have fun?"

"You're asking for me to spend my summer with you? You haven't even kissed me yet."

We're approaching my hotel. I find myself wishing I would have walked slower. He stops walking and faces me, touching my chin between his thumb and forefinger. He's so close as he leans in that I can count the freckles on the bridge of his nose. The night air buzzes between us, my breath lost in the light breeze.

"Would you like me to kiss you?" His voice is so seductive that I almost nod before snapping out of it.

I gently shove at his chest, my heart hammering in my own. "No. Oh my god, no." I try to hide the heat in my cheeks, and he bursts into laughter.

"Right . . . so are you going to give me some of your precious time this summer or not?"

His smile is so convincing, so damn charming.

I twist the fabric of his shirt in my hands, contemplating. "For now. And only the summer. No drama, no ghosting, just a fun summer fling. If we even make it that far."

"Deal," he says, grinning like he won the Super Bowl.

"Deal." I roll my eyes, excited and terrified at the same time.

# Chapter Eleven

When I stretch awake the next morning, I feel every ounce of last night. Of Fabio's shots, of Julián's almost-kiss-then-ditch, him admitting that he's into me. I roll over, press my face into the pillows, dig my fists into the softness, and kick my feet dramatically. What a whirlwind this trip already is, and I've barely gotten my toes wet.

I check the Google Calendar on my phone to see what my schedule for the day is supposed to be. A breakfast with my mom and Lena, a boat tour in the afternoon, and dinner tonight at seven. My entire day is planned for me, and yet all I want to do is find a way to see Julián again. I laugh thinking about how my mom would react if Julián showed up in his flip-flops, board shorts, and tan lines. My mom and Julián are worlds away in every aspect—even imagining them in a room together is comical and anxiety-inducing. The tightness between her brows that never budges are such a contrast to Julián's soft crinkles around his eyes, showing the years of sun, laughter, and life etched into his stunning face.

With the biggest sigh, I drag myself out of bed and mosey my way into the bathroom of my suite. The wooden planked floor is cold against my bare feet. In the mirror, I'm taken aback by the flush in my cheeks, the lack of puffiness and darkness around my eyes. I press my palm into my beating heart, more proof of how much energy, how much life, has been breathed back into me in such a short time. I'm trying not to get ahead of myself, but I owe it to myself to relish the way this feels and allow myself to enjoy it, to savor it, and not go back to the constant brain fog I've been living in. I stare at my pill container. Instead of overthinking it, I turn the shower on.

Anticipation of when I can see Julián again is at the forefront of my mind as I shower and get dressed for breakfast. On top of my navy-blue daisy-patterned bikini, I put on a simple matching set, mocha-brown linen pants and a sleeveless cropped top. The neckline is square, my shell necklace resting just between my collarbones. After pulling my hair back, I drop it down my shoulders, then pull it back up, contemplating which looks better. Deciding on a claw clip so I can take it down if I get the urge, I twist my long hair up and clip it, tugging out a few loose strands around my face.

After my skincare, I opt for tinted sunscreen instead of foundation and a tiny bit of liquid blush under my eyes and the bridge of my nose. I almost pop my contact into my right eye, but remember Amara and Julián's encouragement, so I decide not to put it in after all. I keep my hands busy by tidying up my bathroom counter, the pill organizer practically screaming at me. I cover it with a hand towel, as if that will make it disappear. I'm fine, no side effects yet, even with the strobe light mishap. It's a confusing feeling, knowing I'm making a choice for myself and my body instead of trying to avoid the inevitable, but there's still a weight of guilt inside my chest. Maybe it's because my mom will lose her shit if she finds out, or maybe it's because taking them has just become a habit. If anything, I feel better than ever. I've been on more medications than I can count or remember the names of, since before I could walk or talk. All of that and the tubers still shifted.

"Enough, enough," I say to myself in the mirror.

I take a deep breath, in and out, and roll my shoulders, shifting my mind back to Julián and the way he goofily waved goodbye to me last night in front of the lobby and nearly ran into a pillar as we said good night. After putting on fresh Band-Aids, I slide into my comfiest sandals at the door. I check my phone again. Regardless of how often I remind myself that Julián doesn't have my number and I don't have his, a little bubble of hope is there that he will take the initiative and ask Amara for it. I could always do the same, take charge and just get his number, but since my overly confessional monologue last night on the street, I'd rather have him take the lead this time.

As soon as I step into the elevator my phone buzzes in my hand. It's my mom, informing me that her and Lena are stuck in a meeting and will be late for breakfast. I send back:

> No problem just text me when you're done

I press the L button and ride down to the lobby to see if Amara's there while I wait. The desk is empty when I step out, but I hear her distinct laughter coming from a hallway nearby. I follow the noise and find her pressed against the stone wall, her hands held above her head, with Prisha's mouth on hers. Amara's knee moves between Prisha's thighs, gently pressing between them.

I can't seem to look away. I should, I most certainly, definitely, absolutely should, but Julián pops back into my head and I can't help but imagine him pinning me against a wall . . .

"Oh, Ry. Hey!" Amara says, snapping me out of my voyeurism.

I cover my face with my hands, though it's obviously too late to pretend.

"Sorry, guys! I heard you laughing and came to find you!" My voice is loud and creaky.

*Kill me.*

"It's all good." Amara laughs as Prisha lowers her hands down to her side, still holding them.

Prisha turns to me. "Ry, I hope you got home okay last night." Her face crinkles in worry. "I'm sorry we weren't paying attention to what was happening to you," Prisha explains, sincerity in her large brown eyes.

She's less dressed-up today in tight jeans, a tucked-in black T-shirt, and strappy heeled sandals. Her makeup is subtle and she's even more drop-dead gorgeous in the light of day. Amara seems to agree, not taking her eyes off Prisha as we talk.

"No, no. It's totally not your fault. I'm sorry I got drunk and danced with that creep. One too many Fabio shots." I laugh a little, and the two of them nod, agreeing with laughter.

"I just came down to say hi while waiting for my mom. We're having breakfast, then a boat ride, then blah blah blah . . ." I sigh, leaning against the cold stone wall on the opposite side of them.

"You're not meeting Julián?" Amara asks, nodding in the direction of the lobby.

I shake my head. "I wish," I blurt out.

Both of their brows lift, and they share a look.

"Well, your wish is his command, because he's been waiting in the lobby for you for like two hours," Amara tells me.

Taking a few steps toward the lobby and peering out of the hallway, I search for him. How did I miss him when I passed by? "Really?"

They nod. Amara talks first.

"Oh yeah, realllyyyyy." She draws out the sounds in the most dramatic way.

"You two get back to . . . yeah . . . and I'm going to find him," I say, moving so quickly I'm not sure if they can even hear me.

I turn the corner and there he is, sitting on the arm of one of the oversized couches in the lobby. Seeing him is such a relief and such a rush, it's confusing and contradictory, but god, it feels so good.

"What are you doing here? Don't you have a job?" I tease him.

"I do, but since I'm the second-in-command, I can show up a little late."

"Ah, okay, big shot." I'm touched that he would spend his time here, waiting for me, so I stop the teasing.

"I'm sorry I didn't know you were here and I passed by but didn't see you," I tell him, not able to hide the growing smile on my face.

His lips curl into an equally cheesy smile. "I had to pee. I'd been holding it forever, so I ran to the toilet, and of course, that's when you came down."

"Have you really been here two hours?" I ask, tilting my head and taking him in.

The teal color of his T-shirt looks so good against the color of his skin.

Raising one hand, he rubs the back of his neck. "It was closer to three, but yeah," he admits, shyness covering his words.

"Well, thank you. I really wanted to see you today, and since my day is booked up, I thought I wasn't going to be able to."

"I brought you breakfast." He holds up a brown paper bag. "It's probably not as good now, and isn't warm, but—" I grab the bag from him and stop him from continuing.

"I can't wait to try it." I smile, plopping down onto the couch and patting the empty space next to me.

"Okay, so we've got *ensaïmada*, which is sweet and has a pretty fucked-up story behind it, but I'll save that for another day." He pulls out a thick, swirly bread with a coating of sugar dusted on top.

"Goes perfect with coffee, but that's also cold. Sorry." He smiles, handing me the cup.

"I love cold coffee. I'm a twentysomething American girl, remember? We live for an iced coffee. Okay, what else you got in there?"

He lays out a napkin and sets the first pastry down to dig back into the grease-stained bag. My stomach grumbles. I love anything sweet, and adding bread on top of that—my favorite.

"Okay, so this one is a pan de payas. Super traditional, savory but fucking good. This one has garlic and salt flakes on it. And last, but not least . . ." He sets that one down and reaches back into the bag. "We've got a sort of baguette, in case you're a picky eater. I got two of each, too, in case you're starving."

"Wow, thank you. I'm sorry to keep you waiting so long," I say, breaking off a piece of the sugarcoated one.

"It's okay. You didn't know I was coming, and the sun is brutal today, so I'm not in a hurry to get out on the water."

I shove the bread into my mouth and look at him, taking in the cuts and callouses on his hardworking hands and forearms.

"I was talking to the bread," I tease, with a mouthful of thick, fluffy, salty bread.

"Your charm is really something today." He tosses me a smile, tearing at the food with his teeth.

I wink at him. "Aw, thanks."

We eat in mostly silence, and I down my room-temperature coffee. It's smooth and, like he said, is perfect with the bread. I try each of them, saving the baguette for last, then back to the second sweet bread as Julián watches me, seemingly enjoying watching me eat as much as I'm enjoying devouring it.

He hands me his coffee when mine is empty. "Thank you. I guess I was more hungry than I thought."

"My pleasure."

A family passes by us in the lobby, the two children swatting at each other as the mother tries to break them up, while the father is oblivious on his phone. I would hate that type of marriage. It would be like being married to my mother, never getting their full attention. At least with my mom, she's working. This guy looks like he might just be watching a damn football match.

"Truth is, Ry, I was desperate to see you. I could barely sleep, and I knew I wouldn't be able to focus at work today if I didn't see you even for a moment."

His words catch me off guard and I choke a little, coughing as he pats my back. "Sorry, not trying to have you choke to death."

"You're in a . . . mood today," I note, pressing my shoulder against his.

I am unsure and unable to express how much I love this mood, this open, sarcastic, communicative, desperate-to-see-me mood.

"I took my meds." He laughs, licking his lips.

My scalp pricks a little, thinking about mine.

"Ha. Ha," I say, not sure if he's joking.

"Oh, I got sugar all over myself." I wipe my hands over the tiny white dots across my chest. He raises his hand to help me, gently pressing against my breasts with a napkin.

I take in a big breath through clenched teeth, trying to focus on the slow drum of the lobby music, but it's nearly impossible with the way he's touching me so casually. The air in the lobby shifts, and my breath staggers as his movement slows. Knowing exactly what he's doing, he looks up at me and takes the tip of his index finger and brushes it against my bare skin at the top of my neckline, tracing the square shape of the fabric. Goose bumps rise on my skin; I feel like I'm going to jump out of it. The urge to lean in and close the gap between us and kiss him is stronger than the afternoon tide.

His thumb and forefinger pick up my necklace, toying with it gently, rubbing the pad of his finger over the ridges on the surface of the small seashell. As he clicks it open, I reach my hand up, covering his and lowering it back down. For the first time, I notice his hands are not only calloused but also covered in small scars in the shape of small slices, reaching from the back of his palm up his arms, stopping just below his elbows. Some as thin as a papercut and some as wide as a rope string.

"Does that locket have a photo of your boyfriend back home? Is that why you don't want me to see it?" He cocks a brow, doubt carving into his forehead even though his tone is playful, unbothered.

"Yeah, my kids too," I quip back.

The ache of something I'll never be able to have digs at my insides, but out of habit and a lot of practice, I push it away. A tight smile replaces the heartache.

"Damn. Knew you were too good to be true." Julián's fingers are slowly tracing the line of my collarbone again. He stops and presses his open palm against my chest.

"You look absolutely stunning today. Why?" He moves closer, still gauging my rapidly beating heart.

I can barely speak; my tongue feels heavy and my brain like mashed potatoes. "I . . . I was supposed to have breakfast with my mom, but she was running late." My eyes go wide, and I pull away. "Shit! What time is it? I can never tell if it's been minutes or hours when you're around," I admit in my panic.

His smile says a million words. "What a compliment. It's almost ten."

I reach for my phone and check the screen. A missed call from my mom.

"Sorry, I need to call her really quick," I whisper to Julián, who's now cleaning up the bread massacre we've made on the table.

On the first ring she picks up, and without any type of greeting, she gets right to it. "Ry, I see you're in the hotel but not your room." Annoyance claws at me knowing that unless my phone is dead, she always has my location. I have hers, too, but I've never needed or wanted it. "We already ordered our food. What should I order you?"

"I actually just ate in the lobby. I can meet you guys in the restaurant in a few minutes. I'm finishing up with a friend." I glance at Julián.

"The receptionist from the front desk?" my mother questions.

"No. A different one." I decide not to lie. I'll answer her questions later.

I hear a *hmmm* come through the line and end the call swiftly.

"Sorry. She booked my whole day: breakfast here, some boat ride, a dinner . . ."

"Do you like boats?" Julián asks, intrigue in his voice.

I nod. "I love them. Haven't been on one in a while, but we used to have one when I was a kid. But the busier my mom's schedule got, the less time we had for it, so she sold it and I haven't been on one in years.

"Do you know this one?" I pull my calendar out and click on the link to show him the name of the company my mom booked the tour through and the style of boat.

"That's not a boat. That's a yacht," he corrects me. "You're going to be so far from the water that it's a waste of time and a lot of money. Unless you're just going on to drink and shmooze with rich people and eat their fancy stale food."

The embarrassment I feel is unwarranted. It's not like I booked the huge yacht or spent the money, but he does have a point, now that I'm looking at how massive the size is.

"You won't be able to put your hand in the water as you cruise or feel the waves of the sea at all. They'll serve you overpriced food and champagne, but it's not a true experience," he goes on.

"Sorry, I'm being harsh about it." He shrugs. "But these kinds of tourist traps make me so angry. Inauthenticity makes me so angry." He tugs at the back of his neck with his hand.

"My bias toward it or not, I do want you to have a nice time. Maybe one day when you're not booked up, I can give you the real Mallorca experience?"

I nod, desperately wanting that.

"You should go before you get in trouble," he jokes. "Thank you for enjoying your morning with me. Now my workday will be much better after seeing you."

The freckled spots of his brown eyes seem lighter today. Everything about him seems lighter today. He stands up to leave, and I tug on his hand from where I'm sitting on the couch.

"Thank you for coming here and bringing me food and coffee. It made my day." I hold his hand in mine, turning it around, noting how much bigger it is than my own.

"Let's see each other again soon, deal?" he asks, bending down face-to-face with me. I close my eyes in anticipation, and he double kisses my cheeks. "Adéu, Ry."

"Deal." I watch him leave, soaking in the words he said.

*I was desperate to see you . . .*

My feet dance under me and I pop up, energized and mesmerized. He's enchanting and mysterious. Honest yet private, and though he just left, I'm already counting down to when I can see him again. I don't remember the last time I felt this way about anything; not even my dance performances had me feeling as twirly inside as this man. I'm either about to have the summer I've been dreaming of, or this is going to end in a nightmare.

# Chapter Twelve

My mom and Lena are mid-breakfast when I approach the table. The server rushes over to pull out the chair for me to sit down. I thank her and she hands me a menu. Politely, I take it, though I'm not hungry anymore. My mom tells her in Spanish that I've already eaten, and she apologizes, gently taking the menu away within seconds.

"It's okay, thank you so much." I smile warmly, hoping my mom hasn't been too demanding of her this early in the day.

My mom pats the corners of her mouth with a thick white napkin. "So, who's this friend you've already made? You seem to be making more friends here than back at home."

Lena looks at me, her body shifting from one hip to another in her seat.

I explain, "Just someone I met through Amara."

"The hotel clerk," she retorts as if she's reminding Lena who we're talking about, but erasing her name.

Sighing, I take a drink of water from the glass in front of me.

"Amara is her name, and technically yes, that's her job, but not everyone is defined by their job." My tone is clipped and defensive, but the way she seems to be looking down on Amara strikes a nerve. A big one.

"I'm choosing to ignore that dig. Are you tired?" She leans over the table a little to get a closer look at me.

"No. I'm fine."

"You seem . . . I don't know, different? Off? Did you sleep well?" She sips her coffee, watching me.

I roll my eyes, leaning my back against the chair. Feeling immature and a bit bratty and not caring to hide it, I glare back at her.

"I'm fine. I'm having a great day. Well, I was until now."

My thoughts travel back to Julián, how he waited for hours in the lobby. I can still smell the fresh bread he brought, still feel his fingers trickling along my skin.

"Is it a man or a woman that you met here?" My mom's thick brows rise in question.

"Why are you asking?"

"Why wouldn't I ask? It must be a man." She smiles, placing her lipstick-stained coffee mug down on the table in front of her.

"It's a man, yes. But I barely know him, so I haven't had the time to do a background check."

Lena pops up.

"Should I?" she offers, unfortunately not catching on to my sarcasm.

I wave my hand in front of me.

"No, no way. I'm not a teenager anymore, and he's just a guy. Let's stop talking about it now. Please."

"Be careful in every way, okay?" My mother's eyes soften and there's a hint of something else there, but it disappears before I can take it in.

I agree and work on distracting her by asking about her day, the colors of the balloons, and if yellow lights will work better than the white for the ballroom. I wish it wasn't this way between us, but the most we've ever bonded was when I feigned interest in her work. There've been times when stuck in a hospital room for five-day-long EEGs that we've shared a laugh or two, but ever since I can remember, even during those stays she still took calls nonstop, stepping out of the room constantly to manage some crisis for SetCorp. I spent a lot of the time with the nurses and Child Life specialists who brought me puzzles and played card games with me until I got an iPad, then a cell phone, and eventually pushed my mom to just drop me off for my hospital stays because I enjoyed the quiet of the hospital over her nonstop working.

I try not to resent her. I really do. I know she dedicates her life to her career and that can be admirable, but for me and my heart, I would give anything for her to put me, not just my medical stuff, but *me, a person*, first. Even if only for a short time.

As she drones on about how many tourists and how much money the resort will bring in, I clock out mentally. I nod along as she talks, and Lena takes notes on her iPad. Their empty plates are carried away and my mom orders a second round of espressos for her and Lena.

"I'd love one, too, please," I request.

"Ry, with your medication—" my mom begins.

"I can have espresso. I drink coffee. I'm fine and want an espresso."

Lena's face reddens, caught between the two of us Peras. Not a great place to be.

"Point taken. Ah, hang on. Sorry." Mom picks up her vibrating cell phone and brings it to her ear.

"What do you mean he's refusing? That fucking—" She cuts herself off when her eyes meet mine.

Covering the microphone of her phone with her hand, she mouths *I'll be right back* and walks away from the table, out to the patio of the restaurant. Her body language tells me she's furious. She paces, her hands flying through the air.

"She's a bit uptight today because the seller is attempting to back out of the deal for not only his company, but the land and port it's on, and if that happens . . ." Lena leans in to whisper to me, and her overwhelming Mojave Ghost perfume makes my nose itch.

"Don't tell her I told you . . . but if it falls through, we're all in deep shit. That's the whole reason we came here. So it won't be good. Really, really not good." Lena wipes the literal sweat from her thin brow, and her face crinkles into a terrified, forced smile.

"Aren't you exhausted?" I ask her. "Always having to deal with her moods and take on her stress?"

We've known each other half my life, so it's a fair question, because I can't imagine the pressure she's constantly under to keep my mom at bay, make sure she's fed, never late, crosses her *t*'s and dots her *i*'s. I would have quit or had a heart attack after six months of working under my mom. I could barely handle getting scolded by my dance academy instructor for missing cues and getting blood on the stage during a performance when I had a seizure mid-routine.

"I love my job," Lena robotically responds.

"You're a liar. And a bad one." I laugh, plopping one of the brown sugar cubes into my frothy espresso.

"I value my life, so I know what to say." Lena winks, nodding toward my mom outside. "And she pays me well.

Besides, you should cut her some slack. She's not a bad person. When my niece was sick, she gave me a whole month off with full pay and covered all my travel expenses. Even sent my family food. I'll never forget that."

I've never heard that story or expected my mom to do anything like that for someone, even Lena, who's the closest person to her. I wonder if they talk about personal topics often, or if it was a one-off situation where Lena didn't have a choice. I bet Lena knows much more about my mom's life and personality than I do.

"She's not all stone and curse words," Lena tells me, sipping from her small porcelain espresso cup. It clinks as she puts it back onto the matching saucer.

"Maybe not to you," I sigh as my mom approaches the table, standing over us in her high heels and work suit.

"Lena, we must go to the shipyard ASAP. Ry, sorry, but I can't do the food tour thing with you today. I had a portable charger delivered to your room." She downs her espresso in one gulp.

"Let's go," she commands Lena, who jumps up and calls for the check to be billed to her room.

"It was a boat tour," I quietly say into my half-full cup as they disappear through the arched entryway.

Amara's behind the desk, not making out with Prisha in the hallway, when I step out of the elevator and into the lobby.

"Soooo . . . Julián?" she calls out the moment she sees me.

I look around the quiet, empty lobby. A couple people are spread out, silently working on laptops. I recognize a few Set-Corp faces and gesture for her to lower her voice.

"Are you guys a thing now?"

"No . . . Yeah . . . I don't know? Casual. Stereotypical summer fling." I struggle to respond. "I know you tried to warn me about him, but I'm fine, really. We're just hanging out and seeing what happens. I'm not stupid enough to think it will be more. I only have one summer anyway," I slip, looking down at the floor to brace myself for however she will take that.

I feel her hand on my arm and look up.

"I'm not judging you or questioning you for hanging out with him. Ghosting Master or not, Julián is kind, funny, and a hard worker, and you can handle yourself. I was shocked when he showed up here with food for you, but at a complete loss for words when he waited for *hours*. He must be really, really into you. And the sex must have been something else if he's already whipped like this." She clicks her tongue on the roof of her mouth.

"We didn't sleep together," I tell her, swatting at her like an embarrassed kid.

Her mouth falls open. I reach up and close it for her. "Seriously, we didn't. Yet."

"The woman was too stunned to speak," Amara says in a robotic newscaster voice, and we share a laugh. The internet has made memes and viral clicks universally understood around the world, and I absolutely love that.

I give her a quick hug and head out of the hotel, finding my driver patiently waiting for me outside to take me on my boat—yacht tour—alone. Part of me is relieved I don't have to hear my mom take five hundred work calls during it, but deep down, I had let my imagination create a scenario where we tread the water and she points to different areas along the shore, sharing stories of her upbringing and places she's been. In this daydream, her shoulders would be relaxed, the breeze blowing through her thick dark hair as we laugh and sip wine, bonding over memories old and new. But instead, I'm climbing into a car with nothing but the vulnerable daydream fading and the taste of the bitter espresso still on my tongue.

The car smells brand-new and the air-conditioning is top-notch, a short relief from the sticky summer air. The driver, who hasn't spoken since we pulled out of the hotel, gives me a friendly smile through the rearview. He must get tired of talking to people, so I don't want to bore him or be another obnoxious tourist. I let us both have our peace. He also might not speak English, so I stare out the window at the view: the vast, expansive ocean; the white sand; the wooden fences; and endless paths leading down to the water. A few minutes later we arrive at a dock and I go back to my Google Calendar, read the instructions, and screenshot the name of the company I'm supposed to be looking for.

"Thank you," I tell the driver as I climb out of the car, my tote bag around my shoulder.

The high sun kisses my shoulders, instantly warming them. Sticking one hand into my bag as I walk, I feel around for the extra sunscreen I brought and spray it on. With ease I find the man holding a sign for my tour, and with unease I board the massive yacht full of families and couples and not one person who's alone, except me.

Story of my life.

I impatiently make my way through the people leisurely boarding. Their voices in every language possible. I recognize French, English, and of course Spanish. There are anywhere from twenty to thirty people on the boat, fortunately allowing me to find myself a little private corner on the lower deck. Too big of a boat for such a small number of people, which is likely why my mother chose it. A full buffet of food is available; the smoke coming from the fresh paella being cooked makes my mouth water. Fresh appetizers and seafood are being carried around on little platters by servers dressed in crisp white shirts and black bow ties. Champagne flutes, a full bar, you name it, it's on this yacht. I can't help but think back to Julián's distaste for this level of luxury, and I find myself agreeing with him as a woman carrying a Chanel purse tries to avoid the steam from the food touching her bag. The look of disgust on her face makes me feel out of place and out of touch with reality. These people aren't my type of people, yet technically they are.

With a thank-you, I take a glass of wine and sling it back, earning an eye roll from an older couple whose money I can smell from here. His watch alone costs more than most people's salary in a year; her Hermès sandals can't be comfortable enough to justify the thousand-dollar price tag. Instead of doing a price breakdown of the elitists on the yacht, I try to focus on the water, the ever-changing movements, the dips and divots, the smell of the salty air, as we depart from the dock. Music begins to play, a light piano tune, and I close my eyes, letting the wind caress my face as a group of seagulls speak to one another above me.

"Ry!" I snap my eyes open.

I swear I heard someone yell my name, but that can't be possible. I look around, feeling silly. Who the hell would know my name here? Not a soul. Everyone is doing their own thing: two couples are slow dancing, people are chatting, eating, drinking. Everyone is having a great time, except me.

I reach my hand over the edge, wishing I were ten feet closer to the water and could touch it. Julián was right, of course: I'm too far removed from the water to embrace it.

"Ry!" I hear the voice again, louder this time.

*Julián?*

My mind must be playing tricks on me, a mirage created by the longing to see him again. I rest my cheek on my arm, sighing and look out into the water. There's a medium-sized fishing vessel about one hundred feet away, with a man standing in the center, waving his arms. *It is him!*

"Julián!" I shout, jumping up in excitement.

"Ry!" he yells back, creating whispers and not so casual stares from the snooty crowd.

I wasn't imagining it after all. Julián is somehow here, in the middle of the Mediterranean Sea, coming to my rescue.

# Chapter Thirteen

Julián steers his fishing boat closer to where I'm standing on the deck and I look down and around, wishing I could just jump from this yacht and onto his, but it's too high.

"You look bored out of your mind; I came to save you!" he yells.

Man, the confidence of this guy. He doesn't give a shit if everyone is staring at him or what they might think of him for interrupting their peaceful, luxurious experience.

"I am bored to death!" I admit, calling down to him.

He waves his hand in the air, gesturing to me to come to him. It's at least a twenty-foot drop, and not that I'm scared of heights, but what would happen if I just leaped off the boat? Will the staff call for help? Am I allowed to just leave? It's a paid excursion and I'm an adult, so I guess so, but I find myself second-guessing the permission to do what I want.

"I'll come to you and bring you to mine?" Julián's voice travels easily to me.

He pulls his shirt over his head, tosses it behind him onto his boat, and dives into the water. My heart pounds. As I watch him swim toward the yacht, I follow him to where he's headed, keeping my eyes on him and not the strangers staring at me. When I reach the front of the yacht, there's a staircase, and Julián is speaking to one of the staff. I can tell by the friendly tone and smiles that they know each other. Julián waves for me to come into the water using the stairs. My bag is the only problem. My cell phone and most of the stuff in my bag can't get wet. Including my brand-new copy of a Kennedy Ryan book I haven't finished.

"My purse! I can't swim with it. It can't get wet!"

The scene plays out like we're in a movie, a dramatic grand gesture during the third act of a Kate Hudson rom-com. He's the lead, with wet, slicked-back hair, enough confidence to sink this massive yacht, enough charm to make us all blush and squirm in our seats. Julián reaches for the metal bar on the side of the stairs and pulls himself up. His muscular chest immediately draws my attention, and that of the women around us. I have the urge to cover their eyes.

"Hand it to me. I can hold it up until we get to my boat." He is a fisherman after all, so I take my outfit off, leaving just my swimsuit on and hand my purse to him, trusting that.

"Ugh, how romantic," I hear a woman's voice comment behind me.

I straighten my spine. *Yeah it is* romantic and it's for *me*, and I deserve this. Every woman deserves to have an over-the-top romantic gesture once in their life, and this is my one. So, hell or high water, I'm not going to let it pass me by. Without looking back, I step down the staircase and dive into the water to join him. The warmth of the water washes over me as I go under, my hair slicking back as I pop my head up. Julián wraps one hand around my waist, making me dizzy in the most blissful way. I can feel the slight current of his legs kicking under us.

"I can swim, you know," I tell him, not able to keep the enormous grin off my face.

He pulls me closer to his bare chest. "Yeah, I know."

As promised, not even a drop of water touches my bag as he gently places it inside the body of his boat. He climbs on first, using nothing except his body weight to lift himself. I look for stairs but don't see any.

He notices my hesitation.

"This isn't a yacht, cariño." His hand reaches for mine and he yanks me, fully lifting me into his arms and gently placing me onto my feet.

My god, he's strong.

"How did you even find me?" I ask, wringing my soaked hair out over my shoulder into the water below.

"I have ways." He tosses me a towel. "I know everyone. The island isn't that big when you take out the temps."

"Temps?"

"Temporary visitors. A nice way to say tourists."

"Ah, so now you're being nice to tourists?" I tease him.

"No. Just you."

My stomach flips. The way he makes me feel is dangerous. Not for him, but for me. He seems to be so good at this. Way too good at this.

I look around his boat, to try and stop my heart from palpi-tating. The wooden deck shows its age in the cracks and warps; the blue seats and paint have been faded by the sun. It's an older model; I don't pretend to know the name or type, but it suits him perfectly. It's cozy, feels sturdy. It's much bigger now that I'm on it, nets and hooks and a sail, and a small staircase is in the center, leading to a door with a crooked sign hanging by a thin rope and one single nail. It reads GARCIA FAMILIA in messy handwriting. I wonder if it's his. Just as I open my mouth to ask, he begins.

"It's nothing fancy, but it was my dad's when he was young, and I've tried to keep her together." He looks around, rubbing the back of his neck with his hand. "For the most part."

"What's her name? I know people always name their boats, so what's hers?" I ask, running my hand along the back of the seats closest to me.

"She doesn't have one. It used to, but my pare changed it. Well, I guess erased it is more like it. So I never renamed her, and I like it that way."

"Talk about commitment issues." I look up at him. "Poor nameless boat."

The sun is cast behind him, creating a glow of a shadow.

Though I'm teasing him, it makes me a bit sad that this beautiful, faithful, never-resting vessel doesn't have a name. Like a lot of people, she works so hard but doesn't have an identity. No one to call her name in the light of day or whisper it during the fall of night.

"She doesn't mind," he says with certainty. "She likes not being defined. Why confine her by a title that she didn't choose?" He raises a brow, gently stroking the net hanging on a pillar near him.

"I guess you have a little bit of a point." I nod in agreement. "Also, how many damn crosswords do you do? Because you have a better English vocabulary than me."

"Tons. Vast, plentiful, enormous, astronomical amounts . . . colossal." He grins, and droplets of water fall down his face.

"Okay, okay!" I get it. I gently push his chest. "You're a genius. Don't brag. It doesn't suit you." I put my hand over his mouth, and a gentle prick from his teeth pinches me, making me shriek in surprise.

"And what suits me, Oriah?"

Julián's palm is splayed open cross my bare back, pressing just enough to pull me to him but still give me a choice to back away or not.

"Do you want to have some real fun now?" he asks in a low voice. In my head, he throws me over his shoulder and takes me to whatever is behind that door and has his way with me.

My imagination runs wild, and I hope he doesn't hear my pulse pounding under my sun-kissed skin.

"Aren't you hungry? You didn't touch their fancy food."

My cheeks are burning. "How long were you watching me?"

He shrugs his shoulders, smiling like he's holding a secret. "Long enough."

"I knew you were a stalker the night I met you." I lift my chin so my eyes meet his.

"I wasn't stalking you. Then. Now I have a reason to." The wind and waves around us seem to slow from the tension between us. I can barely breathe.

"And what's the reason now?" I move an inch closer; one tiny movement and our lips will touch.

*Kiss me!* I want to scream.

"Because—" His fingers reach up and tuck my wet hair behind my ear. His mouth moves to the shell of it to whisper, "I have yet to know how you taste."

My knees nearly buckle under me, and he laughs lightly, clearly feeling my body react. This cat-and-mouse game is addicting as sin and frustrating as hell. Even the warmth of his breath against my ear makes me shiver despite the sun soaking into my skin.

"You're driving me crazy," I admit, my breath coming out in short pants.

The tip of his index finger touches my necklace, trailing down the rising and falling of my dripping chest, all the way down to my bare stomach, circling my belly button. I suck in a breath. The floor beneath me feels more than unstable as his fingertip brushes up against the seam of my bathing suit bottoms, going just a touch under them. *My god.*

"I know. And I quite enjoy it," he finally replies, and I can barely remember what he's replying to.

All I can see, hear, and feel is my body aching for him, the wetness and throbbing under my bottoms. He gently pulls away, kissing my cheek, and taps his finger on the tip of my nose. He anchors the boat and I look around. The sea is so vast, yet around us is nearly empty. A couple small boats freckled across the horizon, all different shapes and sizes, but not close enough to make out the people on them.

"Patience. It's a virtue," he tells me, his tongue sliding over his top lip as he steps back and tosses a net over the side of the boat. It disappears beneath the steady waves.

As my body and hormones cool down, Julián shows off his fishing abilities by catching, scaling, and deboning fish. I try not to be squeamish as he works. The muscles in his shoulders flex as he does his thing. I'm impressed and in awe of how natural he is and can tell this is totally his element. We talk about how he spent more time in a boat on the sea than on land as a child, teen, and now adult. He tells me how his grandfather started this family business and how many times they've struggled to evolve and keep up with the ever-changing modern world.

He sails us out to what he tells me is one of the few areas that haven't been polluted beyond repair now because of all the resorts being built. On his phone, he shows me photos of before and after the tourists started flocking here in throngs and tells me how passionately he feels about keeping their ocean clean, their people employed. He asks me about my dancing, how I learned to move the way I did at the lounge. I tell him the fast version, the nondramatic, not lying to him, but choosing to avoid the end of the saga.

"There's so much to know about you. I could talk to you for hours, days, months," he says as he rinses his hands off over the side of the boat.

"Well, we only have one summer, so you'll have to pack it all in," I remind him, and myself, of our limited time together. I hate that I keep doing that, but it's better for both of us to not get too caught up in this. *As if it's so simple.* I mentally roll my eyes at myself for how annoying I can be.

"Don't remind me," he says, and begins to clean up.

He, of course, refuses to allow me to help, telling me to put more sunscreen on and giving me more water in the reusable cup. Despite his harsh persona, he's someone who's used to taking care of people and enjoys it; I can tell by his every move.

A honking noise startles me, and I look over, hoping to god it's not my mom, but instead it's a man on a small fishing boat, waving at us. His hair is shoulder-length and dark, his build is solid, and he's . . . Julián's dad. I can tell even from a distance.

"Pare!" He waves back with a smile.

Am I about to meet his father? Like this? Soaked and awkward . . . I run my fingers through my tangled hair, looking for clothes to put on over my bathing suit.

"Estic en una cita, vés a casa. O en qualsevol altre lloc, però vés!" he yells to his dad, and I keep awkwardly waving my hand and smiling, unsure what to do. A bellowing laugh reaches our boat from his, and he waves once more before turning his boat around and heading the opposite way.

"Was that your dad?"

"Yep. In the flesh."

I widen my eyes. "Why did he leave? Should I have said hi?"

Julián laughs. "I told him to go away. He's fine. You can meet him later. We're on a date, remember?"

I look up at him with a teasing skepticism. "A date, are we? You practically kidnapped me and now you've sent the only other human in our vicinity away?"

He grins, his entire face full of a dazzling, otherworldly smile. "Exactly."

"You're crazy," I tell him as we both settle back into our seats.

"Yeah, so I've been told," he says, a little bit of sarcasm mixed with something else in his tone.

"I should have asked you before, but you eat seafood, right?" he asks a few moments later, his hands busy laying slices of fish onto a metal platter.

"I . . ." I sort of want to lie, but what's the point? He'll be able to tell the moment I pop it into my mouth.

"No, actually. But I want to try it. All of it."

His sparkling eyes widen in surprise. "I thought all rich American girls loved sushi."

I shake my head. "I thought sushi was the roll things? Either way, never had it."

"Technically this is sashimi, but I'm just surprised you haven't had it. I heard in the States they charge tons of money for this." He waves at the growing platter.

He slices a lime and squeezes the juice over some of the fish.

"I think it has to do with my mom's obsession with erasing her past. Even though she's from here, she never really had me try any food from Spain, or seafood in general. I don't know why . . . but she always has. Rich or not, she steers clear from anything that reminds her of this place."

Julián's face is full of confusion. "Your mom's from here? The island or from Spain, or Europe?"

"Here on the island. I know it sounds naïve and clueless of me, but she's so secretive about her past before she became my mom, and we aren't that close. I don't know where on the island, but I'm trying to find out. I would be bragging from the rooftops and visiting monthly if I was from somewhere like this." I wave my hand toward the coastline.

"And you don't speak any Spanish?" he wonders, confused.

Shaking my head, I try to give him the fast version. "No. I mean, I picked up some from my nanny, but my mom never, ever uses her mother tongue, and the only time she encouraged me to learn so much as a few words was right before we came here. Something must have happened here that made her turn her back on where she's from, and I thought I could find out what it was this summer. It's a long, complicated saga, but she barely speaks about her life here."

He studies me and I can almost feel him debating whether to ask me more, but I'm sure he can tell by my tone and the time we've spent together so far that my mom is a sore subject, to say the least.

"Hmph. Your dad is white?" he bluntly wonders, moving on from the subject of my mom.

I'm so curious if he maybe knows someone who knew her or knew my abuelita, or anyone in my bloodline, but I'm not ready to ask him, not yet. Plus, the chances are very slim anyway, so I plan on doing my own detective work to at least find her old home, or a friend she had, something or someone to give me a link to who she was and where she came from. But I won't ask Julián, not today.

I nod. "Yeah, but I look more like my mom. If you saw her, you would immediately recognize this nose and face." I smile, pointing at my distinctive nose.

"Please tell me you're not insecure about your face. You're magnificent."

I cough, surprised by his directness. "I am *not* insecure. I like my face, I was just saying I have her features, and in my town they aren't very common."

"Well, Ry, you're not very common and shouldn't want to be. Look at you." His eyes rake over me, and I feel like I'm completely undressed before him.

"Is that your tagline? You say that to all your girls?"

"Is that your way of deflecting a compliment? Bringing up other women?"

I shake my head, denying the truth he called out. "No, that's my way of finding out how many women you're involved with. I'm not the jealous type, so don't get defensive. I'm just curious." My focus shifts to my hands, picking at my cuticles.

"Truthfully, your question bothers me, but for your sake and mine, I'll answer it. But if you don't believe me, it's your issue and I'm not going to try to prove otherwise. You can either trust and believe me or not." He shrugs, tossing the dry lime into a small, opened garbage bag a few feet away.

"Continue," I urge, my nerves growing.

He's unpredictable, giving me no hints of what will come out of his mouth. I both enjoy and despise his brashness.

"I'm not seeing, dating, or hooking up with anyone. The last woman I was with was a one-night stand from northern France. I didn't ghost her, by the way, and I don't just ghost women. I hate that term. Sometimes it's okay to cut off contact with people without explaining, especially when they're strangers. It doesn't always mean someone's an asshole." He rolls his eyes and continues. "I make it clear that I'm not looking to date or get married, and no tourist Amara gossiped to you about has had that expectation." He pauses, looking toward the clear sky.

"None?" I ask.

"One." He nods. "But I quickly realized she was a little off and she stalked my friends, ran through the streets screaming my name, showed up at my work, until her trip was up and she left the country." His voice is full of relief.

Not knowing her or the full story, but if he swooned her the way he is me, I can't really blame her for her obsession. It's been a few days and I'm nearly there.

"What about you? You came here to live your best life, right? So how many boats have you been on so far? And are you sure you don't have some American football player fiancé waiting for you to have his baby and name it some name with a random *Y* in the middle?"

I laugh at that, thinking of all the Facebook and Instagram posts from people my age who are way further along in their future than I am . . . or will likely ever be.

"No. Sadly, I don't have a fiancé and never have. If I did, I'd like to think he'd be here with me, enjoying the summer together." I sigh, lost in a hopeless daydream.

"Too bad it's just me here. But I can feed you and I'm good with my hands."

"Stop trying to seduce me," I tease, reaching for a bottled water near his leg.

He reaches for my hand and pulls it to him, gently moving me to fall onto his lap.

"I haven't begun yet," he warns seductively, moving my hair to the opposite side of my neck to expose the skin there.

The breezy ocean air tickles my skin just as his lips press against me. My shoulder hikes up as he teases the sensitive nerve bundle at the base of my neck.

I turn my body to straddle his waist. I've had enough waiting. I can't stand it anymore, and if this is his idea of not even starting to entice me, I will combust.

Pushing my fingers through his now-dry hair, I softly tug at the wavy strands, lifting his face to mine.

"I don't believe in virtues, and I don't have any more patience." I move my hips, grinding against him.

His cheeks flush and a low groan falls from his lips. I don't care to look around us to see how near the closest boat is. Julián's face is unreadable. I can feel him hard beneath me, so I know he physically wants me, what the hell is stopping him?

He seems to decide to go further, closing his eyes and wrapping his arms tight around my waist. The thin fabric of our swimwear isn't thick enough to hide both of our arousal. I've never been this forward with a guy, but no man has ever, ever, ever made me feel like this. Mentally stimulated and physically . . . electric. Impossible to control myself.

I lean in to kiss him, but he's faster, closing the space between us with a relieved moan. His mouth tastes exactly like I expected. Like the sunlight against my shoulders in the beginning of June, like wet skin against warm pool tile, like the first sip of ice water in the height of summer. His lips soft and pillowy, wet and skillful. His tongue slides into my mouth and I rock against him, soaking through my bikini bottoms. He kisses me like the water washes over your skin, slowly and powerfully, coming in intense waves and tiding back out.

Salty, strong, and warm. He stands up, carrying me with ease, never breaking his mouth from mine. I can't see where we're going, nor do I care, as we move across the boat. A door creaks open and within seconds, we're horizontal, a soft mattress under my back as he lays me down. The smell of paper and wood envelops my senses before Julián pulls me right back into his orbit. His warm mouth trails down my neck again, focusing again on the spot that makes me squirm. He's a fast learner. I dig my fingers into his soft hair, tugging to pull his mouth back to mine. I feel explosive, impatient. I've never wanted or needed something so badly. No doubt, no second-guessing. I need Julián. Now.

"I can't wait any longer. I really, really can't," I shamelessly admit, breathless.

He cocks his head to the side and gives me a long look. "As you wish."

At the exact moment he finishes speaking, his fingers slide beneath my bathing suit and inside me. I groan, the relief washing over me like a thousand seas. Julián's tongue dips down to my top as his skillful fingers pump slowly, his thumb pressing against my clit, making me press my lips together, trying not to scream with pleasure. He uses his teeth to move the fabric of my top out of the way, revealing my breasts, goose bumps covering them, my nipples hard as his mouth touches one of them. I arch my back, and he uses his hips to pin me down.

His tongue swirls at the same pace as his thumb, fingers still moving in and out . . . in and out . . . slowly, delightfully, building a forgotten pressure low in my belly. I bite down on his shoulder as I come, my entire body tensing and pulsing, the black behind my eyelids filling with exploding light as I stay in the high longer than I ever have. As I come down, my body melts into the mattress, my chest rising and falling at a rapid speed. I can barely see straight as he brings his lips to my ear, gently kissing the center.

"I must taste you. I've craved you since the moment I saw you," he calmly whispers as if he didn't just give me the most intense orgasm of my entire life.

I want more. I need more. I need more than more.

He crawls down my body, the freckles on his broad shoulders like a starry night, the messy waves in his hair. God, he's perfect. I lift my hips so he can take my bottoms off, and I nearly come again at the look in his eyes as his gaze rakes over my naked body. His eyes shine as his tongue glides over his lips, and I've never felt so sexy, so desired. The rush is nearly too intense to stay still. He licks my stomach, the skin on the sides of my hips, circling around, teasing me. I whine his name, trying to pull him by the hair to where I need him. He gently bites the inside of my thigh in return. The stinging, delightful surprise makes my hips rise again; my feet dig into the mattress as his tongue swipes across my still-throbbing clit. He uses his tongue to write poetry, words I'll never forget. My hand flies to my mouth, clamping down as he wraps his thick, toned arms around my thighs, pulling them wide open as he devours me. The first lick of his tongue sets me ablaze.

Flashes of skin, freckles, stars, sunsets, waves, water, the smell of sugar consume me as I climax again.

As I slowly come back to reality, he asks, "Are you exhausted yet?"

There's a playful gleam in his eyes while I catch my breath.

"Absolutely not," I reply quickly, reaching for his shirt, pulling it over his head and tossing it to the side.

His body covers mine and suddenly everything feels easy, feels light and free, and I instinctively know my life will never be the same again.

"We should eat now while it's fresh. In this weather, it will go bad fast, and I'd rather not give you food poisoning," he tells me, his breath much slower than before, but still a little ragged.

He's lying beside me as I count the splinters in the ceiling of this room, feeling my calm heartbeat in my chest. A massive, unerasable grin spreads across my face.

"How long did I doze off?" I ask him, still in disbelief that I was relaxed enough to sleep in a strange place, with a man I barely know, in the middle of the ocean.

"Only about ten minutes. You were awake one minute, then bam, lights out the next.

"Hungry?" he asks.

Sitting up, I clap my hands together, stomach growling like I haven't eaten in a week. I reach over and grab his shirt that I threw, and which is now dangling from an oyster shell–shaped lamp, the light bulb meaning to be the pearl.

"Quirky. I like it." I point to the lamp, and he grins.

"I made it. I used to make all kinds of silly things out of dry clay." He rubs the back of his neck, squeezing a little.

There's a flush in the apple of his cheeks, and I can't tell if it's from what we just did or if he's embarrassed.

"It's not silly. I would buy this on Etsy." I lean up, my body still naked, and run my finger along the cool shell. It's glossy, pearlized white with a tinge of green where the light touches it.

"What's an Etsy?" he wonders, pulling his shorts up to his waist and yanking on the strings.

I laugh a little. "It's a website, well, an app that you can buy handmade stuff on. Something like this would probably sell for at least a hundred bucks, likely more."

His eyes widen. "I'm in the wrong business, then." He smirks, handing me my bathing suit bottoms, standing to adjust my top. There's a darkness in his gaze as he says, "I don't want anyone to see your beautiful, exposed body. Only me."

I swallow, liking the surprisingly territorial way he's claiming me more than I will ever admit. "Hmph, so no nude beaches for me?" I quirk up a defiant brow.

THE LAST SUNRISE    **153**

"Nope. You should have taken that first opportunity you had."

"And you—" I glare at him, feigning seriousness. "No nude beaches for you either, then. Fair is fair."

"As you wish, my lady." He kisses me, tosses me over his shoulder like a sack of air, and carries me back to the deck of the boat.

# Chapter Fourteen

Okay, so what do we have? And how do I eat it?" I gaze over the colorful platter he's crafted.

"Mackerel." He points to a row of white fish with a gray rim. "Sea bream, two types. Sea bream is my favorite, this one specifically." His finger moves above another white fish with a pinkish edge. "And lastly, this is an anchovy. Americans seem to have some bias against them, but keep an open mind." He opens a plastic cooler and takes out a loaf of bread. "With bread and butter."

In another small tub is a red paste with different-colored flakes mixed in. I can smell garlic and tomato.

"Wow, you're so prepared. What if I wouldn't have gotten off the yacht?" I ask him, playfully but curiously.

He rips off a piece of bread, rubs butter and the tomato paste across it, and adds a thin gray anchovy before topping it with large flakes of sea salt.

"You would have. I was certain. But I live here, so I have food. Always."

I look around the boat. "You live here, like on the boat? Or . . ." Confusion draws my brows together.

I guess I should have wondered why there was a mattress on the boat. Jealousy pricks at my skin at the thought of how many women he's slept with on this boat. I almost ask, but he stops me by nodding, and says, "Yeah. My dad has a piso, a flat type, that was his childhood home, but it still smells like my mare, and I can't stand being inside for long. So I've been living on my boat since I was . . . sixteen?"

I wish I would have paid more attention to the room we were in. If I had known it was his living space, I would have memorized every inch of it.

I hesitate before asking, "Can I ask about your mother?"

He nods. "If you eat. Try this and be honest if you don't like it." He opens his mouth, gesturing for me to do the same.

I'm nervous to try something new, but that's why I'm here, and it smells so, so good. I open my mouth and say "ahh" and take a bite as he feeds me. The taste is so much different from what I expected; flavor bursts in my mouth, coating my taste buds. As someone who uses their senses more than the average person, this dish tastes like it was made for me. The smell of garlic and tomato; the salty, earthy flavor of the fish; the buttery crunch of the bread. I chew, nodding in approval.

"Oh my god!" I roll my head back and Julián claps in relief. "It's so good." I talk with my mouth full, not caring about manners.

"So, so good." I snatch the other half of the piece out of his hand and eat it.

The expression on his face should be painted or photographed. It's wonderful and beautiful and proud, like he's letting me in on the secret that food is something very, very dear to him. What a gift for him to share it with me.

"You're always snatching food from me," he teases, light and pure satisfaction beaming from his stunning eyes.

"Now have this one. It's softer than it looks, and you just eat it." He sprinkles the flaky salt on and folds the slice of fish, bringing it to my mouth.

I close my eyes, not knowing what to expect. Again, I'm floored. It's not as full of flavor as the anchovy and bread, but it's so light, so fresh and airy. I open my eyes and nod again.

"More?" he asks.

"Please." I scoot closer to him.

The sun is still high in the sky, but it's lowered since I got onto his boat. I haven't checked my phone, and if it wasn't for my mother, I wouldn't even think about it.

"I can't remember the last time someone made me a home-cooked meal," I say both to Julián and myself.

"Don't you have private chefs at your beck and call?" he says, no judgment, just stating what he assumes.

"We had a housekeeper-slash-nanny for me, who was basically family, and she used to do meal prep for us, per my mother's requests, so she did make everything, but my mom and I never ate together, and by the time I got the dish, it was in a plastic Tupperware. So homemade, yes, and delicious, but not like this. I usually eat alone."

"Meals are meant to be shared, treasured," he says, a hint of loneliness present. I wonder if he mostly has his meals alone too. "And where is she now?"

"She retired." Sadness fills my voice, but I try to bat it away. "I'm happy she doesn't have to work so hard anymore, but I miss her terribly. The house became so quiet after she left, but at least my mom showed her more kindness than I expected and paid her what she was worth, which was a lot. And right-fully so. We still keep in touch. She calls every few months."

I straighten my back, remembering the shock I felt when Sonia told me that my mom bought her a house in her home country of Honduras so she could live near her grandchildren. She had missed their childhood while tending to mine.

"She is where the tiny bit of Spanish I can understand comes from, but it's obviously different from yours."

I look past him, remembering her warm smile, the way she always sang songs under her breath as she worked. The sound was so comforting to me that I nearly asked her to record it for me before she left.

"She must have been lovely to help raise you."

I nod, a lump in my throat. Today has been a roller coaster of emotions, to say the least.

"Lovely, yes, but I feel so guilty that she spent her life dedicated to me and my mom and not her own family," I admit.

"Classism. It's a very real thing, and not that I can relate to the side you're on, the rich side, but I can relate to hers and I'm sure she not only cared about you but was happy to have a job."

"I hope so. You know, I thought I heard my mom crying the night Sonia left. She would never admit it, but I swear I heard it from outside her bathroom door. I, of course, cried for days, and I'm not even a crier. I don't know if I cried out of happiness for her, or because I knew my life would become even more lonely."

He lets that marinate between us for a few moments.

"You're very different from what I expected. Oriah," he says thoughtfully, out of the blue. I smile as my heart soars.

"So are you, Julián Garcia."

"We should both stop being so quick to judge, perhaps?" He raises a brow, and I agree with a small nod.

"Seems so. Speaking of my mom, I should text her just to save myself a headache later."

I get up to grab my bag and send an *I'm alive* text to my mom, and he feeds me another bite.

"Now that I've told you something so personal, it's your turn."

"So, the short version of the story is that my pare, my father, and mare met at a mutual friend's wedding. Not the most romantic story, but my pare was trying to get over his first love and my mare was doing the same. They hung out for a few weeks, she gets pregnant, they try to fall and stay in love, but it just . . ." He pauses, looking away from me.

"It just didn't click," we say in unison.

Nodding, he goes on. "It was for convenience, not happiness. The more they tried, the more they resented each other. Then she got sick . . . and my pare would never leave her, even though we both heard him call out that wretched woman's name in his sleep, night after night. She ignored that, and the longing in his eyes, the photos he kept. My parents were roommates, friends at best, as she slowly died in front of us, never having truly lived outside being a mother."

Wiping the tears from my eyes, I apologize for them. "Sorry, I—These aren't tears of pity. I just . . . I don't know what to say."

"Tragic, I know." He pops a piece of the sea bream into his mouth as I process his life. He must deal with trauma and tragedy with dark humor like me. It's refreshing.

"Wow. His first love must have really messed him up for him to love her for so long after."

"Yeah, she did. They were childhood best friends, then lovers. Promises of marriage, spent every waking moment together, and then one day she disappeared. Not dead or anything, just poof, left the island and didn't even say goodbye. She wrote him letters over the years, and when he tried to toss them, I made sure to take every single one and hide it. I still have them all in there. I'm not even sure why, really." He gestures toward the cabin we were in.

"Have you read them?" I wonder.

"No. Never. I think about throwing them into the sea one day but haven't done it yet. I don't know why, but something stops me each time I almost do it."

He offers me a piece, but I shake my head.

"Don't tell me I made you lose your appetite." He groans, looking down at the nearly full spread.

"You didn't," I tell him, reaching for his arm. "Can I have more of the anchovy one with the bread?"

He smiles, nodding. I decide to share part of my own family mess with him.

"Well, my dad isn't dead, but he might as well be. I've never met him and don't know anything about him aside from his name. I wrote him on Facebook once a few years ago, but he blocked me. I guess his wife and kids don't know about me and he wants to keep it that way." I shrug, remembering their smiling family photos, dressed in matching khaki pants and white linen shirts in the middle of the woods.

"I used to wonder which was worse—death or abandonment." I admit aloud one of my darkest curiosities.

Julián takes it in, his lips moving in a circle as he considers the thought.

"For me, abandonment, because it's a choice. Then again, I have all these memories with my mare that haunt me, all these regrets and guilt, knowing I'm the reason she never got to have a life," he tells me.

I don't know when our bodies moved, but we're inches away from each other now, his hand on my forearm.

"In a way, I'm the reason my mom doesn't have a life either. She works constantly because of all my—" I almost slip.

Oh god, I was so close to saying it. The one thing I don't want him to know. My ultimate sob story.

"My student loan debt and being a single mother," I explain.

The lie slides down my throat like acid, sitting heavily in the pit of my stomach like a rock.

Guilt begins to eat at me the longer I look at him. I know it's wrong to not warn him, give him a chance to run away now, but I can't. It's selfish, but I can't. Thankfully, he chimes in before my lie has another chance to grow.

"So, we have another thing in common. We both ruined our moms' lives and are incredibly judgmental." He smiles, and our twisted laughter drowns out the itch to tell him every single detail that I'm desperate to keep hidden.

# Chapter Fifteen

By the time I get back to my hotel, I'm floating and drift into the deepest sleep of my entire life. I don't wake up once.

The next morning, the water pressure in my shower is just right, the tinted sunscreen and mascara glide on my sun-kissed skin flawlessly. Everything seems to have a pinkish glow. The air feels even more fresh as I peer out my window to the street below. Vendors are setting up for the day, and children run through the streets blowing bubbles. The smell of fresh bread fills my room. My stomach grumbles and I grab my tote, water bottle, and head out. I knock on my mom's suite door, but she doesn't respond and there's no noise coming from inside.

I feel a little guilty for the relief that runs over me. As I step off the elevator, the lobby appears even more sparkling and lavish, the smell of the sea more enticing, and as I pass a ten-foot-tall mirror hanging on the wall, I stop to admire how glowy I am. The deep-green sundress flatters my skin tone. My purple bathing suit straps peek out on my shoulders. Even my seashell necklace flashes under the lights. Something inside me has shifted, and it's such a splendid feeling. I reread Julián's WhatsApp message again and again. It's only one text, a simple:

> Sweet dreams, Ry. Message me anytime and I'll be there.

But those two sentences have my heart rapidly beating out of my chest, my mouth dry, and my fingers itching to message him at least forty million times.

*Am I in love?* I wonder as I twirl in a circle admiring my reflection in the lobby mirror. How do people know when they're in love, and is it possible to love someone so quickly? The heart is such a confusion-inducing organ. It flutters at the thought of him, soars at the sight of him, aches at the absence of him—is that love?

Can you love someone before you know their middle name or what makes them the happiest, or the smell that reminds them of their favorite memory?

I have no damn clue, but the way I feel about Julián is so intense that I can't concentrate on anything else. It doesn't matter if my eyes are open or closed; his beautiful face and warm laughter are ever present.

"Heyyy." Amara waves to me from behind the desk, cutting off my spiraling internal monologue. The landline phone is against her ear as I approach her.

"Give me one sec, don't go yet," she whispers, covering the receiver. "No, we do not allow exotic pets. I'm sorry but it's against our policy . . . and the law," she politely responds in a tone reserved only for her job.

"Mhm, I completely understand, sir, but we cannot allow a tiger cub on our premises." She rolls her eyes and waits for their response.

"Sorry, but I can't help you further," she finally says, hanging the phone up.

"A tiger?" I ask in disbelief, wondering where the ridiculous request is coming from since she was speaking in English.

Nodding, she laughs. "That's far from the craziest request we've had.

"Did you like my customer service voice? I've nearly perfected it," she jokes, flipping her curly hair behind her shoulder.

Through my laughter, I nod. "Very much."

"So"—she leans across the marble counter—"I heard you had quite the adventure yesterday." Her brows wiggle as my cheeks flush.

"How did you already find out?" I chew on the inside of my cheek, flashes of Julián's hands and mouth all over me making my entire body shiver.

"This is a small island, and the service industry is even smaller. My friends were working on the boat and said some American dove off a big yacht and swam out to Julián's boat. Obviously, that has to be you." Her grin is contagious.

"Didn't you encourage me to stay away from him when we met?"

"Oh, that." She waves her hand. "I was just trying to warn you, but you can clearly handle yourself. I don't want you to get tangled up in something that could hurt you, but you seem to be thriving. If that changes and he fucks with you, I'll kill him and dump him in the ocean. Deal?"

"Deal."

Amara's gaze goes over my shoulder.

"Incoming," she warns, nodding behind me.

My mother waltzes into the lobby with an entourage of men in suits behind her like an army. Her expression is serious and determined, slightly murderous, even. She's snapping orders to Lena, who's struggling to keep at my mom's pace as they cross the concrete floor, heading toward the door.

I consider attempting to hide, but my mother is in full work mode. She barely makes eye contact for a second, nods, and keeps walking until she's out of sight.

"Yikes. I feel for whoever has to deal with her today," I sigh, sending Lena strength.

"Has she always been like that? The whole boss-babe, badass, take-no-shit vibe?"

I nod. "Mostly, yeah. I vaguely remember her being a little less work obsessed when I was really young, but sometimes I question my own memories, unsure if that actually happened or not. What about your parents? Are they also work obsessed and that's why you move around?" I ask.

"The opposite. My mom, god love her, she has zero ambition, zero passion for anything outside being drunk and, on occasion, high. Work injury led her to pain pills, which led her to living in a constant state of zombiehood. My dad works but hates his job and my mom"—she smiles—"but puts up with her, thank god. So I moved away the moment I could and will never, *ever*, move back to my hometown. Sorry, I know I unloaded my mommy issues on you before, but it's a habit." She smiles again.

"You don't need to be sorry."

"Thanks, and that's life. I'm just grateful I get to live it."

I lean onto the cold marble between us. Looking up at her in admiration. "Do you feel like that every day? Grateful to be alive, even if life isn't everything it should be sometimes? The ups and the downs? They're worth it to you?"

She nods and begins to gently caress my hair. Her affection heals a part of me that has been longing for a friend since I lost my dearest one, bit by bit, stroke by stroke.

"I'd rather live in chaos and uncertainty. Hearing my own laughter, tasting my own tears, falling in love and back out again, heartache, being loved, all the ups and downs. I can't waste my life wondering what would have happened if I didn't live that way. You know?"

I sigh, closing my eyes.

"I love your outlook on life. I admire it," I say through barely parted lips, hoping to feel that way one day. Less afraid, less trapped in my own body and mind.

Now is the perfect time to explain to her about my very different outlook on life. How unfair it can be, how cruel its expiration date comes to some of us. But when I open my eyes again, she's looking so affectionately at me, almost like she knows I'm hiding something but isn't judging me for not sharing it, so I keep my mouth closed and do my best to etch this moment into my memory while I still have time.

"I'm so grateful I met you."

"It's mutual, babe," she says as the phone begins to ring between us.

"I swear if it's that fucking tiger guy I'm going to lose it." She groans but changes her voice immediately back to her perky customer-service voice.

"Moltes gràcies per trucar a l'Hotel Maricel, com et puc ajudar?"

I wave goodbye to her and head out toward the pool.

Due to my mom's busy day, my morning is free. I pick the lounge chair closest to the edge of the infinity pool and place my bag down, kicking off my sandals. The cement is warm, the grainy texture alive under my bare feet. The sun is high already, though it's barely nine. A group of seagulls converse above me, flying low and steadily in a swoopy circle. There's only one other person at the pool, a man whose face is covered by a newspaper, presumingly asleep.

As I walk over to a lounge chair to put on a fresh spray of sunscreen over my layer from after my shower, my impulse to message Julián has fully taken over my mind. I want to show him the pool, the birds, even the view of the sea that he sees and lives on daily. I don't want to come across as clingy, but truth be told, the only thing I want in my life right now outside of world peace and a magical cure for my medical crap is to cling to him as hard as I can.

What the hell, who cares if he thinks I'm clingy? He showed up on a damn boat yesterday. So why am I nervous to message him? I grab my phone from my bag and send him a picture of the pool.

> Want some company?

His immediate response eases my nerves. I nod, laughing at myself for being so giddy and not realizing he can't see me.

> Yes please. The seagulls are speaking in Spanish and I need a translator ☺

> On my way

As promised, he shows up within ten minutes. I shield my eyes from the sun as I watch him approach; his confidence radiates brighter than the sun. I missed him, I realize, I missed him with a deep ache in my chest, and it's been less than twelve hours since I was with him.

"I missed you," he tells me, as if he read my mind.

He leans down to meet my eyes, his palm scooping around my chin to lift it.

"Your eyes are different again? One's lighter?" He tilts my head a little, inspecting me.

"Shit. My contacts. I usually wear brown contacts so they both match, but I forgot this morning. I keep forgetting lately. I've been distracted." I've been more than a little distracted by the constant thoughts of Julián since I first laid eyes on him.

"Why do you hide them? I noticed before at the cabana when we were drinking, but I didn't want to just ask you."

"It's not that I'm hiding them . . . I mean, I guess I am. But it gives me anxiety to have people making eye contact with me, commenting, drawing unwanted attention over something I have no control over. Sounds like such a silly thing to complain about, but it really started bothering me."

He nods his head slowly. "I get it, really. I do.

"Is the light one blue or green?" he asks, peering closer.

I can't tell if he's teasing me since he's near enough to see the color up close, but his tone feels genuine.

"What do you mean? It's green. I get it, it's weird to look at. I was teased my entire childhood over it, so I started wearing contacts when I was in middle school."

"Not weird. I just wish I could see it clearly. I have trouble with separating blue and green, yellow and red, mostly."

"You're color-blind?" I ask, not sure why I'm so surprised by this.

He nods. "Yeah, always have been." He shrugs and leans in a little closer. "You should stop hiding your beautiful eyes." I close them as he plants a kiss on the lid of each one.

I'm tempted to ask him more about his color-blindness, curious how the ocean looks to him, how I look to him, but I know how it feels when someone is probing you over something you can't control and I'm the last person who would intentionally want to make someone feel like a lab rat, like something about them is wrong or broken.

"I missed you, too, by the way," I say instead.

He smiles, pleased to hear it. "You did?"

I nod. "Mhmm."

"The seagulls said otherwise," he teases.

"Did they, now?"

He nods, pointing at them. "They flew to my place to tell me you're out here in a tiny bikini flirting with some guy." He gestures toward the man and leans in to kiss my chin, then my lips.

My jaw untenses, falling open, and I pull him by his T-shirt to kiss me again. His mouth is welcoming, somehow already familiar to me. I sink into the chair, every muscle and inch of my skin melting around my bones, softening my entire body.

He moves his mouth to my forehead, gently placing a kiss there.

"I don't want to get too carried away and wake up our friend there." He motions toward the sleeping man again.

"Those seagulls have been gossiping since I came out here. I don't know how he's slept through it," I tell him as he sits down on the lounge chair next to mine.

"Ah." He pauses, watching the birds in the sky. "Really?" He pretends to speak with them, and it's so effortlessly funny as he taps his chin, a fake look of concern on his face.

"Oh no. They are worried about me," he whispers, tilting his head to continue the bit. I laugh but feign paranoia.

"Really? Why?" I whisper back, cupping my mouth.

He leans over. "They're worried that I've been brainwashed by a sexy, smart, funny American girl."

"Damn it, they figured it out. Damn seagulls." I raise my middle finger to them, and he falls back laughing.

"They said, and I quote, 'Fuck you too.' But don't worry, I'll cuss them out later and avenge you by not feeding them."

"So, have you?" I sit up, putting my elbows on my knees, taking him in. The freckles on his cheeks are darker today, resembling a map of stars. "Been brainwashed, I mean?" I clarify.

"I'm afraid so," he sighs, scooting the lounge chair even closer to me. "Capitalism wins again."

"Ha. Ha. Well, if it makes you feel any better, I've also been brainwashed by you."

His expression is full of surprise, which I find equally as surprising given our time together, especially yesterday, and the fact that we haven't gone a day without seeing each other since we met.

"It does make me feel better." His grin is cocky yet charming. "Did you wake up thinking about me? I'm asking for a friend, of course."

"Which friend?"

He looks up. "The seagulls."

"I don't think I should give them any more information about me. They're already trying to sabotage me."

"Your humor is perfect," he says, making me flush.

The intensity of the slight language barrier is thrilling in moments like this. Or maybe he's just the type of person who says what he feels? Either way, it's refreshing and not at all what I expected from someone who looks the way he does. He could have any and every woman, and man, on this island, but here he is, sitting poolside with me on a Tuesday morning. I'm not thinking that in a self-deprecating sense, just glad he's going out of his way to show me that he's as into me as I am him.

"What are you considering right now? I can see the wheels spinning in your mind." He circles his fingers around next to his ears, then opens his arms wide for me. I move to his chair, sitting between his legs, scooting down a little so my back is against his chest. Leaning my head back, I rest against his skin. I can feel his heart beating the most perfect rhythm.

"I was thinking how you could be anywhere but you're here with me," I admit at the risk of sounding insecure.

He wraps his arms tighter around my body. His skin is warm against my upper back. Our bodies fit together perfectly; yesterday on the boat was all the proof I needed of that.

"The only other place I could be is work, and this is more enjoyable." Soft laughter falls against my ears, and he continues. "This part isn't a joke." Nervousness plays in his tone. "I mean every single word." His hands gently squeeze my shoulders, kissing the top of each.

"I'm exactly where I want to be, and that's damn terrifying, but I'm going to do my best with how confusing this feels, okay?"

His words come out as a timid warning, but I actively choose to ignore the alarm going off inside my overly active mind and respond with a silent nod. Whatever will happen will happen, and being worried about the potential of something going wrong isn't fair to myself or to our limited time together. This feeling, whether it'll be fleeting or not, is everything I imagined and more, and sure as hell worth any pain that will come later. I'm more of a risk than he is, and I wish I wasn't too selfish to disclose that to him.

"Shall we swim?" he suggests.

Reluctantly I get up from the lounge chair and he pulls me toward the water.

As we float, my body wrapped around his, we glide around the pool, sometimes talking, sometimes letting the silence simmer between us. The water, to my surprise, is salt water, and I should have warned Julián when I smelled it, but he quickly found that out in the worst way, by taking a gulp to spit out at me. Our sleepy guest wakes up as we burst into laughter and Julián coughs, cursing in Spanish. With a grunt, the man mumbles something incoherent and heads back into the hotel, probably to finish his nap.

Julián bounces gently, holding me in his arms, my thighs and arms wrapped around his strong body as we glide through the warm, empty pool.

"It's so easy with you. All my problems from my family's business, my doubts and worries, all the things I usually focus too much on, they don't cross my mind when you're around,

Oriah. I want to spend every waking moment with you. It hasn't been like this before for me. Ever. I don't feel like I need to hide, not from you, Ry."

"Oriah?" My mother's voice slices through our moment; I nearly jump out of my skin and the water, hoping I'm imagining her standing there.

Without thinking, I push Julián away and stand up straight in the shallow water. I was so lost in Julián's words that I hadn't heard the click of her heels approach.

"Mom," I say, letting Julián know who this woman with a death glare directed at him is.

My mother's attention drags between Julián and me, slowly repeating as if she's trying to make sense of what she's seeing. Me in the embrace of a man. I can imagine why it would surprise her, but I silently plead with my eyes for her not to treat me like a child in front of him.

"Hello, I'm Julián Garcia." Julián pops out of the pool to politely greet her, wiping his hand on his wet shorts before stretching out his still-wet hand toward her.

Her face pales, and both of their bodies go rigid as the space between them seems to pulse. My heart quickens. Something's wrong.

"You're . . . wait, you're . . ." He looks over and down at me, his face twisted in confusion, and then straight back to my mom.

"You're Isolde Pera," he says with a stony certainty, my mother's name sounding like a curse rolling off his tongue.

How on earth does he know her name?

His attention snaps to me.

"She's your mother? I knew you looked familiar. This vile woman who came here to demolish our business and bleed our land dry is your mother?" His voice is full of venom, a deep hatred for her that has my head spinning.

I grip my hands around the stony edge of the pool, trying to pull myself up, but the roaring behind my ears makes it hard. It takes several attempts before I join them on the hot cement. Water drips from my body as I try to grasp what the hell the problem between them is.

My mother's face is whiter than a sheet of paper. Her eyes are steel, her chin set. I can practically see her temper flaring. She's trying to appear as unbothered as stone, but I know better.

"How do you two . . . What the hell is going on?" I finally manage to speak through the fog in my brain.

Julián's index finger points toward my mother and she takes a step back.

"She's the one I've been talking about. Her and her greed have come here to steal the land we own and build another useless luxury resort on top of it. She's killing our island, and you—" I can hear the pain in his voice.

"You're her accomplice. That's why you're here." His eyes go wide as if he's piecing together a puzzle that he's spent years trying to connect. "You told me you've been working on a charity thing and came to live a free summer? Bullshit. Your happy-go-lucky summer is putting my family and our workers out of their jobs. How fucking typical."

I whirl to my silent mother. "Mom, what is he talking about? Is the company you've been talking about his?"

She swallows before she speaks, her lip quivering as if she's in the presence of a ghost. Confrontation usually makes her morph into a stronger, bigger version of herself, not shrink the way she is now. I take a breath, wondering if she's going to crush him like a bug as she typically would any man who speaks to her in that type of tone.

"It's more complicated than that, Ry. I can explain it to you, but this isn't personal."

Julián laughs, a sickened, roaring, angry noise from deep in his chest. "You liar. You destroyed my pare's life, broke his heart. You've kept him in an eternal prison, longing for a selfish ghost of a woman he loved as a child, and now you're here to put the final nail in his coffin under the pretense of charity and building a hotel on our land? Disgusting. Both of you." He spits at her feet, and she blinks hard as he storms off.

"Julián, wait!" I try to catch up to him, but when I do, he yanks his arm away from me.

"Do not touch me! Stay away from me! I never want to see your face again. Just go back to where you came from and never, *ever* come back here."

The warmth, the comfort, the familiar Julián I had fallen in love with is gone. The man in front of me is cold, full of ice and metal, no sign of the smiling, endearing Julián. My Julián.

My heart cracks, my knees buckle as I grab on to an umbrella stand to keep my body from collapsing.

# Chapter Sixteen

I sit across from my mother in the dining room of the hotel, my arms crossed around my chest, staring sharply at her until she speaks. I will get an explanation, and she will not get away with sharing the bare minimum as she usually does. A basket of warm bread and butter with flakes of salt sits lonely between us as the server pours my mom's glass full of wine.

"I'll have some too, please." I smile at the server: the same friendly face I've seen at nearly every meal I've eaten at the hotel.

"You shouldn't drink on your medication, Ry. You know—" my mom starts to say.

I cut her off. "I'm having some."

She purses her lips but doesn't argue further. There's a buzzing between us, almost a tinge of fear radiating from her side, which has never been the case in our power dynamic.

"How did you meet him?" Her voice is cool, dripping cold water.

I shake my head. "Answer my questions first. Why did you mislead me about why we came here? You told me you were celebrating a big deal, a merger. You complained about the seller some, but you didn't even hint at what you were actually doing. I would have never come if you had. You know that."

"And what am I doing exactly, Ry? You don't understand anything about my job or how important this deal will be for us. For you, your future."

I slam my hand down on the table, shaking the glasses and cutlery.

"What future?" I glare at her.

"Don't say that." There's pain in her voice as my words land the way I intended them to.

I huff. "You know it's true. So, you brought me here to get revenge on someone and ruin their family's legacy? Are people's livelihoods really such a game for you? Is money the only thing you care about?" I lean back in my chair and guzzle some of the wine. "I already know the answer, but I want to hear you say it."

She mirrors me with her wine, except she downs the entire glass and waves the server over to order a bottle.

"I'm not here to get revenge on anyone. I'm here to make a deal for a valuable piece of land to build an in-demand resort on. Just like I've been doing for years. The family business that they're both obsessed with protecting has been sinking for years. I know it's easy for you to believe that I'm the big bad villain and everything in this world is black-and-white, right or wrong, but you don't have a clue what you're talking about regarding this situation."

Anger bubbles in my chest. Julián's family will be out of business, a business that spans generations. The very one he talked about, in detail, and it didn't sound very small to me.

I sat there listening to him talk about his life, his heritage—not knowing my mom was actively destroying that. I shudder, considering how many times I was oblivious to my mother and SetCorp doing this in the past. I knew they built fancy hotels and resorts all over the world, but I never thought about what or who lived and worked on the land before they came in with their bulldozers and checks. Her hundreds of business trips, promotions, and bonuses were all at the expense of someone else's suffering.

"How did you meet him?" She repeats her question from when we first began. "Julián. Did he seek you out purposely?"

I shake my head, snarling at her audacity.

*He didn't, did he?*

No way. *I have to stop letting her get into my head.*

I sigh heavily out of my nose. "No."

"He appears to be as hotheaded as his father." She tries to keep her voice steady, but I've been studying her mannerisms my entire life, always reading her body language, paying attention to the click of her tongue, the twitch of her brow, the way she looks at my nose instead of my eyes when she's trying to hide emotion.

My throat is dry as I ask, "How on earth do you know his father?" My mind is rapidly attempting to put the pieces in order. Julián said she destroyed his life . . .

There's something there, a deep history with Julián's father. Something that she's been suppressing for god knows how long. Julián said his dad has loved her since they were kids.

My entire body aches down to my bones as I try to piece the puzzle together. Was it possible that she once loved him?

God, what are the chances? The first time I fall in love with a man—on the other side of the planet, at that—my mother and his father have history. Fate continues to be cruel to me, reminding me that no matter how good life can feel, it will always be returned doubly as pain. I've grown used to physical pain but thought I was numb to emotional agony. Clearly that isn't the case.

"Tell me about his father: How did you meet him? Did you love him? Why would you do this to someone you loved?"

She's growing tired and uncomfortable having her hidden past exposed to me. I can feel it before she gets to her feet. Defensiveness covers her like a dark cloak, and her eyes turn to slits.

"I'm doing this *because* I loved him."

She yanks the bottle of wine from the ice bucket next to the table and takes it with her as she disappears from the restaurant.

When I get back to my room, it takes everything in me not to hurl into the toilet. I bet if I had eaten something today, that's exactly what I'd be doing. My mind is a thick fog, my bones feel watery as I mechanically move through my hygiene routine, my mind both empty and overflowing. My ears throb as I wash my hair, not knowing if two or twenty minutes have passed. I step out of the running shower three times to check my phone for a reply from Julián that I know I won't be getting.

If he would just let me explain . . . what would I say? That he should look beyond the fact that my mother is single-handedly destroying not just his, but his father's and all of their employees' lives, while I'm trying on designer dresses for a bullshit charity event?

It's selfish of me to even think of asking him to look past this, to ever speak to me again. I know that, but it still makes my heart feel as if it's been shredded into slivers, painfully floating on top of the sea, not heavy enough to go fully under and be swept away, but never to be whole again.

# Chapter Seventeen

I wake up to my phone vibrating under my pillow. I grab it with haste, only to be disappointed when I see my mom's name flashing across the screen. I ignore it, knowing damn well she's going to call me back or come to my room, but I'm petty enough to smile as I swipe to ignore her call. I shut the phone off, a tiny act of useless rebellion, and walk toward the window. The sun is high today, the street vendors all setting up their carts and tables. My head aches at the temples. I groan and crack the window open, hoping the morning breeze will help.

The air is fresh, and the smell of bakers pulling out their breads and cakes for the day wafts through my room from the bakery next door. My stomach growls, wishing I could teleport a sandwich or pastry to my room. I guess I sort of can, using room service. Using my mother's tainted money.

I scowl, slamming the window shut. I continue to stare out the glass, getting lost in the realization that everything in my life is dependent on my mom. Her money, her knowledge and rolodex of my doctors and scans and medications. I'd always thought I had done my best to learn to advocate for myself medically, but I really just discussed things with her, her always leading. I hadn't done shit. I've let her steer my life, let her be the center of every major choice, every lack of having a choice. In a fairy-tale version of my life, I'd run to Julián, tell him I'm never going to speak to my mother again, and cut her out of my life. It's not only impossible, it's immature.

Everything about me feels immature and selfish . . . Even the pity I feel for myself right now is massively flawed and privileged. A sad rich girl who's spending her summer in Spain in a luxurious suite, with a driver and nearly endless spending money, is sad because a boy she just met justifiably hates her and her greedy mother. I lightly bang my head against the glass, wondering how many times I'd have to do that before I have an episode, before everything goes black.

The way I feel isn't only because of Julián, who I'm devastated about, but it does feel like I'm having an identity crisis. In my head, my mom was just a hard worker. A woman who set out to prove herself and became addicted to her job. But I've been sitting idly living off other people's suffering and loss. On top of that, I'm all too well aware that I haven't accomplished anything in my life and won't have the chance to. Julián's family being ruined by my mom was just the final crack in my delusional mirror of a life I'd pretended to live. I will likely leave the earth and no one except my mother, and maybe Lena, will care. The people my mother has paid to care for me might mourn a little, but I'd be delusional to think their worlds revolved around me. And to Julián I'll always be known as the spoiled American girl who helped ruin his livelihood, if he even remembers me at all.

If banging my head against this glass actually killed me, my funeral would be nearly empty. No flowers, no one to mourn. My mom would probably take a work call and end it early. A flashback to one of my grief therapists warning me about these types of thoughts comes to the forefront of my mind. According to her and her extensive Ivy League education, the imminent question of "What was my purpose in life?" always catches up to you before you go. I had ignored it many times: when I woke up in the hospital after I seized in the middle of my audition for the best dance academy in Texas and bit my tongue so hard that the judges and screaming trainees thought I was dead; when I saw the tubers on the screen covering my right kidney, and my mother's wailing nearly drowned out the doctor's order to remove it; and most recently when staring blankly at my latest MRI results a week before we left to come here. The tubers in my brain had shifted yet again, making for an extremely dangerous surgery, one that stole my best and only friend's memory and life, and my best option for my potential survival. I weighed the options and will keep my promise to Audra, to myself, that I would rather have my heart stop beating than my mind erased.

I climb back into bed, not knowing what the hell else to do. I can't face Amara. I can't stand to see my mother, and Julián can't stand to see me. I should go back home to Texas. A relief washes over me. That's exactly what I should do, *go the hell home*. I came here to have new experiences, to be excited for the time I have, even not knowing how short or long it may be, but now I'm just regressing and feeling sorry for myself. I don't want my plan to find the joy in life, to relish the things that make life worth living, forgotten because of my mom and her work, of all things.

I wake up to a knock on my door. The sheets are so cool and soft against my skin, begging me to stay wrapped in them, but whoever is at my door is insistent, unbearably so. I open the door to my mom and one of the women I recognize from my dress fittings, standing in the frame, a rack of dresses behind them. Now isn't the time to tell my mom I'm getting out of here, that I want nothing to do with her plan or pretend charity, so I concede for now and step out of the way, letting them stroll in. The wheels on the rack creak as I greet the woman.

"Did you just wake up?" my mom asks me, concern clear in her dark eyes.

I nod.

"Hmph." I watch as she looks around my room, taking in everything, seeing if something is amok, or maybe looking for Julián.

"Can we get this over with?" I ask her through a forced smile.

The last thing I want is to seem rude in front of the stylist, but I don't have the energy to fake it today. My head is aching, throbbing at my temples.

"We've narrowed it down to three. A sage green, a cream, and a burgundy. Here's the burgundy." The stylist's accent makes the words sound as beautiful as the deep-wine dress in her hand.

"Let's go with that one," I suggest. I liked them all the last time I tried them on.

The stylist's face falls, and she nods, agreeing. Not wanting to push me, but I can tell she internally disagrees.

"What about the green?" I suggest, and relief fills her eyes. At this point, I don't care what dress I'll be wearing during this bullshit event.

The moment it's over, I'll be on a plane getting the hell out of here. My mind is fully made up; leaving is the only way I can make it through this summer alive, or attempt to. It's better for Julián, too, who won't have to worry about seeing me again.

I try the silky green dress on, and the reaction from the styling team and my mother says it all. It looks great, the silky material hugging my hips, my breasts. The hanging neckline and backless detail make it even more flattering. If I wasn't decaying inside, I would be able to appreciate the dress for the work of art it is. Simple and elegant, unlike the body wearing it.

"It's perfect. You're perfect." My mother smiles, the swollen pockets under her eyes noticeable under the light. Maybe she does feel guilty; she's just become a master at hiding any and all emotions.

After the women pack up their roll-aways, pins, and all things stylists carry, my mom tries to sneak out of my room with them. Hesitation is clear in her eyes when I gently grab ahold of her wrist to stop her. She sighs but gives in, and I pull her to the couch in the living room area of my room.

"What's this about, Ry? The gala?" She doesn't look at me, instead focusing her gaze on a porcelain vase on the table in front of us.

"No. I want to talk to you . . . a real conversation between a mother and her adult daughter."

Her shoulders straighten, immediately defensive.

"You don't need to react like that. That's exactly why we keep butting heads and can't seem to speak the same language."

"We were fine before we came here and before you met Julián," she retorts, crossing her legs. Her foot swings lazily, but I know it's a nervous tick of hers.

"No, we weren't. I was just suffering in silence, Mom."

My words seem to have an effect on her, and she slowly turns her head to look at me. "What do you mean, 'suffering in silence'? I've done my best to take care of you."

"This isn't about you not taking care of me medically," I clarify. "I know you did everything you could when it came to my doctors and medications and finding all the latest research, but that's not what I'm talking about. Suffering isn't only physical, Mom, and you know that."

We sit in a few moments of silence before I continue.

"I want you to see me. Not just my tuberous sclerosis, or a problem you need to handle or fix. I want you—" I correct myself. "I've been aching for you to see me as your daughter who's a grown woman, who has emotions and dreams that were lost, who has a sense of humor and a personality that you don't even know. I'm not blaming you for working overtime, I just wish you could separate me from my condition, especially when we both know the situation I'm in now."

In an attempt to get all my words out before she has the chance to flip them on me, I keep going.

"I want to know what your life was like before you became a mother. I want to know your favorite color or if you ever danced. Did I get my passion and talent for it from anyone in my family? I want to know if you ever had any dreams or hopes. Do you know what it feels like to be loved? Have you ever been heartbroken? What was your favorite snack as a child? Do you even know mine? I don't know anything about you, but I've spent my entire life practically glued to your side. I don't even know if you have friends or family here. If *I* have family here . . ."

My mother's eyes have softened since my speech, but she's still wildly uncomfortable. It breaks my heart for her.

"Ry," she finally says. "I didn't know you felt any of this. I didn't have a clue that you thought about any of this. I wanted you to be able to breeze through life and not worry about my mistakes or my past, only your future."

"None of what I'm asking or wanting to know is about you making mistakes. I really wish your mind didn't always go to that," I tell her, meaning it. "You can't protect me from every-thing, and I don't want you to. Are you planning on living your entire life for me, and then what? When I'm gone—"

"Don't." She raises a hand, her voice feeble and gentle. "Please don't say that. And yes, I am planning on living my entire life for you, just as I've done since I heard your heart-beat inside me."

"That's not living." I wipe the tears from my cheeks, trying to stay as calm as possible.

She turns her body to face me, taking my hands in hers. Her touch is unfamiliar, so much so that it nearly breaks me. "It's the greatest joy in my life to be your mother. I know I didn't do everything right, but to me, taking care of you is the way I choose to live my life, and I have never, and will never, regret that. You must understand that we are different people, Ry. I work so hard and so much to distract me from the pain and guilt of knowing how I've treated the people who have loved me. I work so I can feel like I owe SetCorp a little less for all they've done for us. I work so I can have a little pride, knowing I came from nothing and have been able to provide you with the life you've had. I'm sorry I'm not as emotionally available . . ."

She's nearly crying, a sight I never thought I'd see outside a hospital. "But I can try from here, taking it slowly. I'll try to open up with you a little more, okay?"

"Okay." I nod, not getting all the answers I want, but satisfied by what feels like a massive breakthrough compared to any and every conversation we've ever had.

"And I do see you. I see you every day, and I love you more than anything. I can see how you would feel the way you do, and I'll try harder to show you."

She swallows hard and shifts her body again. Her exit is coming any second, and I'm okay with that. A tiny part of my unseen inner child was healed by her acknowledgment, and the fact that she didn't cut me off as I shared my feelings with her.

"I need to go get my dress pinned, but to answer a few of your questions"—she begins to stand up, and I follow her toward my door—"I can't dance to save my life, and my favorite snack as a child was rubiols that my mother made around Easter." Her hand is shaking as she opens the door, turns to face me, and sighs.

"And I've been in love only once, but you already seem to have figured that out."

"Do you ever do your makeup at home?" I ask Amara as I approach her at the desk.

"Not when I can do it on the clock and get paid." She winks, blowing a kiss to her favorite camera in the corner.

"I'm going back home early," I tell her as she drags a mascara wand across her lashes. Her hand jerks and black smears across the apple of her cheek.

"Excuse me, what?"

"Sorry for the shitty timing." I point to the mascara on her face, and she looks in the mirrored wall behind the desk, shrugging.

"How early are you talking?" She puts the tube of mascara on the counter.

I hesitate before replying, sealing my fate. "Tomorrow. Before the event."

Surprise flashes in her eyes.

"What? What happened? Did Julián . . . what did he do?" Her reaction is so quick, her temper flaring, ready to go full force on Julián.

"He didn't do anything. It was me. Well, my mom, which by proxy makes me guilty too."

She's confused, rightfully so. I give her more context, starting and ending with what happened yesterday.

"Oh no. So, the evil company we're all going to be protesting tomorrow is your mom's?" She cringes.

"Protesting?"

Nodding, she explains that their group of friends, along with a ton of fishermen and their families, have a protest set for tomorrow at the Garcia shipyard. The time is just a few hours before the event.

"I guess the protest is going to bring awareness, and if it gets too out of hand or word travels too fast, it could ruin the fancy party." She apologizes with her eyes.

"I don't give a shit about the party. I can't believe my mom is the one causing all this damage and I've been parading around here, wasting Julián's and your time. I'm sorry."

She waves her hand. "Don't be. If you didn't know, why the hell are you sorry?"

I shrug. "Even knowing that, I still feel so shitty. The least I can do is say sorry."

"No, the least you can do is stay here and try to make it right," she suggests.

"How can I make it right?"

I've gone through every scenario in my mind, trying to think of ways to stop it, even wishing my mom was allergic to something that I could give her to make her sick enough to go home. Her immune system is stronger than her work ethic, and that's saying a fucking lot. Even after our heart-to-heart, there's no way in hell she would cancel it.

"I'm not sure, but there has to be a way. Just packing up and leaving is never the answer. Imagine if Romeo and Juliet just gave up!" she says with passion.

I can't help but laugh at her comparison. "They wouldn't have died."

She laughs, despite the circumstance. "Oh yeah. Bad example. But you get my point. You can't just leave."

The phone in front of her rings, and she groans. I smile, nodding to deceive her, knowing that I'm getting on that flight tomorrow night and nothing and no one can stop me. As I head to my room, I begin to type out an apology text to

Julián, knowing nothing I can say will make it all better, but I don't know if I can live with just leaving and never saying goodbye. This summer was supposed to be about no fear, no regrets, and I sure as hell will regret not attempting to say goodbye to Julián. I sneak past the elevator, making sure Amara doesn't see me, and I head out of the hotel. I slowly make my way to Julián's dock, not having a clue what I'll say or do when I see him, or worse, what he will say or do when he sees me, but I'm letting my heart lead the way and hoping it steers me correctly.

When I get there, his boat is gone. The water is silent, still, almost eerily so. I look out onto the water, but his vessel is nowhere in sight.

I try to call him, but it goes directly to voicemail. Not even an ignored call; his phone is powered off. God, he must hate me so much and feel such deep betrayal.

"Oriah?" A voice behind me has me whirling around before I realize it's Julián's father. They look more like brothers than father and son, but the resemblance up close is uncanny.

"Mr. Garcia?" I stumble over my words.

"Mateo . . . you can call me Mateo. Are you looking for Julián?" he asks, his accent much more prominent than his son's.

I nod. "Is he here by chance? I know his boat isn't, but I thought maybe . . . Sorry, I don't know much Spanish."

Mateo's long hair shakes with his head. "I know enough English to get by. Had to, to adapt to the tourists." He smiles a little, and my heart melts when I see the twin smile of Julián's.

My favorite smile that I've had the pleasure of witnessing but may never see again. "He's not here. He took off earlier without a word."

"I'm sorry. For everything. I know you must also hate me."

He holds one hand up, a gesture his son also does. He's even dressed similarly in a sun-faded cutoff T-shirt and shorts, his feet bare against the wood dock. His hair is much curlier than Julián's, but they look so similar it makes me want to sob right there on the shore, and try as I might, I can't stop the tears as they begin to fall down my face.

Julián's father, a man who loved my mother once upon a time, and potentially still does, steps forward and wraps his arms around me. He smells like wood and ropes, like the comfort of the sea, like a warmth I've never felt from an adult. Despite everything, he consoles me as I cry and cry, my tears falling between the cracks in the old wood and washing away in the sea.

"I will never hate you," he eventually says. "I can't speak for my son, but I don't have any room for hate in my heart," he tells me, and I wonder if it's because my mother has left no room for anything else.

"How is that possible?" I ask, shamelessly wiping my snotty nose on the fabric of my shirt while his attention is on the sea before us. "To not be angry at me, when my mom . . . according to Julián, has ruined your life and is now going to tear down your family business and build a resort on it, and I'm here crying over your son. I swear I'm not usually this selfish," I say, wondering if that's true or not. Maybe I am selfish, like her. Maybe the type of person I convinced myself that I am isn't real at all and I'm the kind of person I've always tried not to be.

The possibility makes my heart sink further.

Mateo sighs, clicking his tongue on the roof of his mouth. "You and Julián have nothing to do with Isolde's and my mistakes. Our debt is not yours to pay."

I don't know what to say, so I just stare at him for a moment and he reaches for my hand, gently gesturing to sit down on the dock with him. "Your mother didn't ruin my life. I know my son has taken to blaming her for everything that has gone wrong." He smiles, the crinkles around his eyes so charming and nearly nostalgic somehow. I can easily see why my mom fell for him. "He holds grudges unreasonably, and it's easier for him to be angry at a woman he doesn't know than deal with the fact that his pare isn't a saint and that life isn't always the way it should be. But my life, through its ups and downs, isn't in ruin. I'm not the kind of man your mother would end up with, I never was, but that didn't stop me from living my life. So please, Oriah, don't get even more angry at your mom because of Julián's words. You're all she has."

"That's her fault," I retort, sniffling. "She's boxed herself into a lonely life where the only thing she cares about is her job. She's never brought me here, never showed me where she's from. I don't know anything about my heritage, my family, whether they're alive or dead. I don't even know her, honestly, so it's really hard not to blame her for all this. Not only how I feel, but everything."

"It's easy to blame her, but it's brave to try to understand her. She lost her mare at such a young age, and it takes a lot to deal with that alone. She loves you deeply, I know that. Her life has been dedicated to you, to her work because of what it offers you. She's ambitious and was once just a girl your age, with a baby, no family, and scared of failing. You and Julián probably will never understand it, but part of me is proud of her, even during this mess."

"You really are a freaking saint." I admire his grace, the empathy he has for my mother regardless of what she's done, and is still doing, to him.

He shakes his head. "I'm far from a saint. We're all just human, trying our best. Her too."

"No wonder she loved you," I quietly remark, half wishing he was angry, bitter, and ready to tell me all the awful things she's done in her life, but the conversation is far, far from that.

"So, can you tell me something about my family? Or something about my mom? You know her better than me. Why would she turn her back on this place?"

"I don't know." He's suspiciously hesitant. "She suffered a lot here, too, and wanted to break the cycle. Maybe that's why she turned her back. Only she knows," he admits, and finally a flash of anger shows in his eyes, in the tick of his jaw. "Did you know your mom was the first of your family to go to university?" He changes the subject.

"No. I didn't. I don't know anything about anything." I wrap my arms around my legs and curl into a ball.

"She was the top student in every year when we were kids. From the day she learned to talk, she impressed everyone. She was a complete menace"—he laughs lightly—"but the best student. No one could understand how someone so mischievous could also be the perfect student."

"My mom? Mischievous?" I ask in disbelief.

"Sure as hell. She was always in trouble with your abuelita or the local police, even. She once chased down a man who stole my wallet and pummeled him, nearly drowning him in the ocean."

"I can't even imagine that," I admit. "Well, the pummeling I can, but she's so . . . reserved. Calm but deadly." I smile at the idea that my mother was once a wild woman. The hunger to know more grows with each of his words.

"Do I have any family left here?" I eventually ask him.

I can read the sadness, near guilt, on his face as he shakes his head.

# Chapter Eighteen

It's a bright, cloudless day. The sky feels too big, too blue for my sunken-in state. My stomach twists with hunger, but just the idea of eating makes me exhausted. My eyes are swollen from crying with Mateo for hours. I got back to my room after midnight. Mateo walked me back to my hotel, generously telling me a little bit about the neighborhood he and my mom grew up in. He didn't go into too much detail, but it was more than I'm owed, and it gave me a little bit of what I've been searching for. He told me she never wore shoes, that she was always trying to sell anything and everything, even paper airplanes a few times, and of course, she had a few loyal customers. He was somber as he described little bits of their past, but I appreciated every word. As I sip my water and take Tylenol for this massive headache, curiosity gets the best of me. I google the symptoms of medication withdrawals. All the years spent in hospitals, labs, offices have taught me to never, ever google anything to do with medical advice. You'll be convinced your stomach bug is cancer or your allergies are a mysterious airborne illness.

I've never considered the withdrawals of my meds, because I'd never considered not taking them until the latest medical news, until boarding the jet to come here. I've been so distracted by Julián that I didn't feel anything wrong, and I'm still not convinced that any of this is from the withdrawal. My brain, aside from the random headaches, has never been clearer. Ironically, I miss the fog I've felt for years, as if my emotions had been subdued by the meds. Logically, I know it wasn't the stopping of them that awakened me, it was him. And now he hates me, and even worse, I hate myself for not being able to stop all of this.

As the morning comes, I open my window one last time as I slowly begin to pack my bags in a way that won't alert my mom if she were to come to my room. I dump every single pill from my container down the toilet and flush, watching as they disappear. Feeling lighter, feeling agency over my own body for once.

I keep running through conversations with my mom in my mind, trying to think of something, anything, that will change her mind or make her back out of this deal, but I know it's bigger than me. Now bigger than her. How had I missed the signs and the hints that it was Julián's family they were talking about this whole time? For someone who prides themselves on being smart, I'm sure as hell not.

I wonder if my mom or her team know about the protest. They surely don't, or she would have mentioned it. A small smile touches my lips at the thought of the people here turning on her and ruining the deal, or at minimum, making it miserable enough for her to suffer at least a fraction of what Mateo and Julián and their employees will. I take another shower and finally get dressed.

With the most confidence I can gather, I straighten my back and march to my mom's room. Lena opens the door instantly as if they expected me.

"Oriah, what's wrong?" my mom asks as she covers the bottom of her phone.

"Nothing." I know she's only referring to medically. "I need to talk to you. Alone." I give Lena an apologetic smile, as she turns to my mother for approval.

Knowing that Lena will clear it up, my mom ends her call without an explanation to whoever was on the other side. With one nod, Lena's released like a dog by its owner. It bothers me deeply, but I have another issue at hand, one that is eating me alive.

"What is it, Ry?" She sits back against the plush couch in the center of her suite. The fabric of her high-necked plum dress goes perfectly with the grayish jewel tone of the couch, her dark hair and dark makeup making her seem like the lady of the manor. I take a deep breath, doing my best to not allow her to intimidate me before I even begin my plea.

"It's about the Garcias," I begin.

She sighs, harsh and exaggerated. "Not this again. I told you; this is about business. You're too young to understand, you don't know the magnitude of this deal, Oriah. You—"

I cut her off. "I'm not too young to understand, you're the one who treats me like a child. I'm also not done speaking. So don't interrupt me, and for once let me talk." I stare at her, not blinking, and her shoulders relax a bit, though I know it's for show as she crosses her legs and sips her coffee. Probably the only way she can physically keep her mouth shut for longer than ten seconds.

"What you're doing is not ethical. I didn't know that building this new hotel would mean taking away someone's family business that they've had for generations, and I was ignorant and naïve about what 'development' typically means and the damage that it can cause." I use air quotes to add to her point. "You're from here, Mom. This is your birthplace; these are supposed to be people you care about, yet you don't even have an ounce of remorse for destroying their lives. Mateo and Julián have worked their entire lives to keep that company running, and you forcing them off their land, their docks, it's so wrong. How do you not see that? Digging up the beautiful beaches . . . It's so, so wrong."

A few passing moments feel like hours as she leans forward and sets her mug down on the table between us. "Ry, I'm offering them money. And lots of it. More money than he's ever made in his life. He can retire, his son can live a good life and not work himself to death like his father does, like Mateo's father did. I'm not kicking them out to become destitute. They should be thanking me, especially Mateo, for trying to give him the type of life he's never had, due to his own stubbornness and sense of loyalty to some family legacy that's been disintegrating since I met him."

"Not everyone's only concern is money," I bite back, my head reeling from just how callous she truly is.

"Well, it should be. Whether you like it or not, life requires funds to be able to live comfortably, and anyone who says otherwise doesn't have a clue what it feels like to have financial freedom. Don't forget that I've had it both ways, Oriah. I know the pain of hunger, the desperation of wanting more and knowing it's out there. But"—she looks me dead in the eyes—"it's not here."

"And that's why you left the only person you've ever loved?" I feel my question hit her like a wall, but her need for control and composure is somehow stronger than my words.

"Yes. I loved this island, these people, and my family. But if I had stayed here, what would have become of my life? At best, I'd be working in this hotel. At worst, I would have been haunted by what could have been for the rest of my miserable life. I loved Mateo, and I don't know that I will ever be able to stop . . ." Her admitting this nearly knocks me over, but I stay quiet and let her finish.

"But I love myself and you much, much more. Even as a teenager, I knew I could never settle for the type of life he wanted, that a quiet life wasn't enough for me. I know it's enough for some, and I don't slight them for it, but it's never been enough for me. I asked him to come with me, but he wouldn't leave that damn company behind, and here we are. And thank god he didn't, or I wouldn't have you. So whose side are you really on, Oriah? Use logic here, not what feels like love. I'm able to afford the life we live, and he's latching on to a sinking boat."

I've heard enough. She's never going to back down. She thinks by throwing money at them, she's doing them a favor, and nothing I say can or will change her mindset. She's been this way her whole life and always will be. I stand to leave, and she watches me through waiting eyes.

"You aren't living a whole life, Mom. And neither am I."

I turn on my heel and leave her room. She calls my name once, but of course she doesn't make any real attempt to try and stop me as I slam the door behind me.

Lena is in the hallway, looking unwell and worried as hell. "Ry, are you okay?" She reaches out and gently squeezes my shoulders in her usual way.

I nod, lying through my damn teeth, but the last person I can or want to vent to is my mom's earpiece. I quietly go into my room and finish my packing, replaying the conversation with my mom over and over. In wanting to learn more about her, I've failed in nearly every category, except I came to find out that she's even more ruthless and selfish than I thought.

I stare out the window and back to my dress hanging from the front of the wardrobe, then back out the window again. My head is pounding, and I feel like I haven't slept in a week. I don't know how I'll manage to look at my mother at the event, but I've decided to take it one step at a time. My conversation with her has me more fired up than before, and more helpless. The feeling of helplessness is not one that sits well with me. I've lived with it as an old friend, and enough is enough. I decide to take the first step, grabbing my purse and checking Amara's location, which she shared with me our first night out, and join their protest.

# Chapter Nineteen

As I arrive at the Garcia shipyard, it's nearly deserted. I find Amara and Prisha holding cardboard signs that say STOP SETCORP'S GREED! NO MORE RESORTS! LESS TOURISTS, MORE LIFE! YOUR PARADISE IS MY NIGHTMARE! Cars honk as they pass, and the small group chants together.

What the hell am I doing here?

Will my presence actually help?

Or will I just be a spoiled brat joining their protest to make myself feel better about what my mom's doing to these people?

I begin to regret coming just as I spot Julián from across the street. My chest aches at the sight of him, my body and mind miss him in a desperate way. I'm going to tell him that I will do anything I can to stop this, to save his family. I'll give him every dime that my mother has been pouring into my bank account since before I knew what it meant.

I rush across the street, dodging a motorbike and two cars, only to have his expression stop me dead in my tracks. The look on his face burns into me; the pure disgust, the visceral hatred cuts me in half.

I begin my desperate plea from a few yards away. "Julián, please listen to me. Just hear me out. I had—"

As I reach him, he continues his death glare at me. His face red with anger and his eyes wide and bright, but his voice flat as the pavement under our feet. "What are you doing here?"

I look around, taking in the small group of people gathered. Families, I assume, who work for his fishery. Nearly all of them, including Amara and Prisha, are watching us.

"I want to help. I want to try to—"

He cuts me off. "And how are you going to do that?"

"I don't know, but I can't just let this—"

"Stop with your savior complex. There's nothing you can do, and you know that. You're here to make yourself feel better, when you might as well be by her side, signing people's livelihoods away." He says the very thing I've dreaded to hear.

I reach for his hand that isn't holding the sign, and he steps back from me like I'm poison.

"Even if you could stop this, which you can't, you think I can look at you and not see her? How am I supposed to look at this coast and not be reminded every time I see that hotel where my family used to be?" He waves around at the protest. "I can't look past what that hotel will do to my island, no matter how I felt about you, or our summer fling. Your life will be the same after this, but with even more money, and mine will never be the same. How can I accept that? When you live off her and your trust fund grows off of my familia? You're part of the problem, not the solution."

A *summer fling*. His voice echoes and his words repeat in my mind as he waits, daring me to respond.

"You know this isn't a fling," I manage to say through the dizziness growing in my head. My heightened state of emotion is making me shaky, foggy.

He takes another step away from me, lifting his arms in the air at his sides. "You're right. It isn't. It *was*."

My hands wrap around my torso as if he has physically attacked me. I wish he had. I'm utterly speechless, only finding the strength to breathe in and out, and barely that. I can't defend myself, or defend her, or make things right. I'm just a girl who fell in love with a boy who will hate her until she dies, not knowing just how soon that may be. My mother was right, I am naïve and I'm clueless; Julián was right, I'm just as bad as her. I'm her flesh and blood, and I will profit from his family's pain.

Julián turns away from me, his back to me and his attention completely on the protest and passing cars. Watching him smile at a group of men, shaking their hands. Slowly they seem to realize who I am, and one by one they glare at me, nodding and shooing at me for me to leave. He doesn't stop them or seem to even notice. Heartbreak is another kind of pain that I'm used to. I would take all the pain I've had in my life, bottle it up, and down it to replace this feeling in my chest, running down my spine, from the tip of my scalp to the bottom of my soles, I'm lost.

My feet under me are unstable as I begin backing away from the crowd, my vision a little blurry. My fingers begin to twitch, and I can feel the blood rushing in, that familiar yet distant spiral into nothing and everything. No, no, no. Not right now, not near Julián and not during their protest. Please, not now. I somehow make it back to the ocean's side of the road and begin to run until I feel my knees hit the sand and all control disappears. I stare up at the expansive sky as my mind and body leave the present, the past, and possibly the future.

# Chapter Twenty

As I blink my eyes open, my mother is standing over me, her eyes small slits, examining me. There's a beeping noise in the background, jolting me up. I'm not in my suite, not on the beach. Everything rushes back to me.

"Ry. Oh my god. Be careful, lie down." She eases my shoulders back against the hospital bed.

I look around the room, taken aback and flustered as the rest of the details come to me. Julián, the words he spoke, the honking cars, the ocean waves, and the low voices as I faded.

"I'm fine." I sit up again, using my stretched-out arms as a shield from her to get any closer to me. "I'm okay. Julián . . . he . . ."

She shakes her head, not able to hide the anger she feels at hearing his name from my lips the moment I came to. "He wasn't there; he didn't come to your rescue," she tells me with venom in her voice.

"I didn't ask because I thought he would rescue me. As you know, nothing can or will rescue me from any of this." I yank my arm up, the IV pulling at my vein.

"I'm sorry for wording it that way. I'm just . . . terrified and glad you're okay. And why were you there? Thank god Jordi found you when he did . . ."

"Who?"

Lena rushes into the room, a phone in her hand.

"Isolde is right here, if you could hold on for a moment." She looks at my mom, afraid of being barked at but clearly needing her on the phone.

No matter the time or place, SetCorp will always need her, and they'll always come first.

"I'm sorry, Ry. I need to take this." She grabs the phone from Lena, and to my surprise she does look sorry for once.

Even so, I'm so fucking angry at her, I don't let the opportunity to let her know pass. "Of course you do. I just woke up in a hospital, but hey! There's someone's money to take, right?"

"Ry . . ." Her voice is soft, a little broken, but nevertheless she exits the room, phone to her ear.

"Unbelievable," I say to myself, the anger from earlier filling me again.

"I'm ready to go," I tell Lena and the nurse as soon as the nurse enters the room. The event will start in less than two hours, which means my flight is in less than six hours. I have to get out of here. Far, far away from this place at any cost.

"You just woke up, Ry," Lena tells me.

"How long was I out?"

"Only ten minutes or so. This hospital is only a few blocks away from where you had your episode."

"I'm not sure we can release you." The nurse looks into the hallway toward my mother.

"I'm an adult. I've had plenty of seizures in my life. There are no aftereffects that anyone here can do anything about. Aside from being a little tired, I'm completely fine. But there's nothing that a hospital can do that I can't do from my hotel. There's no aftercare for a seizure, unless I have injuries." I look down and around my hospital gown–covered body and move my arms and legs.

"Which I don't. So, I want to be released. Now. Unless you have a tuberous sclerosis specialist on this island who says otherwise?"

I don't like taking my frustration out on the innocent, now speechless, nurse, but I'm not a child and I have every right, legally, to leave this hospital. They can't keep me against my will, and I won't allow them to.

"I understand," the woman says, her accent beautiful and thick. "I'll work on your discharge with the doctor now."

"Thank you," I tell her, and turn to Lena. "Don't let her keep me here." I try to get my mother's only ally on my side.

"Please." My voice cracks as I beg. "You know there's nothing to keep me here for."

She blows air out of her mouth; her brows furrow and she tucks her short hair behind her ears. "Okay. She's thinking of canceling the event."

"No, no. She can't." I begin to panic, knowing that if she does, it will be impossible for me to escape.

"Mom!" I yell her name, and she whips around, ending the call she's on, heels clacking as she rushes to my side.

"Don't cancel the event. You said it was for a good cause and the Arts Center needs all the funding it can get. I don't want to ruin that," I say to her, the words burning in my throat. "And everyone has worked so hard. I want to go." The lie coats my tongue. "I really want to go. Please, Mom." My eyes fill with tears, but not for the reason she thinks.

"Ry. Are you that out of it? There's no way you can go. Even if I can't cancel because of the donors and sponsors, there's no way in hell you can go. You're in the hospital, for god's sake."

"And I've been in the hospital a million times in my life," I remind her. "This was the one thing I was looking forward to, Mom." It makes me sick to my stomach, but I reach for her hands and squeeze them. Her eyes fill with tears, and I know I've won as she blinks them away, slowly pulling her hands out of mine.

I can see the options weighing in her dark eyes. The guilt, the pressure from her bosses and people who wrote checks for a lot of money. "Are you positive you feel okay?"

I nod. "This isn't the first time, Mom. And it doesn't seem to have been a bad one. I'm fine, and if I feel anything other than fine, I'll go back to my room. I really, really want to go, Mom." I manage a smile, playing on the rare vulnerability I sense from her. I don't think I've ever said "Mom" so many times in my life.

I'm not fine. I haven't been fine in a long, long time, but I've known that for a while, and so has she. I don't want to waste any more time. As I sign the discharge paperwork, my mom asks me over and over if I'm sure I can manage the charity gala. I assure her that I can, and she orders the stylist, the glam team, and lord knows who else to be in her room waiting for us when we arrive back at the hotel.

# Chapter Twenty-One

The hotel ballroom has been stunning since I arrived in Mallorca, but tonight it's astonishing. White silk ribbons hang from the ceiling to the floor, draping the gigantic room in a pillowy dream of delicate lights and wavy chiffon. It feels like I'm inside a marshmallow, beautiful and elegant and soft and dreamy. There are twinkling lights everywhere, reflecting off the ballroom floor, filling the room with small golden stars. Hundreds of translucent LED balloons hang in the air, the lights making them appear as if they are full of glitter. As much as I complained during the process, the room truly is magical and breathtaking. The space is slightly dark, making it more whimsical and dreamlike. It looks more like a fairy-tale wedding than a celebration disguised as a charity event.

"It's stunning, isn't it?" My mother's familiar voice fills my ears.

I nod. "It's unbelievable. You've outdone yourself."

"You worked hard on this, too, Ry."

"Barely," I admit. I spent most of my time here with Julián, and I don't regret a single moment. I will always treasure the memories.

I turn to her, and she smiles, golden flakes reflecting in her dark eyes. "Still excessive and a waste of resources, though, right?" she asks, taking a sip from a champagne glass.

"Absolutely wasteful, but beautiful nonetheless."

"I'll take that compliment." She eyes me up and down, and I do the same to her.

I've seen her dressed to the nines a million times in my life, but she looks more striking than ever. The satin fabric of her turquoise dress clings to her body like a glove. She looks insanely powerful, her hair slicked back into a tight bun at the base of her neck, and dark mauve lipstick painted onto her full lips. We couldn't be more different, with my hair styled into voluminous pillowy layers, curled at the ends with little flowers pinned throughout, and lighter, more natural makeup. The contrast isn't lost on me as I take in the details of her smoky black and gray eye shadow. I went for the opposite look, just a dusting of bronzer swept across my lids and minimal foundation. The makeup artist assigned to me worked wonders and nailed the minimal-makeup look, enhancing my features instead of burying them.

My mother clearly went in the opposite direction even with her jewelry, a chunky onyx necklace made of thick rocks resting against her sculpted chest bones. My mother is as elegant as they come, and as vicious. The combination makes her even more chilling. She's the enchanting villain in every fairy tale; one smile and she can crush you without a single hair out of place.

"Mrs. Pera." A man in a tuxedo nervously approaches the two of us at the arched entrance, a tray of champagne in one hand. She plucks a glass and downs half of it before turning to him.

"Miss," she corrects him, the way she has the hundreds of men and women throughout my life who assume she's married. It's one of her biggest pet peeves, rightfully so. She's fiercely proud of herself for being the moneymaking career woman she is. She's always loved seeing the moms in our community's shocked expression when she tells them she can't do Pilates with them in the middle of the day because she has a job. Ironically, I was always so envious of the kids around me whose moms were home with them and not on the phone day and night or hopping on a flight somewhere.

"Miss Pera," he fumbles. "Is there anything I can get you? Anything at all?" the man asks with an accent and a smile. I'm surprised by how much English is used around us on this island.

Julián pops into my mind, him and his damn crossword puzzles and perfect English. My mother answers the man in Spanish, and he nods, disappearing just as quickly as he appeared.

"Are you sure you feel okay?" she asks me again, making me internally scream.

I nod, asking her not to ask me again, and she swirls the champagne flute between her long fingers; the maroon paint on her nails goes with her dark goddess theme of the night. A stark difference from the angelic wonderland style of the event. She walks away from me without another word, blending into the growing crowd of guests.

Nothing surprising. I roam around a bit and stop in front of a huge mirror. My sage-green dress fits the theme perfectly, the massive tree acting as a centerpiece of the party, the smaller trees lining the edges of the expansive room, and the twinkling seashell necklace at the base of my throat matching the lights wrapped around the plants and dangling from the ceiling. I can't stop thinking about what Julián would think of seeing me dressed up like this. Would he like it or hate it? He's so unpredictable, it's hard to guess. But guessing and wondering about him is all I have left, so I keep doing it as I walk around the room.

The dress is loose and tight in all the right places, and the slit up my left thigh reaches higher than I would have worn at an event in Texas, but this summer, I've committed to doing things differently, especially knowing I'm leaving soon. I still need to figure out how on earth I'm going to escape this hotel and get a taxi without my mother or anyone on her team being alerted. I had to use a new email to even buy the ticket. I sigh, knowing I don't want to leave but it's better for everyone if I do. Lost in thought, I stare at my reflection a couple seconds longer when Amara pops into the mirror wearing a bright golden-yellow dress with ruffles covering the bodice. Her wild red hair is loosely tied back, but stray pieces of it cascade down her cheeks and touch her neck.

"Oh my god, Ry! I'm so glad you came after all." She hugs me to her. She was the first person I texted when I decided to come to the event before leaving.

"This place is insane! And holy shit, look at you! Your back . . . turn around!" She swirls her finger in the air, and I smile, confidence simmering in my chest. "You should always, always, always wear backless everything!"

She spins me around and hugs me. Her bubbly mood softens me a bit; I just wish she didn't remind me of Julián. I will never see him again, and the pain at that thought makes my stomach twist into a knot. I understand there's no way in fucking hell he would step foot in here, but god, I wish he was by my side right now. I would do anything to see him once more, even if that meant him cussing me out or banishing me from his sight like he did a few hours ago.

"You look remarkable too. Wow! This color . . . only you could pull this off," I say, meaning it and wanting to keep my attention and affection on my only friend here. She's been incredible to me and seems to have no idea about what happened at the protest. I couldn't be more grateful. I take her in, her sunshine soul: her matching makeup is magnificently detailed, and little gold flakes surround her eyes and are sprinkled up toward her cheekbone until they disappear behind her hair.

"Prisha might come too. I know she's not on the guest list, but since I know Javier, the security guy, she'll be fine, right?"

"Of course! My mom won't notice anyway. No one here is paying attention to anyone else, per usual." I roll my eyes and Amara squeezes my back with one arm.

"I know it sucks that Julián isn't here, but you should try to have fun. He was a dick to you earlier. I told him so, and more. But dance, drink, act as fire as you look," she suggests.

"I swear you're more American than me," I tease.

Her casual slang always cracks me up. It would be so cringy coming from literally anyone else, but she makes it funny and charming.

"It's what the kids are saying on TikTok. Now, let's go have fun?" Her tone is wrapped like a question, but she pulls me by the arm straight to the full bar. The bar matches the theme, sparkling and shimmering and elegant.

The man behind the bar is shaking a drink in a mixer as we approach, and Amara asks him for two shots of the fanciest liquor there. I don't argue. I won't be drinking a ton, but the warmth of alcohol to mask some of the loneliness and anxiety inside me from Julián's absence and my last few hours on this island sounds like exactly what I need. Even the slightest bit of relief would feel monumental right now.

There are servers of both genders scattered around the ballroom dressed in tuxedos and carrying trays full of appetizers, champagne, and wine. Guests grab what they desire and the men on my mom's legal team barely give them a second glance, but the locals, including a few fishermen I remember seeing at the docks, smile and thank them. I wonder if those fishermen sided with my mom's company, or they just wanted to attend the over-the-top event, knowing they couldn't stop the acquisition anyway. The party is in full swing, except the space around and under the massive tree in the center that's intended for dancing. Then again, I don't expect this kind of crowd to dance. Amara and Prisha, who couldn't look more like freaking goddesses if they tried, are dancing, like always, to the beat of their own drum. Prisha came in a silver gown, perfectly contrasting with her bronzed skin and luscious black hair. Amara and Prisha are hands down one of the hottest non-official-official couples I've ever laid eyes on.

I watch with a tinge of delighted envy as their hips move together, deliciously curling around each other's bodies as Amara wraps her hand around the back of Prisha's neck and brings them nose to nose, chest to chest. The bottom of my belly aches, and I look away from their sensuality and, yet again, think about how much more fun I'd be having if Julián were here. If none of this would have happened. His anger toward me erased, his body pressing against mine, his mouth on my neck, his hands digging into my hips . . .

I sigh and try to tell myself that everything will somehow work out in the end, for him at least. Thankfully, my mom has the decency to at least pay his family enough to live off after dismantling their company and building a useless resort. I look around the room and see my mother standing with a group of men in suits and laughing the fakest laugh I've ever seen her perform, and find myself grateful that my life will never be like hers. I've at least known how it feels to be desired, to laugh in the middle of the ocean, to love someone, even if it's unrequited. Julián has given me so much, and even though it was taken away at the hands of everyone here, I'm grateful that it happened in the first place. Yep, that's where I land, gratitude instead of bitterness, and it's an unwelcome but surprisingly nice feeling. I turn around to find another drink and run straight into the heavy chest of a man in a black button-down shirt. I look up, relief and shock washing over me in waves.

Julián.

# Chapter Twenty-Two

Julián! You came!" I can't hide my excitement at seeing him, though there's a chance he came to crash the event, to protest more.

It kills me, but I wait a moment before I say anything else. His chin is lowered, and he looks at me through drawn brows. I sense shame in his brown eyes. My heart pounds against my rib cage, attempting to break free. Pressing my fingernails into my hands, I wait for what feels like an eternity before he speaks.

"I'm sorry, so fucking sorry," he finally says, pulling me into his arms and lifting me off my feet.

I have so much to say to him, so many apologies and attempted explanations to give and demand, but right now all I can focus on is the way his arms wrap around me as if he hasn't seen me in a month, as if he hasn't been able to breathe without me, as if he hadn't been so brutally dismissive just hours ago. He squeezes so tightly that it's hard to breathe, but I would give my breath for Julián, again and again.

"I'm so unbelievably sorry, Ry," he says against my hair, gently petting my head with one arm, slightly loosening the grip on my body. My feet are still off the ground as I bury my face in his neck, smelling the warmth and salt of the sea on his skin.

"Julián, you have nothing to be sorry for. This is my mom's company's fault, my fault," I tell him, stroking the back of his neck with my hand.

I feel someone's attention on us, burning into our embrace, and I look up to find my mother's direct eye contact as he continues to hug me. Her eyes narrow and I can see them piercing Julián's back, but she simply grabs another glass of champagne from a passing tray and puts on a smile for a group of men in bright-colored suits I've never seen before. She throws her head back in fake laughter and I hold on to Julián. She must be tired of all the fake laughing; I know I would be.

"My dad told me about the conversation you two had, and he finally told me the whole story about them . . . their tragic love story and all that. And I was wrong to act the way that I did. None of this is your fault, and it was fucking stupid of me to say it was. You came here with hope and understanding that you were doing something meaningful by helping with the fundraiser for the Arts Center, and I let my family baggage and stubbornness ruin that for you. I know I'm all over the place. I'd blame it on my depression, but that doesn't seem fair." His cheeks flush and his eyes go to the floor.

I'm embarrassed and relieved that Mateo told Julián the truth about his history with my mom and that I confided in him. I don't want to spend any more time talking about our families. I want to enjoy the sight in front of me, while appreciating his presence and apology. He doesn't seem to be aware of my seizure earlier, and I'm so grateful for that. It would kill me to have him show up only out of pity.

He moves his hands to my arms to put a little distance between us, and my skin burns as his dark eyes scan me from head to toe. I do the same to him and, good god, he looks incredible. Even though I prefer him shirtless at the beach with water droplets falling from his long lashes and full lips, this dressed-up version of him is sexy as hell. My thighs press together, and my mouth immediately goes dry just looking at him dressed in a black button-down shirt and pants.

"I didn't have a suit." He shrugs. "You are . . . Ry, you're . . . I don't have the words . . . speechless," he says, his eyes sizzling with a heat that makes me nearly break into a sweat. Julián's hands travel down my bare back, stopping just above my backside where the fabric begins.

"I also don't have the words," I admit, admiring his strong shoulders pulling at the silk fabric of his shirt. "Except no suit needed." I gulp.

"You look like the moon," I tell him, not knowing where the words come from. It's true though, he is bright and fenced by darkness, lonely but never alone, constantly surrounded by twinkling stars. Powerful. Strong. Everything revolving around him.

"That's a pretty big compliment." He smiles shyly and rubs his hand across his freshly shaven chin.

"I know how much it must have taken to come here. I thought I would never see you again. I'm so sorry for—" Julián stops me from speaking by touching his lips to mine.

"No more sorrys." He spins me gently and we begin to dance slowly, barely moving our feet. In my entire life as a dancer, this is by far my favorite performance.

Time is an illusion with our bodies pressed together, his skillful fingers tracing the length of my spine, up and down, again and again. Every inch of my bare skin is raised, my back arched, a puddle in his arms and between my thighs.

"Julián," I groan as he presses warm, splayed palms against my skin, sliding the tips of his fingers under the thin material of my dress.

"No panties?" he whispers against the shell of my ear.

My entire body flushes as I shake my head. "They don't go with the dress."

A low growl falls from his lips, and I shiver as the sound fills me head to toe. "If we didn't have an audience, I would rip this thin dress from your body and fill you against that wall." He nods his head toward the faux-grass wall behind us. My vision blurs and I'm not sure how I'm standing.

"Julián," I beg him, to either stop teasing me to near death or to give me some sort of release. I can barely handle the ache low in my belly, the pool of wetness between my thighs, now dripping down the tops of them.

"Julián, what? What do you want, Oriah?" His mouth presses against the base of my jaw, just where it meets my ear.

"You. I need you." I forget about the ballroom full of people and slide his hand to the front of my dress, pressing the silk against the pool there.

"Fuck." He circles a finger around the wet cloth and brings it to his lips. I nearly combust.

I can't take it anymore. "My room. Now." I yank him by the hand, and we crash into the elevator mouth on mouth, tongues touching every exposed inch of each other's mouths, necks. When we reach my floor, Julián lifts me up, my dress riding up at my waist as I tell him through ragged breaths the number of my room.

"I can smell you from here. Fuck." He runs his nose along the side of my cheek, my neck, my collarbones, as my shaking, anxious hands find the little circle chip of a key and press it against the lock. It opens and we barrel in, the door slamming behind us.

Julián takes me immediately to my bed, not gently, but with a ravishing hunger as he yanks my dress up and splays my thighs open; the breeze in the room makes me catch my breath as it touches my exposed, sensitive core. I clamp my hand over my mouth as his tongue swipes across me, my legs kicking and heels digging into the bed as he sucks on me, his tongue and lips taking turns, his growling appreciation for my uncontrollable thrashing as I grip the blanket in one hand, squeezing so hard it feels like my hand will shatter. He continues to lick and kiss the apex of my thighs, his fingers replacing where his tongue and lips were, slowly pumping in and out of me, bringing me just to the edge, then pausing before I slide over it. He continues to devour me in a calculated yet famished way.

"Not yet." He lifts his head just as my back bows off the bed to climax. I nearly scream at the physical frustration, the need to release. He blows a puff of cold air, kisses my core once again, this time his teeth scraping gently, dragging them to the top of my thigh. "I want to feel you come around me."

I spring up, catching him off guard and pushing him back onto the mattress, yanking at his shirt, not caring as at least two of the buttons pops off and skitter across the hardwood floor. I kiss and suck at his broad chest as I remove his shirt, my hands fumbling for the button of his pants, trying my hardest not to destroy them. I do the same with his briefs, pulling them down his thick, muscular thighs, and my mouth waters as I take in the length of him as it springs free. Throbbing, hard, waiting for me. Mine.

He's quicker, stronger than me as he wraps his arms around my back, flipping us over, hovering over my face, nose to nose. He pulls at the thin straps on my dress, and I feel the fabric ripping somewhere in the distance, but I can't be bothered to care, not as Julián teases my aching entrance, pressing gently, but not fully entering me.

"Stop torturing me," I whine, lifting my hips to meet him.

With a wicked smile and one swift movement, he plunges inside me. I cry out, screaming in surprise and ecstasy as he slides back out, and in, and out, and in. My nails rake across his back, his beautiful eyes never leaving mine as he fills me, body and soul. Fast, then slow, deep then shallow, he pulls himself out and has the nerve to rub his cock across my aching clit. Release immediately rolls over me like a crashing wave, one after another, after another as he thrusts back into me, kissing my mouth again, my name falling from his lips as his control slips and his body stills and he finds his release, slowly moving in and out again, to draw out my pleasure as I go limp, my arms and legs fall open onto the mattress and his warm body collapses onto mine. Our breathing in unison, harsh and shallow at first, slows into a deep pattern as I gently run my fingers up and down his sweat-covered back.

"I'm so sorry, Ry. I was so wrong for how I treated you earlier. It's wrong, but I felt like it was easier to just shut you out . . . I do that sometimes, when life gets too hard, too heavy. I shut down and run. I didn't know what else to do but run away from you and I couldn't do that, so I pushed you away instead. None of this is your fault, Ry. I know that, and I'm sorry I didn't try . . . for you. I just let the anger and the darkness pull me in and shut you out. I know your heart, and I know you would never be responsible for what's happening. I'm sorry. I'm not good at this, at being with someone, but I'm so sorry. And I'm sorry for how many times I seem to be sorry for being an asshole."

"Shhh, Julián. I should be apologizing to you. You were right, I did show up there for my own selfishness, but also for you. I meant it when I said I would do anything to help, and I tried and still will, but don't apologize anymore. We're here now, that's what matters." I put my hand on the back of his neck and his eyes pour into mine as he shakes his head.

"What matters is respecting you, hearing your opinions and your side of what's happening, and I didn't do that. I failed you and was wrong. I need to apologize for taking my anguish out on you." His tone is so serious, so calm, with zero room for his typical sarcasm or either of our deflections.

"You deserve an apology, and you deserve respect. I will never disrespect you like that again. I will never treat you like that again. Whatever happened with our parents is between them, and I know you had nothing to do with it. It's not going to be easy, but please, please, forgive me for my lack of control, lack of thinking before lashing out at the wrong person."

His mouth presses gently against my nose and I smile, not only at his sincere apology, but for the way his words fill the gaping hole that had been burned in my chest since I saw the way he looked at me when he found out who my mother was.

When I open my mouth to speak, he rolls me over to lie on my stomach, perching his chin on his elbow. "Don't say you're sorry. Anything but that. You shouldn't spend one more moment of your life being sorry for things you don't have control of."

I nod as he caresses my back, tracing circles and shapes against my skin, stopping at the spot above my tailbone. "I love your birthmark." His lips touch the ash leaf spot on my lower back, and I tense.

"Thank you" is all I can manage.

A half-truth. Technically, I was born with it, but it's not just a simple birthmark. I have other ones, too, scattered across the tops of my thighs and a few tiny ones around my ankles that he probably, like most people, hasn't noticed, or assumed were just spots from the sun, despite their lack of pigment.

"Your poor dress," he says, thumbing the now-disconnected strap between his calloused fingers.

"Your poor shirt." We both glance around us. "I don't even know where it is." Our laughter matches as he sits up, pointing to the chair across the room. How it got all the way over there, I have no clue.

"What are we going to wear to go back down? I can wear my shirt open, but your mother and her donors may take issue with that." A satisfied, mischievous grin spreads across his hauntingly beautiful face.

"You're not going down there with your shirt open, not because of my mother or the bullshit donors and investors," I say as I trace the plane of his chest with my fingertip. "But because I don't want the women looking at you, and trust me, they will." Jealousy pangs my chest, and I press my finger to my chin, thinking of a solution.

"I have an oversized button-down. Not the same color, but it'll do. And if anyone notices, they were looking too closely at you in the first place." I glare from the thought.

"Since when are you jealous and territorial? That's supposed to be my role," he teases, kissing my shoulder as he helps me from the bed and onto my feet, heels still on.

"Since you came back to me. I don't want to share you."

"I'm yours, Oriah. And yours only. I don't have eyes, or space in my heart, for anyone else."

The words sing through my ears, filling my brain with sunshine and joy. I want to tell him that I love him, that I love him so much that it might rip me in two, that I love him so much that I want to fight to stay with him as long as I can. Not only our circumstances and distance, but my body, which is our biggest threat. Before I got on the plane to come here, I had given up on fighting, was exhausted even at the thought of continuing to do so, but now, looking at this man and feeling love, true and infinite love, gives me the strength to want to try.

"And I'm yours, Julián," I finally say as I kiss his flushed cheek and open the wardrobe, hoping there's a backup dress inside.

"Problem solved!" I smile, holding up the burgundy dress that I almost chose to wear tonight. Julián helps me into it and removes the dangling flowers from my now messy hair. I run my fingers over it, not really caring what I look like, still floating from Julián's presence.

"This room is . . ." He glances from the sitting area to the couch, to the massive bed, to the expansive bathroom. "Much bigger than I thought."

I nod as I step back into my heels. "Yeah, it's too big for one person. But there is unlimited water, and the hotel does its best at being eco-friendly." I cringe at my excuses. "I keep telling myself that so I don't feel guilty staying here, anyway."

He's quiet and a little on edge. The tick of his jaw makes me nervous, but with everything going on, he has every reason to be.

"Is your home in Texas like this?" His voice is quiet.

I nod. "Yes and no. It's new, so the architecture is nothing like this, not nearly as beautiful. But . . ." I hesitate. "It's a really big house, honestly. Too big for two people, and shows firsthand how classism and socioeconomic systems work in the States."

I can imagine Julián, disgusted by the nearly ten thousand square feet of my house in Dallas. With two kitchens, four living rooms, massive TVs that we never use in every room, the pool and hot tub, the perfectly manicured lawn, and three-football-fields length of a backyard . . .

"I'm sorry if it sounds like I'm bragging. I just didn't want to lie," I admit, sucking on my bottom lip with anxiety.

He smiles, a tiny but real one. I can tell he's uncomfortable being here, but he still says, "Don't be. Everyone's lives are different, and yours and mine couldn't be more so."

I try not to decipher his words during our walk to the elevator. He hugs me closely, kissing my forehead and keeping his arm wrapped around my waist as we exit and head down the labyrinth of the hallway leading to the grand room.

As we reenter the ballroom, I wonder if anyone noticed my absence, but my curiosity is very quickly answered as I realize the servers are clearing the plates of the first course of dinner and the seat next to my mother is empty. I had forgotten completely about the meal part of the evening, even though most of the menu—the roasted duck, garlic seared shrimp, and mushroom ravioli—were my choices to add.

"She doesn't look happy," Julián warns as we walk toward the table, hand in hand.

I laugh, rolling my eyes. "Does she ever?"

His shoulders rock to stifle his laughter as we approach.

"Ry." My mom's smile is wide, friendly, as if welcoming an old friend, not her only daughter and the son of the man she loved and is now destroying.

"Julián, thank you for coming." My mother's acting is Oscar-worthy.

"You may know Julián Garcia," she performs for the table, pretending like we're all on the same side of this. A little confusion rustles over the men at our table, but it quiets down as my mom looks at each of them.

"I'm so glad you're feeling better, Ry." She looks around the table to comfort the investors there by sealing in the lie she must have told them about me not feeling well and disappearing.

A mild panic arises. What if she told them I was in the hospital just hours ago? What if one of them mentions my epilepsy or tuberous sclerosis? The timing could not be worse.

I manage a smile. "I spilled something on my dress and just needed a little break from the noise. I'm sorry for the delay." I bow to the guests, giving my best feigned innocence, as my mother's piercing eyes take in the change in my hair, the smudged makeup on my face.

I raise a defiant brow to her as the rest of the table continue talking among themselves, as if to say, *Yeah, it's exactly what you think, and there isn't a thing you can do about it.*

Lena notices the tension and, as always, swoops in to make sure nothing gets out of hand, glaring at one of the lawyers who opens his mouth to address Julián but decides against it. Lena, the peacekeeper, waves toward Julián, moving her own chair over to fit another between hers and mine. My mother wants to react; I can tell by the way her hands are gently gripping the edge of the round table, scrunching the dark gray cloth ever so slightly so it's unnoticed. But she knows better than to interfere or say one wrong word to Julián right now, given the circumstances.

"Have a seat next to Oriah and let's finish our meal." Lena smiles warmly at him and he thanks her, sitting down slowly, as if he has an open wound in a pool of sharks. In many ways, that's very, very true.

# Chapter Twenty-Three

Dinner seems to drag on endlessly. Once it's finally over, Julián and I leave the table at our first chance. He kept one hand on my thigh during the entire meal and didn't utter a single word. I hated every moment, but we both knew it was necessary to show my mom that we will not be separated, no matter how much tension is surrounding us. The air feels less constrictive the further from the table we get, and Julián finally talks, telling me how awful the food tasted and how he doesn't know how I've sat through those stale, emotionless business dinners my whole life. He leads me through the crowd as the music picks back up, and we make our way to find Amara and Prisha's still-dancing bodies. Makes sense that they didn't eat, since there was assigned seating and neither of them was technically invited, but they certainly didn't seem to mind.

"You showed up." Amara pushes at Julián's shoulder and turns her eyes to me. "Better late than never." She smiles, knowing how desperately I wanted him here, or anywhere I am. She gets me.

"Wait, weren't you wearing a green dress?" Amara asks, looking me over.

Her eyes fall on my hair, my obviously changed appearance. She giggles, looking back and forth between Julián and me.

"Okay, okay. I see." She clicks her tongue. "Well, glad you two lovebirds made up, because I didn't want to have to pick a side and really, really didn't want you to leave tonight, Ry. You're not leaving now, are you?" She grabs both of my hands between hers and my stomach drops.

I really hope Julián missed what she said about me leaving. Now that he's here, physically and mentally back with me, I can't imagine leaving. Deciding to do so was impulsive and wouldn't have helped anything. What will Julián think of me running off, back to the States? I can't bring myself to look up at him to find out. I can feel his eyes on me, but I purposely focus on Amara.

"Who's in charge of the music? It sucks. We're trying to make the best of it, but it's getting a bit snoozy," Amara says, tilting her head to the DJ booth.

An elderly man stands there, unmoving, very far from your typical DJ at a party. His shoulders aren't moving to the beat, his eyes are downcast, not caring to notice if the crowd is enjoying it. But this is a fancy charity event, so I'm not shocked that my mom hired the stuffiest DJ in all of Spain. Frank Sinatra's crooning voice fills the room. Frank himself is a legend but couldn't be more opposite of what Amara is looking for.

"We're the youngest people here, what did you expect? And the crowd isn't exactly fun . . ." Prisha half smiles, and all four of us look toward my mother, who is anything but.

"Maybe you can request something? Who knows, the DJ might also be bored."

She smiles, and Prisha shakes her head but follows Amara's bouncing body toward the booth.

"They seem to be going well," Julián notes, nodding toward their hands intertwining as they walk away.

I smile for them. "I'm so glad, even though the whole *temporary, accepting the relationship may end in a few weeks* thing still freaks me out a bit, but different strokes for different folks." I shrug.

Julián lets out a laugh. "What an American expression."

"Isn't that what we agreed on too? Being temporary?" I remind him and myself.

"Don't remind me." He pulls me close and leans in to kiss me, but just before his lips touch mine, his eyes widen at something behind me, and his body stiffens.

I jerk my head around to see what he's focused on, and a chill runs over me as I recognize that the man in the crisp suit striding toward us is Julián's father, Mateo. His thick, dark curls are pulled back into a sleek look, banded just above his neck. A far cry from the cutoff shirts, board shorts, and flip-flops I've seen him in on the docks or on his boat. He nods to his son and passes us, heading straight for the center of the room. Beelining to my mother. She blinks rapidly, losing her composure for a moment. It's refreshing to see on the one hand, but I'm worried for her on the other.

There's a nervous twitch in my mother's mouth I've never seen before as Mateo approaches her. She straightens her back and lengthens her neck. She refuses to appear shaken in front of everyone. At least she's consistent. The air in my lungs disappears and Julián squeezes my hand to comfort me.

"Should we stop them?" I whisper through the mild panic bubbling at the base of my neck. As angry as I am with her, I don't want to see her humiliated in front of a crowd, especially by a man she once loved.

Julián's hand moves to rest on my lower back. He shakes his head. He gently caresses me, attempting to reassure me, and even in this intense situation, his touch gives me goose bumps.

"This is their business, not ours," he reminds me.

"It doesn't feel as simple as that," I tell him, looking for even a touch of worry in his eyes, but there is none.

After a few seconds he adds, "Nothing is simple, Ry. But they cannot avoid each other forever. Do you want to go outside so you don't have to see whatever is about to happen?"

I contemplate that. Running away with him into the night sounds like the easier and certainly less-stressful choice, but staying here and seeing the two of them together firsthand is something I've been curious about since I found out about their history. And Julián's right, this isn't our problem to solve.

"I guess my invitation got lost in the mail, Iz?" Mateo steps closer, directly in front of my mom, and her eyes continue to blink rapidly, as if a ghost has just appeared.

I'm sure, and hopeful, that no one except me notices; that despite her cool expression, she is absolutely flailing inside.

"What are you . . ." She trails off, clearly trying to compose her thoughts and hide her surprise in front of the hundreds of eyes in the room. She takes a few steps away from the group of investors she's entertaining, trying to divert Mateo from their earshot.

"Mateo, to what do I owe the pleasure?" She adjusts her tone. Performative, professional, sickening.

I know that tone all too well; I've heard it on hundreds of her work calls throughout my life, and now she's using it on someone she once loved. The more I learn about my mom, the more confused I am. On the one hand, I feel for her, the life she could have had; and on the other, I blame her for so many wrongs and so much damage.

As they size each other up, parts of the crowd begin to notice, little by little. Julián and I move closer too.

"The pleasure? The nerve you must have to come back here and try to swallow up my business, my workers' lives, my son's future? The only one who finds pleasure in hurting people is you."

His words sting me by proxy, and it takes all my self-control not to defend my mom, even though Mateo is right and is completely justified to feel that way. It's a stark difference to how forgiving of her he was with me, but maybe he finally snapped now that reality must be setting in.

"This is a celebration of a new Arts Center for the island, a charity event . . . if you hadn't noticed." My mom sweeps one arm through the air in front of her and her gifted vintage Rolex sparkles under the lights. It's nauseating.

"Oh, I noticed. The whole island noticed," he sneers, pain in his eyes and splashed clearly across his face. He's not someone who hides his pain or emotions, not like her. She's managed to guide him to the door, away from most of the ears. I nod to Amara at the DJ booth, and she understands what I mean. The volume of the music rises.

"I tried my best, Mr. Garcia," my mom coos, and I can tell by the gleam in her eye that she chose his title very carefully, very callously. "We're paying you handsomely, more than the company is even worth, and your workers, and *you*, agreed to sign the contracts. We both know the company can't withstand the demand of resorts here, and if we didn't bail you out, the next buyer would completely take advantage of—"

"Bail me out? Is that what you think you did?" Mateo's voice is full of disbelief.

My mom nods, and the thick necklace moves in unison with her heavy sigh.

"Think of the tourism this will bring to the area. More tourism, more money." My mom's voice is beginning to break, and I've never seen her run out of steam so quickly in my entire life.

"We have the oldest fishing company on the island, and we would have done just fine if you didn't keep bringing tourists here and destroying our land and resources. You know, like you used to complain about before you turned into this." He waves his hand from her head to her toes.

"This isn't personal." She swallows. "It's business, and it was going to happen whether I was involved or not. I tried to make the best of it, which is why we're here, to give back to the community with the Arts Center, and that's only the beginning. Think of the jobs the resort will bring."

"Everything between us is personal, Miss Pera." Mateo takes a step back from her and leans against a tablecloth-covered high table behind him as if my mom's callous treatment has cut him straight to the bone.

"Don't give me that shit about helping the community. What we need is programs for the kids, jobs for their parents, yes, but not another resort polluting our ocean and ruining the land. If you cared about your homeland, you would be building the Arts Center without forcing us out of our land. This is where you're from! Aquesta és la teva gent!" Mateo's voice rises with every word.

"How can you do this without an ounce of sorrow or regret? Without any hint of respect for me and my family? You are not the woman I knew, and not a woman your mother would even recognize. She would be devasted that you turned out this way. T'has tornat cobdiciós i menyspreable."

"No, I am not the woman you knew. She was a careless, romantized child. And how dare you speak of my mother. And my greed? My greed has fed my family. I can't say the same for you. This money will be life-changing for you, Mateo. You'd never have to work again." She shoots, aiming to kill.

"Stop deluding yourself into thinking you're saving me when you know damn well that's not the kind of man I am! And I will speak of your mother and your greed because she didn't have a greedy bone in her body, unlike you."

My heart breaks for both of them at the mention of my mom's mother, who I never had the chance to know, as Mateo makes a cross shape across his chest by tapping his index finger in the four spots. When I was young, my mom talked about her occasionally and told me a handful stories about her. Before my mom started to harden over time, I could tell she loved her mother and that her death affected my mom more than she would ever say to me. The more she pretended she didn't exist made that even more explicitly clear. My mom's face is a shade of pale I've never seen outside a hospital room.

The black necklace around her neck seems to tighten, choking the breath from her. Her free hand pulls a little at the heavy jewelry. "Mateo, you need to leave."

"Why? It's been too long since someone has called you on your shit, Iz. I'm not one of your yes men and, no, everyone"— he turns to the thankfully small crowd of spectators—"I'm not drunk. Not one drop." I wonder why they're speaking in English, then realize that the only people Mateo wants to hear this seems to be SetCorp, and it appears to be a direct decision made by him to prove a point, a point that's clearly working.

"Mateo, let's talk outside. There's so much you don't understand," my mother urges. His mentioning her mother shakes her, because even the glass in her hand is swaying slightly and her legs look wobbly in her heels. That, or she truly does put everything below her company, her ego and reputation.

"You've had so much time to call me yourself. You yet again made a choice for me without asking me, and you can't just throw money at everything and fix it like you always do! You knew how important this was to me, but you still moved forward. I waited, thinking you would call me yourself about this, and you didn't. I don't have anything else to say to you. I just wanted to come to your fancy party and look you in the eyes one last time, hoping, praying that there was just one ounce of the woman I knew and loved. But now, looking at you, there's nothing inside you that I can hold on to. You've become someone you yourself would have hated, and I can finally go on with my life without you haunting me, without thinking about what it could have been like with you. It would have been hell being with you, you soulless woman. Enjoy your fucking money, Isolde. Enjoy destroying our land and toast with the millionaires who are the only ones who will be able to survive here if this doesn't stop! Toast to all the families whose lives are ruined now because you just had to have one more hotel built! Cheers, everyone!" Mateo holds an imaginary glass in his hand and lifts it into the air.

A few people I recognize from SetCorp are staring, worried looks covering their usually smug faces. It pisses me off that this is all falling solely onto my mom's shoulders. My mom's complexion has lost all color, and I have never, ever seen someone speak to her the way Mateo just did and live to tell the tale. Her eyes are shining, her chest moving up and down, the black stones bouncing off the lights. The flute in her hand shakes so much that the champagne splashes over and onto the shiny floor. She doesn't even look down at it as a man in a server's tux dashes over to wipe it up.

I want to rush to her side, but part of me is desperately hoping that his words will resonate with her. I want her to process them, not shut them out like she does with every emotion since I can remember.

She stares blankly ahead, watching Mateo's exit as he shouts, "Good job, everyone! Ho estàs arruïnant tot!"

"He said, 'you're ruining everything,'" Julián whispers. "I'm not going to tell you the rest. You don't need to hear it." His voice is sympathetic, caring for me even though his own father is hurt.

I can't take my eyes from my mother. Even though her expression looks empty, I know her well enough to know she's anything but. She's lost somewhere in the past, in pain, and still watching Mateo's back.

"Go to her," Julián urges me, pushing gently against my back.

I'm torn. I want to comfort her, but in a fucked-up way, I want her to learn something from this, even if it's only temporary. I watch her for a few seconds and can't take it anymore. I kiss Julián's cheek.

"I'll be back," I sigh.

"I'll be here," he promises.

I grab ahold of my mom's hand. Reluctantly she attempts to stop me as I lead her out the closest door. She hesitates a little more, and I yank at her, not giving her a choice but to come with me. I know she must be humiliated, hurt, and already trying to think of a way to explain what just happened to the people at her company.

As soon as I push the door open, she lets out a huge gasp of relief mixed with panic as the night breeze hits her. She lets go of my hand and grasps at her chest with both hands, then pulls at the necklace, ripping it off in one pull. The heavy stones fall onto the concrete in a cluster of thuds, and I bend down to grab them, knowing they must be worth a ton of money. She grips my shoulder, pulling me up.

"Leave them," she tells me.

"Do you want to go to your room?" I ask her.

Her dark eyes are stormy, and her breath is blustering. She shakes her head.

I'm stunned by the words that follow. "We should have never come here."

I think back to the flight across the Atlantic, the excitement she tried to hide in her eyes as we landed on the runway. So much has changed since that day, it feels like a lifetime ago.

"We should have never come here. I shouldn't have brought you here; we shouldn't have—" She struggles to speak, as if she just ran up twenty flights of stairs.

"Mom, I know it had to be hard to face him. But—"

She holds her hand up to cut me off.

"It's not as simple as that. Facing him . . . I've been starving inside for years without seeing him, unbearably missing him, full of regret for decades. Facing him was every nightmare I've ever had come true. He's disgusted by me. My mother would be disgusted by me."

In my entire twenty-three years on this earth, I've never had a vulnerable conversation with my mother until we got to this island. The fact that she had this great love and never even mentioned him to me is evidence of that. She's never talked about herself, her feelings, her anguish, not one mention of regret. Not ever.

"He's missed you, too, I know it. I've spent time with his son this summer, Mom. Stories about you, about your life, your mom, our family. I'm sure he feels angry and betrayed right now, and that's why he said those things, but he loved you more than you can imagine. He's kept letters from you . . ." I don't want to share everything Julián has told me, but I need to salve a little of her pain in some way.

Her eyes fill with tears, and she blinks them away like the inconvenience she's always labeled them as.

"How did you even meet him? You never told me how you met his son. You said you were with Amara and her friends. God!" she shouts. "I don't even know what my daughter has been doing since we arrived because all I've cared about and focused on is this damn company and building this resort. I brought you here to show you how beautiful it is, how wonderful life can be when you just let the energy of the city into your soul, but I've been so blind. I owe this company my life, and yours . . . and you know what?" She smiles, but it's the furthest from happy as it can be. "I've given it to them at the expense of everyone. I've convinced myself I was doing the right thing by taking over the acquisition and build because of the money I knew it would bring to his family, knowing damn well that man doesn't care about money. They were going to do it anyway, Ry; the plan had already been set in motion, but I took over, knowing I could get Mateo a better deal, more money. God, even as I'm rationalizing what I've done, everything is about money, and I don't know when I became like that."

Tears fall down my cheeks and I wipe them away, mirroring her movement. "His son is the boy I was going to tell you more about," I hesitate but add, "when you canceled our boat tour."

She shudders. "Ry, I know you hate me, but I wouldn't change anything I've done, because it's kept you alive. But I wish—" Her chest continues to heave. "I wish I would have done better, by you, by my mare, by Mateo . . . my god, Mateo." My mother presses her palm against her chest as if to keep her heart attached to her body.

"Mom—" I struggle to authentically comfort her because it's been so long, if ever, that I've seen her truly open and remorseful. I wish we hadn't lost so much time. And more than that, I wish it wasn't running out.

"Do you love him? Julián?" she asks me, grabbing ahold of the banister closest to her. Her shoulders slump as if she can barely hold herself up.

I nod. "I do."

"You must hate me."

"I can't hate you. I hate what SetCorp did and what they made you do . . . Julián and Mateo's lives have been turned upside down and I don't know how they will recover from this, but I know how much your work means to you and how much theirs means to them." I gulp, staring at the glimmer of lights reflecting off the pool water.

I will never understand how she, or anyone, could put

money or a job before their morals, but I keep that thought to myself in this moment. She's been through enough for one night, and hurting her more isn't going to make things right.

"I can't go back in there. My colleagues, the hotel employees, I'm so embarrassed. It wasn't supposed to go this way . . ."

I can't tell if she's referring to the event or the chain of events since we arrived here in Mallorca.

"Let's go around to the front and to your room," I suggest.

She shakes her head. "I can't be a coward. This is my event, my job, my responsibility. I can't just run away."

"Why not?" I ask her.

She looks at me like I've grown an extra head or two. "Why not? Because I can't."

"But you can. What makes you think you have to go in there and finish out the evening acting like nothing happened, when you're clearly upset and heartbroken? You don't have to keep suppressing yourself, Mom, you have every right to 'run.'" I hold up my fingers in air quotes. She isn't running, she's been working her ass off for months on this event. Her job is done.

"Heartbroken?" she snarls, the look in her eyes changes from hurt and distraught, and a slight chill runs over my bare arms at the shift. "I am not heartbroken, Oriah," she scoffs, lying through her teeth with a voice full of defense.

"Mom, it's okay to be—"

"Do not tell me what's okay and what's not. You don't have a clue about the real world, or what I'm thinking or feeling right now. I am not concerned about some man I loved thirty years ago. I care about my reputation at the company that has done so much for me, for us. Who do you think pays for your treatments? Your MRIs? Your private hospital rooms and medication? Your livelihood is directly connected to my career. Not Mateo or his son. My priority is you, no one else. I'm not going to let anyone or anything chance that, Oriah. Not him, not this damn island, nothing."

Here she is, Isolde Pera, in full force. Acting cold and disconnected from her emotions and reality. Using my condition as a wall, a never-wavering excuse to not care about anyone or anything else.

"I may not have a clue about the real world, and that's because you have never allowed me to, but I do know you, whether you're aware of that or not, and I know that you don't only care about your job. Why is it so hard for you to admit that you care about something other than your fucking work? And stop using me as some sacrificial lamb for why you behave the way you do! I'm not my condition, Mom, I'm so much more than that, so stop blaming it for your emotionless, empty heart!" I'm getting angrier by the second.

I try to take slow, deep breaths and ignore the pounding sound and throb of pain behind my earlobes. The low sound of water trickles and I know what's coming. I can't stop it.

"You told me you were going to show me where you came from this summer! You promised me that you would spend time with me before I fucking die, and you haven't looked up from your phone long enough to know that I haven't even been taking my medication! Julián has shown me and taught me more about this island and where I came from, my culture that you robbed me of knowing anything about my entire life! It wasn't yours to take away from me, but you did, just like you do everyone else! Julián—"

Her eyes are nearly popping out of her strained face. The veins on her neck and forehead are angry and deep purple.

"What do you mean you haven't been taken your medication? Did he tell you not to?"

I throw my hands into the air. "No! I made the choice myself. I made a choice for myself, and for once it has nothing to do with him or you, or anyone except me!"

"I don't believe you. He's influenced you enough to stop taking your medication, and you had a seizure today! You could have died, Oriah! You're not to see him again. I'll file a report against him for stalking, and you know what money can buy. You've seen it and lived in luxury your whole life. Better yet, you're going home. I'm putting you on the next flight out tomorrow and you will not involve yourself in this any longer."

Rage rips through me and I scream at her, knowing I have seconds at best.

"Do you have any idea how much I resent you? How lonely I've been my entire life, desperate for love and affection and starved of it? I've never been this happy and I've never felt love from someone else like I do now. I'm not leaving this country until I die, which lucky for you will be sooner than later. The fact is that I stopped taking my medication the moment we got here, and you didn't notice because you barely fucking look at me! I heard the doctor tell you that my tubers shifted, so I went and saw him alone and I know the truth. Julián has been the best thing to happen to me, and I love him, and you will not keep me away from—" My vision begins to blur, and I imagine Julián there behind her, rushing toward me as I lose my footing, and someone screams my name. The warm pool water wraps me up, hugging me, pulling me under . . .

# Chapter Twenty-Four

As I come to, I'm shivering and in Julián arms. His face is covered in worry, confusion, and I realize half of the trembling of my body is from his. His hair and clothes are drenched as he slowly rocks my body, pushing my soaked hair off my forehead.

"Don't call the hospital," I choke out, coughing up a good amount of salt water from the pool. "Please."

"Oriah." My mother's voice makes my body tense.

"Hem de trucar a un metge?" Julián's attention doesn't leave me, but I know he's speaking to my mom.

She looks at me, then him. "No, no si ella no ho vol. Però ha d'anar a la seva habitació i ficar-se al llit."

"Let's get you to your room." Julián lifts me up from our place on the cement, and water pours off our bodies, pooling at his feet.

"Can you go the back way so my—" my mom begins, but stops herself at Julián's death glare.

"I will go the way that's easiest for Ry. I don't give a shit about your party," he tells her, but takes me the back way, making sure no one sees me.

Not for her sake, but for mine. I'm dripping wet, and my dress feels heavy against my body, even though I'm being carried. The way back to my room feels like the longest stretch of silence I've ever experienced.

Julián scans my room key from my handbag and carries me into the room, passing the entryway, the living space, and heads straight to the bathroom. The intensity of his stare makes me uneasy as he gently places me on the cushioned mat on the floor. His fingers unzip my dress and remove the clasp of my necklace, dropping it to the floor. He struggles but manages to take my earrings off, putting my jewelry in a neat pile on the tile.

"Are you able to stand?" he finally asks me.

I nod. He turns on the bath faucets and blasts the water, gauging the temperature with his fingers. Gently grabbing on to my hands, he pulls me up, holding me with one arm behind my back to keep me steady.

With ease, he lifts me up again and places me into the bathtub, a few inches deep of water. The hot water gives a rush of relief, nearly instantly stopping my shivering. I lay my head back and close my eyes, but the burn of Julián's on me doesn't lighten. He's probably so angry, so confused . . .

It would be easier to keep my eyes shut, to tell him it's okay if he runs away now that he saw firsthand that I'm a ticking time bomb. Too much to handle, too much of a risk and hassle to be with.

"I'm sorry, Julián." I blink my eyes open and muster the courage to face him. His back is against the wall closest to the tub, his hands clasped together, white-knuckled.

"Sorry for what? What on god's earth could you possibly be sorry for?" His voice is full of exhaustion.

"Aren't you upset with me?" I meekly ask.

He sits up, his back no longer touching the wall.

"Upset with you? I'm damn terrified for you, I thought you were dying, Ry. I saw you . . . spasming and then falling into the pool. I'm fucking scared for your life, not upset with you."

"I'm sorry, Julián," I whisper, the water still rushing from the faucet.

"Do not say sorry again, please. I don't need an apology; I need an explanation. Even just a little bit so I know what the hell just happened."

"I should have told you."

"Then tell me now."

Where to begin? From birth . . . from now . . . I don't want to overwhelm him, but he deserves an explanation of some sort.

"The fast version is . . . I was born with a genetic condition; it's called tuberous sclerosis. There are many, many different versions of my condition, varying from nonverbal, severe autism; blindness . . ."

His lips are purple, and not from the cold. "For me, the part of the condition that affects me the most is epilepsy. I have these things called tubers, not to be confused with tumors, that I was born with in my heart and brain. I developed them in my kidneys over time also, but my brain is the reason you saw what you saw."

His voice is barely a whisper. "Is there a treatment?"

I shake my head. "Yes and no. There are medications to control the seizures, but they've only worked on and off for me. So I gave up taking them when I arrived here, because a few of the tubers shifted recently."

He's as still as a statue as I wait for him to jump up and run far, far away from me and my health burden. "How often has this been happening?"

"Over my lifespan, but . . . this was the second one today."

"Today? When was the other? Please tell me it wasn't when I . . . oh god . . . Ry. If I would have known, I would have never—"

I sit up a little, adjusting my body in the tub. "The one thing I ask from you is to not treat me differently. I know it's nearly impossible, but please don't say you wouldn't have reacted the same if you knew. You didn't cause the seizure. I believe it was my emotional overload that triggered it at that exact moment, but no one and nothing caused this or can fix it."

"I want to hate you for not telling me, but I can't seem to get past the pain of the idea of losing you." Julián's body shakes with a sob. His hands cover his face, and I lean over him and turn the water off. I reach for him, the water splashing around me as I gently pull his hands away from his face. Tears pour from his eyes, and he launches forward, wrapping his arms around me and pulling me to him.

"Shhh . . . It will be okay . . . it will all be okay." I promise him something I can't keep.

"I should be the one telling you that." He hugs me harder. The fabric of his top is so cold against my heated skin. I reach my hands between us and start to unbutton his shirt.

"You're freezing; come in with me," I suggest.

He seems to realize that his clothes are still wet. I push the shirt down his shoulders, and he silently removes the rest of his clothes, climbing into the opposite side of the bathtub. I don't pressure him to move closer to me, even though I want nothing more than to hug him again, to hug him every second of every minute of every hour of every day, until the end of mine.

"Are you afraid?" Julián asks me after a few minutes of silence.

"Yes."

His shoulders rock, my heart breaking again and again as he tries to hold in his tears.

"I wasn't afraid before. I was at peace with what would happen when I came here. I stopped resenting fate, I accepted it, welcomed it even. But then I met you . . . and I started to grow angry again. I found myself wanting to curse the world, destroy it. I had stopped fighting it, stopped fighting everything. I was okay . . . but you, you make me want to live, and that's what I'm afraid of the most. That now I want to fight to live. And that makes me more afraid than dying. Knowing that now I want to live, and can't."

"You can. There must be a way. My pare knows a doctor in Madrid. I can ask him; there must be a way. I refuse to accept that your life is over. Even if you're tired of fighting, I am not. I will never be."

I sigh, wishing I could make him understand that the only solution is way too risky and not one I'm willing to take. Is it better to let him waste his energy fighting a battle he can never win?

"Let's fight, okay? Please, Ry, I can't lose you. You can't . . ." He struggles to say the word. "Die. You can't. I can't lose you. You've become everything to me, and I can't lose you."

I move across the water, holding on to him long after the water is cold, long after his body has run out of tears. Eventually, he wraps me in a thick robe and carries me to the bed. He watches me until I fall asleep, and I wonder if it's because he's worried I won't wake up.

# Chapter Twenty-Five

The next few days, we don't leave my room. We order room service that Julián curses at the prices of for every meal. We watch TV, and I use my suite status to have a pile of crosswords delivered to my room for Julián.

We play house and it's wonderful. We make love all over my suite, against the walls, the tables, couch and chairs, the bed, in the tub. My mom gives me the space I've begged for for years, only having Lena come by once with a nurse and fresh refills of my medications. I take them as Julián scribbles the names of each one inside the cover of his crossword book in his hands. He promises that his pare doesn't need him to work right now, with the transition and up-in-the-airness of the situation with the fishery. We barely speak of our parents, silently agreeing that this is our bubble for now and nothing and no one is going to pop it.

I read, I nap, I eat. Julián doesn't ask more details about my tuberous sclerosis, but I saw the words on his phone screen while I pretended to watch *Mamma Mia!*, one of my favorite comfort movies. It's almost as if nothing happened. Julián's behavior hasn't changed aside from watching me even more closely, which he had basically done anyway since we met.

"I can't eat any more of the food on here," I finally tell him one morning, scrolling through the room service menu on the TV.

I've lost track of the days, but I don't care to know where we are in time.

Julián's relieved groan lets me know he's been waiting to hear those words from me.

"Wanna go back to the world today?" I ask him. He sits down on the bed, scooting closer to me and leaning down on one elbow, looking up at my face.

"Only if you're ready to."

I smile, leaning down to kiss him. "I am. And I'm ready to wear something besides this robe, honestly." I pull at the neck of the thick fabric. As plush and lush as they are, after wearing them so much, it's suffocating me a bit.

"Well." Julián presses his lips against my shoulder, pulling the robe down, and down, and down, his fingers untying the bow at my waist. It falls from me, and he lays me back onto the mattress, hovering over my bare body.

"I'm ready for you to be out of that robe too. And we should celebrate our release." He follows my eyes down to my tight, heavy breasts and matches my grin before disappearing between my thighs.

Once we're dressed, me in a thin white cotton sundress with a crochet cutout pattern across the torso, and him in the clothes I had Amara help me have delivered here, not without protest, of course. Julián wanted none of the small stack of brand-new T-shirts and shorts we had the concierge get him, but I used my mouth and body to shut him up eventually, and he was glad to have fresh underwear and clothes, even though the price tag made him look physically ill. He asked if we could return them at least ten times since, but I convinced him it was a good thing to spend my mother's money, as much of it as possible. And I didn't say this part, but those outfits, socks, underwear, all of it, would be about as noticeable in her account as her almond milk lattes she orders every morning.

I let the air dry my hair as I've been doing since we locked ourselves in my room and don't bother with my contacts. I do, however, bother with my medication, and Julián watches me like a hawk as I take each one, handing me my water bottle to wash them down. A little of my brain fog is creeping back, but even with it, I refuse to break the promise I made to him to fight to live for as long as I can manage. I put on sunscreen and Julián groans like a toddler as I rub the white cream across his skin, telling me he's never worn sunscreen a day in his life. I shut him up by reminding him that skin cancer is a thing, and if I'm going to try to stay alive, so is he. He takes photos of me with his phone as I dab a little blush on my cheeks, and I blow a kiss to his phone camera.

Julián has me pick out his outfit, a beige T-shirt from Polo and linen shorts to match. He looks devilishly handsome in everything, but I'll admit, I like him in his usual sun-faded clothes the most. As we stare into the mirror before leaving, I slide a pair of sunglasses onto his face and his mouth drops open.

"What in Saint's name are these?" He pulls them off, examining them like a species of fish he's never encountered, but with much less excitement.

I can barely speak through my belly laughter. "They're sunglasses. Trendy ones. Amara picked them out and they look great on you!" I put them back on his face.

"The hell they do! And I'll be sure to give Amara an extrasweet *fuck off* when I see her."

I knew the sleek, black, Wayframe-style glasses were a step too far, but Amara insisted, and I was looking forward to Julián's over-the-top reaction I knew he would have. It was beyond worth it. I stare at our bodies in the mirror, his much wider than mine, dressed in similar colors, looking like a picturesque couple on a vacation in Europe. I lean my back against his chest, and he wraps an arm around me, resting his hand on the top of my belly.

"We really are great together," he says, more to himself than to me. "Thank you for coming into my life, Ry. I needed you and didn't even know it."

With his free hand, he pulls his phone from his pocket and takes another photo, this time posting it on Instagram. I tease him about it as we leave the room, but the validation and giddiness of being his first official Instagram relationship have me floating the rest of the way to his boat.

"I'm not sure what food I have left that's not gone bad, so let's stop by the market and grab what we want? Anything you're craving?" He squeezes my hand as we walk down the tiny, winding street.

"Just you," I remark, half teasing, half not.

"You've become rather insatiable." He nudges against my shoulder, coming close enough to swipe his tongue across the shell of my ear. A shiver runs over me.

I can feel the heat in my cheeks and between my legs, so naturally I use humor to deflect from the way he can instantly turn me on.

"Insatiable? Are there any words that you don't know? You're not even just fluent, you have a bigger vocabulary than any English-speaking man I've ever met."

We pause at a crosswalk, waiting our turn. The streets are slightly crowded but quiet. Julián's grin is wicked, cocky, sexy. "Are you saying I'm smarter than all the men you've ever met?

"I've been doing crosswords since I was a kid. I was obsessed with learning English because my pare kept saying I'd need it, with the way the island was changing. Then they became a distraction on my worst mental health days, so my thirst for knowledge became a form of therapy as well."

I'm impressed by him yet again.

"I hate to make your ego any bigger, but sadly I must admit it's true."

He doesn't say a word, but he straightens his back jokingly, walking on his tippy toes. As an old man pulling a cart of apricots passes us, Julián turns to him. "I'm the smartest man she's ever met," he brags, and the grandpa shoos him away, cursing us as we crack up and cross the street.

"I would have helped him with that cart if he wasn't so damn grumpy," he says, pointing his finger toward a covered stall down what looks like an alley but is likely just a narrow street.

"This is my favorite market. Pollensa is the best on the island, but it's only open on Sundays and a far drive from Palma and today is . . . well, I don't know, but there would be more people out if it were Sunday.

"Do you have markets like this in Texas?" he asks as we approach.

An abundance of colorful fresh fruit and vegetables overflow their cardboard boxes.

"We call it a farmer's market. We have them in major cities, but I've never been to one. I've seen them online though, if that counts." I wince.

He nods, his lips making a pouty shape. "It counts. We have many, many different markets here in Mallorca. Every part of the island has their own, multiple in many, and we pride ourselves on our fresh produce, fruit, and seafood. Each one is open on different days, but if you're lucky, you can find one open every day, like this one."

An elderly couple behind the stall smile and greet us in Spanish, calling Julián by name. He introduces me and I do my best to say, "Hola, és un plaer conèixer-te." My attempt at telling them it's so nice to meet them seems to go over well and Julián tells me he's impressed by my Spanish.

I tell Julián to surprise me with whatever he feels like making and he goes to work, picking up and inspecting a pepper, onions, fresh garlic cloves, a chunk of beef. The bag is full as he pays, against the couple's wishes. I can tell by their body language and a word here and there that they insist he doesn't pay, but he puts cash down on the table and playfully grabs my hand, half running away from them.

When we make it back to the boat, Julián's face drops when he opens the unlocked door. "It's, um . . . Sorry, it's so dirty in here, compared to your place . . ."

I push past him, not acknowledging the difference and not caring in the least. I'm so thrilled to be back in Julián's place, to be able to take in the details this time. I look around as quickly and as sharply as I can. Stacks upon stacks of cross-word puzzles, books, newspapers. Giant aluminum cans that have pictures of tomatoes on them. Wine bottles, empty and full. With how much he works, it makes sense that his priority isn't cleaning. He's also a single man living on a boat, so why would he? Like the mind reader he is, he grabs an empty wine bottle and a stack of paper from the wooden dining table near the kitchen space, trying to organize them.

"Sometimes I go through phases when I clean and when I don't. You're seeing this in the middle of one of the bad times. It's been much worse than this, but I'm trying to stay on top of it. Internet says it's common with people with depressive episodes, so I'm trying." He looks embarrassed and I want to hug him and comfort him, but I know how it feels to have someone draw attention to something you're not ready or tired of talking about.

"Well, the best we can do is try. As we know, I'm struggling with trying as well, so let's just keep trying together? Deal?"

His embarrassment melts away slowly and he nods. "Deal."

He walks over to his dresser and grabs a T-shirt, the one he was wearing when we first met, and changes into the cut-sleeved T-shirt and cloth shorts. Neatly folding the new outfit and placing it on top of the dresser. We purposely left the rest of his new wardrobe in my room for the times, many, many more times, that he'll stay over.

"Not because I hate them, but because I'm about to cook and I'm a pretty messy cook as it is."

"Mhmm," I tease him with a smile. "Can I help?"

He regards me for a moment. "Actually, yes. I'd love to show you how to make arros brut."

"Arros brut," I repeat.

He smiles at my pronunciation. "Every region has their own version of this dish, even in the States. The direct translation is 'dirty rice.' Have you had it?"

"Once, from a barbecue place outside Fort Worth, but it definitely didn't have any vegetables in it." I laugh, excited to help him cook.

"I have my own touch too. You'll see." He tosses me an apron and leads me out to the dock, to a little corner between a few empty boats. Not a person in sight. There's a grill and some contraption that looks like an outdoor stovetop. There are at least eight chairs set up, bottles of wine and beer cans, coolers, and plates scattered around small stumps of wood being used as tables. It's lively, lived-in, and a place where I can tell many memories have been made.

"This is our . . . communal kitchen. Where we come to eat, talk about work, complain about everything, fix marriages and contemplate divorces," Julián explains with a rough laugh.

"Plus, it's too hot to cook inside and the flavor is better when you sear the vegetables and roast the beef over real flame. There's also this view, which is much better than in there." He nods to the boat gently wading, anchored and parked at the dock.

"You had me at 'complain about everything.'" I wink, tying the apricot-printed apron around my waist.

"You sit while I chop. Have some wine, it's for everyone."

I reach for a bottle of white wine and read the label, even though I don't know the difference between any sort of wine, just that I prefer white. I pour it into a plastic cup from the stack and take a drink.

"Good?" Julián asks me, spreading out a bundle of ripe tomatoes onto a wooden surface that's clearly multi-use: a cutting board, an island, and table. It's waist high and the biggest of the table-like pieces.

"Wait, shit," he says in a panic. I jerk up, hoping he didn't already chop a finger off. "Are you allowed to drink? Does that make you more likely to have a seizure?" he asks, guilt written all over his face.

I walk over to join him. "I can drink. I'm not going to get wasted, I just want a little wine. But no, it doesn't make me anything . . . don't worry about me. Unless you don't feed me soon, then you should be afraid . . . very afraid . . ." I tease and stand on my toes to kiss him. He wraps his hand around my neck, pulling me in as his tongue savors mine. A groan escapes from his throat, and I swear every time he kisses me feels like the first time. The bubbly confetti exploding in my tummy, the swimmy marshmallow feeling in my head, swirling my thoughts around in glitter.

I reach my hands up and wrap them around his broad shoulders. A throat clears and I jump back away from him. I move to hide behind him like a child, a trained reaction from having such a helicopter mother my entire life. Mateo is standing there with two other men I haven't seen before. The three of them are dressed in full work gear, and one, who looks to be at least ninety, has a thick net wrapped around his arm. I look more, peering around Julián's shoulder, and feel him shake in amusement. The one in the middle grabs a bottle of vodka from the ground below him and the net-holding grandpa grabs a small pack of beer. His eyes are skeptical, not exactly happy to see me, but I wave to Mateo, and

he smiles warmly at me, waving back. The little old man follows Mateo's behavior and manages a smile for me. Whatever
anger Mateo has toward my mother isn't present on this dock,
and I couldn't be more relieved.

"Soparem per a dues persones," Julián tells them, and they
nod, grinning, leaving us just as quickly as they appeared.

"Did we take their dinner space? They could have joined
us. I feel bad," I tell him.

He turns around to me with a small smile. "They're fine. It's
not dinner yet and they just finished work, so they were coming here to drink. They got their drinks and now they'll be out
of our sight." He kisses my forehead, reassuring me.

"After everything my mom and SetCorp have done, the last
thing I want is to be any more of a burden or intrude on anyone
else's space here."

He takes my face between his hands, brushing a gentle kiss
against my temple.

"This is my space, and you will be intruding on it every
single day if it's up to me. Got it?" His voice is soft and playful,
nothing but a murmur on my skin. I can feel his smile and
breath, warm against my own, and that quickly, we're back to
our own world again. Just a woman and a man and a dock,
wishing and pleading to have all the time in the world.

# Chapter Twenty-Six

"What's running through that brain of yours, Ry?" Julián mumbles, his lips brushing against the curve of my ear. I shiver.

"How long did you know I was awake?" I ask, somewhat avoiding his question, not wanting to ruin his morning by telling him that I've been thinking about my mom, that I might have a little separation anxiety from being under her finger for so long that now that I've had what feels like months of freedom, and I kind of miss her? It's fucked-up and doesn't make a lot of sense, but I keep finding myself wondering if she's alright, if she's lonely . . . even more than her usual loneliness.

"A while." He nuzzles his face into the crook of my neck, the stubble gently brushing against my skin. I shiver once more. "Are you okay?" he questions, breath warm against my bare flesh.

My mom continues her stay in my head. The thousands upon thousands of times she's asked me that very question, but never once did she mean it the way Julián does. He's asking about my mental health, not physical. It warms me from the inside out. Last night as we stayed up late, staring and counting the stars, making wishes on them, some out loud and some silently, I wished my mom would find love again. Even if that meant finding peace and love for herself. I woke up thinking about her again, how her life played out, how I wish I knew more about her past but knowing she will never share it.

"Actually, if you really want to know, I've been thinking about my mom. Thinking about how much of her life I know nothing about. How much of myself I know nothing about because of the way she tucked her own history away. Her pain must have been so unbearable that she just shut it off, literally, and decided to never care again. She was so young, younger than me, when she not only moved across the globe, but had me.

"I don't think there's ever been a time when I've thought of her as a young girl alone determined to make something of herself while raising a child completely on her own. I've never once stopped being resentful toward her long enough to consider that she's been working herself to death for me. Not to say she's not addicted to the power and has a scarcity complex when it comes to money, but what started as a drive for more ended in a miserable, lonely life, and how unfair is it that the only person she has in her life, who she can't fire, is me? When I'm gone, she's not going to have anyone. The only person she's ever loved is your dad . . . which I still can't wrap my head around and imagine a world where her and your dad were in love . . ."

Julián's hand runs along the side of the opposite cheek, tucking my hair behind my ear and nuzzling further into the crook of my neck.

"My pare is a good judge of character. He would never love someone who didn't deserve it. The parts of her that are the most lovable are probably parts only he has seen. As kids, even though we aren't kids, we never truly see our parents for who they are. Don't get me wrong, I've despised your mom my whole life, sorry"—he winces and continues—"but the woman he wrote those letters for was worth loving and the cold, distant, and controlling woman you know is also worth loving," he says confidently.

"Do you really believe that everyone deserves to be loved?" I let my thoughts roam into the air between us, not sure I agree with him, but wanting to believe it the same way he does.

"I don't. Not everyone. I don't think most people even know what love is, and I don't believe that whole idea of humans being born good and all that either. I think our instinct is to be evil and we have to work against it, so those of us who do deserve love, but most people don't."

"How cynical." I close my eyes, focusing on the way his fingertips drag lazily across my skin.

"And my mom would be considered evil by most people. Especially the ones who don't have jobs because of her and the ones who won't be able to see the ocean they call home because her resort is blocking the view," I argue.

"An evil person and a woman trying to survive and support her daughter in the only way she knows how aren't the same." His words cause a heavy lump in my throat and my eyes to prick, fighting tears.

"What about babies? Don't you think they're born pure innocence and good?"

"Not all of them. Some of those babies grow up to do bad shit. Jails are full of adults who were once someone's baby. The world isn't black-and-white, and it's certainly not a bright place, Ry. For you, I wish it was. I'm a cynic, just like you, and I think humanity may be doomed, but I'm happy if you're happy and I'm so fucking thankful I met you and I don't wish ill on anyone or these random babies you're asking me about." He lifts his face up slightly to kiss my cheek.

"But you're a good person and only good things deserve to happen to you. That's all I care about."

My heart sinks. And soars. God, the world truly is unfair. Julián is going to end up hurt by me, one way or another, and there's nothing I can do to stop it.

"Can we talk about something else?" I ask. My mind is too heavy and I'm fighting to not let the guilt consume me.

"Sure can. What about turtles? Do you like turtles?" he asks with a smile.

A laugh escapes me, and it works, he distracts me from reality. I love the way he never pressures me to ruminate or elaborate on a subject that I don't want to.

"Turtles?" I laugh again. "That's the first thing that popped into your head when I asked to change the subject?"

He joins me, his body gently shaking against mine. "Well, I didn't think you would want to talk about climate change or politics . . ."

"You're right." We're both giggly and buzzed off each other. "I do like turtles. Doesn't everyone?"

He shakes his head. "No. I hate them. Fucking turtles. They're the worst." My breath catches in my throat from laughing, and I begin to cough.

Slight worry covers Julián's face instantly and he sits up a bit on his elbow to look down at me. He hands me a half-full bottle of water and I down it. The light from the dock is shining on his face so gently, caressing the strong structure of his jawline, the plane of his nose, the thick of his brows. Such a wonder to behold, his beautiful face. It's beyond me how close we've gotten, how much has changed, since the day we met at the beach. The grumpy, annoyingly hot man has turned out to be a deep, enchanting, caring soul who I'm bone-crushingly in love with.

Curious if he does or was just trying to make conversation, I wonder, "May I ask why on earth you hate turtles?"

"They're just annoying. Everyone pretends to love them because they're endangered, but they're full of germs and just poop everywhere. Sea urchins are more my thing. They're misunderstood and ignored just because they're a little spiky, and the turtles are stealing all the attention, if you ask me."

The random pettiness of his annoyance toward turtles is way funnier than it should be. I feel drunk, like I had another one of Fabio's famous flaming shots. My stomach rumbles at the thought. No more Fabio for me this summer. That night feels like a fever dream.

"I mean, fair. But random. Do you have any other grievances with animals that I should know about?" I ask him.

He nods. "Too many to name. Dolphins, pigeons, rats, cats—" I cover his mouth with my hand.

"Dolphins and cats? I don't know if this is going to work," I tease, and he gently bites the tender skin of my palm.

"Have you ever read how dangerous dolphins can be? If you want to be terrified, I suggest you google it."

"No way. Not googling it."

"Do you have a cat?" he asks, reminding me of how little we know about each other on a personal level. He seems to be able to read my mind yet doesn't know if I have any pets. If only we had the time.

I shake my head. "My mom hates animals."

He nods. "Not surprised."

"And your dad probably feeds strays all the time."

Julián cracks a smile that makes my insides melt. "He does. It's ridiculous. Dogs too."

"And charming."

"I guess so. But they never come back, they just take what they need from him and go on their way. Just like everyone else." Julián's tone turns serious, and my stomach twists.

*Like my mom.*

"Don't think that way. It has nothing to do with you," he says, literally reading my mind for the zillionth time.

"We aren't going to pay for our parents' mistakes." He presses his lips against my forehead, and I close my eyes. He's so much like his father, it and continues to show in the best way.

I try not to think about how lonely my mother has been for the last twenty-something years, or how different her life could have been if she had chosen Mateo over herself. Julián's lips cover mine, drowning out the fading image of my mom's alternative life, and I'm grateful that I'm choosing to embrace this feeling, however temporary, however painful it may be for both of us in the end. My mom will suffer, too, but she's had twenty-three years to spend time with me and has chosen not to, and like Julián said, I'm not responsible for her mistakes.

Julián kisses down my bare body, stopping at my lower stomach.

"Can I ask what happened here?" he says, touching the ragged puffy scar on my lower abdomen. "I wanted to before . . . but I didn't want to make you uncomfortable." He touches his lips against it and I hold my breath. I've never had a boy, or a man, even see my scar, let alone touch and kiss it. I'm not embarrassed by it one bit, I just don't know how much of the can of worms I want to open by telling him, but I also don't want to hide anything else from him.

"I got into a knife fight in San Antonio." I try to make a joke out it, my go-to when I'm unsure what to say. I use humor to deal with my trauma; it's the only way I can stay afloat.

"Not funny," he says with a contradictory smile. "You don't have to tell me," he adds, sympathy in his eyes.

"I'll tell you if you stop looking at me like that."

His brow rises. "Like what?"

"Like you feel sorry for me. It makes me feel awful. I hate sympathy and have had enough in my life to last ten more."

Julián adjusts his expression and leans himself up onto his elbows at the side of my hips. "I definitely don't feel sorry for you. Epilepsy or not, you're still a spoiled rich girl," he teases me.

"I had a kidney transplant when I was thirteen." I brace myself for a dramatic reaction from him, but it doesn't come. He studies my eyes and my scar, without a single trace of weirdness or panic on his face.

"Hmm, they must have really gotten you with that knife, what a badass you are." He smiles.

I breathe, not realizing I hadn't in a while.

"They really did." I laugh, appreciating that Julián can handle way more than I had ever expected anyone to.

"I have something to tell you. I wasn't going to, but I opened your locket when you slept when we first met, so I suspected something was going on. Most people don't always have their blood type and emergency contact on them. You started to stir awake before I could read the rest, which I guess was the epilepsy." His fingertips brush along the apple of my cheek, down the plane of my nose.

"I really am sorry I didn't tell you earlier."

Shaking his head, he says, "As traumatic as the way I saw it firsthand was, you weren't ready to tell me and that was your choice."

"Yeah, I guess seeing me fall into a pool was probably pretty traumatic." I cover my dark humor with a small smile.

He nods. "Sure as hell was. I kept waiting for the anger to come, to feel like you lied to me or purposely deceived me, but I guess my love for you outweighs any anger I could muster."

"How poetic." I touch the tip of his nose, and he grins.

"You can tell me the bloody details of your kidney transplant later. We have all the time in the world," he says with a smile.

My heart sinks and soars, from the deeply understanding way he handles me and his naïve optimism when it comes to time.

"What if we didn't?" I clear my throat, elaborating, teetering on the edge of honesty. "Have the time, I mean?"

"Don't you worry about time. I haven't told you, but . . ." He sits up, back straight and proud. "There's a legend here, that the first-born son of Mateo Garcia can start, stop, and re-create time. So you, my mortal love, have nothing to worry about—"

"For research purposes," I interrupt with an ironic laugh, "what if we only had a limited time together, what would you do then?"

The idea of living in a fantasy world felt so damn good, but slightly unfair to Julián since he would be the one dealing with the aftermath.

"Just what we're doing now. Thinking about changing things leads to disappointment and we've both had enough of that, correct?"

I laugh louder. "Yeah. I guess we have."

"So, Ry, let's focus on now. On what's in front of us and hold on to it with our lives."

His words comfort me as they tear me apart. He doesn't understand that my life isn't capable of holding on to a single thing. Not even him.

# Chapter Twenty-Seven

Wear comfortable shoes, we will be walking a lot today," Julián tells me as I wake up.

"Huh? Where are we going?" I stretch my arms out, trying to grab ahold of his waist but he dodges me, grinning. I reach for one of the down feather pillows and chuck it at him.

"Come on, baby. Time to wake up." He's buzzing with excitement, but I have no idea why.

The room smells like espresso and sugar. He must have been up for a while. Dressed in a denim button-down shirt and beige shorts from his stash of clothing in my room, he looks delicious and ready to take on the day. I can feel the crust in my eyes as I groan, rubbing at them, wishing for some of his energy. The sunglasses he claimed to hate just days ago are already on, pushing back his curly hair out of his face and off his forehead.

"You changed your mind on the glasses?" I can't help but tease him.

He shrugs. "They're here, I'm here . . . We'll be out in the sun today."

"Just admit you like them." I stick my tongue out at him.

With a wink, he pops another Nespresso pod into the machine. "Never."

"You're insufferable." I plop back against the mattress.

"As are you, amor meu." I know enough Spanish to know what that means. I flip over and bury my face in the pillow, making fake snoring sounds.

The soft whir of the espresso churning and filling the cup is the only noise I hear. Just as I'm about to pop my head up and see where he went, I'm yanked by my feet and dragged out of the bed. I shriek and he belly laughs as he throws me over his shoulder, carrying me into the bathroom as I kick my feet and try to tickle his sides. Just my luck, he's not ticklish at all.

"Time to get up, princess. Your coffee's done and you should brush your hair." He points to my head as he softly lands me on my feet. I look in the mirror, but my hair is fine, mostly.

"Gotcha. I'll give you twenty minutes before I become even more obnoxious."

"Is that possible?" I ask, lifting the shirt of his I slept in over my head and tossing it onto the floor.

"You have no idea, baby."

"Okay, okay. But can I have a hint?" I whine, pouting my lips.

"We're going to the past," he says simply as he hugs me from behind.

I cock my head, staring at him in the mirror. Excitement brushes over my skin at whatever he's planned for today.

"You should change, though you look incredibly sexy in my clothes." His eyes touch me, caress me as they scan his cutoff shirt barely touching my thighs.

I get dressed, a swimsuit under trouser-style shorts and a white tank top. The neck is high, my shell necklace twinkling in the center. Julián brings me the espresso he made me, and my medication, and about one hundred kisses, distracting me and smearing the lip gloss I keep attempting to apply. It's all over his chin and cheeks by the time we go to leave, and I rub a wet hand towel across his face, before making him wear sunscreen again, much to his dismay.

"I haven't seen you two in ages!" Amara's voice is a scream when we reach the lobby.

Julián grumbles as she comments on how chic and grown-up he looks, how she knew he would love the sunglasses after all. He curses her out in Spanish, and she laughs, looking around the lobby behind us.

"Word has it your mom and her suits have been on a warpath the last few days, so be careful roaming around here, since I know you're trying to avoid her," Amara whispers.

I wonder if word has spread from the event that Isolde Pera's daughter passed out in the pool during the most important event of SetCorp's plan here, or if the partygoers were oblivious, continuing to drink and stuff their faces as it happened. At least there's resolve there, knowing that while they were drinking and enjoying themselves, money was being put toward a good cause. I make a mental note to ask Lena how much money was raised later. I know my mom won't offer the information easily. I can imagine my mother waltzing back inside the event, saying my health declined again, using something minute like a stomachache, so I had to return to my room. I feel guilty as I look at Amara, debating what I should divulge to her and not, but before I can get too in my head, Julián gently tugs my hand, and I kiss Amara goodbye before we head out for the day.

"Let's hang out soon! Don't keep her to yourself!" she yells at Julián with a smile. He flips her off and out we go.

The air is warm; my driver is leaning against the car I've barely used this summer. He tips his head to me, knowing I won't be using him. He's probably relieved to be paid still and not have to drive me around.

"Do you think I should tell Amara . . . about my health stuff?" I ask Julián as we leave the entrance of the hotel.

"Do you want to tell her?"

A sigh lifts and lowers my shoulders. "Not sure. I feel like I'm doing something wrong by not telling her. I've come to care about her so much so I don't want to hide it from her, but I also don't want it to become the main topic of our time together. I want to be the fun, normal Ry she knows and not ruin that. For her sake, and mine," I admit.

Julián stops walking and stands in front of me, bending down to kiss the corner of my mouth. "You get to decide who and when and why you share anything about yourself and what you're going through. Amara will understand either way, and it's your body, your life, and most importantly, your choice."

I kiss his lips and slowly, gently, wrap my arms around his torso, burying my head in his chest. How have I lived my life without making my own choices up until now? It's so free-ing to be reminded that this is *my life* and I can choose to do what I want with it. I'll tell Amara someday, but it won't be today. Today I'm going to enjoy the company of the man who's brought joy, peace, and so much strength into my life and not think about anything except that.

After twenty minutes or so of strolling through tiny cobble-stone streets hand in hand, Julián stops in the center of a street corner, holds me gently by the shoulders, and turns me to face a home with a small pink door and flower baskets on all the windows. He opens the tote bag he brought with him that he wouldn't let me so much as touch or peer inside of and pulls out a stack of what looks like photos.

"What . . ." I begin to ask as I immediately recognize the women in the top photo. The colors are faded, the corners are turned up. "How on earth did you . . ."

Julián hands me the photograph and I stare at my mother's younger face and relaxed posture, with her arms stretched out to the side like a flying bird. She's in a pair of shorts with her shirt tied up her stomach and the smile on her face makes my heart ache. I can't recall a time in my entire life when I've seen her smile that way. Her mother is next to her, staring at her in wonder, with her head slightly turned. Their resemblance is uncanny, their smiles identical. My grandmother's hair had just started to turn gray on the sides, and the now-pink door is red in the photo.

I look at the photograph a few seconds longer before turning to Julián, who's watching me with a satisfied smile on his face. He knows how important it is to me to try to understand where I came from, where my mother came from, how she became the woman she is today . . .

"Thank you. This is so meaningful, Julián. I barely have words."

His thumbs wipe at my wet eyes and he nods, knowing that sometimes silence is better than words. I love that about him. He points for me to stand in front of the door and pulls a small disposable camera from the bag. I hand him the photo and spread my arms wide, just like my mom's. I try to match her smile and a sense of peace trickles through me as the sunlight washes over my skin.

He clicks the camera and I throw my arms around him. "Thank you for this, so, so much. I'm so grateful. Especially knowing how you feel about my mom . . ."

"How I feel about your mother has nothing to do with how I feel about you. How I love you is not related to her, or to anyone except you and me. This is about you and my joy in making you happy, giving you good memories."

"How you . . . what?" Only Julián would declare his love in such a casual way. As if the earth underneath my feet wasn't shifting, as if the breath in my lungs wasn't evaporating.

"How I love you," he repeats slowly, like I couldn't hear him clearly the first time.

The shock is still settling in, and I ask, "You love me?"

He moves closer, kissing me on my forehead, the sun beating down on us, the chirping birds falling silent. "Of course I do."

"I love you," I manage. "I love you so much." It seems almost silly to say and the way we're both just casually declaring our love in the middle of the street is so us, so causal, so messy, so ridiculous.

Julián's smile is wide. Slightly crooked, it makes me want to wrap my arms around him and never let go. "I know you do."

I roll my eyes, gently pushing at his chest. "Don't ruin the moment," I growl.

He shrugs. "I'm not. I'm simply saying the obvious. You had to have known I love you more than my own life, more than the sea, the sky, the air that I breathe. My love is simple, as it should be."

I lean into him, unsteady and on a high. I love him so much it hurts. It might kill me, but he's worth my last breath.

"I love you, my Ry. And you love me, simple as that, and we have an audience." He looks up to the windows above, and sure enough, more than a few nosy heads have popped out of their windows to listen and watch us. I bury my head in his chest, and he laughs, waving to them.

As the sound of their windows closing fades, he pulls the stack of pictures back out and passes them to me, reaching back to grab ahold of my hand. He knocks on the door with a heavy fist. The old wood echoes and hollers under his touch.

"Julián, we can't just—" I stop as an elderly man opens the door, and I can tell by his expression that he knows Julián well.

"Julián! Mirat! Feia temps que no et veig. Has crescut molt, fill meu!" he says, grabbing him into a big hug and nearly lifting him off the ground.

"Sí, he estat ocupat treballant i ajudant el meu pare. Aquest és el meu amic, Oriah." He turns to me and I reach my hand out to shake the man's hand.

His eyes are the color of melted, gooey honey and his smile is warm and comforting to match.

"You again, Oriah," the man says, a knowing insinuation in his voice. "Isolde, your . . . mother. I can see." He touches my face, which would normally make me uncomfortable, but I feel incredibly at ease with him, despite having never met him before, it feels like I have.

He knows my mom—well, an old version of her who slipped away a long time ago—and possibly my grandma, who I didn't get the chance to know the way I wished I would have. But maybe now is my chance to learn even a little bit about her through this home, through this man. This is everything

I wanted this summer, to have a connection to my mom and where she came from and what made her who is she is.

The man puts his hand on Julián's back and Julián holds on to my hand as we walk into the house. It's clean and simple, oil paintings and greenery hanging from the ceiling and covering the archways. It's not big, but it's perfect. The walls are made of stone and each door is in the same shape as the front door, a lovely arch. I instantly feel at home, rooted to a part of my family that I didn't dream I'd ever get the opportunity to feel. Julián introduces his great-uncle Jordi, whose name pushes at my memory from a place I can't recall. They carry on casual conversation in Catalan and I look around the living space. I try to image my mother here, carefree and smiling, in love for the first time, before she hardened and the world and greed got the best of her.

"Look around and meet me in the kitchen when you're done, my love. Take your time." Julián kisses my temple and continues to talk to the man who I assume owns this house now. He's got to be at least seventy or so, but his young, bright spirit feels like wildfire, even with the language barrier.

I move into the kitchen, taking in the details. It looks like something from a romance movie from the 1940s set in Spain. The details are so plentiful, they're hard to take in in one pass. The wooden cart used as an island is covered in choppy knife marks from decades of meals prepared. I run my fingertips over the marks, wondering how many were from my abuelita. I imagine her cooking here, the thick smell of garlic and tomato in the air, dancing around with the windows open, the breeze full of ocean water, singing the songs she used to make up that my mother always told me about.

There's a bowl of lemons, another of limes, fruit and fresh vegetables filling the nooks and crannies of the kitchen. Long strands of garlic bulbs hang near the edges of the windows. There's color everywhere I look. So starkly different from our white and stainless-steel kitchen back in Texas. There's never a single item on the island, nothing on the countertops. In the rarity that my mom does cook, she cleans up before she serves us and it's always spotless and untouchable, like her. Not here, though. Here in this home moments of life are etched into everything. My heart aches at the loss of something I've never had and my mother took for granted. My hand presses on my chest as I walk toward the paned window, following the dusty sunbeams shining through. Did my mom dream about her future here as she watched the neighbors laugh and smile with their families? Did she know that her life would be so stale in comparison, so lonely and colorless?

A colorful line of clothes sways, drying in the breeze, as a woman and her child play hide-and-seek between a woven quilt as it waves, making a rainbow. The shrieking laughter of the child makes my eyes wet. I turn around, holding the happiness I feel for them in my heart, not able to watch them for a moment longer. The white porcelain sink is cold against my back, helping me regulate my emotions before I go find Julián. The last thing I want him to see is me crying, mourning a childhood and family history that will never be mine.

Spaces like this make me wish I was a creative, a writer or a photographer. A painter. There's an emotion that comes along with being in places like this that's hard to explain or convey, but it feels so deep, as if a core memory is being made right now. The camera clicks and Julián smiles behind it, lowering it from covering his eyes.

"Identical," he says, showing me a photograph of my mother in the kitchen. It's almost eerie how similar the background still is, how my mom's posture used to be so much more relaxed, like mine.

"Can't I see the rest yet?" I grab for the stack of photos, but Julián is quick. He blocks me and presses his mouth against mine, rendering me blissfully helpless.

His mouth becomes hungrier, surprisingly so, considering Jordi is in the small house with us. Julián's hands push into my hair, and he grips it, making my eyes water a bit. I bite at his bottom lip, and he lifts me onto the counter. His mouth moves to my bare neck, and I gasp as his hands grip my bare thighs below the line of my shorts.

A quiet cough breaks us apart. With swollen lips and wide eyes, I wipe my mouth off, trying to look anywhere but at the man in the doorway with a huge smile on his face. I'm mortified but Julián doesn't mind one bit. Men.

Julián apologizes with a laugh and helps me down from the counter. Jordi says something to Julián and Julián translates to me.

"He wants to know if you want to hear some stories about your mom and abuelita. Apparently, the men in my family have a long history of loving the women in yours." He winks, and I look at the man.

"Wait, he couldn't be my grandpa, right? Oh my god, what if we're related?" I whisper.

Julián bursts into laughter, kisses my temple, and shakes his head. "Your grandpa hasn't been alive for a long time." He gently reminds me that my grandma was also a single mother for most of her life. "And we are not related. I may be morally gray, but that's where I draw the line."

I nod at how ridiculous the thought was, but today's been a whirlwind of emotions already and my mind is clearly on a high.

"Can you tell him I'd love to hear anything he can tell me?" I lean into Julián's side, and he wraps his arm around my waist, leading me into the main sitting room.

We sit on the floor and Jordi comes in from the kitchen with a wooden platter covered in bright food. Peppers, Romanesco broccoli, sweet potatoes, eggplant, cabbage, all cut into small, wonderfully placed pieces. In the center, there are three types of dips, one green, one reddish, and one white with little green flakes. Pieces of fragrant roasted garlic and shallots are sprinkled among the fresh food. The smell is beyond decadent, making my stomach growl. The aroma from the yeast in the just-out-of-the-oven bread, the almonds everywhere: it takes all my self-control not to dig in like an animal. The two shots of espresso I downed before we left the boat this morning were not much of a sustainable breakfast. But this, this is fresh and heavenly. I thank him and he begins to tell me tales and memories about my family. Julián takes the time to translate every twenty seconds or so.

I learn that my mom used to be called "tomàquet petit" because she was so feisty and was always eating whole, raw tomatoes, which is weird to me because she has always told me she hates them, despite her vegetable-heavy diet. As Jordi shares memories of the version of her who grew up here and of my abuelita, who he was head over heels for, I feel so close to them. I can imagine them in this home, my mother yapping away and my grandmother cooking. I had never gotten to know her, or anyone in my family here. The moment my mother's mom passed away, my mom at just seventeen packed a single suitcase and less than one hundred dollars and came to the States to live with her aunt, who had married a man in Texas years back and encouraged my mom to study business there.

Barely out of high school, but a whiz at charm and street smarts, my mother blew through her studies; with a full scholarship from the University of Texas, she graduated at the top of her class, and then got pregnant with me. Parts of the timeline didn't add up in my brain, but I didn't need to question every single detail when the past differed from person to person, each one putting their own stamp on what happened from their perspective. And I was okay with that; it made us all more human.

One thing was for sure: giving birth to me, having my sperm donor run off and never come back, and my . . . complications had drastically changed my mom's life and who she was to the core. My mind wanders as I dip a piece of broccoli into the thick red sauce and close my eyes, imagining for a moment that my mom sat here in this exact spot on the floor, with this man and his delicious food, music playing softly in the background, daydreaming about the happy, fulfilled future she would never have. She left the only love I've known her to have, and there had to be more of a reason than anyone else knew. I would never be able to ask her, but curiosity eats at me as we feast.

After we finish our meal, Julián leads me outside to the back patio. A row of luscious almond trees and an iron table fill the small but enchanted space. The sun is out, bright and glorious but not scorching. It really is the perfect day. Another photo is held in front of me, my mom lying back on the iron table, her feet dangling off the edge and her face propped up on her elbow. She's using the other hand to block the sunlight.

"Who do you think took all of these?" I ask Julián as I awkwardly climb onto the table.

I would normally feel insanely silly doing something like this, but he's making it feel so fun, so immersive, that even as the table creaks, we both laugh and Julián pulls the camera back out, studying the shot and the photograph in his hand.

"My pare did. I found them in a chest in the boat. He took them all, I asked. Of course, I was pissed and wanted to rip them to shreds but I couldn't bring myself to. Just like the letters."

The click of the camera surprises me as the flash goes off. I reach up to cover my eyes and Julián rushes over to me. "I'm sorry, are you okay? I don't know why the flash turned on." He examines the camera and presses a button, then another. "I'll make sure it doesn't happen again." The tone of his voice is so serious, as if he's studied what flashes can do to me.

"It's okay. Can you show me my mom's old room?" I climb off the table quickly, letting my heart rate slow and my panic dissolve as Julián's hand wraps around my own and he leads me back inside and upstairs.

The room is vibrant and more colorful than I thought it would be, and if it weren't for the lack of dust anywhere, I would assume it's been untouched all these years. I go to the window first to see the view she had for years and jump back in surprise. I blink and it's gone, but I could have sworn . . .

"Are you okay?" Julián's voice brings me back to reality.

"I think the photos and being here is messing with my mind. I swear I saw my mother walking there." I point to the corner of the street. It's empty and she's not there . . . of course she's not. I definitely imagined it.

There's a bed next to the window, a small desk, and a few stacks of schoolbooks. I walk over to the desk and trace the thick, curved wood. There's something carved into it: *Iz i Mateo* is etched deeply into the desk. I open one of the books, again, no dust to be found. I'm a little nervous to tell Julián what I'm thinking, but it comes out anyway.

"Imagine how much happier they would have been if they stayed together. I know we wouldn't be here, but take us out of the equation for a moment. Neither of their lives has been the same since. My mom is miserable and doesn't so much as look at a man. Your pare has been cooking her favorite foods, keeping memories and photographs. How is it possible they were so in love, but separated? It seems cruel and like their lives after are a punishment from the universe."

Julián sits down next to me on the bed and takes my hand in his. "Let's never find out how that feels, okay?"

I nod, knowing it won't do any good to remind him that our time has an expiration date and not only the end of summer. Something more infinite. I send a silent prayer to the universe to punish me for all eternity for the pain he will feel when I'm gone.

# Chapter Twenty-Eight

We walk hand in hand, as we do each day now. The sun is low in the sky, and the birds have begun to quiet down, the city rolling itself into a slumber. The reflection of the sun on the glassy ocean surface illuminates the calm beauty of something so massive, so welcoming. Julián sets a blanket down on a dark rock big enough for both of us. There's no one else at this beach, only us and the sea. He packed our dinner inside a basket, a simple woven thing, romantic and so Julián to not realize how adorable it is. As we eat our sandwiches and rice and fruit, he tells me about how he can't stomach the taste of oysters because they remind him of his mother as they were her favorite food, about his childhood friend who moved back to Bangladesh when they were teens, about how he used to never wear shoes around the town until he was seventeen and got a nail stuck in his foot. He shows me the scar and I run my finger across the bubbled-up little dot.

We talk about anything, everything, and nothing as the sky grows darker. Purple-edged clouds slowly roll past as I stare up at the sky, tilting my head back. I hear the click of a camera and look over at Julián with a smile. A small sense of ease settles over me, knowing he will at least have photographs of me to look back on. Then again, they may end up like the stack of my mother's, shoved into a box, hated and unwelcomed but always kept. I wish I could just have the beginning of a thought like that and cut it off before the cynicism pushes its way in, but here we are.

"Let's walk a bit to digest?" he suggests as I groan and rub my hand over my stomach.

I'm so full I could burst, so I gladly accept.

As we walk, I decide to tell him about one of my most special but buried parts of me that I never share with anyone. The one that brings all my fears to the surface.

"I also had a friend who was so, so dear to me. She was my best friend." I pause as we walk, wanting to share her with him but afraid I won't be able to handle saying it out loud. I haven't tried since it happened, but if I'm capable, it would be Julián who could make me able to finally share her with someone.

"Her name was Audra, and she was my age. We had the exact same birthday, even. We became friends by a chance meeting at the hospital where they accidently scheduled our EEG appointments and hospital stays for the same time but only had one tech and one room. My mom was pissed off, of course, and refused to be rescheduled, and her mom was just as feisty as mine, so our only option was to take the appointment together. We shared a room and bonded with these little wires stuck to our heads. It ended up being so fun, and she had tuberous sclerosis too.

"We became friends outside and inside the hospital. Her TSC affected her in different ways, more intense ways than mine. She had mild autism, and her epilepsy was more severe than mine, but we had so much in common. She loved to watch me dance, I loved to watch her paint. We became inseparable, and she was truly the only friend I've ever had. My mom paid for her to go to my private high school, and we did everything, I mean everything together . . ."

Flashes of her big smile as I twirled and whirled around the empty gymnasium after school, the sound of her voice cheering my name, her paintbrush dancing across the stretched linen surface of a canvas flash through my mind. I've been trying so hard to keep her out, to avoid the pain, that I haven't allowed myself to think of the joy she brought. The Cheeto-dust stains on our fingers, the way she cackled when she laughed, the way she always, always made me feel less alone in the world. She was like a homecooked meal, a warm bath when my life felt like a constant icy lake.

"We were only friends for two years, but it felt like a lifetime. Our bond was . . ." I clear my throat, willing myself not to cry, not until I finish the story at least. "Strong. The tubers in her brain shifted, like mine, and I'll spare both of us the details, but the choice she made to try to save herself was to get them removed. At this point she was having over one hundred seizures a day. It got to the point where she couldn't leave the house anymore. Removal was the only choice, they said. With where they were located, it was risky. Beyond risky, but she, the doctors, and her mom were adamant that the surgery would not only remove the tubers that were causing most of her seizures, but improve her overall quality of life. We were so enthusiastic, positive that this would change everything . . ." Julián squeezes my hand as he listens to me. His way of letting me know I can stop if

I want to. But I don't want to, I want him to know why the only thing that might save me is not an option for me and never will be.

"I was at the hospital waiting for her to wake up and when she did . . . her entire memory was gone. Not like in a movie where they forget who they are, and they don't recognize their family and loved ones . . ." Hot tears fall down my face remembering the pain in her mother's and sister's faces as we all realized what happened.

"Every memory, including how to talk, how to walk, had to be retaught. Her mind was wiped clean, she was back to infancy. She couldn't paint, she couldn't even hold a spoon to feed herself. It was devastating. It . . . her mom . . . her life . . . my friend was gone and wouldn't return. I waited, hoping that the neurologists were wrong, that one day she would wake up and my sunshine of a friend would remember everything. But she stayed that way, trapped in a familiar body but no memory or understanding of how she got there. She's alive, and it's not my place to decide if that's better or not for her, but I wouldn't and will not make the same choice she did. I've tried to completely erase her from my own memory. My mom stayed in contact with hers for a while, but it just became too hard on everyone when she never came back."

"My god, Ry. I'm so sorry. I'm so, so sorry." Julián pulls me into his chest, hugging me fiercely as if it were possible for him to hug me hard enough to transfer my pain to him.

My voice is hysterical, and my chest is caving in, the grief threatening to swallow me right there on the shore.

"The only sunshine never came again, and I stopped looking for it. I obsessed more and more over my dancing, my schoolwork, never wanting to allow myself to become emotionally intimate with anyone, this damn condition or not. I did everything my team of doctors and specialists told me to, but here I am; the same thing happening to me." His hand wraps around the back of my neck and he holds me tighter.

"I can't get that surgery, Julián. I'm sorry that I dragged you into my life knowing we wouldn't be able to have a happy ending, but we won't and I'm sorry. I didn't know I would love you. I'm sorry you fell in love with someone like me." I sob into his embrace.

Audra, as painful as the loss of her was, deep down I knew that my avoidance of her name, her memory, was rooted in my own fear of having the same fate as her. The irony is not lost on me that I came to Mallorca hoping to have an exciting summer and bond a little with my mom's past, but instead I've found my other half, and our fate is decided. Torturous and melancholy.

"Oriah." Julián sucks a breath through his teeth. His face is blotched with emotion and tears as my eyes meet his. "I love you, every part of you. From your charm to your intelligence. Your sense of humor to your empathy. Your way of drowning out the noise in my head when I'm desperate for silence. I love every." He pauses, kissing my chin.

"Single." His mouth lifts to my mouth.

"Part." He sweeps his lips across my temple.

"Of you." His mouth lands on my head, behind my ear, where the biggest cluster of tubers are located.

"I would not change a moment with you, knowing what I know now. Nothing would have changed." He lets a moment pass. "Except I don't think I would have been so quick to put you on the back of my bike." Julián tries to make me smile, and it works. "If I had to do it over, I would love you again and again, even if it meant losing you again and again. In this lifetime and the next, and the next, I will find you and I will love you."

"I'll be waiting for you. I'll wait at the door of every lifetime for you, Julián. I never dreamed that I could feel this way, know what it's like to love and to be loved, and I'm so grateful that it's you."

The sun is fully down by the time we break away from each other, repeating our endless love, our devotion. Our tears are long dried.

Tucking ourselves away into the inside of a rock that looks like a tiny cave, the perfect size for two people, we sit down on the sand, both out of exhaustion and the need to be close to each other. It's shallow enough that it doesn't freak me out.

"There's no monsters inside." Julián scoots closer to me, draping his arm around my shoulder.

"How do you do that?"

His head tilts. "Do what?"

"Always know exactly what I'm thinking. Even about monsters in a cave."

With a shrug of his shoulders, he pulls me closer. "I told you, I'm observant. Especially so when it comes to work or something I adore. Which, funny enough, is only you these days."

"Same here. I haven't found myself able to adore something for a long time." A yawn escapes my mouth, and I stretch my arms above my head. The blanket he spread out beneath us is so comfortable, inviting me to lie down, to snuggle closer.

"Your place or mine?" he asks, noting how tired I am. From the long day in the sun, from the full-body crying.

"Hmm, could we sleep here?"

Julián looks around. "Are you asking about comfort or safety?"

"Both?"

"Safety, yes. Comfort . . . it's a far cry from your suite bed. Even my shit mattress is softer than the sand."

"I don't mind. Do you?"

A proud grin covers his handsome face. "I've slept on the sand more times than I can count. Our bodies weren't originally made to sleep on fluffy mattresses, you know. As a society we've become so disconnected from nature that we pay for the experience. I heard a tourist from France asking Amara where he can buy something called a grounding mat. When I looked it up online, it was the artificial version of lying in the damn grass! I couldn't believe it. Same with these cold-plunge bullshit wellness scams. Yeah, it's good for our bodies to experience shock and it can help with recovery, but have these people never heard of jumping in a lake or cold sea? Consumerism is the doom of humanity, truly." He rubs at his temples.

"Sorry, it just drives me mad how far from nature we've gotten. Sitting in little boxes the entire day with screen light on our faces, going to work before the sun is up, coming home after it's down. No family meals and if there are, everything comes from a box. No one cares about the quality of our natural water because they'd rather just spend a few euros and drink it out of plastic. Amara spent like hundreds of euros on a red light for her face, when red light comes from our natural sunrise and sunset." He shakes his head. "I was born in the wrong time. The modern world makes me crazy sometimes."

"I get it," I tell him, meaning it. He's so right and he would have an absolute heart attack if he got wind of the wellness industry in the States. I decide to wait until another time to tell him some of the craziest things I've seen and heard even my mother do and buy.

"So, are you really okay to crash here?"

I nod at his uncertainty.

"If you're uncomfortable or can't sleep, we'll go. Just say the word. Deal?"

"Deal." I smile and scoot my body against his. I've never felt more comfortable, safe, and at home than in his arms.

I wake up to the sound of the waves crashing. What a perfect alarm clock. The sky has just started to turn orange, preparing for the rising sun. Julián is asleep behind me, his arm draped over my body, hugging my waist. I try to wriggle out without waking him, but his eyes softly open.

"Everything okay?" he asks in a raspy, sleepy voice.

I nod. "I just wanted to see the sunrise."

He sits up, situating his body behind me so I can lean my back against his chest. "You know, I've never watched a sunrise," I tell him.

"Ever?"

Shaking my head, I turn to face him. "On top of my epilepsy medication, I usually have to take sleeping pills, too, and they knock me out and keep me out, so I've never been awake early enough."

"Thank you for saving your first sunrise for me." Julián's mouth meets mine and it's a gentle touch that whispers against me.

"You can have all my firsts and my lasts," I promise him.

"Is that a promise? I'll do anything and everything to make sure we have many, many sunrises together, deal?"

I nod. "Deal. And I'll do anything to stay here with you and this breathtaking sunrise."

"I've always loved watching the sunrise from my boat. It sounds cliché, but it's such a good reminder that every day is a new start, every sunrise is a new beginning. No matter what happens during the day and night, we get another chance, another beginning each time it rises."

It's hard to remember what my life was like before I met him, how empty my heart was compared to now when it feels so full it could burst. We sit in near silence as the sun rises, filling the shore with its spectacular light, starting a new day, a new beginning like he said.

"What does it look like to you?" I ask him, wondering how muted the tones of red, yellow, and orange are.

"Mostly gray . . . I can tell the differences in light reflection, though, so I know that it's bursts of color, and even though I don't see the same sunrise as you, I know it's still just as beautiful, and now my view"—his eyes meet mine—"is even more incredible."

My eyes sting with emotion and I look back toward the horizon. The feeling washing over me is all the proof anyone needs that we are meant to experience life, sunrises and sunsets, laughter, birds singing in the sky, waves crashing against the coastline. I'm overwhelmed by the beauty, by the years I've wasted sitting in my room, in my bed, with the curtains drawn shut. I promise myself to never close my curtains again.

"I love you, Oriah. Insanely so." Julián's lips press against my shoulder just as orange bursts across the sky. The sun is flaming yellow, no clouds obstructing its full glory.

"I love you, Julián. More than the sun." I face him once again and throw my arms around his shoulders, causing both of our bodies to fall back onto the blanket and the sand.

The light reflecting on Julián's face takes my breath away.

"Déu meu ets tan bonica, Ry. So, so beautiful." He lifts his chin to reach me, licking softly at my mouth, and I straddle him.

A hiss of pleasure comes from him, and I swivel my hips, settling in, enjoying the feeling of his hardness between us. Julián's hands grip my hips, digging his fingers into the bone, nearly shaking to keep himself under control. One of his hands moves to my belly, and it aches as he makes his way up my chest, palming my breasts as they tighten and he runs his thumb against a peak, flicking the sensitive bud, making my eyes roll back, friction growing between us as I move slowly. Every groan he makes, every quick breath from him has me high, so high. I cover my mouth as he sucks on my nipple, one then the other, his palm spread across my spine to keep me upright. When I can't take it any longer, I shove him back, yanking frantically at his shorts, and move to ride him. He gently stops me, and confusion rolls over my mind.

"Look at the sunrise while I fill you," he orders. My mouth goes dry, and I turn around on my knees, the morning air caressing my bare skin as he licks and kisses down the length of my spine. My back arches, a cry falls from my parted lips. The wetness pooled between my thighs is dripping between them. I feel it run down my skin as Julián's tongue catches it, licking all the way to the apex of my thighs.

The pleasure ripping through me makes it so hard to hold myself up on my hands and knees and just as my climax gathers, the warmth of his mouth disappears and he fills me with a low growl, his hands holding my hips in place, his cock filling me to the brim. Stillness, the stillness and feeling of being so incredibly full of him with the sunrise and sea in front of me, is pure ecstasy. As he begins to thrust in and out, I clench around him, saying his name, telling him how much I love him, how good he feels, matching the rhythm of his free hand between my thighs, pinching and circling my bundle of nerves as I come, losing all sense of whatever blissful reality he's created for us. He continues to move his cock and hips, dragging slowly, gripping one of my breasts in his hand as he reaches his own climax, shouting my name as the warmth fills me. His body goes rigid, and his chest falls against my back, heaving slightly as he catches his breath.

I turn and fall onto his chest, our bare skin on the sand and each other's bodies, and the light of dawn washing over us is better than any dream I've ever had, any imaginary world I've fantasized over while reading my favorite novels, inserting myself as the main character. To be loved is to be seen, and to be seen is to be loved. I've heard and seen different renditions of the quote throughout my life, but I never fully understood it until right now, in this moment, with this man.

Eventually we get dressed and make our way to standing. I wipe and swipe at the sand stuck on my skin as Julián helps adjust my bathing suit top.

"Do you want to swim?" he asks, nodding toward the ocean. The sun has taken her place high in the sky now and the idea of the warm water washing my body is too good to pass up.

He leads me to the edge of the water, and we walk into it, side by side, soul by soul, heart by heart, the warmth of the water kissing my skin matching the warmth inside my chest.

Nothing could be more perfect. Nothing will ever take this memory from me. The sea will remember us, the imprint of our bodies in the sand, the whisper of our promises made and love shared. I won't be forgotten, and that gives me unexplainable peace.

# Chapter Twenty-Nine

We walk hand in hand down the sandy shore. The feeling of the warm sand under my feet is something I know I'll never forget once I leave this magical place. The summer is nearing the end now. Time hasn't made a lick of sense since I arrived, and I have no idea what I'll do when the clock strikes and it's time for me to go back home. I can't imagine going back to my normal life now that I know what it feels like to live.

"What are you thinking about, Ry?" Julián stops walking and pulls me into his side, wrapping his arm around my waist.

He always knows when I'm lost in thought.

"Just thinking about when the summer is over. Am I supposed to go back to Dallas like none of this happened? That seems impossible."

"Go back to Dallas? You really think I'm going to let you leave?" he says, hugging me tightly to his side.

I look up at his expression, landing somewhere between serious and not.

"Yeah, sure, I'll send for my stuff and just tell my mom this is my new home." I play along, but a part of me wonders if I could actually do it.

I could travel back and forth for doctor stuff if I had to, but there must be a medical system here, maybe not on the island, but somewhere in Europe there must be a tuberous sclerosis specialist, and I'm sure Julián would help me find the best of the best. I look at him, knowing he would do anything for me, knowing that I need to tell him more about my condition and stop sprinkling bits of information here and there. My life has become so complicated and so full of excitement and intimacy and love, but, most of all, confusing as hell.

"Would you ever move to the States?" I ask out of curiosity as we continue to walk.

The sun on my shoulders feels so good, I've never been so tan in my life. Never been so happy.

He shakes his head. "No. I would never."

The happiness evaporates in an instant. His quick and certain response reels me for a second, even more so because I thought we were being hypothetical and daydreaming.

"Really? Never?"

He shakes his head again. "I could never live there."

"What if your family's business wasn't a factor. Would you then?"

"Nope."

This time it's me who stops walking. "Why?"

He uses his free hand to rub his fingers over the slight stubble on his chin. "Why would I?"

My breath catches for a moment and I'm not even sure what it is I want to hear. "For me? Or to get an education, or a good job?"

He scoffs and drops my hand. "If I wanted to, I could get an education here and it would be free."

"Yeah, but the schools in the States are—" I begin, not sure why I'm even defending a system I don't agree with in the first place.

"Are what? And do not say better. Your generation of Americans are broke from their loan debt and they can't get jobs with their degrees or buy homes, and sorry, but I've looked at the rankings of the education systems and the States is pretty low. So, no thanks, I don't want crippling debt in a country that's becoming unlivable and nearly impossible for immigrants to get into. The American dream is not real anymore."

"My mom's an example of the American dream," I snap, defensive enough to use my mom as an example.

Anger flashes in his eyes but he doesn't raise his voice. "Yeah, she's a great example."

"I agree with most of what you're saying, but don't you ever want to do more?"

"What do you mean *more*?" he asks.

"I don't know, live for yourself and go to school. You're so smart, Julián. You could study anywhere and do anything. Find your own passion outside the pressure of a family business."

"How is that more? My passion is this community and being a part of something that makes me proud, which isn't hanging a useless bullshit degree on my wall and thinking that's all life is. I have enough and I'm not a greedy person who always pushes for more, more, more when some people can't even afford to feed their families."

"You could get a great job, do more than just barely getting by on this boat. The company is collapsing. If SetCorp doesn't buy the land now and develop on it, someone else will come along. The world is changing, Julián, this island included. Look how much it's changed even since my mom left."

His tone changes. "Wow."

I try to match it. "'Wow,' what?"

"Why are Americans always like this? They think everyone should just toss out their morals and beliefs over money. Your only ideas in this lecture you're trying to give me involve money or school. Neither of those will bring me happiness. I don't want to always chase more and never be satisfied. Look at your mother—you're right about her being the perfect example of people who can't stop when they have enough—and look how miserable her life is."

"Your dad's life is also miserable. And I was trying to help, Julián."

"Well, you're not. You sound like you think your life is so much better than mine. I don't need a fancy house or chasing the next hustle. I want a quiet life here on this island with my pare, a family, continuing something my lineage has built. And I'm sorry to say this, Ry, but maybe you should take a moment, look in the mirror, and ask yourself who and what you're living for. You don't seem to have any passions outside of pleasing your mother and judging me."

I try to let his words bounce off me, but it's impossible. He's spot-on and it strikes a nerve, a big one. The mention of him having a family, with a woman who obviously won't be me, sends me over the edge. The rage, jealousy, and despair of imagining him smiling his crooked smile at a baby with a matching smile, while looking lovingly at a woman who he marries . . . selfishly, I can't take it.

"So what's the point of all this?" I ask him. "Why are we just wasting our time? You won't move to be with me, and I can't just stay here. So why are we wasting our time?" My temper flares. I don't have time to waste and it's fucking insane that he won't even consider coming to the States with me.

"You're the one who told me we were a summer fling from the beginning. You've reminded me of it every chance you get," he defends.

"That was before. Before all this!" I wave my hands between us, to the invisible string tying us together. "Now it's clear you've kept that mentality and are just wasting both of our time and not all of us have the privilege. So again, what's the point of wasting any more time together?"

"If you feel that you're wasting your time, then stop wasting it. You're the one who started this pointless argument with me, and the more right I am, the more you lash out at me because Miss Perfect Ry can't fathom for a moment that someone else could be right."

"That's not fair." I meet his eyes again. "I was just hoping that you would be at least considering coming with me, even for a little bit. You didn't even think about it, and I have actual reasons preventing me from staying here. Unlike you." I know it's wrong as I say it, but my god, I can't control my temper.

"Unlike you"—he tosses my words back to me—"I don't need to measure or analyze or tear apart every part of my life because I'm miserable. I'm happy, Ry, I've never been happier. Success and happiness in my life aren't measured by money or power. I have food, my boat. I love someone, they love me, my pare is healthy. My community came together to fight corporate greed.

We may have lost this time, but we still tried. That's success to me. Maybe not to you but to me. And let's not forget you were going to leave; you had a flight booked the night of the gala!"

"I was going to leave because you pushed me away and abandoned me, again! You probably only stayed around this long because you'd feel bad if I died! And stop talking about greed, it's hypocritical when at the end of the day your dad will have more money than ever! It's easy to say money doesn't matter when you don't have it!"

Julián's mouth falls open and I wish I could shove the words back into my big, stupid mouth.

"Wow. You're just like her. And the saying is, it's easy to say money doesn't matter when you have too much of it, which you obviously fucking do. I was wrong about you. So fucking wrong," he says, stalking off, leaving me standing in the sand.

"Fuck you!" I scream after him, knowing damn well I took it too far, but there's nothing to say right now to make it better and I need to think, to breathe, to calm down and not hurt him more than I already have.

Nearly every word that came out of my mouth was from a place of anger. I let my fear of being ripped away from him push me to say things to him that I didn't mean and regret to my bones. I can't make excuses for being such a bitch to him, and I don't want to. He deserves more than my childish, emotional ranting and half-ass apologies. I wander around for a while, not knowing where to go, or what the hell to do. Another reminder of a dynamic with my mother I desperately wish I had. One where I could rush to her and get advice. Since that's not possible, I make my way back to the hotel and hope Amara is working.

As I approach the entrance, I find her walking under the arched door, her bag and phone in hand.

"Ry!" She lights up when she sees me. Relief, guilt, anxiety fill me and I bite down on my lip, trying not to cry.

Her expression changes as she looks at me. "Are you okay? What's wrong?" She pulls me into hug her before I can answer. She squeezes me, gently petting my hair.

"I was a raging bitch to Julián and said so many awful things and need to apologize but want to give him space . . . at least for a little bit. I don't know what the hell to do or who to go to, so I came here hoping to find you, hoping you'd be here," I tell her, letting myself melt in her arms.

"Well, you came to the right place." She unwraps herself from me and takes my hand, leading me to sit on a set of stones near the circular driveway of the hotel. Out of sight from guests, with a beautiful view of the coast painted in the early morning light.

"How are you and Prisha?" I ask, and she smiles.

She's wearing her work uniform with dirty, well-lived and -loved sneakers with little charms hanging from the laces. There's a purple heart, and one of those little characters from her bookbag, from the band she loves so much.

"Good, really good. Too good, I think. She's going to have to go back to Sweden soon when her summer break ends, and I didn't think too much of it in the beginning, but it's killing me now that we're getting closer to that day."

I reach for her hand. Why do things always have to end? Why is everything always so damn complicated and time-stamped and full of endless roadblocks?

"You guys could always have a long-distance relationship? Instead of just ending it?"

Amara shakes her head, a sour look on her face. "I'm not a long-distance kind of girl. I know myself well enough to know that won't work. I'm too jealous, too impulsive. If it were a shorter period maybe, but she's in medical school, which takes years and years. Ugh, why does she have to be so great? She was supposed to be a hookup for a few weeks, but now I . . . I think I love her, and I don't know what to do about that."

I can't help but laugh, not because it's funny but because I know how she feels and have absolutely zero credentials to give her advice when my own love life is a complete shit show.

"Ironically, we're in the same situation. Different circumstances, but the whole summer fling, now in love, and have an impending expiration date thing is the same."

"We should have just hung out together and partied all summer instead of going and falling in love with people we can't have a future with," she says, and I nod in agreement. "And no offense to either of us, but I don't think we're going to have any good advice for each other. We don't know what we're doing, clearly."

"Clearly."

"Enough about me, I don't even want to think about it, so tell me about the mess with Julián."

I give her the fast-ish version, and she grimaces a few times, both at my awful behavior toward him and his refusal to consider coming to the States with me. I feel bad not telling her about the whole medical situation, but everything is already complicated enough, and I don't want to become my condition, not with her.

"I think you're both brats, honestly. He's stubborn and you have a wildfire temper." Amara reaches up to touch my shoulder as a flashy black sports car without a top pulls into the circular drive in front of the hotel.

"Julián has always had a major issue with classism, so I can imagine this is hard for him, but at the same time, it's not your fault your mom's wealthy. It seems like the problems are outside both of your controls, you just have to decide whether the small chance of this working out or not is worth the battle."

We both stare at the couple climbing out of the car. The man waltzes over and takes the woman's hand, helping her out of the passenger side. She's either his daughter, or . . .

"See, people who have more than others are everywhere. If you can't beat them, I say do like that girl and join them."

The woman smiles brightly at her walking ATM, and I fight my judgmental thoughts. Good for her, honestly, and at least he seems like a gentleman, helping her, tipping the valet, carrying her bag.

"What if I can't beat them and have involuntarily been on the wrong side the whole time?" I wonder.

"Then you just make sure you know you're doing the right thing for you, and Ry, you're a good person with a good heart. You're too hard on yourself. You aren't the villain here."

"Then who is?" I expect her to say my mother.

"No one. Just life being complicated. There's not always a villain to fight."

"Your advice is better than you think," I tell her, nudging her knee gently.

"Did you figure out what the hell you're going to do about Julián?"

I shake my head. "No, not even close." We both crack up, our laughter covering our heartache.

As I sulk my way back to the boat, I stop at two bakeries to bring all his favorite breads as an olive branch. I'll miss the smell of fresh-baked bread when I get back home. Driving to the local HEB and grabbing a bag of bread is not the same experience. I sigh, swinging my oil-spotted bags of pastries gently as I think about how much I've grown to love this place. The people, the breathtaking views, the way the sidewalks and streets feel as if they have their own heartbeat. Everything is so alive here compared to the boxy modern architecture taking over my town.

I walk a little slower than usual, taking my time to face Julián again. Not knowing what I'll be met with, I hesitate as I open the door. A slight panic bubbles up. What if he left? I'm immediately relieved to see him sitting on the bed, his hands clasped together on his knees, head bent.

"Julián . . ." I close the door behind me. The sun is blasting through the small windows of the boat. The dust flakes dancing in the light distract me for a moment before I speak.

"I'm sorry, Julián. For everything I said. For everything that happened. I can't believe I said any of that to you." I approach him slowly, unsure which one of us is the predator in this moment.

He looks up at me, his eyes bloodshot and cheeks flushed. I hold out the bags of bread between us and his lips pull into a fraction of a smile as he takes them from me and sits them on the table next to the bed.

"I'm sorry, too, Ry. I panicked at the thought of you leaving and knowing I can't go, and I don't want to lose you. I can't lose you, so I lashed out."

"So did I. It's so selfish of me to just expect you to drop your life and come with me. I think reality set in and I also panicked. I don't want to be away from you, but lashing out isn't going to get us anywhere. I just couldn't control my temper and I'm sorry."

He doesn't say anything, but he keeps his eyes on mine and lifts his hands to my thighs, gently touching the sides of them. I push my fingers into his hair and his head drops, resting against my stomach.

I softly run my fingers over his scalp. "I'm sorry for screaming at you and saying 'Fuck you.'" I try to remove the humor from my voice but fail.

It's not that the situation is funny, but my reaction was so stupid, so childish that it almost is. "I really can be such a spoiled brat. It was wrong of me to push you like that and to disrespect your hard work and the things you care about just because I want you to choose me when I know that's not fair or logical."

"Can I ask you one thing before we move on? Do you really feel like this has been a waste of time, Ry?" He doesn't look up at me, just squeezes the back of my thighs with his open palms, pulling me closer. His head pushes into my stomach as if he's holding on to me for life.

"No. God, no. Every second here with you . . . fighting, laughing, learning, all of it has been unforgettable and I would never regret a moment of it. Never," I repeat, making sure it's clear.

His voice is nearly a whisper when he says, "It feels like I've caused you more pain than happiness and I hate myself for that."

"Not only is that not true, it's ridiculous. If anyone should be saying that, it's me. Everything in your life was fine before we came here."

He shakes his head in my hands. "It wasn't fine. I wasn't living. Just going through the motions, doing what I need to until the sun sets and doing the same when it rises. Again, and again."

I gently pull at his hair to lift his face so I can see his eyes. He's closed them, and I push my hips forward. When he still doesn't open them, I take my fingers and touch his eyelid, tapping the thin blue-lined skin. "I'll pry them open if I have to." I keep my voice light. "Look at me, Julián." Gently, I tap his eyelid again.

He opens his eyes and the pain in them is deep. I hate that I caused most of it, and I hate that we seem to be at the mercy of "whatever happens, happens" and it's unbearable.

"I love you. I love you. I love you," I tell him, never moving my eyes from his. Leaning down, I kiss his forehead. "I love you."

The storm in his dark eyes begins to lessen to a breeze as I keep repeating the words.

"Flaws and all?" he finally asks in a soft voice.

I nod. "Flaws and all. I love you. I'll love you forever."

"I love you, Oriah."

"Flaws and all?" I ask, a smile on my lips.

"Flaws and all." He stands up, wrapping his arms around me, and lifts me up. I wrap my thighs around his body, feeling so at home I could die now and know that I truly lived.

# Chapter Thirty

The next morning, we take a morning swim before the sunrise, watching it float up as we wade into the soft current. After showering, we decide to take a walk as the streets are beginning their regular sounds, trucks and brakes squealing and voices picking up. We stay down on the coastline as we walk.

"This rock." Julián bends down to grab a pebble a bit bigger than the size of a quarter, but flat on one side. "It's the exact color of your eyes. Both of them." The corner of his mouth turns into a smile.

I study it as he turns it around in his palm. "It's what they look like to me anyway." Julián rubs the back of his neck, suddenly shy.

"I love it. How freaking corny and sweet." I lean down and plant a kiss in the middle of his forehead.

Though the colors are more muted due to his color-blindness, it's fascinating to see how my eyes look through his. I kneel on the rocky shore and search for one to match his. The deep brown with little gold specks of his eyes is harder to find in a rock than I thought it would be.

He teases me as I refuse to give up, scouring through pebble after pebble, turning each one over and comparing them. I pick up one covered in muddy sand and hold it up to his face. "This'll do," I joke, and he grabs it, tossing it into the ocean with a faux-offended look on his face.

"You can give up, you know. This isn't a competition," he reminds me as I wipe a bead of sweat from my brow.

"I'm not competing, I just want a rock that matches your eyes, too." I pout, and he softens, giving up on trying to get me to stop my search.

"Ah ha!" A joyful scream pushes through my lungs as I turn over the most perfect rock. "It's exactly the same." I do a little happy dance, lifting the rock to his eye level. "Even the little flakes are in the same spot!" I squeeze it between my hands, pressing it tightly to my chest.

Julián's happiness is clear on his face, his amusement singing in his laughter and shining in his eyes.

"Good job, baby. I'm glad you finally found your rock." He presses his shoulder against mine and I lean onto him. The irony of his word choice is not lost on me.

When we get back to the boat, we've gathered bread, meat, and cheese to have for breakfast. Julián's hands are full, the picnic basket in one and the spoils from our shopping in the other, but he refuses to let me help him, so I stroll along, my hands and mind free. Julián drills little holes into our rocks and ties fishing wire through them, creating a necklace for each of us. We vow to never take them off.

"We look pretty good as rocks." I smile at our somewhat-matching jewelry.

"What if we're rocks in the next life?" he asks as he finishes tying mine around my neck.

"As long as we're on the same shore, I'll be a rock with you anytime." I smile at the thought. With all the times Julián has brought up past lives and future lives, I desperately hope he's right and that we get another chance after this one. I don't mean to be greedy; I know most people never get to experience love like this, but now that I have, I need it to breathe. This life and the next, I need him to breathe.

A gentle knock at the door has Julián on his feet, mouth full of the bread I gathered yesterday. He casually yanks the door open and takes a step back when my mother is standing in the threshold. Bracing for something negative, I try to shield myself emotionally. I've had the best weeks of my life, and with the space she's allowed me, I've accomplished everything I wished for this summer.

"Julián." My mom's voice is soft, rehearsed, but still polite. "Is Oriah here?"

Julián looks to me, to get my permission to allow my mom to come inside. There's panic in his eyes, like he's being yanked awake from a deep sleep. I nod and he turns back to her.

"I'll come out," I announce, not wanting her in Julián's space. Not wanting her to have another reason to judge him.

I grab my phone just in case and slide on a pair of his flip-flops by the door. "I'll be back in soon, finish eating. I love you." I kiss his cheek and lead my mom out of the boat and onto the dock.

Wanting to give Mateo the courtesy of not having to see her either, I have us walk back toward the street, away from the water. Just as we are about to step on land, she bends down and runs her fingers over the wooden plank under her feet. Carved there is the same thing as in her old bedroom.

*Iz i Mateo*

"It's been ages since I've been here, this close. I've had to come for . . . meetings, but not this close to the house . . . to this dock."

I let her take her time, not interrupting her quiet walk down memory lane. Though she has no idea, I feel closer to her than I ever have. I don't think either of us is ready to fully talk about it all, and the last thing I want to do is argue with her, so I need to get a gauge of her emotional state. Is she mad at me for avoiding her? Has the time apart given her the clarity she needed to realize I'm not a helpless child? Has she changed her mind about what her company is doing?

"How have you been? You look well." She finally breaks the silence between us.

I smile. "I'm good. Never been better, truly." I mean it. I know she can tell by the color in my face, my sun-kissed skin, the extra weight I've put on from not having meal-prep every day and eating until my stomach aches and a yawn escapes.

"I missed you." She stumbles over the words. I don't think I've ever heard them from her. It might be her first time ever saying them. "I just wanted to make sure you're okay. This is the longest we haven't seen each other, and I wanted to make sure you're taking your medication and that you're okay. I tried to give you space, but it . . . I couldn't take it anymore." A rare glimmer of humor crosses her face. "So here I am." She waves her arms in the air.

I laugh, surprised by her calmness, her good mood.

"Are you okay?" I ask her as we walk down the quiet coastline. She's not dressed for a walk, but if anyone can do long distances in heels, it's her.

"I don't know if anyone has ever asked me that," she admits, looking genuinely puzzled. "I'm okay. In most senses of the word. Work is . . . work, and we're near closing the deal, so everyone has lightened up a bit. It's been hard not knowing how you are or what you're doing."

"You literally have my location." I make sure the lightness of my intention carries through my tone.

"Just because I have it doesn't mean I checked it," she lies, her eyes diverting from mine.

I giggle. "How many times did you check it? Be honest."

The air between us is warm, no tension present. I feel like I'm floating.

"Each day you mean?" She tries not to smile but fails. Her hand covers her mouth to further attempt to hide it and we both laugh when I move her hand down, exposing her.

"At least ten times per hour." Her laughter sounds different, lighter, not practiced or forced.

"Thought so."

"How's Lena?" I ask, realizing that my mom and I don't have much to talk about outside of her work, and I'd rather not hear the details of that when the damage will hit so close to home.

"Stressed as ever. I think she was more worried about you than me. And things got a little rocky with the deal. A lot of locals ended up turning on us, not wanting another resort built." She pauses. "Sorry. I told myself I wasn't going to bring anything Garcia related up. I'm truly sorry."

I take an audible breath through my mouth. It's second nature to her, so I decide to brush it off and give her another chance. I don't want to disturb this tiny bit of peace between us; who knows how long it will last?

"You didn't come here to drag me back, did you?" I finally ask her once we run out of things like food and weather to talk about. She's shocked that I ate so many different local foods, but I can tell by her expression that she's happy to hear it.

"No. I did not. I'll be at the hotel waiting for you when you get tired of playing here. Your worlds are so far apart, Ry. I know you're young and in love, but your worlds are impossible to merge. Trust me, I've tried.

"Believe it or not, I'm trying . . . really damn hard, to let you enjoy your time here like I promised. And it seems like you are, aren't you?" There's a little worry in her eyes but she doesn't tack anything to the end of her question.

"I am." I beam, not hiding an ounce of the happiness I feel. "I'm having the time of my life, mare. Thank you for giving me that."

Her eyes instantly water at the word "mare" and she surprises me by pulling me into her arms. At first, my body doesn't know how to react, so I'm stiff, hands at my sides, but after a few moments, I hug her back. She clears her throat, and I can tell by the noises she's making that she's trying her best not to be emotional but failing.

"I need to get back," she says, pulling away from me, straightening out her dress with her palms, and I swear for a second I think she might try to shake my hand. "Please let me know if you need anything. Okay?" Her eyes blink rapidly to stop any tear that dares to fall.

"Okay," I agree, wanting to hug her again, but not wanting to push it.

As she walks away, her back still to me, I hear her voice call my name. When I turn around, she resembles the teenage girl in the photos I saw and re-created. The world hasn't hardened her yet. Her voice comes out weak and nervous, but I can hear it clear as day. "Let me know if you have any time to get dinner or something sometime?"

My entire face, chest, and body break out into a smile. "I will," I promise her, meaning it.

I watch her walk away, my heart full and proud of her ability to come here and not demand anything. She even hugged me. Outside of a hospital room, my mother hugged me and meant it. I practically bounce back to the boat to tell Julián about the revelation we've had.

"Babe! My mom hugged me! And she didn't try to drag me away!" I shout as soon as I reach the dock. I kick off my sandals and go to step onto the stairs, but the stairs are gone . . . the boat is gone. I blink. Surely I'm out of it and imagining things.

What the hell?

My tote bag is perched neatly on the dock, safely leaning between two wooden planks. "Julián!" I scream, my heart shattering with each letter of his name that falls from my mouth.

I pace back and forth, calling him over and over. He had no reason to leave, and if there had been an emergency, he would have come and found me. Something inside me just knows . . . he ran. He ran away from me and left me again, just like he did all those weeks ago on the beach.

This time I don't have the anger to curse him. I don't have the strength or clarity to do anything except slide to the floor of the dock and wail until my body runs dry.

# Chapter Thirty-One

Days go by and nothing from him. My despair has turned to anger, and I've grown tired of waiting in my hotel room. Too ashamed to tell my mom what happened, and too protective of Julián's friendship with Amara, I hide in my room for days, allowing both to think he's here with me. But I've had enough. How could he abandon me and not say a word? Not answer a single fucking call or desperate text I've sent. I tried to wait for him to come back, to have him bang at my door and fall to his knees to apologize, but he hasn't, and I realize now that he won't, and I will not allow him to never have to see my face again. At least not without telling him to go to hell first.

Amara's not behind the desk as I sneak past, rushing out of the hotel before anyone can see me. This is ridiculous. I shouldn't be hiding. I have no reason to hide. But I am, and I continue to do so as I walk to Julián's dock, my breath stuck in my lungs as I approach, praying to god his boat is there. It is.

That fucker.

My shoulders slouch in relief and I breathe in, breathe out. Having absolutely no plan, I march right up to his boat and knock on the door. No response.

I knock again, still no response.

Fuming, I pound harder.

"I know you're in there!" I put my mouth as close to the cabin door as possible.

"Fucking asshole," I groan, leaning my cheek against the old wood. I knew he would do this eventually; I was warned many, many times. Even by the commitment-phobe himself. But disappearing after everything we've gone through up until now? Just to run away? After showing me the home my mother lived in as a child? After telling me he can't imagine a world where I don't exist? After telling me he will love me in every lifetime we're gifted? What a damn joke.

"Julián Garcia! Open the fucking door!" I scream through my burning throat, tears falling down my cheeks.

"Oriah, is that you?" A male voice behind me makes me jump.

I turn to find Mateo, Julián's father, standing on the dock. His face is drawn and his shoulders slumped.

"He's in there, isn't he?" I harshly accuse.

I can't control my emotions. There's a hurricane inside my chest, and I'm ready to unleash it and flood everything in my path.

With a sigh he responds. "He's been in there for days. Engine off, lights off, phone off. I know he's in there because the boat's rocked a little, and occasionally the light in the toilet turns on and off." He rubs the back of his neck, the same way his son does when he's emotional or trying to regulate said emotions.

"I'm sorry for screaming. I just . . . I need to talk to him. I need him to talk to me." It comes out as a plea.

A desperate one, from a desperate woman.

I try to swallow down the anger, attempting to not make Mateo uncomfortable. He must already feel uneasy around me, with my eyes and nose reminding him of my mother. The woman ruining his life nearly since it began. The woman just days away from closing this whole dock down.

"It's alright." Mateo waves a hand for me to sit down next to him on the dock. "Come have a seat."

The wood feels stable under my body, bringing in a little clarity. Just a little.

"I can go, I really didn't mean to interrupt your day. I'm sorry," I tell him as he sits next to me. I don't want to leave without seeing Julián, but I will for Mateo's sake.

"Stay for a minute. I owe you an apology." His voice is low, his accent beautifully coating every word.

"An apology? To me?" I shake my head.

He has this backward; I owe him at least twenty thousand apologies. And then some.

"I know my son can be . . . hard. He doesn't know what to do when someone cares for him. That's my fault. I never taught him how to allow love into his heart. I closed mine off so long ago." He looks past me, probably not wanting to look at the face of my mother.

"You raised him well," I sigh, meaning it.

"All of our children's struggles come from their parents." He does a double take, noting that he's referring to himself, too, and he clears his throat. A sympathetic look on his face, around the small crinkles of his warm eyes.

"Not meaning your . . . medical things." My heart drops as he says it.

So he knows. How much he knows or what details he's privy to is unclear, but he knows something. He's had to have known since before I met Julián, but he didn't tell him?

"You . . . why didn't you tell him?" I wonder.

He looks back to the boat where his son is hiding out like a coward.

"It's not for me to tell. I know you care about him, and sometimes things are better left unsaid until they need to be." His cryptic response certainly has a double meaning.

What that is, I'm not sure. I'm not sure of much these days.

"If you can love someone through their darkness, their loss of faith, you can love them through anything," he says, his gaze out on the open water before us.

Its quiet splashing against the wooden deck feels like a gentle caress directed at both of our struggling souls.

"Is that how you loved my mother?" I ask, my filter vanishing into thin air. Before I can apologize, he nods his head slowly.

"I loved your mother with the burn of one thousand suns. I would have gone to the ends of the earth for her, and still would." Tears prick my eyes, and my heart feels heavy as a brick in my chest.

"But why? She's awful to you. She's been awful to you."

Mateo chuckles, reminding me of Julián. "My soul burns like the sun; your mother's like the moon. Cold, surrounded by darkness, but steadily there. I would have done anything to be just a star near her, but the moon and sun stay separated, since the beginning of time"—his eyes meet mine, and there's decades of pain there as he finishes with—"for a reason."

I take that in. All of it. Someone loving my mother, my cold, ambitious-to-a-fault mother, in such a way.

"Please tell me why she left here. Can you tell me? I'm sorry to ask again, but she doesn't tell me anything. I barely know her. I sound like a broken record, but you're the only source I have." Sadness draws my knees to my chest, and my toes dangle over the ledge of the dock.

"It's unfair to tell her truths, but I can tell you mine. I mentioned that she suffered, and she did. The woman I knew wanted more for her life than not knowing where the next meal was coming from, if her pare was going to break another window, punch another hole in the wall. When the house was under threat of getting taken, and your mom did everything she could, I saw something in her break. As her mare's health got more unstable . . . she had the same . . ." He pauses, looking for a soft way to say whatever's coming next.

"The same condition you do. But your mother didn't know that, and here in Europe we don't have as much research, and Iz was just a child, a teenager with the world on her shoulders and within her reach. Once her pare left and then her mare passed, she fled. I watched your mom take care of your grandma her whole life, and I think she was afraid the same thing would happen to her, that she would have the same fate. I supported it, only wanting her to be happy, even if I was in misery. I kept thinking, dreaming, that she would come back someday, once she felt she could take care of herself. But the woman I knew faded, and I couldn't accept it. Couldn't let go, no matter how much time passed."

"My grandma had tuberous sclerosis?" I gape.

I had no idea. All these years and my mom never mentioned it once. Maybe she disassociated, maybe she didn't want to make me afraid that I would end up dying young like her grandmother and mother.

He nods, his thick hair blowing in the night wind.

"No one knew what it was at the time. Your mother didn't know either until you were diagnosed, but everyone in our barri, that's our neighborhood, knew about the seizures, so we all kept an eye out for her, like we always did for one another. That's how things are here, and that's why I couldn't leave with your mom, Oriah, even though she begged me to come with her. My family needed me. My pare was ill and I couldn't just let the company go to some stranger. I was never going to aim to live among the stars, I was fine just admiring them from down here. Not because I didn't love her enough, but because I love this island and I would only be holding her back. I couldn't be at fault for dimming her bright light. She needed more than what I could give her, and I can't hold that against her."

"Please don't take this the wrong way, but my mom's life, outside of her job, has been beyond miserable. You two should have been together through all of it, both of you would have had a chance at happiness. I'm sorry if that's rude or too honest. But if you would have fought for each other, everything would have been different."

His eyes watch me, a strong sense of wisdom and pain swirled together. "If we would have fought then, neither of you would be here to fight for each other now." Mateo places something cold in the palm of my hand.

A key.

Without a thought, I jump to my feet and scramble a thank-you as I rush to Julián's door, slide the key in, and push the wood as hard as I can.

# Chapter Thirty-Two

The heartbreak I had felt until now can't be compared to the sight in front of me. The entire living space is trashed, not like he has broken everything, but like he hasn't bothered to touch, clean, or move. I look around the trash-covered room and find his body curled up in the corner, his back to me, his knees pulled into his chest. I rush to him, putting my hands on his face; it's burning up. The entire boat is burning up, the air conditioner not even turned on. His eyes are blank as he looks at me. Deep purple circles are etched under both eyes, his eyelids the same deep purple as he closes them.

"Julián . . . what . . . what happened?"

"You should go," he tells me; his voice sounds like sandpaper. I look around for water but don't see any. I stand up, go to the fridge, and find it empty. Kicking my feet through some of the trash on the floor, I stub my toe on my metal hotel cup, half-full of water. Without a thought, I bring it to his lips and make him drink it. He empties it, and I use every bit of strength I have not to scream at him when I take in how sunken his face looks, how dead behind the eyes. He's a shell of the man I love, and I want to know where the hell my Julián went and what brought this on.

I ignore his pleas for me to leave and begin to collect the trash around the boat, shoving it into a bag. An episode, he had a depressive episode, likely triggered by my mother being here in his space, in his only safe space. I use the rational, methodical part of my brain to power through, opening the windows, wiping off the surfaces of dust and stickiness and trying not to gag when I remove a plate of uneaten, rotten fish from the bedside table. Pages of crossword books have been torn out, thrown, and scattered across the room. My chest aches with each one I pick up and throw away. All the anger I had toward him evaporates by the time the boat is clean. He's still huddled in the same corner, and I approach him slowly, carefully.

"Let's take a shower," I suggest, gently touching his shoulder, fully expecting him to jerk away.

Instead, he begins to shake, sobs breaking through his hoarse throat, shame covering his face, deeply burned into his eyes.

"You shouldn't be here," he cries, squeezing his knees closer to his chest, rocking on his tailbone.

I refuse to cry, and I absolutely refuse to leave. I sit up taller. I give him a few minutes of silence, making sure I say exactly what I mean.

"Here with you . . ." I pause, touching his shoulder again. "This is the only place I belong."

He slowly turns his head to face me, the rocking slowing. "You should never have to see me like this . . . cleaning up my trash . . . I'm worse than a goddamn animal."

I move behind him and wrap my arms around his sweat-soaked body as sobs continue to rake through his body.

"I didn't want you to see me like this; I never wanted you to see me like this. I've been trying to keep it together."

I hug him tighter. "Yeah, well, I never wanted you to see me seize and fall into a pool either, but here we are."

"Ry . . ." My name is wrapped in relief, sorrow, shame, agony as he turns around, grabbing me into his arms. I don't know how long we sit like that, but when his body finally stops shaking, he eventually looks up at me, making eye contact. I can't stop myself from crying any longer.

"I'm so sorry. I just . . . with the fight we had, the realization of this ending soon, then seeing your mom here . . . She looked so pristine and perfect, and my place is a fucking wreck. Seeing her on the land that will be destroyed soon, it was too much for me. Hearing her remind you of how separate our worlds should be, how we can't ever make it work, knowing that they tried and failed. You deserve more than me, than what I can offer you. I don't have anything to offer you— no money, no security, my mental health is all over the place, and you need someone who isn't fucked-up, who isn't a stubborn fucking mess. You shouldn't have to worry about me . . . take care of me. I should be the one taking care of you." He's frantic, panicked, having a breakdown.

"We can take care of each other," I reply. "We will be okay." I pet his hair, my fingertips getting stuck on the tangles.

"I can barely take care of myself; how can I promise to take care of you?"

"Let's take it one step at a time. First step, shower." I stand up and pull on his hand, leading him to the shower. I don't say a word as I wash him, his hair, his entire body. Slowly, rinse by rinse, the color comes back to his cheeks, the light flickers in his eyes. I stop him each time he tries to apologize.

"Just like you, I love every part of you. And will be here when things get dark to help you. I try to think of myself as someone who tries to see the light no matter how dark it is around me. Even though I'm a cynic most of the time, I try. Flaws and all, remember?"

"I'm all flaws, Ry. Hell, I can't see the hint of light most days. Until I met you, I used to have these sorts of things all the time," he admits.

Amara's initial warning to me wasn't Julián just ghosting people and being a flake, it was due to his mental health, but she doesn't know that.

"I can pull you into the light, Julián. You just have to let me and stop running when shit gets hard, because I'm not going anywhere. I'll always find you."

"It's not that simple." He buries his head into my chest, taking a deep breath to smell my bare skin. "I'll try to never run again, but god, I wish it were that simple."

"Just follow me, always? That's as simple as it can get," I whisper, massaging his scalp with my fingernails to calm him.

He gets himself dressed, and we cook together from a bag of groceries that appeared with a knock, but Mateo had disappeared before I could thank him. After three servings, Julián's stomach finally stops groaning in hunger. We don't talk about it; we don't need to. I love him, every dark and light part of him, and I will never leave his side, until my fate pulls me away. And even then, I will fight like hell.

# Chapter Thirty-Three

I wake to the slight rocking of the boat as the ocean swells as always. There's something beautiful about the way it's in constant motion but never changing. The light outside the small windows is creeping in, draping the room in a deep orange. Julián is fast asleep, and I unwrap his arm from my waist and lean up to glance out the window. The sunrise peeking over the horizon of the sea takes my breath away once again. Instead of focusing on all the sunrises I've missed, I smile at the fact that my first one was with Julián in such a special place. The more time I spend with Julián here and immerse myself in his way of life, the easier it is to not resent the way my life has been lived so far. It feels like every new memory made washes away the anger and resentment I have toward the hand I've been dealt, piece by piece. The clouds are thin and stretched out, hanging low in the sky, as the sun passes them, blindingly hanging above the water. I watch until my eyes burn, relishing in the beauty. Once the sun is high in the sky, I turn to face Julián, looking at his sleeping body, his newly cleaned space. He must have a spidey sense, because his body begins to move a little as I watch him, the morning sunlight making him look like a golden god.

Julián mumbles something in his sleep—my name, I think—and I glance back at him. He stretches his long arms out like a cat and reaches for the empty space on the small mattress where I slept peacefully in his embrace the entire night.

"Ryyy." He draws out my name. "Venir al llit." He taps the top mattress, and I smile, knowing exactly what he's saying without needing a translation.

I climb over toward him, and he pulls me on top of his body, wrapping his arms around me and rocking us back and forth.

"I missed you, my Ry," he whispers against my earlobe.

A shiver runs down my spine and I move my hair to one side of my neck.

"I was only at the window for a little while. I watched the sunrise." I smile, loving the way our bodies feel pressed together.

"One second away from you is absolutely unbearable," he says with certainty. I wish on everything that he's right.

"You could have woken me." He tucks my hair behind my ear and pouts, making me playfully poke his chest.

When did we become this way? Intertwined so deeply? When we met, I thought we would be a fling, the first of my life—but here I am, madly, desperately, devastatingly in love with this man. The promise of a meaningless summer romance couldn't be further from what we've become.

I can't look into his eyes because I know I will say too much, or too little, not sure which would be worse right now, so instead I close my eyes and find his lips with mine. He inhales as I open my thighs to rest on either side of him and my hips press against his. He lifts them gently as I tease him, circling over his waist, brushing over him ever so gently.

"We're going to watch the sunrise thousands of times together, remember, no matter what," he promises as he lifts my shirt over my head.

"No matter what," I repeat softly.

His warm mouth covers my skin, making my mind go nearly blank. The peaceful silence that Julián brings to my life is such a gift. I will never take it for granted. His tongue runs along the skin in the center of my neck to the edge of my shoulder. His teeth gently bite into me, and I groan, head falling back, in complete euphoria. Reality slips away as the boat rocks us gently and my hands pull at Julián's underwear. He lifts his hips, and I toss them to the side and climb backward a bit. His eyes burn into mine as I take him into my mouth.

His head falls back briefly as I move my mouth up and down his length. He brings his gaze back to mine and locks it there, keeping eye contact with me as I please him. I can feel the wetness pooling in my panties with each of his moans. He brings one hand up to hold my hair back, never breaking eye contact. I've never felt so sexy, so in control and seductive in my entire life. I use my tongue to tease the tip of him, and his eyes roll back in his head. I smile and keep going, beyond pleased with the way his legs jerk as I continue to move my mouth and his grip on my hair tightens, gently tugging at the roots, and I nearly come undone without him even touching me. His body stiffens as release tears through him. Warmth fills my mouth as every muscle in his body relaxes, collapsing into the thin mattress.

His breath is staggered as I move to lie on him again, rubbing my nose against his and kissing his flushed cheeks, his stubbly chin, his closed eyes, his sweat-beaded forehead. He's impossibly beautiful.

"Jesus, Ry," he puffs. "I love you."

"Because of what I just did or . . ." I tease him. He laughs, cupping my face with his hands. They're so big they cover the span of it.

"Both, of course." He winks and we share a laugh. Mid-laugh he kisses my eyelids, his soft winded breath is warm against my skin.

"Do you love me? Even after last night?" he asks, his tone more vulnerable than I expected in this playful moment.

I nod. Beats of silence rest between us as his breathing evens. "I've never loved you more."

"Would you love me if I was a fish?" he asks, breaking the tension.

I laugh. "A fish?" I tap my index finger against my chin. "Hmm, what kind of fish?"

"A hideous one."

"Would you always be a fish, or would you turn into a human at night or something, like a werewolf?"

Julián breaks into laughter. "You do read too many books, my love. For entertainment purposes, I'd be a fish at night only. Each morning when dawn arrives, I become human again. So, would you keep me on your shelf and feed me every night? And not allow my father or the hungry fisherman to chomp me up?"

"As long as you don't piss me off that day. Then I might get you confused with the other fish and eat you," I tease him.

"Oh, now you're suddenly a seafood lover, right?" He gently tries to hit me with a pillow, and I catch it with one hand.

"I played softball for a year. Well, not a whole year, like three games before my mom found out and totally lost her shit because—of course I'm too fragile to play sports." I stop myself from indulging in too many details, but it feels good to give Julián a little more context of my experiences and life.

"I want to know everything about you," he tells me, the lit candles in the room shining in the pupils of his dark eyes.

"Well, let's take it step-by-step and finish what we started. What about a worm? Would you love me if I was a worm?" I ask him.

"A worm . . . hmmm. Yeah."

"How about a chicken? Would you want to eat me?" I ask, and both of us are hysterically laughing now.

"Depends if you piss me off that day," he repeats my words, and I fall back against the wall of the boat in laughter.

"Well, it seems like you're going to piss me off every day, soooo . . ."

He pulls me into his chest, sitting on his lap with my thighs on either side of his, his T-shirt hanging loosely on my skin.

"I wanted to tell you that I found a therapy center online last night when you were asleep . . ." He sucks in a nervous breath. "Weird timing to tell you, but I signed up for a session and submitted a request to the pharmacy for a refill of my meds. So, thank you."

"You only need to thank yourself." I kiss the tip of his nose and pet his hair back. "I'm so proud of you."

"You make me want to be in the light, Ry. No more hiding here in the darkness." He looks around the room. "I'm going to fight like hell to stay in the light of life with you."

Conflict fills me, knowing that I've also joined the fight for life. I had come here to Mallorca completely hopeless, wanting—at best—to make a few memories and find out more about where my mom and my heritage come from. I'd never felt so free as when I flushed my epilepsy medication down the toilet, knowing it wasn't going to save me. I was ready to meet death as a friend, but now I'm prepared to fight it like an enemy. For Julián, for my mother who I haven't gotten the chance to know yet, and most of all for myself.

I hold his face between my hands. "I'm so proud of you, Julián. I know it's so hard and you should be so proud of yourself."

"I swear I won't let you clean up my mess again." His eyes roam around the extraordinarily clean room. "I'll do my best to keep it this way."

"I'll help you; don't you worry. Plus"—I shrug—"nowhere except my mom's house stays this pristine, so it's okay to let it be a little more lived-in."

"I'll never be able to thank you enough. I didn't know I needed that. The release, to just let go and look around at how I was living. It's all thanks to you. My life is . . ." His eyes are glassy, and I hug him tightly, not pressing him to finish, knowing exactly how he feels and what he's struggling to say. His body shakes gently as he lets the tears come, and I hold on to him until the seagulls start their midmorning screaming and wait for the storm inside him to pass.

The days go back to our version of normal—Julián nervously begins therapy, both of us make sure to take our medicine. An odd bonding experience, but it continues to bring us closer. I even have a nice dinner with my mother, and she doesn't talk about work once. I don't tell her about my plan, and I don't tell either of them that I can feel something in my body shifting, that sometimes when I stand up, the world around me jerks and spasms for a moment. We spend our time between the hotel, the beach with Amara and Prisha— who are still going strong as they wait for Amara's transfer to go through, because of course she's going to move to Sweden to live near Prisha after all. I approve of her madness, because we all only have one life, and why not travel the globe in hopes of a lifelong love?

SetCorp begins to put their construction permits up around Julián's family's shipyard, even though the ink hasn't been drawn on the final contract yet. Mateo, stubborn as his son, wants to make things as hard as he can, postponing the final signatures, and rightfully so. My mom doesn't comment when I flip the SUV full of SetCorp employees off every single time they drive by. Julián and I go out on the boat nearly every day, soaking in the last bits of summer. Things are great; from the outside they seem perfect, and that terrifies me.

Julián spends all of his off time taking me around the island. We take at least a hundred photos a day. I snap photos of our dinner at Fera Palma, where Julián nearly chokes on his dessert when the bill comes. I grab it quickly, and he sinks back in the chair but doesn't protest. We go inside the Catedral-Basilica de Santa Maria, and though I can't remember the last time I stepped foot in a church, I find myself silently wishing to whoever is listening, begging for more time, for a lifetime with Julián. We walk around Alcudia Old Town until my feet ache, and Julián carries me on his back, despite my protests. We eat and eat, breads and paella and much seafood that I can barely keep my eyes open at the end of the day. He's the ultimate tour guide, especially on the sea, taking me to all of the best views, and the smile never leaves his face or mine. I never want to leave here. I never want to leave his side, and not even beautiful castles or aqua-blue water can distract me enough from wondering when the last time I'll see him will be. Out of desperation, I have him take me back to the church to beg again for that time to come when my hair is gray.

# Chapter Thirty-Four

I startle awake. It's still dark out, the stars bright and the ocean waves crashing gently against the shore just twentyish feet away. Julián is sound asleep with his arm hooked around my waist and a soft snore falling from his lips. Something isn't right.

I grab for my phone on the sand next to our blanket, and the screen appears to be moving as I type as fast as I can. I hit send and the screen dances faster, but I know it's not really moving. My heart begins to race.

Not now.

Not yet.

Please not yet.

My hand jerks involuntarily, and the phone moves out of my reach. I know I only have a few more seconds of consciousness and I don't know what's on the other side of it, but I know what I've been preparing for, what I thought I was ready for. But please . . . please . . . whoever is listening, not yet. I need more time. I need more time with Julián, with my mom, with this island. I look at Julián and almost wake him up, but I can't let him see this, it will traumatize him beyond repair. I bend down and kiss his parted lips, and lie down, trying to keep the awareness in my body for just a few more seconds. My eyes start to twitch, and I can barely see his face before they close. I want the last thing I see to be his face, the outline of his stubborn jaw, the curve of his neck.

I've never been one to think too much about fairness or self-pity. But now that my time has run out, my hourglass empty, I'm livid. I've done everything I was supposed to do: I went out of my way to not hurt people, I smiled at babies on the street and ate vegetables. I've done it all to the best of my ability, but this is my fate and it's not fucking fair. I have so much to do. I never got to show Julián my home country, I didn't get to see my mom get married or meet Julián at the altar as my husband. I didn't realize how badly I wanted these things: the baby with golden eyes that Julián and I daydreamed of . . . All of it is being taken away from me, and there's nothing I can do about it. I can feel my body spasming as my ears fill with the sound of flushing water.

Images flicker behind my lids like the ending credits of a film as I lose all control of my body. Amara, her bright smile and sunshine soul. I'm so grateful to have had time with her, even briefly, and I hope her grief won't consume her. I wish she will spend the time thinking about our chats, our laughs, and I pray that she knows how much she taught me in such a short time. My mother's face flashes, images of her holding me and dancing around the kitchen, her burning brownies and us laughing, her trying her best to do what she could for me. As my body trembles, I send a silent plea to the universe that she will somehow know that I don't hold any resentment toward her, and maybe . . . just maybe, the rest of her life will be easier without having to worry about me.

And Julián, my Julián, who is lying on the sand next to me, the love of my life, the one man I've ever loved . . . The pain of knowing I will never see him again is the most devastating and painful part of all this. Even though I know it's impossible, I try to control the muscles in my body one last time, desperate to crawl away from him, for him not to be the one who finds me.

I always wondered when my clock would run out, when my Cinderella story would be over, and this, the man I love, who I know loves me more than himself, on a beautiful beach in the Mediterranean Sea, gives me the peace I need. This summer was a dream, a whirlwind of finding and losing myself, sharing moments that I never thought I would have. I lived, I was loved, and I loved with all my failing heart. My vision begins to fade, my dream coming to an end, and I desperately hold on to the vision of Julián's dimply crooked smile, his infectious laugh, and his warmth, and I slip away into the consuming darkness.

# Chapter Thirty-Five

## JULIÁN

The annoyingly familiar sound of seagulls fills the breezy air. Ry is still asleep in my arms. I'm shocked she hasn't been woken up by them and their calls. The sun is bright, beaming on our skin. I hug Ry's body closer to mine and she doesn't mumble or make that little sigh noise that she usually does. Then again, we did spend most of our day in the sun yesterday, so she must be worn-out. I close my eyes and listen to her breath, planning to fall back asleep until she wakes me up. She is so incredibly, magnificently breathtaking. The sun reflecting off her tanned skin, her beauty is so much more than the surface. Saints, I fucking love this woman. I don't know what the hell I did in my past lives to deserve someone like her to love me, but I vow to never take it for granted, to never take her for granted. I haven't imagined loving anyone outside of my bloodline in my life. I lean over and kiss her slightly opened lips.

Her breath is so quiet I can't hear it over the sound of the sea, and I don't feel her back moving up and down against my hand. I don't hear the soft breaths of air escaping her lips like I always do. Something inside me churns. I jump up, putting my hand on her chest, and she still doesn't move.

"Ry." I shake her shoulder gently. Her head rocks to the side.

"No, no, no. Ry!" I grab her shoulders and lift her to sit up. I feel for her heartbeat. It gently pumps against my palm. Thank fucking god.

Her head falls back in an unnatural way, and my entire world collapses, folding in on itself, and I pray to the saints that I disappear with it, like the sand does into the sea, with her.

# Chapter Thirty-Six

## JULIÁN

The hospital is mayhem, voices echoing, whispering, screaming. My hands tremble as I beg the woman behind the desk for any information on Ry's consciousness. Isolde and my pare come rushing in, Isolde collapsing to her knees, while my pare pulls her up, carrying her weight as we all try to understand what's happening.

"She must get the surgery to remove them. They've shifted, and there's nothing outside of surgery we can do," the surgeon and his team explain to the three of us.

"She doesn't want that. She's never wanted that." Isolde is hysterical. Her voice pure agony.

"She must. We have to," I interrupt.

"It's her choice, Julián, and I can't take her choice from her. I've tried for years. She won't even hear of it. The surgery is extremely dangerous, even with the best surgeon, and she would never want it. I've tried. I've tried so many times." My father wraps his arms around her shaking shoulders.

"I'm sorry, Julián. I know you love my daughter, but I have known and loved her her entire life and I know she will never forgive us if it goes wrong."

"At least she will be alive to be angry! I made her a promise to keep her here with me, and I refuse to break it! I don't care if she never speaks to me again, and you can hate me all you want, as long as her heart is still beating! We have to give her a chance!" I shout, slamming my fist against the desk. The nurse behind it jumps in shock.

"Her heart may beat, but her mind could be gone! Do you know what happens when it goes wrong?"

"I know about Audra, yes. But I've spent weeks doing research, and there are many cases of success—many of them—and she will be one. I promised her, Isolde. Please, we have to." I shove my shaking phone with its shitty cracked screen toward her face, scrolling through article after article, post after post.

"But she's always been so against it. She's refused more times than I can count. I've taken so much from her. I can't make this choice for her. You may have spent weeks with her, but I've spent her entire life with her."

"That was before! She has so much to live for, so much to do. Please don't take her away from me." I feel my knees hit the hard tile floor and I try to stand back up.

"You think you're the only one who loves her? The only one who wants her to live? I'm her mother, and I'm the reason she has this condition. I passed it to her and she's the one suffering." The anguish in Isolde's guilt-ridden confession pains me.

"No." I reach for her hands to beg, but she pulls away. "You aren't the reason. You didn't know and you spent her entire life trying to keep her alive, so don't stop now! We both need her. I know how much you need her. Who are you without her? Who are any of us? The world needs her. Please, Isolde. Please don't take her chance at life away."

Conflict, anguish, absolute devastation, and the tiniest bit of hope flash over her face as she stares at me in silence. "I don't know . . ." she finally says, and I stand fully.

"I'm not going anywhere. Neither is she. I will never leave her side. If something goes wrong, you can blame me for the rest of my life. You can take my life; I'll gladly trade it for hers." I swallow, meaning every word.

"I will never forgive you if my daughter doesn't come back. I will spend my life making sure you suffer," Isolde promises, and I hope she keeps her word if that were to happen.

Grief can make people lose all sense of grounding, of their tempers and reality. I know the cold touch of grief all too well, and Isolde may hate me now, but when her daughter wakes up with her memory, everything will be fine. She finally nods to the waiting surgeon, and they rush to get to work. The room is spinning; the relief of Isolde changing her mind has me nearly jumping up and down.

I don't care how long it takes, but I know Ry will be okay. She has to be. Life can't be this unfair, not to her. Not to that warm heart and kind soul. It's taken too much from her already; it cannot claim her memories or her life.

Once Ry and the medical staff are out of our vision, Isolde pivots to me. "She will hate both of us if this goes wrong! You must know what happened to Audra after her surgery, and Ry was never the same. I swore to her I would never allow that to happen to her! What will we do if it doesn't work? What will we do?" Isolde repeats as she collapses, and I hold on to her this time, knowing she doesn't want a response, and let her curse me in both languages and sob until she has no tears left.

My father takes over holding her, and shocking us both, she allows him to comfort her until she falls asleep, half in his arms, and half of on the cold hospital floor. She's terrified, her heart is worried and nearly shattered, and I would feel guilty for convincing her if I didn't know I was doing the right thing. Hours later, I ask the nurse again for an update, and she tells me Ry will be moved to recovery soon. My heart is a heavy anchor as I hear that word—*recovery*. So she made it through the surgery. Relief, like the waves of the sea, washes over me, and I take one look at Isolde and know to keep quiet until we know what state Ry is in before speaking to her again. I wait, trying to distract myself with crossword puzzles, but every thought goes back to Ry. The day I met her, her sarcasm and attitude immediately drawing me in. Her reluctance to admit she was wrong and her stubbornness were so intense, I knew I had met my match. She's my other and better half; she's all that's right in this cruel world, and I may be a poor fisherman's son, but I will scour this entire fucking planet to find a better surgeon, another surgery, some kind of cure, if anything goes wrong.

The hours feel like years until the doctor comes out to us. Isolde is asleep, her body resting against my pare as he strokes her hair. Maybe they are soulmates, I realize. He's loved her his whole life, and she didn't make it easy, yet here he is, comforting her in the most important moment of her life. The surgeon, who came from Madrid on an emergency flight, comes to me first, and I hold my breath, trying not to vomit up my empty stomach as he speaks. He tells me the surgery was technically a success, but she hasn't regained consciousness yet. Both good and uneasy news.

He tells me that we can go see her, but to allow her to wake up on her own. Even though it's hard as hell, I have Isolde go into the small room first to see her daughter alone, but she comes out rather quickly and rushes back to my pare's side, sobbing again.

When I enter the room, the beeping and the smell of stale saline remind me of when my mare was dying. I gag a little but swallow it down and approach Ry in the bed. The sight of her like this is devastating, even though the machines tell me she's stable, the steady beeping is a positive thing, but saints, seeing her this way, I pray to a god I've never believed in that she's going to be okay. I will pray and worship for the rest of my life if she's okay. And if not, I will wreak havoc on this world, unlike anything anyone's ever seen. If I somehow manage to survive it, I simply won't accept it. I sit down next to her still body, counting the movements of her chest as she breathes in and out, in and out.

My lids are heavy, but I refuse to sleep until she wakes up. I attempt again to do a crossword but fail. I turn the page to a new puzzle and notice scratchy handwriting. Ry's scribbling in random boxes that, as I read, spell: **I LOVE YOU JULIEN.** In the margin, her scribbles appear again: "Sorry they didn't have the boxes for the right way to spell your name, so I had to use an E."

Smiling for the first time since we got here, I take the pen and write back, *I love you, Oriah*, then reach for Ry's hand. I drag the tip of it down her palm, extending her lifeline, willing it to be.

# Chapter Thirty-Seven

## RY

There's a hammer racking against the side of my brain. It's constant, along with a voice in the distance . . . it's familiar, my mother. Through the heavy throbbing, I listen to her.

"I tried everything to be a good mother to you, but I ended up being the worst person for you," my mom says through her tears. The medicine in my IV bag fills my veins so much that I can taste it, but I can barely keep my eyes open. My mom's voice is soft but desperate as she begins to speak into the empty room. I wish I could open my eyes, my mouth, move my hand to tell her I'm okay.

"Please save my daughter. If there's anyone up there," she begs. I've never heard my mom pray or even mention god or saints in my life, but many people search for meaning or help from the sky during grief.

"Please—" she continues. "If I ever get to be your mother again in another life, I will do better. I will cherish you with every part of me. I will hug you and kiss you. I will only encourage you to live. I will be a better mom, a better person.

I promise, Oriah. I swear I will let you dance, god, you can dance all day long and I will never stop you. I will only turn the music up and even dance with you. You deserved a better mother, a better life than this. I will tell you I love you every day and show up to your recitals. I will walk you down the aisle on your wedding day and always allow you to make your own choices. I won't suffocate or abandon you. I will do anything for you. Anything you ask of me, Oriah. I'm so sorry I was such a horrible mom. I'm sorry I didn't hug you or tell you how brilliant and vibrant you are. I tried to protect you, to make sure you didn't suffer the way my own mother did, but I erased your sense of self in the process." Her voice is barely recognizable as I try to stay alert, letting her words and wishes soak into me.

I would have given anything to live a life with a mother like the one she's promising: hugs and kisses, hair braids while we talk about boys and school and life, a home full of laughter instead of silence. Words of encouragement and not judgment. She's squeezing my hand, and I can hear the machine next to my bed beeping as she continues. The pad of her thumb is running over my palm in one of the most affectionate ways she's ever touched me.

"I will do anything, please don't take her away from me, not yet. I wasted my life and hers, please take mine, please. I was such an awful mother, please give me another chance, in another life, and I will do better. I will do better; I will do better. I hope you can forgive me if . . . when . . . you wake up . . . forgive the teenage girl who fled this place after watching her mother die at seventeen, who always wanted to be a mom, your mom, and was awful at it. The first thing

I failed was you, the most important part of my entire life. I didn't know . . . I couldn't have known, but my guilt has been eating me alive since your diagnosis." I feel the gentle pressure of her head falling onto my arm, and my hospital bed rocks as her body collapses, breaking down, still repeating her plea.

I try to lift my hand to pet her hair or squeeze her hand to tell her it's okay, that I know she tried her best and that I don't resent her. But I don't have the strength. The medicine is stronger than me. The only thing I can feel is the warmth of the tears rolling down my cheeks and the bed shaking from my mother's heartbreak.

When I wake up, my mom is asleep on the chair close to my bed. My vision is so blurry, like my eyes have been painted with some sort of gray coating. I try to move my hands, but they're as heavy as cement.

Julián! Oh god, where is he? Does he know where I am? I frantically try to will my eyes to work better, for my mouth to open to yell his name. I need him. I need to see him like I need air. I try so damn hard to open my mouth, but I can't. A movement in the corner of the room catches my eye. It's Julián. He's pushing himself up from the couch in the corner and walking toward me. God, I wish I could speak. I know they're both probably frantic, heartbroken, unsure if I will remember them or not. If I'll still be me, or not.

"Jesus, Ry. Oh my . . ." He begins to sob, falling to his knees.

This wakes my mother up. She blinks and stands from the chair. Her eyes are swollen nearly shut. The stack of photographs of her as a teenager falls from her lap. He must have given them to her, along with the ones of me. Julián bends down to pick them up for her on his way to the other side of the bed to be close to me, but out of her way. She doesn't thank him, but her eyes are softer than they've ever been when directed at him.

"Oriah." Her voice is a whimper, barely there and in desperate need of water. Julián, my intuition-filled Julián, is always able to read my mind, and hands her a small bottle from my bedside as she moves closer to my hospital bed, leaning over me.

I try to tell them that I remember everything, that I'm so glad they didn't listen to me when it came to getting surgery, that I'm sorry for causing them worry and pain. But I can't . . . I can feel myself drifting away again, and no matter how hard I hold on . . . I can't.

# JULIÁN

Ry's mom and my pare convince me to leave the room for a few minutes. I do so only to give her mom time with her without me, but I find myself pacing back and forth in the hallway, brushing off concerned nurses every time they dare to approach me. I'm aware that my expression is not a welcoming one and they're trying to help, but this is the most devastated, helpless, miserable . . . Even my crossword books don't have enough words to describe this dread clouding my mind. I find an empty spot on the floor, near Ry's room, in case anything happens, but far enough to give Isolde a little space. Pulling out my hand phone, I realize it's turned off. Makes sense, given that I haven't looked at it, let alone charged it since I got to the hospital. If I didn't have so many pictures and videos of Ry, I wouldn't care if my phone stayed dead, broken, lost at sea, but right now, outside of her lying there, in and out of consciousness, all I have is the content on my shitty phone. Flagging down a nurse, I ask for a charger, showing her the input cable so she's aware not to bring me some fancy Apple charger. She nods, glad to help, and as a caregiver for a living, I'm sure her empathetic nature can sense my extreme distress. Leaning my back against the cool plaster wall, I plug the device in and wait for it to power on.

Quickly tapping and swiping, I open my photos, to relive the moments we've had together. Her scrunched-up nose when she tried to play it cool and have raw sashimi for the first time, her eyes growing wide in delight as she actually enjoyed it. Her head floating above the water as she waved for me to join her in the sea. The candid moments are my favorite, the sparkle in her that is glimmering even through my cracked screen, the bewitching way she smiles and rolls her eyes at the same time. The natural curve of her neck when she laughs so hard that she can't hold it up straight.

I scroll and tap, scroll and tap, and something unusual catches my eye. The thumbnail doesn't match anything I've taken. I click it, and Ry's face appears on the screen. Confusion, excitement, and a dash of fear have my hands shaking, barely able to hold my phone as I press play on the video.

The sound of the waves rolls softly in the background and the flash of the phone camera is bright on her face in the darkness. "You're asleep, obviously, and here's proof that you do snore, even though you always deny it." Her eyes draw into thin lines, and she smiles, so wide, so full of life that I don't know if I can handle continuing to watch, but I do.

"I've been trying to sneak away from you long enough to make this video every night for a week, but you always wake up, so this is my only shot. I'm going to speak as quickly as possible before you wake up and ruin it," she teases.

"You've made me promises, so many that I can't even remember half of them, but I need to ask something else of you. I need this more than anything, Julián. Please, please, do this for me. Try to live a happy life, as happy as you can. Smile sometimes, take it easy on the American tourists, and please think back on our time with a full heart, not an empty one. Try your hardest not to resent meeting me, to be grateful instead of spiteful for the time we had together. It's selfish of me, but even if I'm not here, I can't stand the idea of you being unhappy. No matter where I am, just know that you're the reason I know how it feels to be loved and to love. A gift I never thought I'd receive in my short life. I was so terrified of feeling anything, good or bad, that I shut everything off so long ago, so thank you for making me feel everything. Anger, annoyance, joy, bliss . . ." Her eyes begin to fill with tears, and she blinks away from the camera, trying to stop herself from crying.

"Thank you for making me want to live again. I really tried, and I'll really, really try. Please help me try, no matter how hard

I fight you, make me try even when I don't have the strength or the voice. But even when . . . if . . . I'm gone, I know I'll hear your laughter from wherever I am. I'll count the freckles on the bridge of your nose, I'll smell the salt water soaked into your skin, and I'll never forget the way it felt to be held by you. You understood me, you saw me for the first time. I'm so grateful to have known you, and as angry as I am that our time will be cut short, I feel so thankful to have had even a moment with you. Please keep your promise to me, keep watching the sunrise, and I hope you think of me often but live a happy, fulfilled life like you deserve to. You deserve happiness, Julián, never forget that." Her sobs match mine. Nurses and strangers pass above me, but I can't look away from Ry's video.

"I love you, I'm sorry I'm such a mess, I love you so deeply, and I'm so sorry for the pain I will cause you. Please don't allow my absence to pull you into the darkness. Please. When you feel it coming, try to imagine me, even if you forget my face someday, even if you can no longer remember my voice, try to imagine me taking your hand and leading you to the light. That's what you've been for me since the moment we met. It's my turn to return the favor. Oh, and don't forget to take your meds—I'll haunt you forever if you don't." Her dark humor makes me choke on my own sobs.

"You're waking up, I think, I love you I love you, God, I love you, flaws and all, Julián." The video ends with her panning over the black night, and I can barely breathe as I sink deeper into the wall.

# RY

I'm in a dark room when I come to again. Julián's voice is there, somewhere, but I can't see him.

"I had a dream last night, Oriah. One where you were alone, floating on the water, talking to yourself about the sea and forgiveness." He sighs. "I could hear you so clearly, but I couldn't find you. I circled and circled in the boat and pulled you out of the water the moment your eyes began to close."

It's quiet for a minute before he begins to speak again. "When I fell back asleep, I had another dream, in English. It was my first dream in English. This time of a little girl with two different-colored eyes and jet-black hair who called me pare and gave me attitude just like her mare. Two little boys who couldn't stop yapping and screeching. You laughed, as I tried to calm them—God, I miss your laugh—as our children raced around our crowded kitchen, their bellies and hearts full. You were no longer sinking, Ry, you were soaring.

"It's okay, baby," he says, touching my fingers one by one, lifting one to kiss, then the next, finally pressing his warm lips against my palm. "I know you're tired, you don't have to fight much longer. I'm selfish for begging you to keep fighting this whole time. Just please, please know that I love you. That everything will be okay because your heart is still beating. Please just fight a little more, my love. I can't live in a world without you. I would give my life for you right now if I could. I would have done it yesterday, tomorrow—hell, anytime since I met you. You're such a gift to this world, Oriah, to me. You came into my life exactly when I needed you, though I didn't realize it, and I will always, always thank you for that. No matter what happens, when you wake up, I'll be here. I don't care if you remember me or not, I will never leave your side. I'll move to your capitalist country and won't complain . . . much. I'll teach you to cook. I'll even get a driver's license since you can't.

"I will do anything to make you happy, to keep you safe, anything it takes. I'll dance with you and eat that petrol station food you keep raving about. I somehow managed to make you fall in love with me once. I can do it again. And again. As long as your heart is beating, mine will." His sob breaks my heavy heart, and I desperately try to find the light in the room, but I can't.

# Chapter Thirty-Eight

Here, please have water." Mateo's voice is soft, slowly treading through the fog in my brain.

"I had water. Many times. Many, many times, since you keep bringing it to me every twenty minutes. Why are you speaking in English?" My mother's tone is harsh compared to his.

"They always say when someone is unconscious, you should talk to them and in front of them. Imagine she wakes up and hears Spanish and is even more confused."

"Good point," she admits.

"Thanks. I'm not a complete idiot all the time, you know."

"I know. But you do have a pretty high record."

Laughter, from both of them. The shock of hearing my mom laughing, *almost flirting*, nearly has me jump out of the hospital bed.

"So do you."

"Why did you keep those photos all this time, Mateo?" My mom's voice changes to shaky, nervous even.

"The same reason you wrote me all those letters even though I never responded."

"Did you read them? I can't believe Julián had them. I hope to god he didn't read them, how mortifying."

"I read them and tossed them. Well, I thought I tossed them, but he kept them. But I read every word. I couldn't bring myself to respond, to open that door, but I loved knowing what your life was like, even though I wasn't a part of it. How Ry's life was. I did miss you, Iz. I just—"

"That's enough, Mateo. I can't have this conversation right now. She can likely hear us." She shuts him down as I begin to drift off again.

"It's been days." Mateo's voice is persistent, desperate. "Come with me to the hotel and shower. You can take turns, one of you go now, and one after," he pleads.

"No," they both say at once.

"We aren't leaving," Julián tells his father, and I wonder why they're speaking English. Everything's blurry, but that doesn't make sense to me.

"At least eat something, both of you," he begs.

Flashes of Julián's cheeks sunken in, purple circles around his beautiful eyes, haunt me, pushing me toward consciousness. "I'm not hungry," they answer in unison.

I wonder if the two of them have bonded now, formed an alliance to drive Mateo absolutely mad as he tries to be the voice of reason. My Julián . . . has he been taking his medicine? Has he showered? Clearly not, given his father's plea.

A machine beeps louder than usual, and I try to focus on Julián's voice, Julián's laughter, the tone he used when he told me he loved me for the first time. Another voice enters the room, speaking in English.

"Her vitals are great. The surgeon you brought from Madrid is exceptional. I might need to steal him for our hospital." I know that voice—that's Dr. Steele, the neurologist I've had since I was a child. Why and how is he here? Are we in Texas? Am I awake or is this all a dream?

"He's an old friend," Mateo says. "I'm just so grateful it may have worked."

"She's not awake yet. She might not know anything anymore; she's probably terrified," my emotion-ridden Julián says to the room. I reach for him, and I feel movement. Just before I decide if it was real or not, Julián's hand clasps over mine.

"Ry, please stay, Ry." He breathes a terrified breath to match the anxious look on his face as my eyes peel open.

He's paper-white and in pure distress. His cheeks are sunken in, nearly black half-moons under his eyes. I consider teasing him, pretending to not remember anything, but I fear he may actually have a heart attack if I do, so instead I use all my strength to pry open my heavy mouth and try to speak.

Nothing comes. The orange glow of the sunrise shines through the hospital window, covering the entire room. It hurts my eyes, but I refuse to close them or look away. Another sunrise with Julián. I have so much to say, so much to be grateful for. He did exactly what I'd been afraid to do, exactly what I hoped, to keep me alive. I'm alive and remember everything. Every crooked smile, every kiss, every tear, everything my mother promised me while I was half-conscious. I think back, racking my memory, turning the pages like a cabinet full of folders—my fourth-grade math teacher's name, the mascot of my high school, hospitals, the boat and lake with my mom. My mind is still here, seemingly every part of it.

The panic on Julián's face increases by the second. I try again. I will not let him suffer; I can't let him feel pain any longer. My throat is on fire. Will I be able to speak through the flames?

"Julián," I manage, wondering if the words actually came out.

"Ry! Oriah." He falls to his knees next to my bed, squeezing my hands.

"Are you okay? Do you know where you are? Who you are?"

I nod, and a thousand days of sighs pour from his body as he slumps over, the weight of the world seeming to melt off his shoulders. The sunrise out the window is deep red; the glow is so beautiful. Life is so beautiful.

"I promised to keep watching the sunrise with you," I tell him, hot tears soaking my cheeks and his.

# Epilogue

## One Year Later

Mateo carries a platter of fresh fish and places it on the long wooden table. There are banners and balloons, little pieces of biodegradable confetti. Setting up was simple, a lot more fun than the charity event that brought us here last summer. Instead of tens of party planners and thousands of dollars of balloon arrangements, we blew a dozen balloons up with only our mouths; when my cheeks got sore, I bribed a few of the children playing by the water with candy to come and help me. Julián sang quietly as we worked, Mateo humming along to the song. I was becoming familiar with it, even though it was in Spanish. Julián told me his mom used to sing it to him at night. I've learned so much about his late mother that I miss her, even though I never met her.

Speaking of mothers, mine saunters over, dressed to the nines as if it's her birthday and not Julián's. Some things never change. But some things do.

She wraps her arm around Mateo's back, helping him re-arrange the food to be more to her, and my, liking. He kisses her. I don't know if I'll ever get used to seeing that. She's smiling the way I had always wished she would, living a real life, the way I'd always wished she would. I've begun to speak a little Spanish, which my mom couldn't protest since she was the reason I never did, and she's the one who decided we were never leaving the island again. I'll never forget the shock I felt when she told me, *This is our home.*

We both cried for hours, and she finally opened up to me about so many missing pieces of her life, and mine. We have so much still to learn. About each other, about life, about our relationship, but she's not the same woman she was a year ago, and neither am I. At first I was afraid she would change her mind; the anxiety melted away when she purchased her childhood home and the one next to it. Once Mateo slowly started coming over, and eventually didn't leave, I was over the moon.

Julián and I haven't spent a single day apart. I go to work with him, and he comes with me to the Arts Center for Children that SetCorp ended up opening once the deal fell through, which is now how I fulfill my love of dance and live a life with purpose. I may not be able to dance professionally, but I'm a pretty good mentor.

And I have never been prouder of my mother than when she got the local preservation committee to declare the land untouchable, meaning no one, including SetCorp or any other poachers, could build on it. Too afraid to lose my mom, their top and most irreplaceable employee, they backed off and allowed her to work from here. I constantly nag her to retire but know she never will. She works less and laughs more, so I give her the benefit of the doubt and am happy with the change in our quality of life.

I travel to my home hospital in Dallas every three months, and Julián comes with me. Of course, he dislikes nearly everything about the States, except the Tex-Mex and the size of the houses, but he gladly boards the flight with me and sleeps on the couch in the room during my routine EEGs, entertained and horrified by the local news. We buy too much candy and jerky and brisket and T-shirts at Buc-ee's and go to the giant malls in Dallas. We take road trips to Austin and the San Antonio River Walk. In exchange, he takes me to Barcelona every chance we get, and we've gone to Paris twice. London is next. My mom and Mateo came along on our second Paris trip, and my mom barely touched her phone. I couldn't believe it. Mateo balances her out in a way that I didn't think was possible, and I love him so much for it. Julián and I try not to think about the fact that we're practically stepsiblings; though our parents aren't married, we both know they will be. Seeing my mother be loved and in love is another dream I couldn't have even fathomed a year ago.

I truly can't believe the life I'm living now. I used to think of myself as unlucky, as doomed, even. As a girl with an unpredictable condition whose life was limited in so many ways. I focused on the fact that I couldn't drive, instead of the fact that I can walk; on the fact that I was exhausted from hospitals and doctors, not the fact that I was fortunate enough to have access to hospitals and doctors. I'm still changing, I'm still growing, but I've come to understand that everyone has struggles, and mine weren't any better or worse than anyone else's; all we can do is try each day to live.

Some days I can't believe I'm still living. Other days I panic, paranoid I'll have another seizure and not be able to escape death this time. I know my thoughts are just thoughts, but they're still there sometimes, and that's okay. I look around at the people I love, let my senses take in the smell of the food and the ocean, the noise from the soft waves, the sunset in the backdrop. My life is worth living, and I'm going to live it to the fullest. I do my best to take care of myself; Julián too. My phone alarm goes off daily and we toast with our coffees while downing our meds. It's so us, and we keep each other accountable for our appointments, our health, and everything in between. I know wholeheartedly that I will spend every day for the rest of my days with Julián, watching the sun set and rise, set and rise, and never, ever take a single one for granted.

"Amor meu." Julián's voice finds me. "I want to show you something," he whispers in my ear as he wraps his arms around my torso. I can feel the cold stone of his necklace, the one that matches my eyes, against my skin.

"It's your birthday. I'm supposed to be the one getting you gifts." I lean my head back against his chest.

"Who said it was a gift, Miss Spoiled?" His warm laughter puffs against my earlobe and I shiver, even in the humid summer night.

The table begins to fill up with our friends and neighbors. Even Amara and Prisha came back from Sweden for a week to visit for Julián's birthday. I came here to search for a family I never knew and ended up with one that exceeded my wishes. I mouth to Amara as she looks at us, telling her we will be right back. She opens her mouth as Prisha stuffs a piece of bread into it and their shoulders touch.

He leads me over to the newly renovated boat at the dock, and the look on his face is priceless as he unveils the paint on the hull. No matter how much money the now-thriving business brings in, he refuses to get a new boat, so I bought an apartment across the street and am remodeling it for when we want to live on land, when we want to have the sound of little feet running around the house.

"She finally has a name," we say in unison.

The name is written in Spanish, in a beautiful cursive font: *La meva sortida de sol, Oriah.*

What I once thought would be my last summer, my first and last sunrise, ended up being the beginning of my life.

# Acknowledgments

Writing these each time I publish is harder than writing the actual novel lol. Even after thirteen books, I always forget at least two people, so here's my apology ahead of time. :P

My readers: The love I have for you is indescribable. Your posts, your messages, and your endless support over the last ten years has kept me so encouraged and so motivated. Because of you, all (and more) of my dreams have come true. I'll never be able to thank you enough for believing in me for so long and through so much, but I'm going to continue to try. <3

Flavia Viotti: I could just copy and paste from the last few books to say what I want to say here, but as you know, I'm so grateful to have you as a friend, family, agent, and producing partner. 2025 is our year, and I can't wait to continue to celebrate and bring projects to life with you.

Carrie Feron: This is our first (totally new) book together, but since the moment we met, I knew I was in great hands. Your expertise and experience and general love for romance are so inspiring and so admirable. Being around you feels like a warm hug, and I can't wait to continue this path we're on.

Ali Chesnick: Thank you for all the work you've been doing on my books. Your energy is so great! Thanks for teaching me Adobe, and a future thanks for all the traditional things you're going to have to walk me through. :P

Kristin Dwyer: You've been in every acknowledgements I've ever done, and I couldn't be luckier. You're the best publicist, therapist, and life coach on this planet, and I'm so honored to be one of your OG's and watching your company grow and grow. Here's to a lifetime of stories and stress management together. <3

Asher: You're the reason for everything I do in my life, and you always will be. Even though you will never read this, it's all for you. <3

Erin: You know everything I could type here. and that's why this works. Thank you for everything from top to bottom—you're still my right hand (and sometimes my left). ilysm

Douglas Vasquez: I can't believe we've been working together so long now! I appreciate all of your hard work and your excitement for the imprint. I still remember the day we met—we've come so far! I can't wait to see you in person again to celebrate all our achievements! Xo

Vilma Gonzalez: Thank you for always cheering me on, listening to me vent about everything under the sun, and being such a great friend. I'm lucky to have you in my corner, and we're one book closer to getting to meet BTS through my books haha. Love you so much. <3

Sales and Marketing at Gallery: Thank you for being so proactive, modern, and open-minded! Your work doesn't go unnoticed and is so appreciated!

Jen Bergstrom: Thank you for having me back in the Gallery family. I'm so excited for our future together and love that you're the boss boss now. You're funny, brilliant, and a badass. I'm honored to have you as my publisher. xo